YOU CAN'T FALL IN LOVE WITH YOUR EX (CAN YOU?)

Also by Sophie Ranald

*It Would Be Wrong to Steal My Sister's
Boyfriend (Wouldn't It?)*

A Groom With a View

Who Wants to Marry a Millionaire?
(previously published as *The Frog Prince*)

YOU CAN'T FALL IN LOVE WITH YOUR EX (CAN YOU?)

SOPHIE RANALD

For Jassy and Dion, with very best sisterly love

CHAPTER ONE

"Shit," I whispered to Jonathan. "The buggers have packed Green Rabbit. They must have done. I've looked everywhere and I can't find him."

I looked helplessly around us at the piles of dun-coloured cardboard boxes, all securely and immaculately taped shut, and the even larger pile of tea chests, their tops locked. Even as I spoke, the movers were beginning to carry our belongings out to the waiting van. Somewhere, buried beneath a pile of folded bedding, maybe, or lost within a heap of toys, was my son's beloved comfort object, without which a horrendous meltdown, featuring uncontrollable wailing and rivers of tears and snot, was guaranteed. And Owen would be inconsolable, too.

I was feeling pretty fragile anyway. My ankle hurt from endless trips up and down the stairs. My final, frantic decluttering session the previous night had led to the unwise conclusion that there was no point packing and moving two bottles of gin and one of vodka that were nearly finished, so I'd improvised and drunk a couple of rounds of vesper martinis while I prowled through the bare, forlorn rooms of our flat, wondering too late whether this move was going to prove a terrible mistake, and my head hurt too.

"For God's sake, Laura," my husband said. "Why didn't you... Never mind. There's no point rowing over it. Don't say anything to him; he might not notice until we're on our way."

But he'd reckoned without our daughter's uncanny ability to overhear conversations not meant for her five-year-old ears, and her newly discovered power to make her little brother cry.

"Owen!" her voice rang out over the sound of the removal van's engine idling by the front door. "Owen! Mummy's lost Green Rabbit! She thinks he's in a box. Poor Green Rabbit, shut up in the dark. And he might not even be there. He might have been taken to the charity shop by mistake."

"Darcey!" I tried my best to sound calm yet firm, but I heard my voice rising to a shriek as Owen started to sob. "How many times do I have to tell you that it's not nice to be unkind to your brother? And it's not true, darling. I'm sure Green Rabbit is perfectly safe."

Owen wailed, "I want Green Rabbit! I want him now!"

I picked him up from the car seat where we'd strapped him half an hour before with the distraction of my normally off-limits iPad, to prevent him unpacking and unwrapping even faster than the relentlessly efficient movers could pack and wrap.

"Darling, shhh," I soothed, but his cries increased in volume, and his legs hammered against my thighs. "We'll find him, I promise. As soon as we get to the new house, we'll unpack your room first and there he'll be."

I thought of my master spreadsheet, planned to the last box, with meticulous details of what boxes were to be opened in what order. So much for that – for the two-and-a-half years of his life, Owen had succumbed reluctantly to sleep only thanks to the soothing presence of the ever-tattier neon green plush toy. The platoon of tasteful John Lewis teddies, the adorable smiley monkey his aunt Sadie had given him for his first birthday, the cuddly hippo Jonathan had brought back from a business trip to South Africa – all had been shunned in favour of his precious bunny.

I stroked his blond head, but he ducked away from my caress and yelled even louder, fighting to escape.

"Find him, Daddy!" he commanded.

Darcey watched, biting her thumb, looking as if she might be about to cry too as she realised the extent of the carnage she'd caused.

"Now, come on, Sausage," Jonathan said. "You know what rabbits do if they get a fright? They jump into a hole and wait until it's safe to come out. Green Rabbit's hiding in one of the boxes where it's quiet and dark. He's quite happy. And tonight, in your new bed, there he'll be for you to cuddle. Promise."

Owen's cries abated for a second.

"And look what Mummy's got here," Jonathan said, rummaging in my handbag. "Chocolate buttons! Who'd like a chocolate button?"

"Me!" I lied. "And I bet Darcey would too, wouldn't you, sweetheart? And Daddy. Are there enough for Owen to have one too?"

Owen hiccupped and stretched out a grubby hand. "Me!" he said, his trauma for the moment forgotten.

I blew a grateful kiss to Jonathan, wiped Owen's nose with a soggy tissue extracted from my jeans pocket, and parked him back in the buggy, where he began to savour his treat, smearing chocolate over his face, fingers and clothes with fierce concentration.

I looked again at the moving spreadsheet on my phone.

"Have you put the box with the chargers in the car? And the overnight bags?"

"All sorted," Jonathan said. "And the kettle and stuff. We should be good to go in half an hour."

"And my crusader costume," Darcey said. "You said I could wear my crusader costume when I sleep in my new bed, didn't you, Mummy? In case there are dragons? You promised."

"There won't be dragons in Battersea," I said automatically, for the thousandth time. "Not in our house, anyway. But if there were any, I know you'd protect us all, because you're such a brave girl."

And Darcey wasn't the only one who was going to need to be a brave girl, I reflected. In spite of all the time I'd had to steel myself for the new life that awaited me, I still didn't feel quite ready for it.

Six months before, we'd completed our purchase of what the estate agents described as 'a delightful family home, with endless potential for improvement' and moved into a rented flat while the builders moved into our new house to begin the process of gutting and extending it. A week later, I was made redundant from my job at Flashpoint Communications. And that same day, in a freak coincidence, Jonathan learned that he'd been made a partner in the financial consulting firm where he'd worked since leaving university. Which made me feel just great, of course.

I'd been sitting at the kitchen table drinking tea, having just managed to stop crying, when he arrived back at the flat, which I was just beginning to think of as home, bearing a bottle of Krug from the off-licence, and said we needed to talk.

For a moment I'd wondered if he was going to tell me he was having an affair, and I was going to lose him as well as my job. But even the most callous of cheating husbands wouldn't drop that particular bombshell over a glass of fizz, and Jonathan wasn't callous at all – nor could I imagine him ever cheating.

Jonathan, my sister Sadie once said, is the Ikea dinner service of husbands. Pleasant to look at without being flashy, dependable, able to withstand the rigours of family life. I like to think that's what Sadie meant, anyway; it's possible she meant something quite different.

"Can we sit down and have a chat?" Jonathan said, easing the cork out of the bottle with his usual quiet competence.

"I think we need to," I said.

Then he told me his news, and I told him mine.

"But don't you see, Laura," he said. "It's actually perfect timing. I mean, I know you're gutted, but it's not like you loved working there, really, did you?"

"Well, no," I admitted. It was true – God knows I'd whinged extensively to him over the years about the unreasonableness of my boss, the irrational demands of our clients, the difficulty of juggling a full-time job with two small children and a husband who worked longer hours than I did, for considerably more money, and therefore couldn't be summoned at the eleventh hour to do nursery pick-ups because I was having a crisis over a staff newsletter deadline.

"And we'll be far better off now, even without you working," Jonathan said. "You'll be able to keep the builders on track, which will be practically a full-time job anyway, and once we move you'll be there for Darcey while she settles into her new school. And then you can look for another job, if you want to – but we might decide it's better for you to be at home for the kids, because I suspect my hours are going to be even more crazy than they are now. It's perfect timing."

Reluctantly, I found myself admitting that he had a point. It was often the way with my husband – when he decided he wanted something, the world seemed to organise itself to fall in with his plans, and, incredibly, the world never seemed to mind. Trains ran on time when Jonathan was on them. When we were buying the house and the estate agent turned flaky and refused to answer my calls for a week, all it took was one polite email from Jonathan to get them to reply with a full update and a fulsome apology. Even Jonathan's suggestion that it might be time to try for another baby, because three years was the perfect age gap, had resulted in Owen turning up nine months later to the day.

"Are you getting hungry?" Jonathan asked. "I am, I'm starving. Why don't we order a takeaway? Thai or Indian?"

"Whatever you want," I said. "Either's fine with me. I'm not that hungry, I had some chips earlier with the children." This wasn't strictly true, but Jonathan didn't need to know that.

While he rang the Everest Inn, I scraped the last few peas and cherry tomatoes off the children's plates into the compost caddy and poured myself a glass of water. I went and checked on the children, silently opening Darcey's door then Owen's, tucking Darcey's duvet over her feet and picking Green Rabbit off the floor so he'd be on Owen's pillow if he woke in the night.

The flat was silent, apart from Radio 6 Music playing softly in the kitchen. I sat on the sofa, resting my chin on my knees, and listened. Jonathan was humming along to a jazz saxophone, slightly off key as always. A radiator ticked. Darcey cried out in her sleep and I lifted my head, ready to go to her if she needed me. But she didn't make another sound.

This was it – this calm, this night-time peace that meant the end of another day, another day added on to the end of the end of ten years. Ten years – more or less, not actually to the day, because neither of us can remember the exact date we met – since I'd begun to realise that, in Jonathan, I'd found something I'd never expected to want. Ten years of weaving a web of security, strand by strand, that joined us first to each other, then to the first house we'd bought together, then to Darcey and Owen.

You nailed it, Laura, I told myself. Back when you were twenty-two, you thought your life was fucked beyond repair. But it wasn't. Well, it was fucked – but it was fixable. And now look at you. You're thirty-five, and you've got it all sorted. A house thirty seconds from one of the best primary schools in London, which eventually won't be a building site. Two gorgeous children. A husband you adore, who has just had a shiny new promotion.

I made myself breathe slowly and evenly, in and out, in and out, and felt my shoulders relax. We hadn't had a row – that was good. Jonathan and I almost never rowed, and when we did – even though we'd talk things all over calmly and sensibly afterwards – it left me with a sense of unease that lasted days. I'd give Jonathan my full support in his new job, I promised myself. I'd chivvy the builders and choose paint colours and design a kitchen worthy of *Ideal Home* magazine, even though I never cook. I'd love being a stay-at-home mum. I'd take them to museums, pantomimes and – no, not soft play. I drew the line at that.

The crash of the door knocker startled me, and I waited anxiously for a few minutes to check that it hadn't woken the children. Then I stood up and padded to the kitchen to find Jonathan.

"They brought extra garlic naan and pickles," he said. "I've no idea why, but I didn't say no."

"Of course you know why," I said. "It's your irresistible charm, and the fact that you always tip outrageously."

"Come on – it's not outrageous! Poor guy, having to drive around in the pissing rain and getting paid minimum wage if he's lucky."

I slid my hand up under his shirt tails, which were hanging unevenly over his belt, stroking the smooth skin of his waist.

"Not outrageous at all," I said.

"God, Laura, your hands are freezing." He pressed my fingers between his warm, dry palms, then lifted them and kissed my wrists, his lips running gently down towards my elbows.

"Let's eat," he said. "Then let's go to bed."

Later, as I lay next to my husband's warm, sleeping body, I became conscious of an unwelcome and lingering sensation that wasn't just indigestion from the curry. I felt as if I'd somehow been out-manoeuvred, manipulated by circumstances into a place where I wasn't at all sure I wanted to be.

CHAPTER TWO

"Is your daughter the new little girl who started in Delphine's class last week?" a woman asked, falling into step next to me as I walked away from the classroom where I'd left Darcey.

To be honest, I felt more like the new girl than my daughter seemed to. She set off each morning full of excitement about her day at school, while I dreaded the curious stares the other mums directed at me from beneath their immaculately shaped eyebrows.

Most of them seemed to dress for the school run as if it were a significant social event, requiring full make-up, swishy blow-dries and high heels. And even among this glossy gaggle, this woman and her friends stood out – there was their uniform of skinny jeans, cashmere jumpers and Mulberry handbags. There was the way they chatted to one another, slightly too loudly, then suddenly very quietly again, with outbursts of laughter. There was the way the other women looked at them with a mixture of resentment and envy. In my leggings and T-shirt, which, I noticed with shame, was smeared with banana from Owen's breakfast, I felt shabby and inadequate.

"That's right," I said. "I'm Laura Payne. We've just moved here from Ealing."

"Amanda Moss." She offered a perfectly manicured hand for me to shake. "Settling in all right?"

"I think so. The house renovation was a nightmare, but it's great to be in at last."

"Oh – so it was you who bought twenty-three Millhouse Road," she said. There was a subtle change in her manner – a hint of respect that hadn't been there before. "Congratulations! I heard there was a massive bidding war."

"Not really," I said, knowing she was itching for me to tell her how much we'd paid. "There might have been a couple of other offers. I can't quite remember."

"On your way to work now, then?" she asked, with a slightly pointed glance at my shabby attire.

"I'm not working at the moment," I said. "I've been a housewife for the past few months. Literally – it's felt like I've been married to the place. I've certainly spent more time with the builders than with my husband."

"And what does he do? Your hubby, I mean?"

I told her, and she gave the smallest of nods, as if I'd passed some sort of test.

"You'll be wanting to get to know people in the area, of course," she said. "Why not come along to our book group? It's just a small group of mums who meet at each other's houses, read a different book every month and have something to eat and a few drinkies. It'll help you to get to know people."

This was my moment, I realised – my chance to break into the school gate A-list. Somehow, I didn't feel as honoured at the prospect as I was clearly expected to, but, put on the spot, I couldn't come up with an excuse that was even vaguely plausible. Anyway, Amanda was right, I supposed, I did need to get to know the mothers of the friends Darcey would hopefully make, now that she'd been torn away from her old school and the fledgling network of party inviters and play-date havers we'd begun to develop there.

And my own social circle was limited, to say the least. When I was working, I'd occasionally go to the pub with my colleagues, but more often than not I'd have to bow out because Jonathan was working. The few women I'd met through NCT classes and nursery were the parents of my children's friends, not my own. Apart from Sadie, who rang for a chat once a week.

Sadie's eleven years older than me, and although my mother never said as much, I'm pretty sure she and Dad had intended to stop at one child. By the time I came along, their marriage was a bit like the Cold War – complex negotiations followed by long silences, and the threat hanging over us all the time that it could all go bang.

Sadie, understandably, left home as soon as she finished school, and soon after that she met Gareth, and the two of them have lived in happy chaos on their smallholding in the Cotswolds ever since, surrounded by chickens, ducks, horses and an assortment of cats and dogs.

When I was eleven I went off to boarding school, and I suppose Mum saw that as her chance to escape, so escape she did – all the way to Seattle with her new husband. I spent my summer holidays there for a couple of years, then put my foot down and started spending them with Sadie and Gareth instead. And when I was fifteen, Dad was killed in a car accident.

So it was Sadie who gave me away at my wedding. She was the first person I texted when Darcey was born. Both our kids adore her, and she adores them, even though she and Gareth have remained happily child-free. And it's her I blame for Darcey's obsession with horses – terrifying death traps on legs, as far as I'm concerned. She's my family, and I suppose my closest friend. I missed having a best friend, in some ways – but I'd learned the hard way to keep women at arm's length.

Three days later, I found myself lying on Owen's bed, holding a book up above my head and getting cramp in my arms. It was the only way to read whilst lying, prone and immobile, next to my son. I'd hoped to flick through the final chapters after I'd read Owen his bedtime story, but he was having none of it, insisting, "No, Mummy, stay with me!" when I tried to sneak out.

So here I was, hoping that Owen would fall asleep before the final page, so I could make my escape and not be late. Stealthily, I leaned over and brushed a kiss on to his cheek, but he didn't move. Silently, hardly daring to breathe, I sat up, swung my bare feet on to the sheepskin rug, and crept silently out.

"It's nearly your bedtime, too," I told Darcey, who was slumped on the sofa, transfixed by Charlie and Lola. "Daddy's going to be home soon, and he'll do your teeth and your story, okay?"

"Mmm," she said, her eyes not leaving the screen.

I flopped down next to her and skimmed the last few pages of the book at lightning speed, in contrast to the meticulous, note-taking attention I'd paid to the first chapter. It had been ages since I'd read anything more challenging than Julia Donaldson's latest opus, and to be totally honest I was finding this hard going. Even at the best of times, the plight of unmarried mothers in a Liverpool slum in the 1930s wouldn't have been my thing, and I'd had to fit in the final chapters in between the children's supper and baths.

I dragged a comb through my hair, wound a scarf round my neck and put my coat on, then hovered by the front door, resisting the urge to hop from foot to foot like Usain Bolt on the start line. Where was Jonathan? He'd promised he'd be home early so I could embark punctually on my debut into Clapham society. I took a bottle of white burgundy from the fridge and stuffed it into a carrier bag along with my copy of *The Hard Road Home*. If Jonathan wasn't home, like, five minutes ago, I'd be late, and my standing with the mummy elite would be in jeopardy.

"Mummy!" Owen called from upstairs.

Shit. I thought he was asleep. I waited, holding my breath, to see if he'd call again.

"Mummy, I need to wee."

"Hold on, darling," I said, just as I heard Jonathan's key in the door. "Here's Daddy. You need to take Owen to the loo, like, now. I'll be back around eleven, I expect. Love you."

I kissed him and raced out of the door, fumbling my phone out of my bag and launching the map app to guide me to Amanda's house.

"Glad you could make it," she said, quarter of an hour later. "We thought you'd abandoned us, didn't we, ladies?"

"Hi," I said, waving feebly at the eight women assembled round the table in Amanda's palatial kitchen. I glanced around, taking in the framed artwork on the walls, clearly produced by her children but far superior to Darcey's daubs and Owen's scribbles, the well-stocked wine fridge, the artfully mismatched chairs and the expanse of cream gloss units, miraculously free of sticky fingerprints. And where the hell was the clutter? There were no toys, no scooters, no discarded parkas or muddy wellies. Presumably Amanda had a playroom, a cleaner or most likely both.

"Everyone, this is Laura," Amanda said. "Her little girl, Darcey, has just started in Delphine's class. This is Monica, Carrie, Faith, Helen, Jo, Kate, Sigourney, and another Helen."

"Hi," I said, smiling and wiping my slightly sweaty palms on the leg of my jeans, relieved that no one appeared to want to shake hands and wondering how I was ever going to be able to distinguish one expertly contoured face from the next.

I sat on the empty chair between – I think – Kate and Jo, and accepted a glass of wine.

"So, as I was saying," one of them – it may have been Monica – said, "I went upstairs last night and found Xavier halfway through *The Once and Future King*. Totally unsuitable for a seven-year-old, but I do think it's different when it's a classic, don't you? He's so advanced for his age, I sometimes wonder how we ended up with such a bright child. I'm certainly no genius and Simon might be a merchant banker but he can barely write his own name."

There was a ripple of tinkly laughter around the table.

"With Millicent it's maths," said one of the other women. Faith? Or one of the Helens? "She's only five, but she made me explain fractions to her this afternoon. She says what they're doing in class is so boring. She's already doing long division. I had to download a tutorial online to work through with her because I'd completely forgotten how it worked."

"I always feel that social skills are so important at that age," said Amanda. "Although Delphine's diary is already far busier than mine! She's got three birthday parties on Saturday – I have no idea how we're going to fit everything in when she's older and her friendship group gets even larger. She has such a wonderful ability to get along with people from other age groups and walks of life – she says her best friend is the lady we take out to tea sometimes, who we met through Age UK. Such a wonderful woman – the stories she tells about her childhood in Barbados are just fascinating."

"And tell us about your children, Laura," said Monica.

"Errr…" I'd been too busy working my way through the stipulated reading material to prepare a detailed script of humble – or not so humble – brags about them. "Darcey's five. She likes dressing up as Elsa, and ponies, and tormenting her brother. Owen's nearly three, and he's an adorable little squidge when he's not tantrumming the place down or shoving things up his nose."

There was a pause. I felt like I was on *Pointless* and the answer I'd just given had elicited a big red X on the screen. But there was no "Awww" of sympathy from this audience.

"I'm concerned that school might be putting too much pressure on Millicent," Faith went on. "She's been working with a higher year group for maths for a few months now, and although she's thriving academically I worry that the other children might resent the fact that she's so bright. When you have a child who's truly exceptional, it's so hard to know where to strike the balance between their relationship with their peer group and one's duty to make sure they fulfil their potential. But then I look at Warren, who went up to Cambridge when he was sixteen, and I think, being that little bit stretched doesn't seem to have done her daddy any harm, so perhaps it's the right thing for her, too."

Great – I'd inadvertently signed up for my début Competitive Parenting tournament and crashed out in the first round. I felt a surge of nostalgia for those rare nights out at the pub with my old colleagues, when we were all too busy bitching about our clients and whoever in the team wasn't there at the time to even touch on our lives outside the Soho office.

"Nibbles, anyone?" Amanda said, sliding a baking sheet out of her oven. It was the very same model I'd seen in the kitchen showroom a few weeks ago and coveted, until I showed it to Jonathan and he said, "How much? You're joking, right? It's not like we ever cook anything more challenging than oven chips and chicken nuggets." Which I'd had to concede was a fair point.

"Now, these are gluten-free, made with chick-pea flour, so they'll be fine for you, Monica. And I know you're low-carbing, Sigourney, so I did some tuna sashimi and crab and cucumber rolls. Top-up, anyone?" She passed round the bottle and I held my glass out gratefully.

"So," Amanda said, sitting down and crossing her legs, "I popped into Liberty the other day to buy some fabric – the lady you recommended, Helen, is making up a party dress for Delphine to wear this summer – and I almost literally bumped into Zélide Campbell at the Aesop counter."

There was an intake of breath around the table and Faith and Helen stopped talking about tutoring for the Eleven Plus.

"Zélide Campbell!" Sigourney speared a piece of tuna and ate it. Her low-carb regimen was clearly working – she was model-slender in her black leather jeans. I felt a pang of envy and guilt as I remembered the slices of microwave pizza I'd eaten for supper with the children, and resolved to start drinking bullet-proof coffee the next day.

"She seriously needed her roots doing," Amanda said. "I always thought her colour wasn't natural, and that harsh black is so ageing. But of course she's botoxed to the max."

"It's the shiny forehead that gives it away," Monica said.

"Iranian, my arse," Amanda said, and everyone except me giggled.

"Who's Zélide Campbell?" asked one of the Helens, to my relief – I wasn't the only one without a clue, and I hadn't had to reveal my ignorance.

"She lives just a couple of doors down from you, Laura," Amanda said. "So I expect you'll encounter her soon enough. Her and her precocious daughter – what's she called again? Jennifer?"

"Juniper," Sigourney said, making a face like she'd bitten into an off piece of sashimi.

"Yes, of course, that's right," Monica said. "So pretentious."

Which was a bit much, I thought, coming from someone who'd called their child Taleisin. I found myself feeling a bit sorry for Zélide, whoever she was.

"What did she do?" I asked.

"Constantly disruptive in class, acting out, major meltdowns like you'd expect from a two-year-old, not a girl of eight," said Monica.

"I meant her mother, actually," I said.

"We don't really talk about it," Amanda said.

I was intrigued. Was this woman some sort of suburban witch who'd initiate me into a cult? Or a cougar who'd try and seduce my husband?

"Why?" I said. "Is she going to try and rope me into selling Younique or something?"

"Frankly, I wouldn't put it past her," Amanda said.

There was a ripple of laughter, then another awkward pause.

"Now, if we've all got something to eat," Amanda said, "why don't we move on to our book of the month, *The Hard Road Home*? What did everyone think of it? Jo, you go first."

The rest of the evening was given over to literary criticism, more wine, a cheese platter and coffee. Disappointingly, there was no more scurrilous gossip, although there was another bout between Monica and Kate over the benefits or lack thereof of Kumon maths tuition. At last, everyone said their goodbyes and spilled out into the night, and I practically ran

home to my messy house and my wonderful, ordinary, sleeping children.

Jonathan was still downstairs when I got in, sitting on
the sofa with his laptop, a pile of greasy takeaway car-
tons on the floor next to him.

"How was it?" he asked. "The local Thai place
is pretty good, by the way, we should go there
sometime."

"It was okay," I said. "No, actually, it was grim.
Individually they might be okay, maybe, but as a
group – ugh."

"Turns out my colleague Rick lives on our road,"
Jonathan said. "Their kid goes to Darcey's school, but
she's a couple of years older. He's asked us to come
round for a drink some time."

"Rick who?" I said.

"Campbell," Jonathan said. "His wife's got some
weird name, starts with Z."

"Jonathan, we have to go. Will you sort it out
tomorrow?" I was suddenly very eager to meet Zélide
Campbell.

"I'll see what I can do," Jonathan said. "Coming
to bed?"

"In a bit," I said.

I poured myself a final glass of wine and retrieved
my iPad from its hiding place on top of the fridge,
safe from Darcey and her lethal attraction to technol-
ogy that cost five hundred pounds as opposed to fifty,
and sat at the kitchen table.

A brief scan of Facebook told me that my former colleagues were planning a night out next Friday – "Survivors of the axe – we're off to the Woodsman". Lucky them, I thought. Briefly, I considered inviting myself along, but there was no point – I was ancient history, I wouldn't understand any of the office gossip any more. And then, as I'd done so often, I did a search for Mel's name.

Her security settings were hopelessly lax, I thought. But then, she used her Facebook profile mostly for work, it seemed. That suited me – I didn't care that much about her private life. It was her career I was interested in, her public persona that kept me checking up on her, month after month, year after year, even though it made me feel sick with loss, anger and envy to do so.

"Lovely article in the *New York Times*," her most recent post said. "So awesome to meet a journalist who really gets it. Thank you, Erin Brady, for the amazing interview, and even bigger thanks to Annie Leibovitz for the gorgeous photos – I don't look like this in real life, I promise!"

Enough with the false modesty, I thought, clicking on the story. "Melissa Hammond is a truly phenomenal talent… at the height of her powers at thirty-six years of age… Brings both exuberance and gravitas to the…"

God, what a load of sycophantic bollocks. I could hardly bear to read it – but I did, anyway. I read every overblown, flattering word, and then I spent ages looking at the photos. Mel in her apartment, standing by the window cuddling a Siamese cat, the light falling on her curtain of blonde hair and perfect bone structure. Mel radiant, smiling triumphantly over an enormous bouquet of lilies, her husband next to her, oozing pride. Mel working, lean, focussed and unencumbered. Mel having it all – having what I'd wanted and worked for.

She'd never had Felix, of course. That's where it had all gone wrong.

But I wasn't going to think about Felix. That was a habit I'd resolved to break when I married Jonathan. Jonathan – the perfect man. A catch, all my friends said. And they were right. Why on earth would anyone married to someone as handsome, successful, funny and kind as Jonathan spend time hankering after Felix? Not me. Although, if I were honest with myself, it had been gloating as much as hankering. Unlike Mel, Felix didn't have a Facebook page to show off on. When his name came up on Google, it revealed a series of near-misses, a peripatetic succession of new starts all over the world, chasing a dream he could never quite reach. Not that I searched for his name often – it was an occasional, guilty indulgence that caused pain and pleasure in equal measure, like picking the skin off my feet.

There was no doubt about it: in life, I'd succeeded where Felix had not. My life might not have worked out quite as I'd expected, but now I was a grown-up, and I'd nailed it. Felix was a permanent man-child,

living a life devoid of stability, responsibility, family –
all the things that really mattered. As far as I knew,
anyway – there was no reason to suspect that any of
that would have changed since I'd last Googled him.
Perhaps now I might just have a quick look…

Almost without my volition, by fingers moved
over the keypad. Open quotes, Felix Lawson, close
quotes, enter.

Just as the list of search results appeared on my
screen, I heard Jonathan call from upstairs, "Coming,
Laura? It's late."

I felt a rush of guilt and I closed the browser window, then closed Facebook too.

CHAPTER THREE

March 2001: Class

It was a Monday morning, the day after our day off, when I first saw him. I should have been feeling as fresh as the winter sunshine that flooded the studio with light, but I wasn't – I was dull and sluggish, my thighs still throbbing with a residual ache from Saturday's double show. My stomach felt heavy and sore, a weight like liquid metal where there should have been lightness and space. It was only my period, probably – that and the cappuccinos and blueberry muffins I'd been mainlining all the previous day in the grip of a sugar craving.

I gave the top of my baggy tracksuit bottoms a couple of extra turns to hide the bulge I could feel around my waist, which I was sure everyone else could see, gulped down two painkillers with a mouthful of water, and took my usual place between Mel and Roddy.

"Oh my God, I'm, like, totally broken," Roddy said. "Did you hear me come in last night? Or this morning, rather. It must have been after four, no word of a lie."

"It was three thirty," Mel said. "And you woke me up, crashing around like a herd of bloody buffalo in the kitchen. And you left your eggy pan in the sink. You're disgusting, Roderigo. It's like living with the boy who was raised by wolves."

Roddy's deep olive skin made it impossible to tell if he was blushing, but he ducked his head and grinned contritely. "Sorry, Melba-toast. But they do say you need protein before bed after a heavy session, to avoid a hangover."

"Clearly it didn't work on this occasion," I said.

"How do you know? I might be feeling worse if I'd gone straight to bed. Although I can't imagine feeling worse than this."

"Want some of my ibuprofen?" I offered, but before I had a chance to rummage for them in my bag, Anna arrived and the roar of conversation dwindled to a hum and then stopped.

"Good morning, boys and girls," she said. "If you're all ready, let's begin."

Mel blew her nose and tucked the soggy tissue into the sleeve of her cardigan. Roddy yawned hugely. Around us, the rest of the company sipped water, dropped woolly hats and scarves into their open bags, and finished whispered conversations as they hurried to their places.

I half-listened to Anna's instructions, flexing my stiff ankles and waiting for the music to begin.

"One, two, three, and…" Anna gestured to the pianist and Schubert spilled into the room, as luminous as the morning. I felt the music enter my body, too, compelling my limbs out of their fatigue, swelling inside me and replacing the heaviness with a familiar bubble of excitement.

Anna moved slowly among us, watching and assessing, dispensing a smile here and giving a word of advice there.

"Good," she said, as the final bar ended. "We'll move on."

"See the new guy?" Mel murmured, catching my eye in the mirror. We'd become expert at lip-reading, conducting detailed conversations without making a sound while our teachers' backs were turned.

"Where?" I looked around. Morning class was full, but Mondays generally were, before the stresses of the week kicked in and drove people to Pilates or to the physiotherapist's office instead.

"Next to Jerome. Red jacket." Mel dropped into a deep, perfect plié and I followed, instinctively keeping in perfect time with her and the music.

I scanned the fifty or so heads in the room, looking for Jerome's distinctive ginger one. He was one of our male Principals – this new guy must be either totally clueless or totally arrogant if he'd chosen a place next to Jerome on his first day.

"Felix Lawson," Roddy said, lowering his voice as the music stopped once more. "The boy wonder from the Bolshoi."

Sharing a flat with Roddy might have its disadvantages – his late nights and feral housekeeping standards, for example – but it was worth being woken up in the small hours and having dance belts festooned over the radiators for the stream of juicy and infallibly accurate gossip he provided.

Roddy's looks might be pure Mediterranean – his parents were Spanish – but his accent was deepest Essex and his manner high camp. He was a relentless and extremely successful shagger; a dizzying procession of strange men making tea in our kitchen in the mornings was another hazard of living with Roddy.

"The Bolshoi? Really?" I said.

"Most recently, yes. My spies tell me he's from Warrington or Wigan or some such hell-hole originally. But he escaped to New York and trained there, and then the Russians snapped him up."

I broke my eye contact with Roddy and focussed on the far wall as I found my balance in the first arabesque of the day, feeling my leg wobble and then steady. I glanced around the studio again and located Jerome just as he relaxed out of the pose and turned back to the barre.

Next to him was the man who must be Felix. A head shorter than Jerome, he was wearing a bright red down gilet over his black tights, and a knitted beanie pulled down almost to his eyebrows. London might be freezing, but surely Moscow was even colder – perhaps he'd come back to England in search of a bit of sunshine?

But before I could speculate further, Anna said, "Move the barres please, and let's come into the centre."

Mel and I sank to the floor. As we laced our pointe shoes, I snuck another glance at Felix, just in time to see him unzip his jacket and pull off his hat, releasing a shiny dark fringe that flopped over his face before he pushed it back.

"What d'you reckon?" I said to Mel. "Fit?"

"Short," she said. "You might fancy him, but you'll struggle to dance with him."

I rolled my eyes. "Whatever. You smug cow."

Mel was my best friend and she didn't mean her observation to sting, but it did. At five foot seven and a half (God, I hated that half an inch), I was tall for a ballet dancer – almost too tall. Too tall for a soloist, unless I was exceptional, and I didn't know yet whether I was. Too tall to dance pas de deux with men who weren't well above average height. Mel herself was a perfect, sylph-like five foot four and could partner anyone. In that way, as in so many others, she had the edge over me, and we both knew it.

"Come on then, beanpole," Mel said, standing up from the floor without using her hands, as if pulled by a string. I followed her on to the floor, positioning myself further back in the room than usual so I could take a good look at the newest member of the company.

Being surrounded by beauty all the time had inured me to it. I hardly noticed Roddy's perfect body, six foot three of pure muscle – only the fact that his left leg didn't turn out quite as far as the right. Mel, too, was conventionally pretty, stunning, even – with her blonde hair, blue eyes and tiny waist, she was an archetypal English rose. All the bodies in the room would have appeared perfect to a random observer, I suppose – honed, supple and above all young. But I'd grown so used to them that now all I saw was that Fabia was wearing a knee support, Lisa had gained a couple of pounds, and Connor was going to have to shave off what looked like several days' worth of stubble before he put on his make-up for the evening performance.

Felix was different, though. I told myself it was because he was new, but I couldn't stop my eyes sliding towards him as we worked on our turns, and found myself getting dizzy because I wasn't keeping my eyes fixed in the direction I was moving. I could have sworn he glanced at me, but then his eyes snapped back to where they were meant to be and, unlike me, he didn't lose his balance and his line.

He was beautiful. Now that he'd pulled off his woolly hat, I could see that his hair was dark brown, almost black, and long enough to flop over his eyes. I couldn't see their colour across the room, but they were pale and bright – blue, or perhaps green. His skin was pale too, almost sallow in the bright lights of the studio, stretched taut over the sharp lines of his jaw and cheekbones. He seemed never to stop smiling – a grin of pure enjoyment that made me suspect that this class was just a bit of easy fun for him, not punishingly hard work as it was for me.

"I think you're forgetting to breathe again, Laura," Anna said.

I felt my face turn scarlet, and retreated to the safety of my bag, where I towelled my sweaty back and sipped water. This wouldn't do. I needed to focus – I, of all people, couldn't afford to show myself up. I breathed, I concentrated, I fixed my eyes on a point that wasn't Felix, and I executed the sequence perfectly with the rest of my group.

Then, when I returned to the barre, I saw him watching me. His gaze was steady and appraising, and when his smile amped up a notch, I smiled shyly back.

The class moved on to jumps – the grands jêtés that wow audiences and leave dancers gasping for breath. I found myself in the wrong place – I'd have to go in the first group with Fabia and Tom, rather than hanging back with my friends for the safety of mid-class mediocrity. I waited for the music to give us our cue, then moved smoothly across the floor, imagining that the notes of the piano were a spring lifting me upwards, wings holding me, a cushion softening my descent.

"Good!" Anna said. "Very nice indeed. Just a little higher in the front leg, Tom."

Sipping water, I watched the other groups go through the same sequence. Mel was text-book perfect, as usual, appraising herself in the mirror throughout and earning a nod of approval. Lisa seemed rushed and anxious, hanging her head as she walked back to join us at the barre. And the men, conscious of the presence of a newcomer, were show-boating around, putting more energy than was nec-essary in a regular morning class into their jumps, aiming for the illusion of hovering weightlessness.

None of them, not even Jerome, was as power-ful or as graceful as Felix. His technique was perfect, but there was something else too – an exuberance, a nonchalance, an impression that he was doing this just for a laugh and could do far more if he put a bit of wellie in. He strolled back to the barre when he was done as if it had been nothing at all, and Jerome punched him lightly on the shoulder and grinned at him, but there was a hint of trepidation in his smile. Jerome was thirty-four. His career was at its zenith – there was only one way it could go from here.

Mine wasn't, though. I was twenty-one. I'd spent the past eleven years striving to get where I was, and this was just the beginning. Of the twenty-five stu-dents who'd entered the Royal Ballet School in our year, only Mel and I had made it here. Promotion beyond the chorus was a dream, but it was a dream that seemed to become less distant with every day that passed, every smile from a teacher or director, every step I executed that made me think, "Yes!" I didn't have the world at my feet – not at all. But I had the sense that if I were to go just a little further, just a little higher, there it would be, spread out in front of me, ready and waiting. For a moment I imagined what I'd be like when I was Jerome's age, turning up to morning class because it was the right thing to do, an example to set to the junior dancers, as well as maintaining my by-then-flawless technique.

I was jolted out of my daydream by Roddy saying, "God, I'm fucking Hank Marvin. I want a double sausage bap and a fat Coke. Coming, Meltdown?"

"No chance," Mel said. "It's freezing out there and I've got rehearsal in less than an hour. I'm going to grab a yoghurt and a banana and check my costume for this evening."

"Laura?" Roddy said. I heard my stomach give a great, mortifying gurgle at the prospect of a sausage bap. As if – but maybe I could have a jacket potato. The menstrual munchies still had me well and truly in their grip. But then I saw Jerome make an unmistakeable gesture towards Felix and head towards the stairs leading up to the roof. Like moths to a candle, several of the dancers shouldered their bags and followed.

"I think I'll go out for a fag, actually," I said.

CHAPTER FOUR

In the event, I met Zélide Campbell sooner than I'd expected. It was a typical morning – typically hellish, that is. Owen cried buckets when I dropped him off at nursery, and his piteous howls of, "Don't leave me, Mummy!" were made no less heart-rending by the knowledge that he'd be playing quite happily with the other kids five minutes after I'd gone.

Darcey, by contrast, came over all teenagery and ordered, "Don't hold my hand, Mummy, it's embarrassing," and stalked off ahead of me to join her friends in the playground. She didn't even let me kiss her goodbye. I was fighting back tears as I turned for home, and didn't see Amanda appear next to me.

"Hi, Laura!" she said, in tones of faux surprise. "You're late today."

"Again," I said. "Mornings in our house are mayhem – I'm sure you know how it is."

"I find having a routine helps," Amanda said. "And being strict about bedtime, of course. When they're tired it all goes to pot."

I wondered guiltily if she had some sixth sense that allowed her to envision the scene in our house the previous night, with both children in floods of tears, demanding to stay up until Daddy was home, and me taking the course of least resistance and drinking wine while I read them their stories in the sitting room.

"Yes, well… It's all still quite new to them," I said. "We'll settle in, I expect."

Then her mobile rang. She snatched it from her bag and answered.

"Thank you for coming back to me, Lara. I'm sure you know why I'm calling. Yes, the cake sample arrived. However, I asked for shocking pink icing, and pale pink glitter. And that's not what you delivered. It's more a cerise. And the glitter's too dark against it, it barely shows up at all. Well, if there are limitations to what you can achieve with paste colouring, Lara, you should have let me know when I placed the order – or rather, didn't place it, because I would then have found an alternative supplier. And, as I'm sure you're aware, it's a bit late in the day for that now. What do you suggest I do? Don't you think you're making your problem my problem, Lara?"

She unlocked her car and flung her Mulberry bag on to the passenger seat. I lingered, not sure whether it would be rude to head for home without saying goodbye, or ruder still to stand and listen, fascinated, to her conversation. I opted for the latter.

"Lara, I'll have you know you came highly recom-mended on SWmums.com – a community in which

I am highly active. A reputation like that is entirely dependent on the goodwill of your customers, as I'm sure you're aware. A few bad reviews could mean the end of your business. And I can make that happen quite easily. Not that I expect to need to, of course, because I'm quite confident that you will be delivering what I ordered, before close of play today, at no extra cost. That's what you're going to do, isn't it, Lara? Yes, I thought so. You have the address. Goodbye."

She ended the call, and uttered a sentence I honestly thought no one ever said in real life. "You just can't get the staff these days."

Suppressing a giggle, I said, "Having a party?"

With a flourish, she pulled an invitation from her bag and handed it to me.

"It's Delphine's sixth birthday on Saturday," she said. "And I hope you'll bring Darcey? We're having a Barbie Princess theme, all the little girls will be dressing up and I'm hiring a pink marquee for the garden as a surprise. I had to have words with the marquee company earlier though. They weren't keen to set up at night once Delphine's in bed, even though that's what I stipulated on my order. I gave them a piece of my mind, let me tell you! The man said he doesn't do erections after dark."

I stifled a giggle. "I'm sure you persuaded him otherwise."

"Oh, yes," she said. "One needs a firm hand with tradesmen."

"I… thanks very much," I said, remembering that Jonathan and I had talked vaguely about taking both the children to Legoland. "I'll check the diary. I'm sure Darcey would love it. It won't be a problem if I bring Owen along too, will it?"

Amanda looked aghast. "Laura, I don't want to put you in an awkward position, but it's girls only, I'm afraid. And even if it weren't, we're quite limited on numbers. The seating plan, you know? And everything's been planned for just fifteen children – the party bags, the catering… And besides, you'll want to be socialising with the other mums, won't you?"

About as much as I wanted to eat my own hair, I thought. "He's no trouble, honestly. He's very well behaved for three. But if it's a problem…"

"I'm awfully sorry," Amanda said. "But it's no siblings. I did mention it on the information sheet I included with the invitation. I'd love to help, but it just won't be possible. It's Delphine's special day and I must have everything just perfect for her. If Darcey's not going to be able to come, you will let me know as soon as possible, won't you, so I can give her place to one of the children on the B list?"

And she swung her denim-clad bottom into her car and drove away, leaving me feeling like a bunting supplier who'd delivered the wrong shape of triangles.

I rummaged in my bag for my own phone and called Jonathan.

"Guess what? We've been invited to Amanda's daughter's Barbie princess party on Saturday. It sounds like the seventh circle of hell, but she'll love it and I can pick up some tips for Darcey's party next month. So can you take Owen swimming?"

"Can't, I'm afraid," Jonathan said. "I've said I'll play golf with Rick from work."

"Golf? You don't play golf."

"Yes, I do," Jonathan said. "Well, I can, anyway. Haven't hit a ball for years – not since before I met you. But I used to play with Dad, most weekends. And there's a client golf day coming up that I can't miss, so I need to get my eye back in."

"But we were going to take the kids to Legoland."

"But now you've had a better offer," Jonathan said. "We can go another day, and you can take the kids to this party thing instead."

"No I can't," I said. "Turning up at parties with a sibling in tow is apparently the worst kind of faux pas imaginable. Owen's not invited. Darcey is."

"They won't mind, surely," Jonathan said. "Or just drop her off and take Owen out somewhere, like we used to do."

"Yes, but… it's her first party here. She hardly knows the other children. What if they're horrible to her? She'll need me to be there."

And, I thought, what about me? I needed to make friends, too. If I was going to cast my lot in with Amanda and her gang, then I needed to be there, drinking wine and nattering with them, not turning my back and allowing them to talk about me behind it.

"So what are the other mums going to do, then?"

"Their husbands will look after the other kid," I said. "Or the nanny will, or whatever. I don't know – we've always sorted it out between us, before. But we can't do that now, can we? I'm not being unreasonable, Jonathan – if you can't look after Owen, Darcey and I can't go."

"But you didn't much want to go, did you? Seventh circle of hell, you said."

"Darcey will want to go. She'll be desperate to go."

"She doesn't know she's been invited yet, does she?"

"No, but she will. All the little girls will be talking about it, you watch. And she'll be gutted if she thinks she's been left out. And I'll have to deal with the fall-out while you bugger off and play bloody golf."

"Laura, it's a work thing," he said. "It's not like have a choice."

"Yes you do. You said you know how to play – so turn up at your work thing and play. You don't have to spend a Saturday afternoon working on your swing or polishing your putting or whatever. And I bet there are going to be drinks afterwards, and you won't be home until stupid o'clock and I'll have to do bedtime on my own. Again."

"Laura," Jonathan sighed. "Okay, there are going to be drinks afterwards. But I can come home early – I've hated missing putting the kids to bed, you know I have. You get to have them all day and I get a phone call in the evenings. Do you think I like that?"

"Do you think I like it?" I countered. "I'm knackered, coping with both of them on my own with no help."

"I have to go into a meeting now, Laura," Jonathan said, and that was that.

Furious, I stomped away and crossed the road towards home. Blinded by annoyance, I didn't see the cyclist until it was too late – somehow, my mind just didn't make the connection between the 'LOOK RIGHT' sign on the pavement and the possibility that there might actually be approaching traffic.

Apparently time is meant to go into slow motion when something like this happens, but the reverse was true for me. Everything seemed to speed up, terrifyingly, to a blinding jumble of primary-coloured Lycra, and my hands on the buggy, frozen, receiving no command from my brain telling them whether to push or pull.

He missed me, but he ploughed into the buggy, somersaulting, and landing on the pavement at my feet.

To his credit, he didn't start shouting at me straight away. The first thing he did, once he'd scrambled to his feet, before even surveying the buckled wheel and scraped paintwork of his racing bicycle, was to look inside the buggy, his face white with dread at what he might see there. But there was no child – Owen was at nursery. My only passenger was Green

Rabbit, who Owen insisted must be allowed to come along for the ride to nursery.

"Jesus Christ," he said. "What were you... You stupid fucking bitch. You didn't even look where you were fucking going. What the fuck is wrong with you? Are you drunk?"

Mute with shock, I could only shake my head.

"You – I could have killed your kid. What were you doing? I could have killed your kid because you weren't looking where you were fucking going."

He was shouting now, his face no longer pale but almost puce with rage. In the face of his fury, I found I had nothing at all to say in my defence. My eyes and nose were streaming, and my hands were still clenched in front of me, my knuckles white, as if they were still gripped fast to the buggy's rubber handle.

"Don't just fucking stand there! Say something!"

I opened my mouth, but no words came out.

Then I felt a hand on my arm, and heard a calm voice say, "Can't you see she's in shock? Stop shouting at the poor woman. You were going far too fast, you were riding like an idiot. Don't you know this is a school?"

"She needs to looks where she's going. Stupid cow."

"I could say the same about you," the voice replied frostily. "And I shall, when I take this photograph of you to the police."

"You...what?" The cyclist suddenly seemed a little less confident.

I turned around to look at my rescuer. She didn't look like your stereotypical guardian angel – unless guardian angels had changed their uniform to ripped skinny jeans, over-the-knee boots and pistachio-coloured leather jackets, and replaced their harps with iPhone 6s.

"Yes, I intend to report this," the woman said. "This road is a death trap, the way people drive and park. I live here and I see incidents like this all the time. It's a wonder a child hasn't been killed."

"Well, at least no one was hurt," the cyclist said. "Look, I'm sorry, I probably was going a bit fast but I was running late for work, and…"

"Best you get on your way then," the woman said dismissively, then turned to me. "You look like you could do with a cup of tea. Want to come in?"

"Yes, please." I realised my knees were trembling violently, and if I didn't sit down I'd fall down.

"It's this one right here." She guided me through her front door and into a space-age kitchen, all stainless steel and skylights, and gestured to a canary-yellow sofa. "Here, have a seat and I'll put the kettle on. Unless you'd prefer a brandy? That's meant to be good for shock."

"Thanks," I said. "Tea would be lovely. I've done my bit of irresponsible parenting, I don't want to start drinking before ten in the morning or someone will call Social Services on me for sure. God, what was I thinking? If Owen had been in the buggy…"

"But he wasn't," she said. "No harm done. Would you rather builders' with sugar or herbal something with honey?"

"Herbal, please," I said. "Thank you so much for this, I really appreciate it. My name's Laura, by the way."

"Zélide. Call me Zé, all my friends do. Now, chamomile's good for sleeplessness so I reckon it'll do the job. I did a herbal medicine course ages ago but I've forgotten most of it, and I suspect it was mostly bollocks anyway."

If she didn't quite look the part of a guardian angel, Zélide was stunning nonetheless. Her dark hair hung in two straight wings on either side of her oval face; her lips gleamed with gloss; her fluttery eyelashes were just too long to be real. She sat next to me on the sofa and crossed her slender, booted legs.

"Thanks so much for this," I said. "I'm really sorry to mess up your morning – were you on your way out?"

"Just back from the school run," she said. "Same as you."

"I wish I looked like that for the school run," I said, glancing down at my own jeans, which the label had promised were 'boyfriend' but were really just shapeless, and battered converse.

Zé laughed. "I have a fashion blog. I post every day, and include a selfie. Talk about making a rod for my own back! I spent less time getting ready in the mornings when I worked at *Tatler*. But now I've kind of got into the habit, and if I slack off I'll lose readers. What about you – what do you do?"

"Nothing," I said. "Well, being-a-mum nothing. We only moved here a few weeks ago. I used to work in PR as an account-handler. I expect I'll look for

43

SOPHIE RANALD

temp work at some point but I haven't got around to it yet – you know what it's like."

"Hardest job in the world, innit?" She raised a perfectly groomed eyebrow.

"You know what, it really bloody is. When I was working it was hectic juggling everything, but things seemed to just sort of work, somehow, amid the mayhem. And my husband wasn't working such mad hours, which helped. But how, being with them all the time, it seems as if there's just no let-up. Even when Darcey's at school and Owen's at nursery shit just appears to fill the time and then I have to pick them up again and I've got nothing done."

"Fab names. Darcey and Owen, lovely," she said, and I felt a little glow of pride.

"When I was growing up, I always said I wanted to name my daughter Darcey, after the dancer, obviously. I changed my mind later on, but I mentioned it to Jonathan when I was pregnant and he said he loved it and I hadn't the heart to veto it. Owen's after Jonathan's dad; he died when Jonathan was a teenager, so that one was a given. And your daughter – Juniper?"

"I suppose it's pretentious as anything, but I don't care," she said. "It was a chance to wind up my bitch of a mother-in-law, and I love it, and Juniper loves it, so it works for both of us. Although Rick's mother still passive-aggressively refers to her as June when we talk on the phone. Which, thankfully, doesn't happen often. More tea?"

The honeyed chamomile tea was actually pretty foul, but I realised I was enjoying Zé's company more than I'd enjoyed anyone's for a long time.

"Yes, please," I said, kicking off my shoes and tucking my feet underneath me on the yellow sofa. "You don't mind?"

"God, no. Shoes on, shoes off, feet on the sofa – whatever. Make yourself comfortable." She switched the kettle on again and opened one of the sleek white cupboards, rummaging around a bit before producing a duck-egg blue tin of biscuits. "Elevenses?"

It wasn't yet ten o'clock, but all I'd had for breakfast was half a banana off Owen's plate. "Yes, please," I said.

"So your husband works with Rick?" Zé said. "Small world. Rick went for promotion at the same time as he did, but he didn't get it. He's pretending not to be bitter about it but he so is, and it'll mean him working even longer hours than usual. We barely see each other as it is."

She didn't sound like she minded that a bit, I thought, intrigued.

"How did you two meet?" I asked.

"At a dinner party," she said. "I'd been single for ages, my mid-thirties were slipping away and I wanted a baby. He seemed like a decent enough option."

She grimaced ruefully, took a second biscuit and ate it in two bites. "We'll pay for this tomorrow, I suppose. But now, fuck it."

I reached for another biscuit too, one with a chocolate coating, and caught her eye as I bit into it. The chocolate melted against the roof of my mouth and the buttery crumbs stuck to my lips. We exchanged a small, complicit smile, and I knew she was feeling just the same way I was.

In return, I told her the relatively simple, humble story of how I'd met Jonathan when I was twenty-six and in my first job out of uni, because I'd been a mature student, and he'd come to do the annual audit at my work. I told her how all the women in the client service department had fancied the pants off him, and how elated I'd been when it was me he emailed a week later to invite out for a drink.

"I didn't think I was even in the market for a relationship," I said. "But there was this whole rivalry thing going on between the other girls, and when I got that email I was suddenly the queen of the department for a day. So I couldn't say no. And then he was so lovely, and made me laugh so much. And then I went out with him again a couple of times, and suddenly we were an item, and then we moved in together and a bit later he proposed and I said yes, and we had this amazing wedding and two years later we had Darcey."

I paused for breath and ate another biscuit.

"You must feel very lucky," Zé said, but the way she said it made it a question.

"Oh, yes, I do!" I said. "I love him to bits. I love my children. I'm very lucky. I never expected to have all this."

"Why not, Laura?" Zé said. "You're exactly the kind of woman who has all this – all that. Look at you. You're so pretty, and you're kind and bright. I bet Amanda Moss has had you over for her book group, right? They're super-selective, they only pick the elite."

"Surely they must have picked you then?"

Zé laughed. "I'm hardly the elite. I did go along a few times, but I never read anything. Then Amanda tried to rope me into the PTA, but I told her I can't be arsed with committees, and she threw a strop and blocked me on Facebook, and now I'm persona non grata with her and her gang."

I laughed. "I'll take that as a warning. She's invited Darcey to her daughter's party on Saturday, actually, but now Jonathan says he's going out and I've got no one to look after Owen, who's most definitely NFI, so I don't know if she'll be able to go."

"But you must let me look after him," Zé said. "Juniper adores toddlers. God knows where she gets it from, but she's the most maternal creature. Why not bring them both round in the morning, and your little girl can try on Juniper's clothes – she's got truckloads from when she was that age – and we can have lunch and then by the time you head off I won't be a stranger any more. Owen will be fine with us for a couple of hours, and we'll be just down the road if he needs you. Go on – you know it makes sense."

Before I realised I was going to do it, I leaned forward and gave her a hug.

"Thanks," I said, "I think I'll do that."

"There," Zé said, "Darcey shall go to the ball."

"Do you want to knock on the door, Pickle?" I asked Darcey, when we arrived at Zé's at the appointed time on Saturday.

Her excitement at the prospect of meeting Zé and Juniper, and the party that was to follow, seemed to have deserted her and been replaced by shyness. She shook her head mutely and put her thumb in her mouth.

"Okay, I'll do it." But as I lifted my hand to the brushed stainless steel knocker, the door flew open and a child stood there who could only have been Zé's daughter. I mean, it was obviously her because no other little girl would have come to let us in, but I could have picked her out of a line-up of dozens, so striking was the resemblance to her mother.

She was very tall for eight, with a curtain of smooth hair the colour of black coffee, and brilliant green eyes. She was wearing dark indigo skinny jeans with a rip in one knee that I was pretty certain was supposed to be there, and not a result of falling over on her scooter. Her T-shirt had dozens of tiny sequinned stars on it, which Darcey would have picked off within about ten minutes. She looked like she'd been born stylish.

Darcey stared at her, wide-eyed, and took her thumb out of her mouth very quickly. Owen hid behind my leg.

Then Juniper smiled, the gappy grin of a normal eight-year old.

"Hello. Are you Darcey? You've got a cool name, and you're so lucky to have a little brother. Mummy's outside in the garden, but we can go upstairs to my room and play on my iPad, or do dressing up. Gardens are boring, don't you think? Come on."

She held out her hand and Darcey instantly took it, briefly turning to glance back at me, anxious for permission.

"Off you go," I said. "Owen and I will go and find Juniper's mum."

I scooped Owen up and he buried his face in my shoulder. "Hello?" I called, closing the door behind us and walking through to the kitchen.

"Hi," Zé said. "I'm so glad you came. I'm just making us a bit of lunch, I thought you'd probably rather eat now than join the kids in whatever sugar-laden spread they've laid on for the party. And you must be Owen. What a cutie he is, Laura. Would you like to come and see the giant goldfish in my pond? Last time I counted there were ten, but it's really hard to find them all. Maybe you can help me?"

Owen squirmed to be put down, and said, "Yes! Fishes! I can count up to ten now, because I'm nearly three."

"And very clever," I said, catching Zé's eye and returning her smile. "Thanks so much again for offering to have him. I can't tell you how grateful I am."

"Honestly, it's no bother," she said. "They're adorable at this age. We'll have a lovely afternoon here, and if he gets bored we can go to the park and play on the slide."

"I want to see the fishes," Owen said.

"All right, but you must be very, very careful and not lean too far over the water." I had a sudden, horrible stab of anxiety, imagining a panicked phone call from Zé, a mad rush back to the house, Owen's little body limp and sodden...

As if she'd read my thoughts, Zé said, "There's a net over the pool, Laura. Don't worry. Not just for safety – last winter a bloody heron decided to feed her family for a week on my koi. I was gutted – but not as gutted as I'd be if anything happened to a child, of course. Would you like a glass of wine with lunch? Dutch courage before you face the party?"

I vacillated for a moment, then said, "Yes, please. If you're having one."

"It's just a salad Nicoise," she said. "With lots of olives. Do you like olives, Owen?"

"I don't think he's ever tried one," I admitted.

But Owen said, "Yes! Olives."

We sat in the shade and ate and drank, while Owen made a series of forays into the garden, returning to chatter away about the fish and eat olives off our plates, and soon it was half past two and time to leave for Amanda's.

"Let me go and see what those girls are up to," Zé said, calling up the stairs, "Juniper! It's time for Darcey to go to her party."

Darcey ran downstairs, Juniper following her more sedately. Gone were her grey leggings and pink Barbie top, and in their place she was wearing Juniper's sequinned T-shirt as a dress. Her hair was piled up in a messy bun that was clearly meant to be that way, not just inexpertly arranged the way I did it. A pair of heart-shaped sunglasses were perched on her nose.

"Look," she said, giving me a shy twirl. "Juniper said I could borrow it. Isn't it beautiful?"

"You don't mind, do you, Mum?" Juniper said. "We tried on loads of my clothes but Darcey liked this best."

"Darcey looks gorgeous," Zé said. "You'll be the sparkliest girl at the party, and the prettiest too."

"Are you sure?" I said. "What if she spills something on it, or damages it? Is it dry-clean only?"

"Don't give it a thought," Zé said. "Juniper has far too many clothes. PR people are constantly sending me samples and I never get around to eBaying them. If she doesn't mind lending it, then of course I don't either."

"And I've said I don't mind," said Juniper. "Keep it, if you like. It suits you."

"Say thank you, darling," I said, admitting defeat.

"Thank you," Darcey said. "But I already said, loads of times, didn't I?"

"She did," Juniper confirmed. "When can Darcey come and play again? It's so boring that you have to go to this party. Can't you stay?"

Darcey looked down at her new outfit, then at Juniper, then at me. I could see her suffering agonies of indecision – part of her longing to spend the after-noon with her new friend, part wanting to show off her finery to her classmates.

"We'll come again soon, I promise," I said. "It's so kind of you to lend it to her, and to look after Owen, and the lunch…"

"You're so welcome," Zé said. "Come any time."

"Come next week," Juniper said. "You can see Carmen."

"Our au pair," Zé said. "She's in Romania this week, her sister's just had a baby. But she's back on Monday, thank God. We've missed her, haven't we?"

"Mmmm," Juniper was losing interest in this grown-up conversation. "Do you want to come and make a castle in the sandpit?" she said to Owen, who agreed eagerly.

I kissed him, and kissed Zé, and said we'd be back in a few hours, and Darcey and I departed.

All the way to Amanda's, she chatted non-stop about how cool Juniper's clothes were, how many amazing toys she had, and when she could show Juniper her own bedroom and toys.

And as I steeled myself for another bout of competitive parenting, I found myself thinking how much nicer it would be to still be sitting in Zé's tranquil garden, sipping white wine and chatting while our children played together. It sounds mad, I know, but it felt like the end of a holiday, or like leaving a lover to return to a sour, unsatisfactory marriage.

CHAPTER FIVE

It was a week later, and Jonathan was giving the kids their bath while I tried to make some impact on the chaos that had taken over our kitchen, which I'd tidied just that morning. Darcey had wanted to make cupcakes; Owen had insisted on helping and dolloped chocolate batter all over the floor and made his sister cry. So I'd packed them off to the park with Jonathan, and then it had rained and he'd forgotten to make them take their wellies off at the front door, so the spilled cake mix was indistinguishable from the smears of mud that decorated the so-modern, so-impractical white rubber floor.

Was six thirty too early for a glass of wine, I wondered, and immediately decided it certainly was not. A glass of wine, maybe several, and Jonathan could sort something out for our dinner, and if it ended up being yet another takeaway I wouldn't complain, as long as I didn't have to lift another finger in this kitchen all weekend.

I was just twisting the corkscrew into a bottle of chardonnay when I heard my phone ring. I almost

53

didn't answer – it would be Sadie ringing for a chat, which would be far more enjoyable later over a drink. Or one of the school mums wanting to arrange something for tomorrow, in which case I'd need a bit of breathing space to think of a plausible excuse. Or Jonathan's mother, who infuriatingly insisted on ringing me whenever she wanted to make plans to see her grandchildren, as if Jonathan was incapable of using a phone or looking in a diary.

But when I glanced at the screen, I saw Zé's name, and decided to take the call after all.

"Hi, Laura!" she sounded a bit croaky, as if she had a cold.

"Hi," I said. "How's it going?"

"Been better," she said. "Actually I was meant to be going out with Rick, but the fucker's stood me up at the eleventh hour. We had the most epic row about it."

I wondered whether she didn't actually have a cold, but had been crying.

"Bastard," I said sympathetically. I thought, shall I ask her to come round for a drink? She must have a babysitter sorted if she'd been going out. Then I imagined having to give the house a less cursory clean, put on make-up and wave goodbye to my quiet evening in, and didn't say anything.

"Look, are you busy tonight?" she said. "It's just, I booked this theatre thing. It's virtually impossible to get in, I only managed to get tickets through a friend who's producing it and I really want to go. Will you come along?"

"Okay," I said. "I didn't have any plans, and Jonathan hasn't got work to do, for once. I'd love to come."

"Great!" she said. "It starts at eight, so you'll need to get your skates on, but it's just round the corner, in Battersea Park. You know the bandstand? Meet me there as soon after seven thirty as you can. And wear comfortable shoes, and something warm – it's outdoors and we'll be running around. Thank God the rain's stopped, or they would have cancelled the performance."

And she rang off before I could say that actually running around in a park at night sounded like the least fun thing in the world, ever.

I went upstairs, calling to Jonathan that I had last-minute plans and was going out.

"Out where?" He emerged from the bathroom, his shirt splashed with water and smudged with bath crayon.

"Some theatre thing, with Zé. Rick stood her up. It's in Battersea Park, I've no idea what it is."

"That must be *A Midsummer Night's Dream.* Lucky you – tickets are harder to come by than ones with six winning lottery numbers, apparently. We tried to arrange to take some clients but it's totally sold out. Everyone's talking about it."

"Not to me, they aren't." I pulled my shirt off and glanced down at my jeans. They were too smeared with cake batter to pass muster, even in the dark. I found a clean pair, and a clean black jumper. The rain had made my hair frizz, even though I hadn't been outside all day, but there was no time to do anything about that, or about my face.

"Here, I've found it. Listen." Jonathan read from his iPad. "'The new, ground-breaking immersive production, from Flight of Fancy, the most talked-about theatre company of the century (who brought us last summer's award-winning *Out to Sea*, as if our readers need telling) is a must-not-miss. This magical interpretation of Shakespeare's best known comedy blends theatre and dance with elusive, intimate moments that see cast and audience interacting, and the fourth wall dissolving. The sensational set transforms a suburban park into a sylvan wood, with breathtaking lighting and sound effects completing an enchanted world. And it's not just about smoke and mirrors – there are truly insightful performances from...' Loads of people I've never heard of. Anyway, it says, 'Prepare to be dazzled, amazed and perhaps quite literally swept off your feet – if you can get your hands on a ticket. Rob a bank, sell a close family member – whatever it takes, you won't regret it.' They've given it five stars."

"I'm already regretting it," I said, lacing up my trainers. "She didn't say anything about dance."

"Don't be daft, Laura, you'll love it." There was a splash from the bathroom, and a gale of giggles from Darcey. "I'd better get back and see what those two are up to. Probably causing a flood. Have fun."

"Thanks," I said. "No idea when I'll be back, or in what state. Probably with my head swapped for a donkey's. Bye, Darcey, bye Owen – Mummy's going out."

How hard could it be to transform a park into a sylvan grove anyway, I thought sullenly as I hurried through the streets. Battersea Park was about as sylvan as it got – mud and all. And why hadn't Zé said anything about dance? She'd only mentioned theatre. If she'd said dance, I wouldn't have gone. Oh well, it was too late – there was no backing out now.

"There in five," I texted hastily, making my way along the path to the bandstand, joining a small throng of people heading in the same direction. They all seemed delighted at the prospect of the experience that lay ahead of us.

"Oh my God, I am, like, gibbering with excitement," I overhead one woman say. "It's my tenth time at this. It's bankrupting me. How many times have you been, Stu?"

"Only twice," her companion said. "I'm not as well connected as you, I guess."

"It's not about being well connected!" she protested. "It's about giving Flight of Fancy a fat donation every year – tax-deductible, fortunately – and getting priority booking before tickets go on general sale. I've got another twelve shows booked after tonight and I'm worried it won't be enough. Do hurry up, we've only got twenty minutes."

And she dragged the unfortunate Stu off into the crowd, leaving me shaking my head in bemusement.

Of course, I'd encountered my fair share of obsessives when I was dancing professionally. There was one old gent who sat in the same seat in the front row for an entire fortnight, and sent two dozen pink roses to my dressing room each morning when we were doing *Manon* – and I wasn't even a soloist; that was nothing compared to the adulation some of my colleagues received – Jerome, Mel... But I wasn't going to go there. I was going to find Zé and get this thing over with, and go home to my proper life.

It wasn't hard to locate her, even in the mass of people gathered around the bandstand – there must have been two hundred or more, I reckoned, all standing about drinking prosecco out of plastic flutes and chattering excitedly. But even in the twilight, with only huge ropes of silvery-blue fairy lights for illumination, Zé stood out. She was wearing a shocking-pink cropped leather biker jacket over black jeans, and her lipstick was bright fuschia too. The combination would have been absurdly over-the-top on just about anyone else; on her it was effortlessly stylish.

"Laura!" she hurried over to me, kissed me, and handed me a glass of fizz. "I can't thank you enough for coming, honestly, I was mortified when bloody Rick cancelled on me. You don't get the chance to see Flight of Fancy's *Dream* and bail at the last minute, the fuckwit."

I wondered again what was going on in their marriage – whenever she mentioned Rick it was with coolness at best, contempt at worst. Then, in spite of myself, I felt the air of excitement infect me, too. Zé's normally pale cheeks were flushed, and she was talking even more than usual.

"So, the idea is to split up, do your own thing, explore the set and see whatever scenes come your way," she said. "If you get lost, you can make your way back here and have a drink and a sit-down, and we'll meet up here afterwards, okay? We just need to go through there" – she gestured towards a pair of marble pillars that, although they were obviously part of the set, were coated with moss and lichen and looked like they'd been there for centuries – "and they'll check our tickets, and then we're on our own. Did you see *Out to Sea* last summer?"

"No," I said. "I didn't."

"Of course, it wasn't in London, it was in Newcastle, of all places," Zé prattled on. "Stunning setting, of course, but my God, the wind! My hair was totally fucked."

She grinned and clicked her plastic glass against mine, then her smile was replaced with deadly seriousness. "Look! We're going in! Come on, I'll see you on the other side, and remember – if you see something that looks interesting, stick around and watch, and if you see a character who fascinates you, follow them. They're all in masks, as well as in costume. And switch your phone off if you haven't already, and remember there's no talking once we're through the pillars, they're brutal about chucking people out who they think are being disrespectful."

She grabbed my hand and pulled me towards the entrance, abandoning our half-finished drinks on the way. A robed steward checked our tickets and reminded us sternly about the talking and phones. The audience filed between the pillars, through a kind of dazzling curtain of brightness created by powerful spotlights aimed towards the ground. I blinked, waiting for my eyes to adjust – but as soon as they had, I was plunged into absolute darkness and Zé dropped my hand and vanished.

We must be in some kind of tunnel, I decided, brushing my hand against its sides – hessian, maybe. Then the person behind me trod on my heel and I continued blindly on, feeling my way, unable to see where I was going. There was music, I realised, eerie and soft, only audible now that the babble of conversation had ceased. I moved towards the source of the sound, and as I did so I noticed the darkness diluting slightly, a faint glimmer of green appearing ahead. The person behind me pushed past me, and I felt a sudden surge of adrenalin – who the hell did they think they were, trying to get there before me? I pushed back, dodged in front, and found myself hurrying, almost running, towards the light.

I've never been much of a reader. We 'did' *A Midsummer Night's Dream* at school, but that was long ago – long enough ago to make me feel seriously old. But not quite as old as I felt when I remembered how long ago it was that, aged eight, I'd danced a fairy in a production staged by my ballet school.

Anyway, it was all pretty much in the distant past, and my recollection of the plot was shaky to say the least. So when I emerged on to the set, I was surprised to find it all coming back to me – dimly at first, then more clearly. Here were the king and queen – Theseus and whatever-her-name-was – and their masked retinue, in flowing gold and silver robes, in their palace. The breathless review Jonathan had read to me didn't exaggerate – the set was stunning. Marble pillars soaring up into the darkness, twined with ivy; flaming torches illuminating the walls; a fountain splashing in the centre.

Around me, the audience was dispersing, some moving around to get a better view, others hurrying off into the darkness to find – what? I had no idea. I'd wait here for a bit, I decided, and see what was going to happen.

The volume of the music increased, and the king and queen began to dance. I took a deep, trembly breath and watched, feeling unaccountably afraid. If they were shit, I'd be devastated. If they were good, it would be even worse. And I realised within a few seconds that they were very good indeed. I could hardly bear to look – but I couldn't look away, either.

As the lead woman moved across the stage, seeming almost to float, I felt physically sick with envy and regret. Look at her, with her honed, supple limbs, her command of the audience and the choreography – her career. That could have been me, I thought – that was me. But not any more.

As the routine came to an end and more characters entered – two of the four lovers, I thought vaguely, unable to remember their names or what they were doing there – I realised my cheeks were wet with tears. I dug in my pocket for a tissue and blew my nose as quietly as I could, hoping that if anyone noticed they'd assume I was moved to tears by the beauty of it all. But no one was looking at me – everyone was entirely absorbed in the scene.

I'd wander off and explore, I decided, see more of the set that had received such rave reviews, and try not to look too closely if I came upon any more dancers. I skirted around the palace building and headed towards another island of light in the trees. Some of them were real, I noticed, but the fake ones were so skilfully constructed, so subtly blended into the natural parkland, that it was almost impossible to tell the difference, to separate artifice from reality.

I arrived at a clearing where another stage had been constructed – a rough wooden affair this time. Presumably this was where Quince and his friends would rehearse their play, about which I could recall no details whatsoever. I remembered finding those bits tedious and unfunny during those long-ago English Lit lessons. But the detail was meticulous. An entire village had been constructed around the stage:

there was a carpenter's shop, the floor scattered with shavings, which even smelled of freshly sawn wood. There was a wagon hung with metal pots, pans and cups that rattled as I brushed past, making me start guiltily. The tailor's workroom was festooned with apparel in various stages of repair. I pushed through them, feeling the coarse fabric brushing my face and breathing in the musty scent of well worn clothing. The hanging garments became denser, and I wondered if I ought to turn back, but something made me carry on – I remembered the wardrobe that led to Narnia in another long-ago story, and pushed the walls of fabric aside, finding a path to the other side.

I emerged into another clearing, lit by a full moon, smelling headily of flowers. How the hell did they do this, I wondered fleetingly – and more importantly, where was I? I'd lost my bearings entirely, and lost all sense of time, too. I paused, inhaling the cool, fragrant air. The sky above me was darkening to a deep indigo, and I could see stars. Was this real twilight or a clever lighting effect? It was impossible to tell.

I heard a swelling burst of music and the light of the moon seemed to concentrate on the space between two trees. Almost of their own accord, my feet carried me towards it, and I found myself suddenly joined by about twenty other audience members, who'd appeared seemingly from nowhere. I'd nearly forgotten, I realised, that this was a show, and not some kind of alternate reality I'd stepped into, or a fragment of a dream.

A masked man and woman appeared in the moonlight. There were two pairs of lovers, I remembered sketchily, and they were all in love with the wrong people, before it all somehow got sorted out. These must be two of them. I waited, watching as they danced together. Even though I was shoulder to shoulder with other spectators, it was easy to forget they were there – there was nothing but me, the music and the dancers. I couldn't even hear the man next to me breathing.

The dance – it was part dance, part seduction, tender and erotic – must have lasted a few minutes, but it felt like just seconds before the music became slower and softer, the two lovers lay still in each other's arms, and a cloud passed over the moon – or the spotlight that served as a moon. Immediately, the audience broke up and moved away, one woman actually sprinting off between the trees. I recognised her from earlier on – the woman with the friend called Stu, who'd seen the production over and over. Where was she going? She seemed to know – she must be on her way to somewhere or something specific. I followed her, also breaking into a run.

She'd bloody better know where she was going, I thought, a few breathless seconds later – we seemed to be heading deep into impenetrable forest, dodging between tree trunks, real and artificial leaves brushing my face, fake and genuine roots catching at my feet and threatening to send me flying. Thank God for Zé's warning and my sensible trainers. Abruptly, the woman stopped and so did I, just in time to avoid crashing into her. She pushed her hair off her face and glanced around, catching my eye and giving me an unfriendly scowl. Whatever she was waiting for, clearly she expected to have it all to herself.

I retreated a step or two and waited. It was dark and silent – there was no hint that anything was going to happen. Then I spotted a figure in the shadows – an actor, or another spectator? Or something else? I looked closer, trying to make sense of the unfamiliar, distorted form. Of course, it was the bloke who got turned into a donkey. Bum something? I wished I'd had time to look up the plot on Wikipedia and make more sense of what was going on. Bottom – that was it! His absurd head tilted towards us, and he shambled in our direction, tripping over a fallen log on his way.

I heard the woman, who was standing a pace or two in front of me, give a little gasp of excitement. She shifted a little, blocking my view. I shifted the other way; so did she. Bottom paused in front of us, and reached his hairy mask forward, making snuffling sounds. Then he reached out a hand to me.

I hesitated for just a second, my fascinated need to know what would happen if I followed him overpowered by fear of the unknown. But a second was enough for the other woman to grab the actor's outstretched hand and be led away into the darkness. I followed again, even though I could sense that it was the wrong thing to do, that I'd missed my chance. And sure enough, when they disappeared into a thicket of what looked like birch trees, I heard the unmistakeable sound of a lock clicking shut.

Should I wait until they came out again, I wondered. But I couldn't bring myself to, somehow. I was conscious that I'd failed, that I'd let her get something that should have been mine – and even though I had no idea what it would have been, I felt bitterly disappointed, and a bit ashamed of my disappointment. Besides, I realised, I was very thirsty and also dying for a wee. It's only a play, Laura, I told myself – do get a grip.

I turned back into the forest and tried to retrace my steps, realising that what had felt like a headlong race had only in reality been a few yards. After a couple of false starts, I found the village again, and beyond it the Theban palace. And if I went back through the tunnel I'd find the bar and hopefully the loos.

A few minutes later I was perched on a tree stump sipping another plastic cup of prosecco, examining a long scratch on my wrist that I couldn't remember feeling but must have sustained on my dash through the trees, and wondering what to do next. It was nine thirty – there was only about an hour of the performance left. I was tired and chilly and my ankle hurt, but far more powerful was my regret at having missed out. I wanted what that woman had had – whatever it was. The mysterious interaction with someone who was, as I knew only too well, just a performer doing a job – but also not. Also a poor man under an enchantment on a summer night when the bounds of possibility were stretching and snapping. I wanted to know what would have happened if I had taken his hand.

"Laura!" Zé appeared next to me, drink in hand. "God, isn't this totally fucking amazing! How are you getting on? What have you seen?"

"I saw the king and queen dancing," I said. "I looked round the village thing, and I saw an amazing pas de deux – I'm not sure who the characters were, they went to sleep afterwards…"

"Hermia and Lysander," Zé said. "Fab! What else?"

"Then I followed someone away from there, and I'm not sure what happened. I think I fucked up. The donkey guy – Bottom, is it? – did a thing where he tried to hold my hand, but I bottled it, and the other woman went instead."

"You missed the Bottom interaction! Gutting! I got Puck, it was mind-blowing. Look – he gave me a spell." She rummaged in her pocket and pulled out a tiny glass bottle, removed the cork and sniffed. I leaned over and sniffed too.

"What is that?" I said. "It reminds me of… Something. But I can't place it."

"Mmm," Zé said. "They use scent a lot in their productions, it's so evocative. But we need to get back in there, Laura, come on! And next time you're offered an interaction, for God's sake take it!"

I gulped the last of my drink and stood up. I didn't feel tired any longer – just eager to see more, and frightened of missing out again.

"I'm off," I said. "See you in an hour or so."

I hastened back through the tunnel, suddenly confident once more. I knew where I was going. I'd make my way back to where I'd lost Bottom, and see what would happen there next.

But I overestimated my knowledge of the set. I decided to take a short cut through the palace, bypassing the rude mechanicals' village, and soon I found myself lost in the trees. The full moon was high overhead, but it seemed to have moved, and anyway I'd been the shittest girl guide ever and if I relied on my night navigation skills, in the absence of Google Maps, I'd never even find my way home from the pub.

There was still music, but it was faint and elusive. I tried to find its source, dodging between tree trunks, only the occasional glimpse of another spectator reassuring me that I hadn't strayed off the set entirely. But I was beginning to feel anxious – anxious and frustrated, aware that I was wasting time wandering haplessly about and seeing nothing.

I stopped, leaning against a tree, and wondered what the hell to do next. I could go back, start again – but then I'd be seeing stuff over, not discovering new things. And time was running out. Then I heard the faintest rustle behind me, the sound of stealthy feet on a carpet of leaves. I was about to turn around when a pair of warm, strong hands closed over my eyes.

I wanted to scream, but, as happens when you try to scream in a nightmare, all that came out was a sort of strangled gasp. I could feel gentle breath on my neck, and for a second I thought that this was it, it had all gone horribly wrong, I was going to be raped and murdered in the middle of a sell-out immersive theatre production in South West London. The idea was absurd enough to make me relax slightly, and as I did so, the hands moved gently away from my eyes, but a blindfold was tied securely in their place.

"Come, take hands with me," a voice said. "Let your eyes be blind, lest you should be afeared."

The hand that had been over my left eye moved gently down and fingers clasped my own. I felt a strong arm encircle my waist. My eyes squeezed shut. I was led away across ground that felt surprisingly smooth beneath my feet. My heart was pounding; I was aware that my breath was coming in huge gasps, but I didn't feel frightened any more, only avid to know what would happen next.

I was guided through hanging branches that felt like they might be a willow tree, and I heard running water. For a moment my heart jumped again in my chest, and I thought, fuck, he's going to drown me. But there was something about the calm assurance of my guide – who was just an actor, I reminded myself – that allayed my fear with eagerness. I felt hands on my shoulders pushing me down, and found myself sitting on something soft. My exploring fingers felt velvet, and then hands smoothed my face, removing the blindfold and brushing over my eyelids, and the smell of a garden on a summer night was suddenly everywhere.

"I lay the love potion on my true love's sight," a voice murmured in my ear. "To charm her eyes. And what next she sees, she will dote on in extremity."

I took another breath, the fragrance filling my senses, and realised there was music playing now too. Part of me didn't want to open my eyes; a more powerful part couldn't help it. And when I did, there in front of me was Oberon, king of the magical wood. Oberon, in deepest green robes, a crown of oak leaves on his head. Oberon, who I suddenly remembered I'd had a massive crush on at school when I was eleven, thinking Demetrius and Lysander too laddish and gauche to bother with. It was Oberon who lifted his elaborate, horned mask and softly kissed my lips as the scent of flowers whirled around me. But it wasn't really Oberon. It was Felix.

CHAPTER SIX

April 2001: Recovery

For the next couple of weeks, I followed Felix around slavishly, like a reality TV contestant going, "Pick me! Pick me!" I tried to be subtle about it, studying his habits and altering my routine ever so slightly so it coincided with his. I didn't move from my usual spot at the barre in morning class, between Mel and Roddy, but when it came to the floor work I hung back, trying to find myself in the group just before his, which he'd be watching while he waited for his turn. I stopped buying my morning espresso at the canteen and settled for an inferior, more expensive takeaway version from Pret, because I'd seen him carrying their branded cups around with him and hoped I might bump into him there. I went to Camden on my day off and bought a Metallica sweatshirt off a market stall and wore it as a warm-up top, because I'd seen him in a similar AC/DC one.

Still, our paths remained resolutely uncrossed outside work. The only place where I could count on finding Felix was on the roof, during every break, smoking Marlboro Reds with the health warnings printed in Russian. Before, smoking had been an occasional indulgence on a night out; now, I found my consumption creeping up to two or three, then five a day, then more. I noticed myself becoming slightly breathless when I ran up the stairs, but I wasn't bothered – by smoking instead of eating, I was losing weight, my body becoming leaner and my line cleaner. A thin dancer, even one who wheezed after a series of grands jêtés, was a good dancer.

And a fat lot of good it did me, because I wasn't the only one in Felix's entourage. The number of cigarette-smoking, Pret-drinking metal fans in the company had increased exponentially since his arrival. The weight had dropped off Lisa, too, and I noticed her casting resentful glares at me when I seemed to turn up in the same place as her all the time, because it was the same place as Felix. Even some of the soloists seemed to have succumbed to his allure – the normally taciturn Briony, who rarely cracked a smile when she wasn't on stage, became positively skittish around him, chatting away and asking him for lights, even when I'd seen her spark up a fag with her own Bic lighter just minutes before.

Mel and Roddy mocked me mercilessly. For Roddy, Felix was an object of envy, not of desire.

"Poncy git," he said. "Okay, he can dance, but he's got an ego the size of the Kremlin. Good luck with getting a shag there, Laura – not that you aren't hot or anything, but you'll have to take a number and get in line. Even if he does every girl in the company it could be months before he gets round to you."

"God, Laura, you reek of smoke," Mel said one night as we flopped on the sofa in the flat after a performance of *Giselle*, working our way through a bottle of Rioja to take the edge of our post-performance adrenaline so we'd be able to sleep. "What are you trying to prove, hanging around Lawsonski like a dose of athlete's foot?"

"Don't call him that." I dug her in the ribs with my elbow. "He's the man of my dreams. I'm allowed to have a crush, aren't I? And besides, I think it's working – he smiled at me in class today."

"Whoopee twang," Mel said. "He smiles at everyone. He's a right Mr Happy, that one. Mr Happy Lawsonski. If you want him to notice you, you'd be better off getting Marius to notice you first, so he gives you a good part. Lawsonski knows which side his bread's buttered."

"I'm not sure I want Marius to notice me," I said.

We paused, and exchanged a mutual shudder at the idea of shagging Marius, the company's all-powerful Creative Director, who terrified and fascinated us in equal measure. His lean, black-clad figure had a way of appearing in our peripheral vision just when we'd fucked up a step, were corpsing with laughter or were shovelling doughnuts into our faces after a particularly brutal class. Being acknowledged by him, even if only with the smallest nod, could mean we were about to shoot stratospherically through the ranks to stardom – or it could mean we'd been found wanting and our card was marked.

"I do," Mel said.

"What? You never fancy him."

"Marius? Good God, no," Mel said, but there was something about her tone that wasn't quite convincing.

"Mel and Marius, sitting in a tree, k-i-s-s..." I began.

"Oh, fuck off, Laura." She lobbed a cushion at me, just as she always did when I teased her, but she sounded seriously annoyed, so I changed the subject.

"Speaking of bread, do we have any in? I'd kill for a piece of hot buttered toast."

"There are some Ryvitas in the kitchen, I think," Mel said. "Want one?"

"Nah." I poured more wine into our glasses, half-heartedly mopping up the bit that splashed on to the sofa with my sleeve. It was so stained already, a bit more damage would make no difference to our chances of seeing our deposit when we moved out – if we ever did.

We'd been living in the flat for three years. When we first saw it, we'd been so elated at the prospect of living round the corner from work – work! Actually being paid to dance! Having made it into the company! – that we'd happily ignored the damp, the intermittent hot water and the mouse we'd seen scurrying along the skirting board on our first night there. It was only a matter of time, we told ourselves, until we were promoted, or one of us was, and then we'd move somewhere better, together like the Three Musketeers, sharing our good fortune.

But we were still waiting. We'd seen our contemporaries move on, some promoted, some decamping to other companies and even other countries, some giving up ballet altogether and training as dance teachers, finding modelling work, or just quietly vanishing.

"But we're still here," I said. "That has to be a good thing, right?"

Mel knew me well enough to read the thought behind this random remark.

"Sure," she said. "You're only twenty-one. Heaps of time yet. Only freaks make soloist at our age."

"Freaks and naturals," I said gloomily, draining my glass. "Is there another bottle?"

"Best not," Mel said. "Marius is coming to watch morning class tomorrow, remember? You don't want to be stinking of booze as well as fags."

"I'll shower before bed," I said, contemplating the prospect of ten minutes under a trickle of water with enthusiasm as lukewarm as it would be. I levered myself off the sofa, assessing a new click in my left hip, twin to the one in my right.

"See you later," I said.

"Laura," Mel said. "Just a second, before you go…"

I paused, a sinking feeling in my stomach. She was going to say Felix had asked her out. Or something else – something worse.

"I didn't want you to find out tomorrow with everyone else," she said. "But it's… They only told me today. I've been promoted. First Artist, from tomorrow."

"Mel! How did you keep that quiet all day? When did you find out? My God, that's incredible, I'm so made up for you."

I bent over and gave her a hug. I was pleased for her – of course I was. But I was also horribly, bitterly envious. The jump from being a mere Artist, as we'd been since we joined the company, to First Artist wasn't huge – it didn't mean masses more money or starring roles or anything like that – but it meant Mel was being considered for better parts, perhaps even for under-studying a soloist some time soon. It meant she was highly thought of – more highly thought of than me.

"I'm going to be a cygnet," she said, starting to giggle. "I can't believe it! I thought it was never going to happen and now it has."

"It has," I said. "And you bloody deserve it too, you work so hard."

I sat down again, even though what I really wanted was to go to bed and try to sleep, try not to think about it. "Tell me everything – what did they say?"

Mel put her feet up on the sofa, hugging her knees. "God, it's freezing in here. I swear, my entire pay rise is going to go towards having the heating on more often. Anna called me in – you know what she's like, I was terrified I was going to be sacked, and the way she started it really sounded like that. She went on and on about the importance of good technique, how that underlies everything and without it there's no point carrying on – you know, the usual lecture. And I stood there saying, 'Yes, Anna. I understand,' over and over, and trying not to cry."

"Then what?"

"Then she said she hoped I'd take on board her comments, and I realised I wasn't going to be sacked, because what would be the point if I was. And then she said she'd expect me in rehearsal room eight for *Swan Lake* tomorrow afternoon. And I said, 'But that's the cygnets, isn't it?' And she said yes, and that I could pick up the official letter about the promotion on my way out. And then I did cry – I felt like such a div."

"I'm sure everyone cries," I said. I needed to be more enthusiastic, congratulate her again – but I couldn't find the words. I was saved by the sound of Roddy's key in the door and he came bursting in, carrying a bunch of yellow roses.

"Mellifluous!" he said. "What's this rumour I hear?"

"How the hell did you find out?" Mel said.

"I keep my ear to the ground," Roddy said, thrusting the flowers at Mel. "I may have nicked these from Briony's dressing room. She's knee-deep in bouquets, she'll never miss them. Congratulations, darling girl, you're on your way to stardom!"

"In my dreams," Mel said, but she was all pleased and giggly.

"Come on, let's crack open a bottle," Roddy said. "Oh – you already have. You're way ahead of me. Another bottle, then."

"I don't think we should, really," Mel said. "I was just saying to Laura, Marius is coming to class tomorrow and… you know."

"You don't want to turn up with a hangover on your first day as a First Artist," Roddy rolled his eyes. "Suck-up. Fair enough, though – it is nearly one. Have you girls eaten?"

"I had a salad earlier," Mel said.

"I'm not hungry," I said. "I was just going to shower and go to bed, actually."

"I'll brush my teeth while your water gets hot," Roddy said. "I know you, you take hours in there."

"I suppose it's too late to ring Mum," Mel said. "God, I'm too wired to sleep though. I need to get my shoes sorted for tomorrow."

She picked up her bag and went into her bedroom, her shoulders drooping with tiredness.

Roddy and I collided with each other in the bathroom doorway. He put his arms round me and gave me a squeeze, whispering, "It sucks, Laura, I know."

"It's cool," I said. "I'm thrilled for Mel."

"Course you are," Roddy said, sticking his tongue out at me. "By the way, Lawsonski was asking about you in the pub."

"He was?"

"Mmhm. 'But who is ziz gorgeous girl, ze quiet one, who follows me everywhere I go and who smokes like ze chimneys in Siberia would smoke if zere was coal to keep ze peasants from freezing to death? I fear she is spy sent by ze KGB,' he said."

"Piss off," I said, giggling in spite of myself. "He doesn't talk like that."

"So I said, 'Why, Lawsonski, zat – sorry, that – is the fair Laura Braithwaite, my dear friend and flatmate. Sadly she is betrothed to a high-ranking Kremlin official, and if you so much as sniff her sweaty pointe shoes you will be sent to the gulags forever.'"

"Roddy, don't be such an arse!" I said. "What did he really say?"

"Okay, fine. Don't let me have my fun," Roddy said. "We were having lunch and he said he's look-ing for a flat – he's being put up in some dodgy digs at the sec – and he asked about my living arrange-ments. So I said I paid an extortionate amount to share with the two of you, here, and he looked glum, and then he said, which of you was the short blonde and which was the tall mousy one with the amazing legs."

Being described as having amazing legs slightly took the sting out of being called mousy, but only just – amazing legs were, after all, a quality every single woman in the company possessed, and hardly a dis-tinguishing feature.

"Then what?" I said.

"Aww, not much," Roddy admitted. "Keep up the stalking though, he's noticed you."

The next afternoon, as I rehearsed with the rest of the Corps de Ballet, going through the already-familiar steps over and over until they were perfect, I found my mind drifting away from my work to the upstairs rehearsal room where Mel was working with Briony, Francoise and Steph. I knew I should be happy for her, and I was, but my happiness was tainted with envy, and with anger at myself for feeling envious. Mel hadn't got this through luck or nepotism, but because she worked bloody hard, relentlessly hard. She was talented, she took direction well, she had an innate musical talent that I lacked. Did all those things mean she was destined to be more successful than me, always? Did it mean I'd never catch up? I felt my self-confidence, never particularly solid, becoming even more shaky. Were she and Roddy talking about me, pitying me? My own self-pity was hard enough to deal with, without the imagined sympathy of others.

But I needn't have worried, because if there was anything on Mel's mind other than her own perfor-mance, she gave no sign of it over the next few days. She talked incessantly about the show, how challeng-ing it was learning the dance with just two weeks to go before opening night, how brilliantly Felix was understudying Jerome, how exciting and original Marius's interpretation of the dance was.

It was the coldest, wettest spring I could remem-ber, and the weather reflected my mood. Getting out of bed, braving the freezing flat and the rainy, blus-tery walk to work became harder each day. I felt as if I hadn't seen the sun in months. Everyone had colds – our stage make-up had to be slathered on each night over red, flaking noses and chapped cheeks. Jerome came down with flu and missed two days' rehearsal for the first time anyone could remember, and speculation was rife over whether Felix would get his starring role after less than a month with the company. I desperately hoped he would, but if he felt the same he gave no sign of it – when I hovered on the outskirts of his group as we smoked on the roof, he seemed exactly the same as normal, careless and larky. Despite what Roddy had said, he paid me no more attention than usual, only greeting me with a casual, "Hey there," and offering me his lighter. He didn't even seem to have remembered my name.

On Sunday, our day off, my longed-for lie-in was interrupted by the actors who rented the flat upstairs crashing home pissed after an all-nighter. I checked my watch – it was seven thirty, far too early to get up, but sleep refused to reclaim me. Reluctantly, I threw off the duvet and went in search of coffee.

Mel was on the sofa watching telly, cocooned in a blanket.

"Hi," I said. "You're up early."

"I couldn't sleep," she said. "I've got the most awful headache and my throat hurts."

"Oh God, you poor thing. Would you like tea? Paracetamol?"

"I've already taken two. Shit, Laura, I feel grim. I should go back to bed, I suppose, but that would be…"

"I know," I said. That would mean admitting that she was ill, allowing the possibility of becoming iller still. "I was going to go out. Get a coffee, maybe go for a walk, do some shopping…"

"I'll come," she said. "Take my mind off it. At least it's not fucking raining."

"I'll see if Roddy's up," I said, but when I tapped on his door he mumbled something about what the hell time was this, and couldn't a boy get any rest, so I abandoned that idea.

We bundled ourselves up in coats and scarves, forced our blistered feet into high-heeled boots, and went out. I bought coffee and a croissant, but Mel said she wasn't hungry. She looked drawn and anxious, and she didn't chatter away about the show – she didn't talk much at all.

"Shall we go to Selfridges and try on make-up?" I said. It was a prospect Mel usually relished, making the girls on the counters apply a full face of products neither of us could hope to afford.

"It won't be open for ages," she objected.

"We could get the Tube somewhere," I suggested, realising that it had been weeks since I'd been further than about a mile from the flat. "Or go to a movie, or something. Somewhere warm. Or to the park."

"Whatever you want," Mel said.

Because we couldn't decide, we ended up just walking along Shaftesbury Avenue and through Soho, quiet and ghostly at this time, when the shops weren't open and the tourists hadn't emerged. We walked along Oxford Street, but when I commented on the contents of the windows, trying to engage Mel in our favourite game of 'when I have thousands of pounds to spend on clothes…', but she wasn't interested; whenever I stopped she rummaged in her bag for tissues and blew her nose. The first sign of enthusiasm she showed was when we passed Boots.

"Let's wait here until they open," she said. "I need drugs."

"Look, why don't you go home and go back to bed," I said. "Tell me what you need and I'll get it for you. You're not well."

"I'm fine," she said. "I just need something stronger than bloody paracetamol and I'll be grand."

But she wasn't. As the morning went on, she became paler and more miserable, and at last, when even the prospect of the Chanel counter didn't enthuse her, I insisted we go back to the flat, and we spent the rest of the day slumped in front of repeats of *Friends* drinking tea.

This was my life, I thought gloomily – six days' work a week, from ten in the morning until almost midnight, with snatched breaks for fags and coffee. And on a longed-for day off, being too knackered and skint to do anything fun. It was what I'd longed for and worked for since I was six years old, and now I found it hard to remember what I was supposed to enjoy about it.

It was the worst kind of Sunday afternoon, last-day-of-the-holidays feeling – a gloomy blanket overshadowing everything, blotting out the prospect of pleasure. On the sofa next to me, Mel looked as sunk in depression as I felt. I tucked my feet up, picking at a piece of loose skin on my heel, the legacy of an old blister, feeling the satisfying twinge of pain as it came loose.

"Don't do that, for Christ's sake," Mel snapped. "It's gross. Make an appointment with the podiatrist if your feet need doing."

"No point polishing a turd," I said, stretching my legs out in front of me and surveying them. All dancers have horrible feet, and mine, after a brutally busy winter season, were even more of a mess than usual, covered in calluses, my toes distorted from my pointe shoes. I'd stopped noticing them, and given up entirely on painting my nails – what was the point, when I'd never be able to take my shoes off in front of anyone who wasn't a dancer too, and wouldn't understand?

"No foot-fetishist lovers for us," said Mel.

"No lovers, full stop," I said. My social life felt as drab and featureless as my career. I hadn't had a boyfriend since sixth form, and there wasn't exactly a proliferation of likely candidates for the role. "Felix doesn't fancy me. Roddy was just making shit up to make me feel better. Speaking of which, how are you feeling?"

"Utter toilet," Mel said. She was pale – even paler then usual – and shivering.

"Go to bed, then," I said. "No point both of us sitting here feeling sorry for ourselves."

"No point going to bed, either," Mel said. "It's even colder in my room. Besides, I want to watch the video of the Balachine *Swan Lake* before tomorrow."

"God, do you have to? We've watched that bloody thing about a hundred times. Go to bed – you look terrible."

"Cheers for that, Florence Nightingale," Mel said. "Anyway, last time I checked, I live here too and I'm allowed to watch stuff on telly, aren't I?"

"Oh, watch what you fucking want," I said. "You always get your own way, there's no point me arguing about it."

The atmosphere in the room had suddenly changed, from a reasonably good natured, if narky, Sunday night quarrel to something more serious.

"Grow up, Laura," Mel said. "You're such a child sometimes. There's no need to be a brat just because you're jealous about my part."

It hurt because it was true. There was no denying it, no way for her to take it back now that it was said. I felt tears of anger and self-pity sting my eyes, and Mel looked like she was about to cry too.

"Sorry," she muttered.

"Yeah, that really helps," I said. "Nice one. Say whatever bitchy shit you want and then come out with some half-arsed apology and I'll forget all about it, and you can go back to thinking you're Miss Perfect. Or rather, First Artist Perfect."

I stood up, picked up my fags and lighter, and prepared to flounce out to the balcony, already planning to leave the door open so Mel would have to get up and close it if she didn't want to be surrounded by smoky, freezing air. Then we both paused, hearing voices and laughter on the stairs outside.

"…Not sure if the girls are in," Roddy said, flinging the door open so it bounced back against the wall. "Oh, yes, they are."

He burst into the room, followed by a blast of cold, a smell of beer, smoke and pizza, and Felix.

"God, there's an atmosphere in here you could cut with a knife," Roddy said. "Have you two been having a row? We've been to the pub, and we've brought fuckloads of dirty Domino's. An entire week's worth of calories, right here."

He dumped the boxes on the sofa next to Mel, who queasily averted her eyes.

"And I brought Lawsonski back too," Roddy went on. "He's extra hot but he doesn't have a stuffed crust."

"And more booze," Felix held aloft a blue carrier bag jangling with bottles. "There's cheap, shit red and cheap, shit white – that covers all the bases, right?"

He smiled at me, and I felt myself blushing and wished I'd bothered to wash my hair that morning. Still, he looked pretty dishevelled himself, I realised – clearly the session in the pub had been a long one. His hair was messier than ever and there were dark shadows under his bloodshot blue eyes.

"It's Sunday, right?" he said. "I haven't been to bed since…" he counted on his fingers. "Friday. Well, Thursday night, strictly speaking."

"You need to pace yourself, my son," Roddy twisted the cap off a bottle of wine and sloshed it into four coffee mugs. "Here, get this down you. Hair of the dog that's going to bite you tomorrow."

"A placebo," Felix said. "No, that's not what I mean. Something else beginning with P."

"Precaution?" Roddy said.

"Prophylactic," I said.

"That's a condom, isn't it?" said Felix, and I blushed again, taking a gulp of wine.

"What's up with you, Melancholy?" Roddy said. "Come on, have a drink."

"I don't think I should," Mel said. "I think I'm coming down with something."

"Oh, come on," I said. "Take another of those tablets you bought and have a glass of wine. You'll be fine."

Mel sipped reluctantly. Roddy and Felix sat on the carpet, opened the pizza boxes and tore in. My mouth watered and I realised I hadn't eaten anything since my breakfast croissant hours before, and I was starving.

"Help yourselves," Felix gestured towards the boxes.

I took a slice and bit the end off, feeling the grease coating my lips. I'd pay for this tomorrow, I thought, but it was worth it.

"What's this then?" Roddy pointed at the telly.

"*Friends*," Mel said. "We were just going to put on the video of the Balachine *Swan Lake*, though."

"Bollocks to that," Felix said. "It's the weekend. Let's have some proper music."

He rummaged through our CDs, which were a pitiful mixture of Mel's classical stuff, my embarrassing girl band collection and Roddy's country and western. I watched Roddy squirm – he never let anyone look at his CDs.

"I thought," Felix pointed an accusing finger at me, "you were into Metallica. You've brought me here under false pretences, Roderigo. 'Come and meet my flatmate,' you said, 'you like the same music,' you said. And what do I get? The fucking Spice Girls. It's a poor show, mate."

He ate another slice of pizza. Even with cheese on his chin, he was the most desirable man I'd ever seen.

"I have Metallica," I said shyly, "but it's on tape. Hold on." I went to my room and rummaged around in the pile of clutter on my bedside table until I found what I was looking for. Thank God for the man at the stall in Camden, who, when I bought the T-shirt, had dropped a cassette box into the carrier bag, saying, "Here you go, love, I'll throw this in for a quid." And thank God for me being too polite to say that I couldn't actually spare a whole pound on some horrible music I didn't even like.

"Here," I handed it over to Felix. "I got this the other day. I haven't had a chance to listen to it yet."

He squinted at the blurry photocopied sleeve. "Holy shit. That's the Death Magnetic demo. I've been looking for this forever. Where'd you get it?"

For once in my life, I managed to act nonchalant. I shrugged and lied, "A friend of mine in LA sent it to me. We often exchange music, it's our thing." And I smiled in a sad, secret sort of way that I hoped Felix would interpret as evidence of a deep and passionate long-distance relationship with someone whose knowledge of heavy metal far exceeded Felix's own.

"Rad," he said. "What are we waiting for?"

He slotted the tape into our ancient stereo, and seconds later a loud whine of feedback filled the room, followed by a crashing guitar riff. Roddy and Mel winced; I tried to look enthusiastic.

"Come on! We can't not dance to this. Ever had a mosh pit in your living room, Roderigo?" Felix pulled me to my feet, snapped off the light and started to dance. Well – if it was dancing, it was like nothing I'd ever seen before. His body moved like the flame from a Zippo lighter when you're trying to spark up your fag on a windy day. He leaped and darted, seeming to be boneless and weightless. His hair flew around his head in a wild halo of shining darkness.

I tried my best to copy him, gasping with exertion and laughter after a few minutes. Roddy and Mel watched us from the sofa, providing a running critique.

"Your turnout sucks, Laura," Roddy said.

"Give us a pas de chat, Felix," said Mel.

When the track ended, we collapsed on the floor, panting for breath and giggling helplessly.

"For Christ's sake, no one ever, ever tell Anna I did that," I said.

"But you must headbang all the time," Felix said. "It looks that way, at least."

"Yeah," I lied, "But, you know, not in front of work people." I ducked my head, hiding my flushed face behind my hair.

"So, do you go to Hobgoblin?" Felix asked me. "My mates in Moscow all reckoned that's the best. What's it like? We should head over after work one Saturday."

"Um... yeah, that would be amazing," I said. How the hell was I going to maintain the rock-chick image I seemed to have inadvertently acquired? I was desperate to carry on impressing Felix – if impressing him I was – but conscious that I was on extremely shaky ground. If only I had a bit more time, I could go online and research this stuff, buy a few CDs, pick Sadie's brain – she'd always been the cool rebel one of us, she'd know about this stuff for sure. But I needed to make an impression, and make it now.

I was saved by my phone trilling urgently from the depths of my handbag. It would be Sadie, I knew, making her regular Sunday evening call to find out whether I was okay, eating properly, keeping warm, and all the other annoying, trivial things she worried about. But right now her call wasn't an annoyance – it was a lifeline.

"'Scuse me a second," I said, "This might be important."

And I grabbed my phone and headed out on to the balcony, where I spent ten freezing minutes with my back to the room, trying to look like I was talking to my mystery lover while patiently answering my sister's anxious queries.

When I turned around again, the room was empty. I felt utterly bereft – I'd played it wrong. They'd all gone out somewhere, or Felix had gone home, having got my pretend message only too strongly. Yet again, I'd fucked up, I'd blown my chance. I realised, standing in the dark, silent living room, that in those few frenzied moments of dancing together, Felix had given me a glimpse into another world – a world where letting go was fun, where music didn't mean Tchaikovsky, where it was possible to want to kiss someone even though you both smelled of pizza. But it was too late now.

I washed my face and cleaned my teeth in the freezing bathroom, then poured a glass of water and took it and my phone through to my bedroom. The door was shut – I didn't remember closing it, but I must have done, when I went to find the tape. I pushed it open, turned on the light, and gasped. There, on my narrow single bed, under my duvet, was Felix, fast asleep, his dark hair spread out over my pillow and his impossibly long eyelashes fanned out over his cheeks.

As quietly as I could, I put down my glass of water and squeezed in next to him, pulling the covers over us, breathing in the smell of him, relishing the heat of his body in the chilly room but not daring to touch him. Seconds later, I was asleep.

Chapter Seven

"So how was your thing? You must have got in really late, I didn't hear you at all." Jonathan's voice and the smell of coffee made me open my eyes, which felt sore and scratchy. For a moment I was barely sure where I was, or who he was – then Owen came running into the room and jumped on the bed, demanding a cuddle.

"Come on then," I moved over and lifted the duvet, and he squirmed in next to me and snuggled up, his hands leaving muddy smears on the white pillowcase.

"Where've you been?" I said. "Playing in the garden with Daddy?"

"We were playing dinosaurs," Jonathan said. "It's a bog out there. Sorry he's a bit grubby. He was being a T-rex in the flowerbed."

"That's okay," I said. "Thanks for the lie-in. I didn't get to sleep for ages, I'm knackered."

Owen gave a fearsome growl and pushed his face up against mine. "I'm a T-rex," he said.

YOU CAN'T FALL IN LOVE WITH YOUR EX (CAN YOU?)

"You're the squidgiest T-rex I've ever seen," I said, pulling him against me and going, "Grrrr!" into his tummy.

I'd dreamed of Owen, I remembered – dreamed that I'd been back in the forest, on the set, and Owen was there, somewhere, lost. I remembered chasing his voice through the trees, hearing him calling, "Mummy, Mummy," but whenever I got close to where I thought he was, his cries faded away again. That must have been when Jonathan took him downstairs so I could sleep.

There had been no Felix in my dream, only the endless, dark woods and the sense of futile searching. But now he was back in my thoughts, filling me with longing so fierce it shocked me.

"Where's Darcey?" I forced my mind away, on to other things.

"Downstairs, on her tablet," Jonathan said. "What the hell is unboxing? She's obsessed with watching clips of it on YouTube. I was worried it was something dodgy but when I had a look it's just some weird Brazilian teenager opening Disney eggs."

"That's pretty much it," I said. "I think Zé's daughter got her into it. It's a Thing, evidently. They open one of those plastic egg things and tell you what's inside."

"Then what?" Jonathan said.

I sipped my coffee. "Then nothing. Then they open another one. And another, and so on and on."

"But…why?" Jonathan asked, bemused.

"Search me. She's watched dozens of the things in the past week. We need to enforce her screen time limit. Go and tell her to stop, and watch telly or something. Or we could go out, I suppose. Go to the park."

"It's a nice day," Jonathan said, opening the curtains and filling the bedroom with sunlight.

"What time is it, anyway?" With Owen pinning down my arm, I couldn't see my watch or reach my phone. Suddenly, it seemed very important to look at my phone, see whether I had any texts or any messages on Facebook. Not that I would – Felix didn't know my number. He didn't even, as far as I was aware, know my married name.

"Half ten," Jonathan said. "You were out like a light, I thought I'd leave you to it."

"God. I had no idea it was so late. I'd better get in the shower. Come on, Monster, you go downstairs with Daddy while I get ready. And wash those hands."

Owen and Jonathan went downstairs, and I heard Darcey's voice saying plaintively, "Just one more, Daddy, please?"

I pushed the duvet reluctantly aside and went to the bathroom, wincing as I caught sight of my reflection in the mirror. My eyes were hollow, ringed with black shadows. My skin looked sallow and dull, I had a spot erupting on my chin and my hair was a bird's-nest tangle. That's what Felix would have seen last night, I thought. This middle-aged woman. Most of the time I thought I looked okay for thirty-five. Just a normal mum, with a sensible layered haircut that I could tie up when I didn't have time to blow-dry it, and highlights to mostly hide the grey roots that were appearing in depressing numbers. A slim woman, not particularly tall or short, with good posture and good teeth and okay skin, when I wasn't too tired.

But the last time he saw me – I hadn't been ordinary then. I'd been beautiful, and now I wasn't. And all the things about Felix that I'd managed to convince myself were true – that he was too short, that he was a disappointed, lonely man living in a single room in rented digs wherever he could get work, that he'd have aged worse than I had – simply didn't matter. He hadn't aged badly, not a bit. In those few moments last night when I'd been face to face with him, he'd been as vital and desirable as the first time I'd seen him. And my feelings seemed to have lost none of their power, either.

I turned the shower on to its hottest setting, waited until steam obscured my reflection, and stepped under the needles of scalding water. It was all over. I'd seen him, but it was bound to have happened eventually. It wouldn't happen again, or if it did, if I bumped into him in Sainsbury's when another fourteen years had passed, I'd deal with it, as I must deal with it now. He was in my past, and there he must stay.

By the time I'd dried my hair, dressed and put on a bit of make-up, I was able to face my reflection with equanimity again. In my skinny jeans and pink cashmere polo-neck, I looked healthy and pretty. Just another woman taking her family to the park on a Sunday in the yummy mummy capital of Britain.

"You'll never see him again," I told my reflection, and my reflection nodded back at me. "Smile," I commanded, and it did.

"Who are you talking to, Mummy?" said Darcey from the doorway, snapping me out of my thoughts.

"Nobody, Pickle," I said. "Shall we go to the park? You can go on the slide."

"Okay." Darcey looked down at her trainered feet. "Only first, Daddy said I can go on YouTube for a bit longer."

"I bet he didn't," I said. "Come on, get your coat and let's go. I'll show you the place where Mummy was last night, where the play happened."

"What play?"

"You know, that I went to last night. It was outside, in the park."

"How do you do a play outside?"

Glad to have her attention, I explained as we bundled both kids into their coats and walked down the road.

"It's called *A Midsummer Night's Dream,*" I said. "It's about some fairies who live in a forest, and there are two men and two women who are in love, except they're not in love with the people they're supposed to be in love with. And the fairies cast loads of spells, and turn one man into a donkey, and the Fairy Queen falls in love with him."

"Is that meant to be funny?" Darcey asked.

"Yes, I suppose it is," I said. "Because he's not really a donkey, he's just got a donkey's head stuck on over his, and after a bit the fairies magic it off again, and the Fairy Queen falls back in love with her husband."

"But what about the poor man who was a donkey?" Darcey said. "Who's he in love with?"

I glanced at Jonathan for help.

"No one," he said. "I expect he's got a wife at home, and children, and is quite glad to go back home afterwards, and get a telling-off from his wife for being out in the forest all night. But the story doesn't say, so you have to imagine what happened to him next."

"Look," I said, as we arrived at the bandstand. "They had a bar set up here, and there's the bit where you go through to get on to the set. It's all closed off now. I wonder if there's a performance tonight."

I felt a sudden wild urge to text Zé, see if she could pull strings with her well-connected friend and get us tickets for another performance. I longed to be back inside the forest, in the darkness, exploring deeper, seeing things I'd missed last night. Feeling the adrenaline and wine coursing through my body and turning me, briefly, into someone else, someone without responsibilities, with nowhere to go but deeper into the dream. Seeing Felix again, watching him in costume and in character, knowing, this time, who the man was behind the mask. But that way madness lay.

"You're still thinking about it, aren't you?" Jonathan said, once Darcey had run off to play on the swings.

"About what?"

"The play, Laura. I can see you've got something on your mind."

"I… yes, I suppose I am, a bit. It was pretty amazing. You saw the reviews."

"We can do more of that sort of thing, you know, now we're in London. It would be a shame not to." He lifted Owen up on to the slide. "Down you go, Mummy will catch you at the bottom. We can organise babysitters, book a few Saturday nights out. God knows I could do with a bit of culture."

"Yes, good idea," I said, passing Owen back for another go. I imagined going to see a West End show, having dinner afterwards, being tourists for a night. A few months ago the idea would have seemed like fun; now it seemed dull and stifling.

I looked at Jonathan, laughing with our son as he hoisted him up on to his shoulders. The past ten years had added a few grey strands to his dark hair. He bought thirty-four inch waist jeans now, not thirty-two as he used to. But he was still as handsome as he'd been when I met him. You are extremely bloody lucky, Laura, I told myself firmly.

"I'm starving," Jonathan said. "What are we doing for lunch?"

"There's a chicken in the fridge," I said. "I can bung it in the oven with some potatoes. Make a salad."

Jonathan looked at me, sensing disinterest. "Fuck it, let's go to the pub," he said.

"Daddy said a rude word," Darcey said.

The next week, things returned to their normal chaos, and I had no chance to think about Felix or, indeed, very much else at all. Whether it was a virus or dodgy chicken nuggets I don't know, but both the children were horribly ill, and I spent my days slumped in front of CBeebies with a limp, forlorn little figure on either side of me, and my nights cleaning up sick. It was awful, it went on for three days, and by the end of it I felt like a limp rag, and probably smelled like one too.

When at last Darcey and Owen were well enough to keep down toast and Marmite and watered-down apple juice, I packed them off back to school and nursery with an overwhelming sense of relief. Once I'd handed Darcey over to Mrs Odewayu, assuring her that it had been forty-eight hours since she was last sick, whatever had caused it was now in the past and she wasn't going to infect the entire classroom, I crossed the road and knocked on Zé's door. I felt horribly aware that I hadn't washed my hair since Sunday and had worn the same jeans for more days than I liked to remember, but I was also desperately in need of adult company and a conversation that didn't revolve around how people's tummies were feeling and whether we were going to watch *The Clangers* or *Postman Pat* next.

"Hey," she said, opening it, looking like a creature from another world in her cream leather skirt, over-the-knee boots and linen jumper. "Where have you been? I thought you'd left the country."

"Home," I said. "Battening down the hatches with two poorly kids. It's been grim."

"God, you poor thing," she said. "Coffee?"

I accepted gratefully and entered the serene haven of her immaculate house.

"I'm so bloody glad to have Carmen back, I can't tell you," Zé said, firing up the espresso machine. "Juniper's going through a Phase. She's acting eight going on sixteen, bursting into tears at the slightest thing and slamming doors and generally being a little madam. It makes me want to cry and slam doors right back, but Carmen seems to be able to manage her."

"Do you think she could be unhappy at school?"

"God knows. I've asked her, I've had a meeting with her teacher but Juniper won't tell me anything and apparently she's angelic in the classroom. She's not naturally academic. She's like me, I was bottom in everything at school. So anyway, how did you enjoy Saturday night? We didn't really have a chance to talk about it afterwards."

"It was fabulous," I said. "Thanks so much again for the ticket. I got lost in the forest bit, and I got taken off for a scene with Oberon."

"Really? What happened?" she asked.

I told her about the lifting of the mask, what I could remember about the words, and about the kisses, feeling my cheeks colouring at the memory. I didn't tell her that I knew who the actor was. I don't know why – part of me was longing to talk about Felix, but part of me wanted to keep it secret, keep my feelings buried deep inside me where they belonged.

"It gets to you, doesn't it?" Zé said. "I've been dreaming about it, you know, and I never remember my dreams. I won't tell you what happens in them though, there's nothing duller than hearing about other people's dreams. Anyway, I was going to ask you – any chance you and your husband are free on Saturday night? If you can face my company two weeks in a row, that is."

"Of course I can. Let me check with Jonathan. As far as I know we haven't got any plans…" I took out my phone and checked the diary. Saturday was free. I immediately put 'Seeing Zé, L and J' in the space, so Jonathan would see it and have no excuse for saying he didn't know we had anything on, and arranging post-golf drinks or something. "I'm sure it will be fine. I'll just need to sort someone to look after the children."

"Carmen will do it," Zé said. "Juniper's at a sleepover. Bung her forty quid and she'll be only too happy – she's saving up for a trip to Ibiza with her mates in the summer, she's desperate for extra cash."

"Great, if you're sure," I said.

"I'll check with her, but it'll be fine," Zé said. "I've asked my friend Anton, the one who sorted out the tickets to the show, out for dinner to say thanks. He'll probably bring a boyfriend. And Rick will come, if he knows Jonathan's there to talk shop to. So there'll be six of us. I'll book Le Bouchon d'Or."

This time, I resolved, I wasn't going to be caught on the hop, looking mumsy and frumpy in contrast to my new friend's groomed glamour. I made appointments to have my hair highlighted and my eyebrows threaded, sent the black dress I'd worn to Jonathan's work Christmas party to the dry cleaners and bought a chunky black and silver necklace to wear with it.

I realised I'd achieved the desired effect when Jonathan did a double take at me in my finery and said, "God, you look gorgeous, Laura. We should go out to nice places more often, so I can show off my glamorous wife."

"Your wife's forgotten how to be glamorous," I said gloomily. "It feels seriously weird to be wearing something that doesn't have egg stains on it."

"I can assure you it was worth the effort," Jonathan said, running his hands over my hips and kissing me. "In fact, we've got fifteen minutes and the children are in bed…"

He pulled me close and kissed me again, pulling up the dress and stroking my thighs.

"Stockings," he said. "Is this some kind of special occasion?"

"Just felt like it," I said. "You don't look too bad yourself. Or smell too bad."

I ran my lips over his neck, breathing in the freshly showered smell of him, feeling the smoothness of his newly shaved skin. In my four-inch heels I was tall enough to kiss him without standing on tiptoes as I usually did. I undid the top button of his shirt, then the next one down and the next, stroking his skin with my fingertips.

Then the doorbell rang.

By the time we'd let Carmen in, shown her where everything was, given her the broadband password and checked one last time that the kids were asleep, the moment had truly passed. Still, as we walked hand in hand to the restaurant, I felt a gentle, fizzing undercurrent of excitement. I could feel the tops of my stockings encircling my thighs, and the lace of my new underwear against my skin, unfamiliar and slightly, pleasantly scratchy. The air was cool on my bare spine where my dress scooped low over my back.

The evening felt full of promise, like a first date, only one with a person I knew, trusted and loved. I knew that during dinner Jonathan and I would catch each other's eyes, perhaps brush hands, let our thighs press together under the table, and know that we were thinking the same thing, engaged together in a silent dance of desire. It felt good – I'd missed it.

I was even gladder of my new dress when I saw Zé, polished and stunning in a silver-grey vest top that showed off her slim, sculpted arms. I couldn't compete with her – I didn't have the time, the money or the raw material. I wondered fleetingly how it must feel to be so fundamentally, unquestionably beautiful, for it to be the first thing anyone ever noticed about you, the first thing they thought when they saw you, even once they knew you quite well. I wondered whether it was frightening for her to know that her looks would fade, would slip away and leave her invisible, without currency.

But I didn't have much time for such gloomy thoughts, because I were being introduced to Rick, a silver fox whose tanned skin, perfectly fitting clothes and Cartier watch shouted status.

"Anton's running a bit late," Zé said. "He said they'll be here in twenty minutes, so why don't we have a cocktail while we wait? We've already ordered – I'm on the pisco sours and Rick's having something called a Blue Marine, God knows what's in it."

"I always order the campest drinks," Rick said. "I can't help it, it's a curse."

And sure enough, his cocktail arrived bristling with pineapple slices, maraschino cherries and paper parasols. He laughed, and I found myself liking him better. Jonathan and I ordered martinis, and we all embarked on the kind of conversation you have when the women know each other mostly through their children, and the men through their jobs.

We'd covered the weather, the pleasantness of the restaurant, and were just skirting cautiously around the results of the General Election. Then Rick turned to Jonathan and launched into a diatribe about office politics, leaving Zé and me to talk to each other, and I liked him a bit less again, and found myself understanding why Zé didn't mind him being at work all the time.

Then she glanced over my shoulder towards the door and said, "And here's Anton. So glad you could make it, darling."

"Zé, my precious, you look wonderful." Anton was fey and tiny, with sparkly blue eyes and a waxed moustache that I imagined he'd sported since last time they were fashionable, about sixty years ago. His outfit was similarly extravagant: a velvet smoking jacket and a cravat. But I wasn't really looking at him or his clothes.

"I brought one of my boys along," he said. "It's his night off and I promised him a square meal. We pay Equity rates, of course, we're not vilely exploitative like some theatre companies, but even so it's barely enough to keep body and soul together, is it, sweetheart?"

"I intend to eat all the food," agreed Felix solemnly.

My heart was beating so fast it felt as if it was about to escape my body, either by bashing through my rib-cage or bursting out of my mouth. I pressed my lips together and swallowed hard.

"Are you in the show, then?" Zé said. "How excit-ing. We loved it, it's the best thing I've seen for ages. Rick's gutted he missed it."

"This is Felix Lawson," Anton said. "Meet my very dear, very old – well, not old at all, my apologies, dar-ling – friend Zélide. And you must be Rick, about whom I've heard so very much. And..."

He gestured towards Jonathan and me in a vague, fluttery sort of way.

"My new friend Laura and her husband Jonathan," Zé supplied.

I shook Anton's hand and reached for Felix's, my face still arranged in a polite smile, but my thoughts spinning wildly, ricocheting like a ball in one of the computer games Felix had loved to play, back in the day. All I had to do was say, "Yes, we know each other, actually." But the words didn't come.

Instead, Felix said, "Lovely to meet you, Laura, Jonathan." And he shook my husband's hand and kissed both my cheeks as if it was the most normal thing in the world.

I've never been more grateful for the etiquette of seating arrangements, which placed me opposite Anton and next to Zé, while Felix was on her other side, opposite Rick, and thus almost invisible to me. Even so, as we ate oysters and discussed whether the pâté or the asparagus would be a better bet to start with, I felt as conscious of his presence as if a live electric current were running between us. In the noisy restaurant, I could barely hear anything he said, but the timbre of his voice and the quality of his laugh were unmistakeable. I found myself straining to hear what he was saying and tuning out poor Anton.

"Don't you think, Laura?" Anton said, catching me off guard.

"Oh, yes, I completely agree," I said helplessly, wondering what on earth he'd asked, and what I was agreeing with.

I was saved by the arrival of our waiter and the need to actually read the menu, instead of staring blankly at the sea of swimming words it contained. By the time we'd sorted out whose filet mignon was to be rare and whose well done, ordered sides of buttered spinach, pommes frites and heirloom tomatoes for the table, and witnessed a clash of wills between Rick and the sommelier, I'd more or less recovered my poise. But still, when Zé nudged me and murmured, "Fancy a fag?" I felt giddy with relief, and ignored Jonathan's disapproving frown.

We edged out between the tables and made our way towards the exit, but before we reached it, Zé thrust her pack of Marlboro and lighter into my hand and said, "I'm just going for a wee, see you out there in a second."

I pushed the heavy glass door aside and stepped out into the night, taking relieved gulps of the cool air and, in short order, the blissfully welcome nicotine. I had three courses to get through, probably followed by dessert and pudding wine, if Rick's initial bout of showing off over the wine list was anything to go by. And then coffee. And maybe brandy. The main thing, I told myself, was not to get pissed, and not, whatever happened, to move any closer to Felix. If I didn't talk to him, it would all be fine. Jonathan

107

would know nothing, and my life could return to normal.

I felt a gust of warm air from inside the restaurant and turned to greet Zé. But, of course, it was not her but Felix.

"Smokers' corner," he said, extracting a rollie from his pocket. Almost against my will, I handed him Zé's slim, silver lighter and watched as he cupped the flame and touched it to the paper, exhaling a cloud of smoke in a way that was utterly, agonisingly familiar.

"Why did you pretend not to know me?" I blurted out.

"Because that's what you wanted me to do," Felix said, smiling. "I don't know why, but I could tell. So I did. Haven't you told your husband about us? He seems like a decent bloke."

"I... he is," I said. "And I would have told him. I could have done, it would've been fine. But now you've gone and fucked it all up."

Felix laughed. The street lamp overhead lit up his shining dark hair, shorter now than it had been when he was younger, but no less glossy. His teeth shone too – I didn't remember them being so white and straight. Even though I was the same height as him in my high heels, I felt as if I was looking up to him.

"You can say I'd forgotten, if you want," he said. "We can go back in there and be like, 'Oh my God, we do know each other, after all. It's just we've changed so much, we didn't recognise each other.'"

"You haven't changed," I said.

"And neither have you," said Felix. "Your friend's coming. Dial my number, quickly, so I have yours."

And I found myself holding my mobile, urgently punching out the digits he recited, then ending the call, immediately and furtively, the moment his phone bleeped in his hand and Zé opened the door.

"So that must have felt like a blast from the past," Jonathan said as we walked home. We weren't holding hands any more – I was clutching his arm, because I'd ended up drinking loads more than I meant to and I was feeling decidedly unsteady on my towering heels. I felt my hand involuntarily tighten on his elbow.

"What do you mean?" I said, relieved that it was too dark for him to see how violently I was blushing.

"Just – you know. Being with those arty types. It must have reminded you of when you were dancing."

"Oh." I was appalled by how relieved I felt not to have been caught out in the fiction Felix and I had played out for the rest of the evening – that we were strangers, that we'd never met before. Okay, it was more than a fiction – it was a lie. It was the first time I'd lied outright to Jonathan – lies of omission didn't really count, as I'd told myself countless times over the past ten years. "Dancers aren't arty. I wasn't, anyway. I was more like – I don't know, a netball player, or something. An athlete. And not a very good one. And it was ages ago, anyway. Ancient history."

SOPHIE RANALD

"But that actor guy was saying he used to be a dancer," Jonathan said. "It's funny the two of you never met."

"No it isn't." Through the haze of wine, I realised I was furious with Felix. What the hell did he think he was doing, dragging me into some stupid game, making me play along with his pathetic deception? "It's not that small a world."

"Do you think he's sleeping with that producer guy?" Jonathan continued. "He didn't strike me as gay but I could be wrong. Or maybe he's just stringing him along, keeping an eye on the main chance."

Gay men had always fancied Felix, I remembered. Anton would be no exception. And a rich, older man who could be admired and pandered to, flattered by the idea that he'd still got it, would be fair game. I was stung by the accuracy of Jonathan's analysis.

"I have no idea," I said, more irritably than I intended. "I don't know why you're interested, anyway. It's not like we'll ever see them again. Let's talk about something else, for God's sake."

"Are you okay, Laura? You seemed distracted tonight. I thought it was a fun evening – it's good to get out and meet new people."

"I'm just tired," I said. "It's been a long week, that's all. And the kids will probably be up at some ungodly hour in the morning."

"We'll pay the babysitter and go straight to bed," Jonathan said. "I still want…"

He didn't finish his sentence, because we'd arrived at our door. But I knew what he meant – what he wanted. To resume what Carmen's arrival had interrupted. And although, earlier, I'd wanted it too, my earlier mood of carefree arousal had dissolved. Felix had spoiled it.

I stood in the bathroom a few minutes later, painstakingly removing my make-up, flossing my teeth, spinning out the process of getting ready for bed in the hope that Jonathan would fall asleep and I'd be left alone with my thoughts. But when I emerged into the bedroom he was propped up against the pillows, his tablet in his hands. As soon as he saw me, he put it aside.

"Come here, my gorgeous wife," he said.

"I'll just check on the kids," I said.

"I already did. Completely sparko, the pair of them. Come on."

I took my necklace off, put it in my jewellery box and stepped out of my shoes. My heels felt raw, and I suspected I'd have blisters. My ankle ached, my mouth felt sour from all the wine I'd drunk, and I knew I'd have a hangover in the morning, when it was Jonathan's turn for a lie-in. In short, I felt about as unsexy as it was possible to feel.

I reached up to undo my dress, but the zip caught and jammed.

"Fuck," I said, tugging at it.

"Don't," Jonathan said. "You'll make it worse. Come here." I sat reluctantly on the bed and waited while he

SOPHIE RANALD

eased the zip down. So, he was undressing me after all –
getting what he wanted as he always did. I knew how
I must look, in my black lace bra and pants and the
hold-up stockings I'd put on for no particular reason
other than that my only pair of sheer tights were in the
wash and opaques didn't work with the dress – like a
woman who wanted to seduce her husband. Earlier,
I had wanted to. And although I didn't any more, I
didn't want to say no, either.

We hadn't had sex for… I counted back in my
head. More than two weeks. I'd had my period,
Jonathan had been working late, I'd been out – it
just hadn't happened. Two weeks was too long, I told
myself firmly. Two weeks felt like the beginning of a
slippery slope, one that might lead to not having sex
for months, then never. And besides, I didn't want
to hurt Jonathan, and I knew that rejection did hurt
him, just a bit, every time it happened.

So I stepped out of my dress and hung it in the
wardrobe, watching him watching me, and I smiled
at him and came to bed without taking off my underwear. I made my body relax, tried to empty my mind
and enjoy the familiar, skilful movements of his hands
over my skin. And it worked. Soon I felt the first stir-
rings of pleasure, faint at first, then more insistent
and intense. He knelt over me, peeling down my
knickers, and kissed my thighs above my stocking
tops, and I heard myself gasp with longing. Then his
fingers and tongue were inside me, quickly making
me come.

I laughed up at him, and pulled him down on top of me, relieved that I was able to take the pleasure he so loved to give. But when he started to fuck me, the image of Felix's face came unbidden into my mind, and I found myself imagining that it was his cock inside me, not my husband's – his face above mine in the golden light of the bedside lamp. Not Felix as he had been fifteen years ago, but the man I'd met tonight; the man who'd pretended to be a stranger. I remembered how I'd obeyed him, instantly and without question, when he'd told me to dial his number. I imagined giving my body to him in the same way, not coerced but somehow compelled. The idea was electrically exciting, impossible to resist. I closed my eyes, giving myself up to the fantasy, and came again seconds later.

I couldn't look at Jonathan afterwards. I turned my back to him, letting him wrap his arms around me, feeling his kisses on my neck. We fell asleep that way, almost as if everything was normal.

Chapter Eight

"Yes, it's all very well to say 'cover the butter-cream in desiccated coconut,' you smug cow," I muttered at my iPad screen, "You don't mention that you cover the entire fucking kitchen with it, too."

It had seemed so simple – a white rabbit cake to fit in with the magic theme of Darcey's birthday party. There were loads of tutorials on YouTube, and I'd watched several, wondering airily what could possibly go wrong. Just about everything, I was beginning to realise. I'd burned the first cake and had to start again, then the corner shop had run out of golden caster sugar and I'd had to waste a precious half-hour on a trip to Waitrose. Now I had just forty-five minutes before I needed to leave to fetch my daughter from school, and the cake was still nowhere near done.

"Fuck." I threw my palette knife into the sink and grabbed a handful of coconut from the bag, pressing it into the icing and praying that it would stick. It did – but the warmth of my hands melted the buttercream and I soon had a sticky, gritty mess coating both hands. And then, of course, my phone rang.

Over the past few weeks, the lurch of nervous excitement I'd felt whenever I heard its trill had dulled – none of the calls had been Felix, and this wasn't going to be, either. I glanced at the screen – Jonathan.

"What is it?" I picked up the phone with my fingertips, leaving a greasy, coconutty smear on the screen.

"Hey," Jonathan said. "Is this a bad time?"

"No, it's perfect," I said. "I'm in the process of spackling the entire kitchen with cake decorations, I've got to leave in a few minutes to fetch the kids and I've got a zillion things to do before tomorrow. You couldn't have picked a better moment."

He didn't laugh. "Listen, Laura, I'm actually calling about tomorrow. There's been… There's a problem."

"What kind of… hold on." I put down the phone, washed my hands, and picked it up again. "What's happened?"

"Laura, you're not going to like this. So let me get the apologies out of the way first, because it's not my fault and there's nothing I can do. Okay?"

"What?" I said. "Don't tell me you have to work tomorrow, because you can't. You promised. End of."

"It's not work, Laura. Well, it is – it's Royal Ascot. Remember we discussed it, I told you we have a box for a client hospitality day, and we decided I couldn't go because of Darcey's birthday."

I remembered the conversation well, as it happened. When I say conversation – it had been more of a row. Yes, definitely a row, when Jonathan had been home after ten every night for two weeks running, and I'd finally snapped and said I didn't know how much more of this I could fucking stand, and he'd pointed out that he was doing his best to dial it down, including saying he wouldn't be available for the social highlight of the firm's year, because it was his daughter's birthday, and did I think he wasn't doing his best, did I think he liked being stuck in the office until stupid o'clock every night? And I'd said, did he think I liked coping with the kids on my own every night? And things had escalated from there, as they do.

"You've got to go, haven't you?" I said. "Jonathan, I don't fucking believe this."

"I know," he said. "But Myles's wife has gone into labour, and Rick's had to fly out to Singapore and... well, there it is. I'm the only partner who's available, and I have to go."

"You're not available," I hissed.

"I'm more available than the person on a plane to the Far East or the person holding the gas and air in the Lindo Wing." I heard him sigh, a weary, defeated exhalation. "Come on, Laura, please don't make this worse than it already is. Don't be..."

"Unreasonable," I finished for him. "Okay, I won't be unreasonable. I'll be the good little corporate wife and say it's all fine, and explain to our daughter that her daddy isn't going to be there for her party, which she's been looking forward to for weeks. It's all completely okay."

He must have heard the sarcasm dripping from my words, but he chose to ignore it. "Thanks, Laura. I'll talk to Darcey tonight. I'll be home early. Sevenish, in time to put them to bed. Okay?"

There was nothing more I could say. "Okay."

"Love you. Bye."

Defeated and seething, I turned back to the cake. It needed the rest of its coating to be applied, then the bunny's face to be piped on, then there was the black top hat to be covered in the fondant icing that had refused to go any darker than a dreary charcoal, and the glittery stars to be scattered artfully over the board. And there was no time to do any of it. I'd have to wait until tonight, when the kids were in bed. And then there were the wand biscuits I'd planned to bake and ice, the party bags to assemble, Darcey's presents to wrap… I'd be up until two in the morning, as I'd been before every one of my children's birthday parties, and I'd be a frazzled wreck tomorrow, as I always was.

Still, at least I didn't have to worry about keeping twenty-five six-year-olds entertained. This year, instead of preparing lame treasure hunts and games of pass the parcel, I'd thrown money at the problem. When I'd dished out the invitations at the school gate, Monica had said, "I don't want to interfere, Laura, but if I can make a suggestion…" and pressed a business card into my hand with the air of a woman passing on her trusted coke dealer's mobile number.

And so Magical Larry was booked. Magical Larry, who drove a top-of-the-range white Merc with the vanity plate M8GIK and hadn't stopped staring at my cleavage when he'd come round to deliver his sales spiel and exorbitant quote, but whose website was packed with rave reviews from ecstatic parents saying they'd never bother booking anyone else again, ever. Thank God for Magical Larry, I thought, swathing the cake in bin liners and hiding it in the cupboard under the stairs. He was costing a bloody fortune – more than the rest of the party put together, including Darcey's new bicycle (a poor substitute for a pony, but cool nonetheless) but he was going to be worth it. I'd be able to be a gracious hostess, take lots of photos and if it all got too much, get stuck into the gin.

Jonathan didn't get home at seven. He sent an apologetic text saying that a client meeting had dragged on and he had a mountain of paperwork to get through and was expecting a call from San Francisco so couldn't leave his desk, so I put the two overtired, overexcited, cranky children to bed on my own, poured a massive drink, turned on the radio and carried on cooking. By this stage, I'd passed through the pissed-off stage and was resigned to my fate. But it didn't help that the phone didn't stop ringing. First, Carrie called to say that her little boy was coming down with chicken pox so she wouldn't risk bringing her daughter to the party. Then one of the Helens – I wasn't sure which – rang to ask if I'd like her to come early and lend a hand. If it had been Helen Markham, whose only child was a beautifully behaved, solemn little boy who seemed permanently glued to maths games on his iPad, I'd have said yes – but there was the chance it could have been the other Helen, whose twin daughters I'd nicknamed the Visigoths, and of course by that stage it would have been rude to ask, so I declined graciously.

Then, just as I was piping frosting on to a phalanx of vaguely wand-shaped biscuits, my mobile rang yet again. Not bothering to see who it was, I snatched it up and said, "Hello?"

There was silence, and then a man's voice said, "Is that Mrs Payne?"

God, I thought, the last thing I need now is some poor sod trying to sell me household insurance or do market research on me. "Yes, but I'm extremely busy right now," I snapped.

"Mrs Payne, it's Larry here. The party entertainer."

Oh God, no, please no, I thought. If you fucking cancel on me now my life won't be worth living.

"What can I do for you, Larry?" I said, praying that he'd just mislaid my address or wanted to check on the time, but of course it wasn't that.

"Mrs Payne, I'm awfully sorry, but I have to… I've had some bad news." He sounded a bit hoarse, and I heard a loud sniff and realised that he'd been – or still was – crying.

"Yes?" I said. "Does this – does whatever it is mean you are cancelling my booking?" And if it does, even if your house has burned down and your top hat and white rabbits and coloured handkerchiefs are mere ashes; even if you've lost both hands in a firecracker accident and will never work again, I will hate you for ever and ever, I thought, but of course didn't say.

"It's my parrot, Mrs Payne," he said.

"What?" I said, my voice rising hysterically.

"My parrot. Vincent. He's an African Grey." He didn't sound a bit like the brash, slightly sleazy man who'd called round two weeks before. He sounded pathetic and old, and in spite of myself I felt sorry for him.

"What's happened?" I sat down on one of the kitchen chairs and took a big gulp of my G&T.

"He's been falling off his perch," Larry said. I felt a bubble of hysterical laughter rising in my throat. "And the only appointment I can get with the specialist avian vet is tomorrow at two o'clock. Which of course means I am going to have to – I won't be able to do your daughter's party. I've never let a client down in thirty years, Mrs Payne. I can't say how sorry I am. But Vincent's my friend. I will of course return your deposit in full, and if you book me again there'll be no charge. And I can give you some names of colleagues who might…"

"Don't worry, Larry, I'll Google," I said. "I hope Vincent makes it okay and isn't… Goodbye." I disconnected the call just before I said out loud, "Pushing up the daisies." Then I burst into a fit of uncontrollable giggles that quickly turned to tears.

I cried for a long time, hunched over the kitchen table, getting purple frosting in my hair. Every time

I managed to stop and blow my nose, I remembered Larry saying, "He's my friend," and it set me off again. Eventually I got control of myself enough to pick up my phone and start Googling alternative party entertainers, but then I imagined them, all these lonely men with parrots for company and no children of their own, and worried I'd cry some more. So I put down my phone, resolving to get back to the biscuits and worry about a back-up plan in the morning. It was ten o'clock anyway, far too late to start ringing up magicians.

Wearily, I picked up the piping bag, just as my phone rang again. Jonathan, I thought, on his way home at last. But it was another unfamiliar mobile number.

"Hello?"

"Laura? It's me." Oh my God. Felix. Almost a month of waiting and wondering and jumping out of my skin every time someone sends me a text, and he picks now to call, I thought. Now, of all times.

"Laura? Is this a bad time?"

I took another sip of my drink and a huge gulp of air, almost choked, and started to cry again.

"Laura? Babe, what's the matter?"

"Everything," I said. "It's my daughter's birthday and her party's tomorrow and my husband's got to work and the fucking magician's just cancelled on me and the cake's a mess and it's all shit."

I realised, even through the fog of my self-pity, how pathetic it sounded. The ultimate middle-class nightmare or first-world problem or whatever you want to call it.

"And I'm crying about it and that's just so stupid," I blurted out.

"It's not stupid," Felix said gently. "Look, you've made her a cake, haven't you? With a fuck-ton of sugar, right?"

"Yes, I suppose so," I said.

"And sparkly shit?"

"And sparkly shit," I admitted, feeling the beginnings of a smile.

"Right then," he said. "Job done on the cake. And your magician guy, what was he going to do? Make daft jokes and pull coloured hankies out of a hat and make pound coins come out of the kids' ears?"

"Yes," I said. "But he's not, because his parrot's dying and he's got to take it to the vet."

"His parrot?" I heard the beginning of a laugh in Felix's voice, and started to giggle too.

"I know," I said. "It's not funny, except it is."

"Look, I can do magic," Felix said. "I'm not as shit-hot as your parrot guy, I expect, but I can do the basic stuff. I've done kids' parties. They scare the hell out of me, but I can do them. Want me to come round?"

"Are you serious?" I said.

"Of course," he said. "I'd love to see… to help. If you want."

"Really? I don't want you to go to any trouble."

"Don't be absurd, Laura. It's no trouble – would I offer if it was?"

I paused. He wouldn't, of course. Felix never did anything he didn't want to do.

"I'll pay you," I said. "Of course. I'll pay what I was going to pay Larry the parrot man." And I named Larry's vast fee.

Felix laughed. "No you won't. I'm skint, but not so skint I'd take your money. Bloody hell, though, it's a nice little earner, isn't it? Maybe I should ditch the day job and move into magic. Fuck playing Hamlet, when you can pull rabbits out of hats for a hundred and fifty quid an hour. What's your address, and what time do you want me?"

Before I could think about my decision, before any doubts could form in my mind about the wisdom of letting this man back into my life, into my home, into my children's lives, I'd said yes and told him when and where to come. Then I hung up, just before Jonathan arrived home from work, and just before I could say anything to Felix that I'd really regret.

I didn't tell Jonathan what I'd arranged. Well, I did – I told him that Magical Larry had cancelled, but that I'd managed to find a replacement at the eleventh hour. He didn't ask who, or how, and I didn't volunteer the information. In fact we didn't talk much at all; we went straight to bed. I suppose he thought I was still sulking over his jolly to the races.

I wasn't, though. A shameful part of me that I could barely acknowledge was grateful, because after all, if Jonathan was going to be there, I wouldn't have been able to let Felix step in – not, at least, without long and convoluted explanations that would involve either telling the truth or telling lies worse than those of omission. So I lay in the dark next to my husband, said nothing, and waited for sleep to come.

We were woken the next morning by Darcey leaping on to the bed, literally bouncing with excitement.

"Today's my party!" she said. "Wake up, Mummy! Come on, Daddy!"

Reluctantly, I opened my eyes. "Happy party day, Pickle. Come and give your Mum a kiss, and let's get Owen up and dressed."

The rest of the morning was spent in frantic preparations. I hung multi-coloured bunting from the spotlights in the kitchen and over the patio outside, and arranged Darcey's presents in a satisfyingly large pile in front of which she sat, transfixed and forbidden to touch, for a good ten minutes before dashing outside and spinning round and round on the lawn in a frenzy of excitement. I made the children eat some breakfast and started arranging the party food on platters and baking sheets. Then I stuck them both in front of the telly and barricaded myself in the kitchen to put the finishing touches on the cake.

Jonathan tapped on the door to say goodbye, clad in his race-day finery. It was impressive, I thought fleetingly, that he was still able to get into the morning suit he'd bought for our wedding – my frock certainly wouldn't fit me any more. And with that realisation came a torrent of self-doubt – what the hell was I going to wear? My Mum uniform of skinny jeans and a tunic top would have been good enough for Darcey's friends and their parents, and it would certainly have been good enough for Magical Larry, but Felix? I didn't want him to see me like that.

I washed and straightened my hair and put on a summer dress, wishing there was time for the fake tan I slapped on my legs to develop. I frantically painted two coats of coral varnish on my toenails and slid my feet into a pair of sparkly flip-flops. No amount of expensive podiatry appointments in the years since I'd last worn pointe shoes had done anything to fix my distorted, lumpy toes or disguise the fact that the metatarsal I broke had healed crooked. But Felix knew my feet. He'd spent so many nights peeling tape off them after performances, dabbing antiseptic on bleeding blisters, kissing the pain away. There'd be no surprises for him there.

"God, pull yourself together, Laura," I told my reflection in the mirror. "Why are you even thinking like this? Get a grip. He's helping out, as a friend."

"Who is, Mummy?" Darcey appeared in the doorway, catching me by surprise as she so often did.

"People whose birthday party it is shouldn't ask questions like that, darling," I said. "Not unless they want surprises to be spoiled. And you don't, do you?"

She squirmed with excitement, put her thumb in her mouth, a habit she'd mostly overcome but still resorted to in times of high emotion, and produced a muffled, "No."

"Come on then, let's get you into your party dress."

Soon we were all ready – Darcey in her fairy splendour, layers of white tulle that reminded me of the costumes I'd worn on stage, Owen in a clean T-shirt and shorts, me looking as good as I was going to get. The kids, unable to sit still, went out into the garden and raced around, shrieking. My mother's voice said in my head, "Don't let Darcey get her best frock dirty," but I silenced it. It was her birthday party – she could get as dirty as she wanted.

I found myself unable to sit still, either. I faffed around, arranging and rearranging food and drink, tying balloons to the front gate, peering critically at my face in the mirror, wondering what Felix was going to make of it all – the photo of Jonathan and me on our wedding day hanging in the hallway; the kids' drawings curling beneath a forest of fridge magnets; the plastic toys spilling through the glass doors out into the garden. It was a typical family home – a picture of comfortable conventionality that he and I would have sneered at twelve years ago. And I would have sneered at myself, too – a frazzled stay-at-home mum in last year's summer frock, surrounded by plates of ham sandwiches.

But that's what I am now, I told myself – and why did I even care what Felix thought? He was a relic of my past, and if I had any sense at all, I would have made sure he remained there. I felt a sudden rush of apprehension: regret at what I'd done and fear of what it might mean, and snatched up my phone to call him and invent some reason why he shouldn't come after all. But before I could dial, there was a knock at the door.

"Hello!" Amanda cooed. "I'm sorry we're a bit early, we've come from another party and it seemed silly to go home. It's such a social whirl at the moment – one birthday after another! I swear the kids have busier diaries than I've ever had! You don't mind, do you? Go and find Darcey, Delphine, and say happy birthday. Is she out in the garden? You've got a glorious day for it. How's it going, Laura? Need a hand with anything?"

"It's all under control, thanks," I said, faintly. Amanda, I reflected, was actually quite relaxing company – all you had to do was feed her occasional cues and she'd talk and talk. Much as I longed for Zé's more congenial presence, with Amanda around, there was no need to put much effort in at all.

"Monica tells me you booked Magical Larry," she said. "Good call! He's pricey, but worth it."

"Yes, except unfortunately he can't make it," I said. "But I managed to find a replacement, so – well, as I said, it's all under control."

"A replacement?" Amanda rummaged in her bag for her phone. "You simply must pass on his details. Decent party entertainers are like unicorn poo."

"He's a friend of a friend, actually. He's just doing me a favour. I don't know if he'll even be any good."

This was something that hadn't occurred to me until now. What if Felix was rubbish? What if I – and by extension Darcey – were shamed in front of all her friends? The more I thought about this, the more I realised how truly, deeply stupid I'd been to accept his offer.

The knocker crashed on the door again, and I greeted Jo and her daughter, then Helen arrived to drop off her twins, and soon I was knee-deep in children, laughing, squabbling, wanting juice, asking where the toilet was and trying to play with Owen. I glanced at my watch – I'd told Felix to come at three o'clock, and it was already five past. I wasn't sure which I was dreading more – his arrival, or his not turning up at all.

"No – no, you can't open those, they're for Darcey." Helen's hellion twins were showing too keen an interest in the pile of presents. "Why don't you have a go on the trampoline? Come on."

I grabbed a small, sticky hand in each of mine and led the twins outside. "One at a time, now, you have to take turns."

"I'm first," Darcey said. "It's my party."

"All right, but only two minutes, okay? Then you must let Rosie have a turn."

"I'm Poppy," said the twin, and I forced a smile. It was going to be a long afternoon.

"Laura, there's someone here to see you." Amanda appeared at my side and mouthed, "The magician. He's waiting in the lounge."

"Oh – right. Thanks. Would you…?" I gestured at the trampoline and retreated indoors.

The house was cool and still after the sunny chaos of the garden. I ran my hands through my hair and walked slowly through to the sitting room. Felix was standing by the window, reading the front page of Jonathan's copy of the *Guardian*, his back to me.

"Hello," I said, and he turned around.

I started to laugh. Magical Larry's working attire, I'd gathered from YouTube, was a red polyester clown outfit, complete with white panstick and a yellow bowler hat. Felix's interpretation of what the well-dressed conjuror wore couldn't have been more different. He was part steampunk and part Mad Hatter in a velvet frock coat, a tall black hat, a shirt with a cascade of white ruffles down the front and a fake moustache. He looked both hilarious and impossibly sexy.

"Oh my God," I said. "You came."

"Of course I came," he said. "Didn't I say I would?"

"Thank you." Suddenly shy, I walked over and kissed his cheek, just above the moustache.

"All my stuff's in there." He gestured to a battered leather suitcase on the sofa. "Want to give me five minutes to get sorted and then we'll get the show on the road?"

"Yes, great," I said. I felt as if he was the one in control here, calm and poised, while I flapped around like an idiot, not knowing whether to fall at his feet with gratitude and desire or run away as far and fast as I could. "I'll get them in. Would you like anything? Glass of water?"

His professional demeanour flickered for a moment. "A fucking enormous drink," he said. "I'm bricking it. But that wouldn't really be appropriate, would it?"

I went outside and rounded up the children, who, well trained by their first year of school, filed obediently in and sat in fairly orderly rows on the carpet, their chatter gradually stilling until they were all quiet. I could see Darcey sitting on her hands so as not to suck her thumb, and felt a rush of love for my little girl, who was growing up so fast. I sat on the sofa next to Amanda and tucked Owen on to my lap, whispering to him that he must be very quiet and good.

Felix stood with his back to the children, adjusting a few objects that he'd placed on the mantelpiece and covered with coloured handkerchiefs. One of the little girls whispered something to her neighbour and they both giggled. Delphine said, "Shhh!"

There was a long, long pause. Fuck, I thought, he's going to bottle it.

Then Felix turned around. He looked at the children for a moment, and then he smiled.

"Who here believes in magic?" he said softly, into the silence.

"Me!" they chorused, sounding like a flock of birds taking wing. I felt my own spirits soar. It was going to be all right.

CHAPTER NINE

Felix didn't leave after his magic show, and he didn't leave when the other mums departed, their children clutching party bags and practically ricocheting off the walls from all the sugar (except Jo's daughter, who'd been restricted to carrot sticks and hummus). Amanda, in her self-appointed role of my best friend, offered to stay and help clear up, but I assured her it would be fine.

"You must give me your card," she said to Felix. "We all loved your show, the littles were transfixed. I'd love to contact you later in the year, when it gets closer to Delphine's b-i-r-t-h-d-a-y."

"I'd adore to help," Felix said, with a totally convincing note of regret in his voice. "But this isn't actually my day job, so to speak. I just did it as a favour for Laura."

"Are you sure?" Amanda said. "Well… do get in touch if you change your mind. Thanks for the party, Darcey – Delphine, say, 'Thank you for having me.'"

"Thank you for having me," muttered Delphine, and I closed the door behind them.

"Thank God that's over," I said.

"Mummy, can Felix stay and watch me open my presents?" Darcey said. "And do some more magic? Please?"

"No more magic," I said. "And no presents until we've tidied up a bit, okay? I'm sure Felix would love to see your presents, but I expect he's got other things to do."

"I don't mind," Felix said. "I can stay for a bit."

So he did, helping to sort out the wreckage of the kitchen, which had plates of congealing cocktail sausages everywhere, crisps trodden into the floor, countless half-drunk cups of squash on every surface, the plundered remains of the birthday cake, and, inexplicably, a pair of fairy wings draped over the back of a chair. We watched Darcey rip the paper off her stack of birthday presents, then he showed her some more magic tricks while I put Owen to bed. When eventually I'd tucked Darcey up and watched as she almost instantly fell asleep, I came downstairs to find him waiting with a bottle of wine and two glasses.

"I hope you don't mind," he said. "I thought you looked like you needed a drink, and I know I do."

"Damn right I do." I sank down onto the floor, my back against the sofa, and Felix joined me. It was how we used to sit, I remembered, our legs stretched out in front of us, our hands intertwined, while Mel and Roddy sprawled above us on the shabby leather couch in our flat in Covent Garden, all those years ago. Felix handed me a glass of wine and smiled, and I knew he was remembering, too.

I felt suddenly shy again, although while the kids had been around and we'd been busy with the mundane post-party chores, I'd felt completely comfortable, answering his questions about whether things went in the dishwasher and where I kept the clingfilm as if he was just another friend. But he wasn't, I realised – he was my ex, the man who'd broken my heart, who I'd believed for years was The One, The Only One, the One Who Got Away – even though that wasn't true, that was how it felt. And here he was sitting in my house, close enough to touch, while my husband was out. I tucked my knees up and wrapped my arms around them, then realised that made my skirt slip down my bare thighs, so I straightened them again.

"So," I said. "You haven't told me what you've been up to, all these years."

"You haven't told me, either," he said.

"Yes, but," I gestured at the room around me, up to the ceiling above which my children were sleeping. "You know. You've seen. It's all here. I don't know anything about you."

"You've seen where I am now, too," Felix said. "I stayed in Russia until I stopped dancing. I was still okay, but I was getting slower, taking longer to recover – you know. So I tried acting. Turns out I'm good at it – good enough to be in work some of the time, anyway. When I'm not I do other stuff."

"Like what?"

"Magic shows for kids, obviously," he laughed. "No, I don't do that much. I work in a bar sometimes – a mate of mine has a place in Hoxton and I help out there when it's busy. I mix a mean Blood and Sand. And I train doctors."

"You what?"

"Train doctors. Well, not myself. But when they're learning to have a bedside manner, they use actors. You know – 'Mr Lawson, I'm afraid there's nothing more we can do for your wife.' 'Mr Lawson, you'll need six-monthly prostate checks for the rest of your life.' That kind of thing. It's not exactly a laugh a minute, but it pays the bills when nothing else does. I work with a woman in Brixton who does theatre workshops with young offenders – they're almost as scary as kids' parties. I was in the States for a bit. I had a part on Broadway but the show bombed, so I came back here."

"Where are you living?" I asked – the typical London question that lets you find out almost everything you need to know about a person's life by their postcode. But Felix was unforthcoming.

"A hotel, for the time being," he said. "While I'm doing *Dream*. And after that –" he shrugged – "I'll go wherever there's work. Chasing after my big break. I live in hope, anyway."

"But…" I said again, then stopped, and topped up our glasses. The closeness, the intimacy I'd felt when we first sat down together was gone. I was conscious of the huge gulf that had opened up between us – how different our lives were, our aspirations. Not, I realised, that I really had any aspirations any more, beyond my children's happiness and safety. And losing half a stone, obviously.

"Laura, there's nothing wrong with this, you know. What you have. It's wonderful."

Anyone else would have thought that I felt sorry for Felix when he told me what his life was like, but he knew me too well. He'd realised I was worried that he pitied me.

"It is," I said, defensively. "Anyway, I couldn't have carried on. You know that." "I do," he said, and reached over, almost putting his hand on my bare knee, then withdrawing it. "I was married, you know."

I felt a sharp, unexpected stab of jealousy. He what? When I'd imagined what Felix was doing in the years since we last saw each other, that had somehow not crossed my mind. Sometimes, I'd tortured myself by imagining him on the red carpet with a succession of glamorous, A-list women on his arm – sometimes so vividly that I'd been too frightened to look at the *Daily Mail* sidebar of shame lest he appear there in a dinner jacket next to a beautiful model in Valentino. But mostly, I'd preferred to imagine him single, alone and lonely, success eluding him as he lost his looks and became a fat, disappointed shadow of himself. The second scenario was pretty accurate, I realised – apart from the minor details of Felix being as gorgeous as he'd ever been and, apparently, not disappointed in the slightest.

"She was a dancer," he said. "Of course. Tatiana, I mean. We met not long after... about twelve years ago. But then she decided she wanted a family, and there was just no way I could do that. I couldn't jack in my career for two kids and a picket fence and I wasn't earning enough to let her jack hers in and try and do something else. So that went tits up. And now she's married to an accountant and living in Omsk."

Maddeningly, he didn't even sound particularly disappointed about that.

"Funny how history repeats itself," I said, cattily.

"Hilarious," Felix said.

I tipped more wine into our glasses. The bottle was nearly finished.

"He's an accountant, then, your 'hubby'?" I could hear the careful quotes he put around the word.

"A management consultant," I said. "He's just been made a partner in the firm where he works. And I'm not working. I was, but I got laid off."

I knew how prickly I sounded. Jonathan's success, and my lack of it, was something I avoided thinking about.

"What does a management consultant do, then?" Felix said, steering the conversation on to safer territory.

"I'm not exactly sure," I admitted. "Jonathan said when I met him that the definition of a consultant is a guy who knows ninety-nine positions to have sex in, and no women."

"And does he?" Felix said. He was looking at me sideways, from beneath his impossibly long eyelashes, and his gaze and his words reminded me of all the times we'd fucked, all the positions we'd done it in, all the places.

"He knows me," I said, deliberately misunderstanding. "His boss is a woman, actually. Things have changed. There's lots more equality now, Jonathan says."

"Is there," Felix said. It wasn't a question. He stretched his arms up over his head, pulling the silk shirt out from the waistband of his trousers, and yawned hugely. Fuck, I thought, I was boring him. I'd changed too much, we no longer had anything in common, and now he was going to go home, and tomorrow he'd tell all his mates at work about his adventure in middle-class Wandsworth, and laugh about how conventional, dull and shallow his ex-girlfriend, who used to have a brilliant career as a ballerina, had become.

And then I thought, rightly so. Let him fuck off and live his life, hoping that his big break is just around the corner, even when it's not. Good luck to him. I've succeeded in my life – he blatantly hasn't. He's a failure, even if he's the most beautiful failure I've ever seen.

Then Felix said, "Laura, I've wanted to say sorry for fifteen years. For what happened. I tried to tell you then, but you wouldn't let me. And then I was in Russia – there was no Facebook then, it was harder to find people. I tried, once I was back in London. But you were married by then and I couldn't find you. And even if I had…"

He stopped, but I knew what he'd been about to say. It would have been too late. And now he had, and it was.

"I know," I said. "I'm sorry, too. It wasn't your fault. It felt like it then, but I know it wasn't, really. I've grown up, I guess."

I didn't tell him that I'd had very little difficulty tracking him down – that his name had been almost the first I'd looked for when I opened my Facebook account, and Googling him had become as tempting as picking a scab.

He reached over and took my hand, and we sat there for a moment, feeling the warm pressure of each other's fingers, remembering.

Then I stood up, pleased that I was still able to uncurl myself from the floor without using my hands. I meant to say – I genuinely did – that it was almost eight o'clock, and he should go, but what came out was, "Shall I open another bottle?"

Felix said, "Only if you put some music on."

Half an hour later, we were dancing around my sitting room like lunatics, the music quiet enough not to wake the children, but loud enough to drown out our tuneless attempts to sing along. I discovered that although my mind didn't remember the way I'd moved back when I still could, my body did. And Felix's did too. It was late, far too late, when we

collapsed on the sofa in a laughing heap, our acri-
mony forgotten and the second bottle of wine history.

"Laura," Felix said.

"What?" I said, gasping for breath, and we both
started to laugh again.

"Look, I need to go," he said. "And you need me
to go. But I want to see you again. Not in a – not like
that. But you liked the play, didn't you?"

"The play?" I'd forgotten all about it. "Yes, I did.
I loved it."

"I can get comps. If I send you some, will you
come? Maybe we could have a drink in the bar after."

"I'd love that," I said. "Thank you." Then I offered
to ring a taxi for him, and said I'd pay for it, and we
were able to say goodbye, kissing each other on the
cheek at the front door like old friends, because we
knew we were going to see each other again.

CHAPTER TEN

April 2001: Rehearsal

I may have fallen asleep quickly, but my sleep wasn't deep, or restful. All night, it seemed, I dreamed strange, anxious dreams, in which I was on my way to rehearsal but couldn't find the right studio, and when eventually I did I'd forgotten my shoes, and then when I rushed off to find them, the rehearsal room had moved again, and suddenly I was out in the street with no clothes on, and people were laughing at me.

It was laughter that woke me fully. Felix was sitting up in bed next to me, his eyes bleary and his hair tousled, and Roddy was in the doorway with two mugs of coffee.

"What's this then?" he said. "Sleeping Beauty, the Porn Star Years?"

"Fuck off, Roderigo," Felix said. "I can assure you that your flatmate's virtue is unsullied – by me, at any rate. Unless I was too pissed to remember, but I don't think so. Was I, Laura?"

140

"You must have been pretty pissed," I said, sitting up too. "Or do you make a habit of passing out in girls' beds?"

"I've been known to," Felix said. "But generally only once I've driven them to extremes of ecstasy, and I'd have remembered doing that to you. Wouldn't I?"

"No extremes of ecstasy here," I said. "You were rubbish, to be honest."

Felix's face fell, then he realised I was taking the piss out of him. "Hand me a coffee, Roderigo," he said. "I feel like utter shite."

"What time is it, anyway?" I asked. "We haven't missed class, have we?"

"It's only seven thirty," Roddy said. "Melodrama hasn't surfaced yet."

That was unlike Mel, who was usually up at six on work days, doing her Pilates in the living room.

"I'll go and see if she's okay," I said. I clambered out of bed, shy in front of Felix in the T-shirt I'd slept in, which barely covered my bottom. I wasn't wearing anything underneath. I hoped I hadn't snored. This was the moment I'd longed for – waking up next to Felix – but it wasn't happening at all as I'd imagined.

"I'll take this to Mel," I said, grabbing one of the cups of coffee from Roddy.

"Here, you have this one." He handed the other to Felix. "Your need's greater than mine, Lawsonski. I'll stick the kettle on again. Breakfast will be served in ten minutes, so make yourself decent. This is a respectable establishment, not one of your Moscow bordelloes."

Felix chucked one of my pillows at Roddy, but it hit me instead.

"Sorry, Laura," he said. "For taking over your bed, not just for my crap aim."

I looked at him, too shy to meet his eyes, and found my gaze drawn to his bare legs, impossibly long and muscular, sticking out from under my faded flowery duvet cover. I felt myself blushing and ducked my head again.

"That's all right," I said, and scurried off to knock on Mel's door. I was longing to have an urgent, whispered chat about what had happened – or not happened – between Felix and me, and what – if anything – it meant. Would he have slept in my bed if he didn't like me? If he did like me, what should I do about it? Or was it all just a stupid, random, drunken thing that had happened, which I needed to put out of my mind once and for all?

But as soon as I heard Mel's croaky, "Come in," and opened the door, I knew that wasn't the conversation I was going to have with her. The room smelled odd – stale and musty. Mel was lying down, curled in a foetal huddle, her lank hair sticking to her face, which was ghostly pale. I could see that the pillowcase next to her was damp, and realised she'd been sweating, or crying, or both.

"Hey," I said softly. "How are you feeling? Are you okay? You look awful. I brought you coffee."

I put the mug down on the floor and sat next to her, reaching out to stroke her hair.

"Don't touch me," she groaned. "It hurts. Everything hurts. Could you bring me a glass of water, please? If I drink coffee I'll spew. And those tablets I bought yesterday."

"You should see a doctor," I said. "You're not well."

"Don't be ridiculous." She struggled upright. "It's just a cold. I'm fine."

"You're not fine," I said. "Mel, seriously, you need to rest."

"Fuck that," she said. "I can rest when I'm dead. Right now I need to get to class, and then to rehearsal. You don't chuck sickies when you've just been given a promotion, Laura, as you know full well."

I did know. I'd seen it happen before – Iris, who'd joined the company in the same year as us, had been identified as a rising star, a dancer who was going places. Then she'd started getting migraines. Her doctor said they were caused by stress, and advised her to take it easy for a bit. Iris certainly did take it easy – she stopped getting any parts at all, sank back to the Corps de Ballet with the rest of us, and left a year later, her promise come to nothing. So I pushed my worries to the back of my mind, fetched Mel her tablets and had a shower.

Class that morning was different from usual. I could sense that more eyes were on me than had ever been before – the company's rumour mill had clearly been working overtime, and the whispers that always followed Felix now followed me, too. I felt proud and excited to be the one who was watched, was talked about – but also frightened. Nothing had happened between us, after all – probably nothing was going to. But every time I glanced at Felix, I saw that he was looking at me, too, and every time our eyes met we smiled at each other. His smiles gave new sureness to my steps, new height to my jumps, a sense of freedom and pleasure in my work that hadn't been there in the weeks before. But all too soon, class was over and Felix and Mel departed with the soloists while I had my break and prepared for my own mundane rehearsal with the rest of the mere Artists.

I, along with the rest of the dancers who'd been with the company for a while, knew *Swan Lake* pretty much inside out. I'd been dancing bits of it since I was a little girl, after all. So rehearsals like today's were a strange mixture of comfort and frustration. Here we were, practising the same, familiar steps, albeit with slightly different artistic interpretation, but basically it was all the same, as easy as putting on a favourite pair of jeans, but with the niggling knowledge that you'd really, really like a new pair – ideally a gorgeous, designer pair that would turn heads when you walked down the street.

I slotted into my place behind Lisa, the pianist began to play, and we all flowed seamlessly into the choreography, our shoulders identically angled, our hands identically placed. Always let the audience see your palms – it was a message we'd had drummed into us for so long that it was automatic, like breathing or swallowing.

Anna moved along the line of dancers, criticising a tempo here, demanding more turnout there, correcting the tilt of a chin or the angle of a spine. I worked on autopilot, my thoughts straying to Felix and when I'd see him again. His rehearsal finished half an hour after ours – I'd loiter on the stairs and wait for him to go up for a smoke, and then maybe we could talk, if he wasn't surrounded by his usual fan club. And even if he was, perhaps he'd single me out, invite me for a coffee – I'd be satisfied with anything, if it meant being close to him. And while I waited I'd text Mel and ask how she was feeling. She'd seemed to be okay in class, her face set with determination, although paler than usual.

The background hum of my thoughts was broken by a ripple of – something – through the line of dancers. It wasn't a sound; it wasn't even visible, really, unless the routine was as familiar as cleaning your teeth. It was more a tension, a series of tiny adjustments that began with Rosa at the front and spread like a game of Chinese Whispers from one girl to the next, and on and on. Gestures, while still identical, became ever so slightly more extravagant. Spines were held straighter. I noticed Lisa across the room suck in her abs and minutely alter the angle of her body to the mirror. I didn't have to look – I knew. Marius was in the studio. I could literally smell him.

"Thank you, girls. Thank you, Paul." There was a final chord from the piano, then silence. We always thanked the pianist at the end of a class or rehearsal, bowing deeply to show our appreciation, but when Anna said thank you, it meant stop.

It was our cue to relax and look at Marius while pretending not to. It wasn't unheard-of for him to look in on rehearsals – as Artistic Director, he was notorious for knowing exactly what was going on in every part of the company at any time, down to the tiniest detail. Inez, one of the seamstresses, had shown me just the other day a deep wound in her finger where she'd shoved a needle into it through sheer fright at smelling Marius behind her in Wardrobe as she took up a hem.

"Thank you, Anna," Marius said. "That was very pretty, girls. A little more... perhaps." He gestured with both hands, knowing even after watching for just a few seconds that we hadn't been trying as hard as we should. "But I won't keep you. You're all hard at work. Anna, could you spare Laura for just a moment?"

Instantly, I wasn't a part in the machine any more, one small and anonymous form in the flock of dancing swans. I'd been singled out. Thirty pairs of eyes swivelled around the room to find me. Girls shifted to see me better, or to allow their neighbours to. I could hear thirty pairs of lungs giving almost identical, tiny gasps, then exhaling, all together. I felt sick.

"Marius." I walked to the door, trying to keep my head high and my back straight, imagining a wire pulling up through my spine so I crossed the floor like a marionette carried by its string, gliding and graceful. Only when I reached him did I dip into a deep bow.

"Yes, thank you," he said impatiently. "Come along."

Clumsy in my pointe shoes, I hurried through the corridors behind him, conscious of the sweat beading my upper lip and trickling down my spine. I was worried I'd get cold – we weren't allowed to get cold.

"Melissa Hammond," Marius said. "She's a friend of yours?"

"Yes. Yes, she's my friend and we share a flat, us and Roderigo Silva." My breathing was rapid and uneven. "Is she okay?"

"She fainted in rehearsal." There was a slight but definite note of scorn in Marius's voice. "She'll be fine, but not for this show. Some sort of virus. Let's hope it doesn't spread through the whole company. So, for now, her part is yours. We'll get the paperwork sorted ASAP." He pronounced it ay-sapp. My mouth was as dry as my body was wet – I wished I'd brought my bottle of water almost as much as I longed for my warm top.

"Thank you, Marius," I said.

"Here we are then. Studio Eight," he said. Then he took my jaw in the fingers of one hand, turning my head this way and that, so I had to force myself to meet his eyes until at last he let go, giving me a small, paternal pat on the shoulder. "Off you go. Any problems, you know where to come."

Jesus, I thought, I'd rather go to Ozzy Osbourne with my problems than to you. The idea made me giggle, and I wrapped my arms around my freezing shoulders, trying to summon up the courage to open the door and go in to the soloists' rehearsal room, where Briony, Jerome and the others had been working for the past few weeks, remote as planets. I understood now how Mel would have felt – how terrified and daunted, while all I'd been aware of was my own jealousy. And then another thought occurred to me – Mel wouldn't like this. Not one bit. Her illness wasn't her fault, any more than my promotion was mine, but I knew that, deep down, she'd see this as an unwelcome reversal of the natural order of things, in which she led and I followed, some way behind. She'd blame me, and I wondered if she'd ever be able to forgive me.

Then I realised that Felix would be there too, rehearsing with the others. I thought of his easy banter and his smile that made me feel like a candle had been lit inside me, and I remembered the way his body had felt next to mine in my bed. And that gave me the courage I needed to open the door.

CHAPTER ELEVEN

Felix was as good as his word. Two days later, an envelope arrived on the doormat addressed to me in his distinctive black scrawl – using a fountain pen had always been an affectation of his. I tore it open eagerly, and found two tickets and a note.

"Come next Friday if you can. It's the final night and there'll be a party after."

He'd signed it with a large, sloping F and three kisses.

I logged on to our online calendar and checked Jonathan's diary. Meetings – bloody six o'clock meetings every evening, for the next two weeks, except Thursday when he had a dinner. I was going to have to call in the cavalry.

"So," I said to Zé the next morning as we sipped coffee together in her garden. "Fancy seeing the show again?"

"The *Dream*? Hell yes. Or I would if I could get hold of tickets. There were some on eBay but they're like three times the face value and I'm not quite that desperate yet."

"I've got two," I said. "One each."

"Seriously? How did you manage that? Do you still have both your kidneys? And both your children?"

I laughed. "Friends in high places. Or rather, one friend."

And I told her the same half-truth I'd told Jonathan the day after Darcey's birthday party – that Felix had mentioned to me when we were having our cigarette outside the restaurant that he did magic as a hobby, and I'd remembered when I was in dire straits when Larry had let us down, and Googled him.

"And he sent me a couple of tickets," I said. "Which was lovely of him, don't you think?"

Zé looked at me astutely. "He fancies you."

"No! No, of course he doesn't! He's just being kind."

"Do you fancy him? You must do, he's fucking gorgeous. Such charisma – I suppose you have to have that, to act. And his voice! I so would. We can get Carmen to babysit, at yours if you don't mind Juniper sleeping over? The girls will love it. Thanks, Laura."

I walked home and sat in the kitchen and drank more coffee, staring blankly out of the window. The wave of jealousy I felt when Zé had said she found Felix attractive had completely blindsided me, especially as I could see exactly how Felix – or anyone else, for that matter – would be attracted to her, too.

It was my own fault for not having owned up to her, and more importantly to Jonathan, about the role Felix had played in my past. At the time it had seemed like a simple glossing-over of a time I preferred to forget – a way of protecting my feelings and my husband's. But at the time I hadn't imagined ever meeting him again, and now I'd begun to spin myself into a web of deception that I couldn't see a way of unravelling.

The sensible thing to do, of course, would be to return the tickets to Felix, with a note explaining that I'd had a think and decided it was better if we let things lie – that there was too much potential for hurt. But he hadn't included a return address on the envelope.

So hand them in at the box office, I told myself, and send him a text – or call him – and explain. It's simple. It's what any adult in your position would do. Or give the tickets to Zé – let her go with another friend. Just do it, Laura. Do the right thing.

But I didn't want to.

We'd be in a public place, I rationalised. There was no harm in it. Zé would be with me, probably hitting on Felix herself, if what she'd said that morning was true. And with her around, no one was going to give me a second glance – certainly not Felix, for whom I was ancient history anyway. And I'd loved the play – I wanted quite desperately to return to that world, that night-time forest, and discover more of its secrets. It wasn't about Felix, I said firmly to myself – it was about me, about discovering a new interest, a new passion, something to relieve the monotony of my life.

And it was just an evening – an evening at the theatre. After that I wouldn't see him again, ever.

There was no reason for our paths to cross again – they hadn't before, so why would they in future? An evening at the theatre, and then Felix would be consigned to my past where he belonged and normal service would resume in the Payne household – no more ex-boyfriends, no more chasing after actors in a park at nighttime, no more not telling Jonathan everything. Especially that last bit.

My conscience uneasily appeased, I opened Jonathan's and my shared calendar app and entered "Laura out, Juniper sleepover", before I could change my mind.

"So where are you off to next Friday then?" Jonathan asked that night over dinner. He'd come home late again – I'd more or less given up mentioning it. No amount of protest from me was going to change his workload and arguing about it just made both of us angry.

"The play," I said. "The one in Battersea Park? I wanted to see it again before it finishes, and Zé managed to get more tickets."

The lie came out before I could even think about it. Shit. Why couldn't you just say, Laura? Just tell him? But once again, it was too late.

"Cool," Jonathan said. "It must have really made an impression on you; I've never known you to be into this stuff before. Although, of course, you must have been – you were a dancer. You hardly ever talk about that."

He forked up some salad and looked at me.

"No – what's to talk about? You worked at Pizza Hut when you were at uni and you never talk about that either."

"I can if you want," Jonathan said. "Although my hilarious anecdotes about pilfering bacon bits to take home to my brother wouldn't be as interesting as your stories."

"I haven't got any interesting stories," I said. "I started ballet classes when I was six, I was good at it, I did it professionally for a bit, then I got injured so I stopped. Then I did my degree and then I met you. The end."

"You know, Laura," he said, "I sometimes think… I sometimes worry that, now the kids are bigger and you've got more time, especially when I'm putting in these hours, you need something else in your life. Have you ever thought, maybe, that you could teach dancing? You'd be amazing at it. It would give you an interest, outside of us."

"I don't want to teach," I said. "God! We always used to say only losers taught. Or people who were too old to dance, obviously. Look, Jonathan, I don't know where this has come from, suddenly. I'm perfectly happy. I'll go back to work when Owen starts school – there are loads of comms agencies in London who are just desperate for mid-thirties women who have to leave on the dot of half five for after-school pick-up and take endless days off when the kids have chicken pox. It'll work out brilliantly."

"Laura…" He reached across the table and brushed the top of my hand.

"What?"

"Sometimes I worry you're not very happy."

"Of course I'm happy!" I said. "Look at my life. It's brilliant. I've got two gorgeous children, we live in this beautiful house, we go on fab holidays – why wouldn't I be happy? And I've got you, of course."

I realised as I said it how much like an afterthought that sounded, but it was too late to change it, to make it better.

"Okay," Jonathan said. "I just wondered… I worry."

"Well, don't," I said. "Look, this thing – it's just a play, all right? If I was going to Les Mis you wouldn't think twice about it."

"You wouldn't go to Les Mis twice," Jonathan pointed out.

"Too right," I laughed. "I wouldn't go once. Come on, let's clear up and go to bed."

So we did, and we had hasty, comfortable sex before we both fell asleep, and Jonathan didn't say anything more about my past life or my sudden obsession with an immersive theatre production, for which I was grateful.

I didn't either – but that wasn't because I wasn't thinking about it. I counted down the days until I'd enter that world again, waking up every morning thinking, that's another sleep over, just like Darcey did when she was looking forward to a party. The eight days became seven, then it was the weekend and Jonathan was home, blissfully content as he pottered in the garden and took the children to the park. On Sunday we had Amanda, the nicer of the two Helens and their families round for a barbecue. The sun shone, the children played happily together, Jonathan made burgers using his secret recipe – it was all perfect, and it made me wonder why on earth I hankered, deep down, for something more.

But on Wednesday morning I woke up to find that Owen had been sick in the night. Grey sheets of rain were battering against the windows, and real life descended on me again with a thud. I cleaned up the mess, rang the nursery to say I'd be keeping him home, and we walked an unusually silent Darcey to school, huddled together under Jonathan's golfing umbrella.

I spent two days on the sofa with Owen's warm body on my knee, cuddling him and cautiously giving him sips of water with apple juice in. He felt floppy and listless, unlike his usual boisterous self. It was just a bug, I told myself – nothing to worry about. But I did worry, and the more I worried, the guiltier I felt, because I knew that I was concerned not just about my little boy, but about whether he'd be well enough for me to leave him in two nights' time.

To deflect my anxiety, I found myself obsessively checking the BBC weather app. If it carried on raining like this, the show would be cancelled, and none of it would matter. I found myself bargaining with my phone – if Owen's okay, it can rain all day on Friday and I won't care.

But in the event, by Thursday evening Owen was devouring banana on toast and the sky had cleared, and Darcey was saying, "Only one more sleep until Juniper comes to stay, Mummy!"

And I was thinking, "Only one more sleep until I see Felix again."

Owen made a full recovery from his lurgy, but whatever bug it was that was going the rounds claimed another victim. I was getting ready, applying my makeup with far more care than I had the first time I prepared to go and see Flight of Fancy's *Dream*, as I was learning to call it in my head, when my phone rang.

"Zé? How's it going? Are you excited?"

"I fucking was," she said bitterly. "I've been like a kid waiting for Christmas, but now I'm ill. I've been spewing all day and I feel terrible. I'm not going to make it, Laura, I'm so gutted."

"Oh no, you poor thing! Have you got flat Coke? That's meant to be the best thing."

"I can't even face a glass of water. I'm in bed right now, and I literally feel like if I move I'll be sick again."

"Oh no." Poor Zé, poor Darcey missing her longed-for sleepover with her friend, and poor me. It looked like I wouldn't be going to the ball after all. Maybe it wasn't too late to book a babysitter online – but I couldn't do that to my daughter. I'd have to stay in with her and think of something fun to do, and hide my disappointment.

"Anyway, Laura," Zé continued dolefully, "Do you mind if I send Juniper and Carmen over anyway? You'd be doing me a favour. Unless you're worried about the children catching whatever it is?"

"Owen's had it," I said. "Unless what he had was food poisoning from my cooking, which is possible, but I think not. Are you sure, though? That's so lovely of you."

"It really isn't," Zé said. "It's the most selfish thing I've done all week. Juniper keeps coming to check on me and see if I want cups of tea, which I don't – at least this way I can get some rest. And you can see the show and go to the party. What are you wearing?"

"Jeans, I guess," I said, remembering the require-ment for practical clothing.

"Don't you dare! Wear something sparkly – I bet people will dress up. Ugh, I have to go. Have a great time. Carmen and Juniper are leaving in ten. Call me tomorrow."

"Feel better soon," I said, but she'd already ended the call, presumably to race for the bathroom.

I ransacked my wardrobe and found a white shift dress that had a few sequins round the sleeves and hem. I hadn't worn it for ages – it had been a lucky find in a charity shop when I was uni – but it still fit-ted, just. I combed my hair, slicked on a coat of bright red lipstick and went downstairs just as the doorbell rang.

"You look amazing, Laura," Juniper said.

"Mummy always looks beautiful," Darcey said loyally. I kissed her and Owen, gave Carmen money for takeaway pizzas, and headed out into the balmy night.

Until the moment I closed my front door, excitement and adrenaline had been carrying me. All that mattered was that I got to go out – that I didn't have to abandon my plans and send Felix a sheepish text saying I wasn't going to make it after all. But now, the reality of my situation hit home again. I felt more like a woman going to meet her lover than like a suburban housewife out for an evening at the theatre. And, in my sparkly frock and lipstick, I must look like one too.

A passing group of teenage boys in hoodies gave me a long, appreciative stare and one of them said, "MILF." I knew I ought to feel outraged, but instead I burst out laughing and they scuttled off, shamefaced. With my laughter came a new sense of carelessness. This was, honestly, just a night out. I should enjoy it, not encumber myself with needless guilt when I'd done nothing wrong, and wasn't going to. Jonathan was at work, my children were being safely cared for in their own home by a girl they adored. Even Jonathan had said I needed to do more for myself, and now I was. It was just like booking a spa day. I was going to have a brilliant time.

My sense of elation carried me all the way to the park, and I backed it up with a hastily gulped glass of prosecco. Zé had been right – people were dressed up. A few women had even come with fairy wings strapped to their backs, and one man was wearing a donkey mask on his head, until a steward made him take it off.

The sense of anticipation was almost palpable. I joined the crowd by the marble pillars, and wished I'd come earlier to have a chance of being in first. The idea of being alone – truly alone, even for a few seconds – in that magical world was intoxicating. But I was a few minutes too late, and there were about a dozen people ahead of me. I wasn't first – but I knew where to go.

As soon as the barriers opened, I hurried through the curtain of light. I knew what I wanted to do – find Felix and follow him all night, seeing the play through his eyes, watching every move he made and trying to understand what it meant to be Oberon, what it felt like to have this power to enchant, to command a night-time world where love was a game and mortals were nothing more than toys, or pieces on a chessboard to be moved around in a contest of power.

But I'd forgotten the sheer size of the set. I took a wrong turning leaving the village, and found myself watching an amazing, acrobatic dance performed by five of the fairies. There must surely be wires involved, I thought, astonished by the sheer height and duration of their leaps. My plan forgotten, I stood transfixed, overwhelmed with admiration and envy, because once long ago, I'd been able to do this, or something like it.

Even though I was lost, I'd come to the right place. Soon I saw Puck, then Oberon, and I spent the next hour racing after him along the narrow paths through the undergrowth, until my breath was coming in gasps and the hem of my dress was wet with dew. I knew he'd seen me, because when he rounded a sudden corner and I was sure I'd lost him, he'd be there a second later, waiting for me. Every time his eyes behind the great, horned mask scanned the audience, I was sure they paused on me, resting for a moment in acknowledgement. Once I was sure I caught a glint of blue through the elaborate bronze visor.

And then I did lose him. He darted behind a tree, I followed – and he wasn't there any more. I stopped, listening, but all I could hear was my pounding heart and the eerie, unearthly music. I wasn't alone – there'd been a group of five or six of us all night following the same route, and now we'd all been thwarted. We looked at each other, keeping to the rule of silence, and exchanged baffled shrugs. Two women went back the way we'd come; one turned away to the left, I thought in the direction of the palace, and the other two went on ahead.

I paused, indecisive. I could wait here, see whether he returned to find me. But I knew all too well that this wasn't about me – Felix was a professional playing a role, and he'd be governed rigidly by his cues, the orders given to him by the music and the lights. There was no time for messing about. I'd see what lay beyond the thicket of trees to my right, I decided, and then I'd head back to the bar and have a drink and sit down for a bit, and see if I could catch the wedding scene at the end, which I'd missed before. It was fine – I was having a wonderful time; the twinge of disappointment I felt was ridiculous and would pass.

I found a gap between the trees, and emerged into a clearing I hadn't seen before. I stopped and looked around, a gasp coming unthinking from my throat. It was beautiful. The full moon – even though I knew it was a spotlight – cast an ethereal glow over the trees, the moss that covered the ancient stone floor and the flowering vines that twined over a pair of stone columns in the centre. For a second, my brain acknowledged the genius of the set design, but I was in no mood for analysis – I was transported entirely, charmed by the illusion as powerfully as if a spell had been cast on me.

And then I saw Oberon. He appeared from behind one of the columns, lit now from above in a way that made me realise he'd been there all the time, the lichen colours of his robes blending into the stone like camouflage, as long as he was still. He wasn't still now.

I would have forgotten that it was Felix behind that mask, only the beauty with which he moved was unmistakeable. There was a wild savagery to his dance, but total control and effortless grace, too. The professional I'd been years before marvelled at it – Felix's ex-girlfriend felt a stabbing, familiar pulse of desire so strong I could hardly bear it. He might have quit classical ballet, I realised, but he'd acquired new skills and an amazing athletic ability I hadn't seen before. He moved between the pillars like a gymnast, seeming to ignore gravity as his body moved sideways, perpendicular to the floor, upside down – and then he ran, as if it were part of the choreography, towards me and swept me up into his dance.

As it had in my living room a few days before, my body remembered what to do. I wasn't as fit or as supple as I'd been, I was a stone heavier, I was wearing Converse instead of pointe shoes. But I was dancing – dancing with Felix, and it was heaven. He spun me and lifted me, and I followed his lead effortlessly, as if we'd rehearsed this moment for weeks.

It lasted just a minute or two – any longer would have killed me. But I realised a small crowd had gathered round the clearing, watching in silent admiration. And when Oberon took my arm and ran with me away from our small stage into the trees, I heard a brief smattering of applause – although that might just have been my brain remembering the past as my body had done.

Once again, we were alone in Oberon's grotto, his fairy cave, dimly lit and drenched in soft, strange music. Once again he covered my eyes and spoke his lines, and took off his mask and kissed me. But the kiss this time was deeper and more intense, and there was a moment when I reached up to touch his sweating face with my fingertip, which I hadn't been brave enough to do before. And then, for one second so fleeting it might not have happened at all, he stopped being Oberon and became Felix, and whispered, "Wait for me afterwards, Laura."

In a haze of happiness, I watched the finale from the steps of the palace, seeing the lovers reunited in their natural order. I screamed my appreciation with the rest of the audience as the choreographer and the creative director were carried on to the stage on the shoulders of the cast, and I cried actual tears into the woman next to me's shoulder as we exchanged fervent hugs and said, "I can't believe it's over!"

Everyone flocked to the bar. I bought the woman I'd hugged a glass of fizz and a total stranger bought me one, then someone else bought a round for a random group of about ten of us who were exchanging breathless memories of what we'd seen and what had happened to us.

Someone nudged me and said, "Look! There's Lysander," and I realised that the cast were starting to emerge, mingling with their fans, and that the man whose dance I'd watched and admired when I saw the show with Zé was a household name, an actor who'd been on the cover of *Hello* magazine and was properly famous.

I noticed through my haze of prosecco and happiness that the crowd was beginning to thin, and the woman I'd befriended said, "Oh no, chucking out time," just before a steward approached our little group and told us politely that it was cast and VIPs only from now on, please, and could we make our way to the exit over there, where we'd be able to collect our bags.

I wanted to say, "No! Not me! I'm supposed to be here. Look, I have an invitation."

Then I remembered that the precious pass to the after-show party was in my handbag, which I'd checked in with my coat when I arrived. Fool! Anyway, there was nothing to be done. I'd have to go home with everyone else.

Then, suddenly, I felt a warm arm encircle my waist and smelled fresh soap and shampoo, and Felix said, "Don't sling Laura out, Marco, she's with me."

I was woken the next morning by Jonathan singing 'What shall we do with a grumpy Owen?' to the tune of 'What shall we do with the drunken sailor?' It was one of the collection of joke songs he'd made up when our son was a tiny baby and wouldn't sleep, and it brought back memories of lying in bed, exhausted, my breasts sore from endless feeding, trying desperately to get the sleep Jonathan said I should have while he took over on rocking and bouncing duty for a few hours. I felt no less exhausted now.

It had been long after two when I got in, I remembered blearily. The house was dark and silent, except for the cooker hood light, which someone had left on for me. Jonathan must have paid Carmen and sent her home when he got back from work. I took my make-up off, made a cup of tea and sat in near-darkness in the kitchen, too wired to go to bed. Memories of the evening spun through my head – dancing with Felix, with the famous actor who'd played Lysander, with a series of faceless people taking in turns to wear Bottom's donkey mask. Wandering around the dark, empty set, wishing that it would come alive again with characters and music. Walking home with Felix through the quiet streets and saying good night to him outside our front door.

Saying goodnight – that was all. We'd kissed each other on both cheeks, and he hugged me close, and I thanked him again for inviting me. But that was all. Nothing had happened for me to feel guilty about.

Yet I felt guilty all the same. Guilty, hungover, and full of regret.

I resisted the urge to pull the pillow over my head and try to go back to sleep. Instead, I pulled my body out of bed – why was I aching all over? I felt like I'd been hit by a bus, or been to a Pilates class or something. The room tilted alarmingly as I stood up. I must have drunk far more than I'd realised. The stairs felt strange under my feet as I walked down to the kitchen, as if the height of their treads had been altered while I slept. The sunlight pouring through the skylights hurt my eyes.

Jonathan and Owen were perched on stools at the kitchen counter, which was splattered with what looked like porridge.

SOPHIE RANALD

Owen said, "Mummy!" and stretched out his arms to be picked up.

"Look at you, mucky face," I kissed him.

"My breakfast offering wasn't up to standard," Jonathan said, "and Jay Rayner here expressed his disapproval by tipping it out of the bowl."

"Well, if you will serve him snail porridge," I joked lamely. "Where are the girls?"

"Still asleep," Jonathan said. "You weren't the only one who had a late night – I could hear them chatting for ages after I went to bed. How was the party?"

"Okay," I said. "It was fun. It went on for ages."

"So I see," Jonathan said, raising an eyebrow at my dishevelled appearance. "Coffee?"

"Please." I sat down next to him, Owen on my lap, and took a healing sip.

Darcey and Juniper came clattering down the stairs, Katy Perry playing tinnily on Juniper's mobile.

"Good morning," Juniper said.

"Mum, please can I go to Juniper's house to play? Zé says it's okay." I'd noticed that Darcey was calling me Mummy less and less often. There'd come a point, I realised, when she'd call me Mummy for the last time, and Mum would take over for good, but because I wouldn't know it was the last time I wouldn't be able to treasure it.

"If she's not still poorly… I'll text her and check."

Zé replied saying she'd love to have Darcey for the day.

"Okay, I'll drive you both over once I've had a shower. What would you girls like for breakfast? Toast? Porridge?"

"Nothing, thank you," Juniper said, so I gave up and handed them each a cereal bar.

"And what shall we do? Picnic? Swimming?"

"I'm afraid I have work to do," Jonathan said.

I opened my mouth to protest, to point out that he'd worked late every single night that week, that it was Saturday, that surely he wanted to spend some time with me and with his son. But what was the point? It would only lead to an argument, which would be resolved in half an hour's time by Jonathan going upstairs with his laptop anyway.

A few months ago, when I'd been working full time, the idea of a day alone with my little boy would have felt like heaven. I'd make playdough or we'd blow bubbles or I'd Google sensory play and make magical clouds out of flour and Fairy Liquid, and generally behave like a model mum, straight out of *Junior* magazine.

(Although in reality, of course, the day would be spent with me chasing my tail, frantically catching up on housework with a toddler underfoot, stressed and snappy.)

Now, though, once I'd dropped the girls off, I felt totally at a loose end. I looked after the children on my own all week and now it was Saturday and I'd have to do it all over again. I thought about sticking Owen in front of the telly – where, I had to admit, he'd love nothing more than to spend the day – and getting out my laptop and seeing if there was anything new on the Outnet. But guilt stopped me – I was not only a rubbish mother, squandering my little boy's childhood on CBeebies, but I was a rubbish wife, too, resenting the time Jonathan spent working to support us.

Firmly suppressing my urge to look at shoes online, I took Owen and his scooter to the library and chose a selection of suitable books. Then we went to play on the swings and feed the ducks. The park on this glorious summer morning seemed to be full of couples. Of course, there were people alone and families with children too, but it was the couples I saw. Lounging on benches, one with their head in the other's lap; leaning over the balustrade looking at the river; reclining on picnic blankets with bottles of cava and packets of crisps and an air about them that said, "Once we've finished this, we're off home for a shag."

Looking at them, I remembered what it had been like when Jonathan and I were first going out. I remembered how much fun we'd had together – going to restaurants, art-house films, or galleries, or on mini-breaks to Paris or Prague, all of it punctuated by endless sex. At first, I'd thought it was all a bit of fun, a way to experience a life of luxury with a man who, inexplicably, seemed to worship me. But after a while, I'd started longing for the evenings and weekends I spent with Jonathan, missing him when I wasn't with him, storing up snippets of my day to recount to him, knowing what would make him laugh or what he could give me advice about.

Then he went away, to spend two weeks skiing with his brother. To my amazement, I was bereft. I missed him – his companionship, his jokes, the sense of effortless joy he brought to my life. I had to stop myself phoning him every night to tell him what had happened at work, or what I'd read in the newspaper, or what I'd like to do to him in bed. It had snuck up on me entirely unexpectedly, but I couldn't deny it – I was in love. I was subsumed by desire and longing in a way I'd never thought I could be again.

I forced myself to play it cool, not to contact Jonathan until he got back – and even after I knew he had, I resolutely didn't dial his number. Then he called me, just two days after returning from Switzerland, and suggested we meet up on a Sunday afternoon for a walk. The walk turned into a picnic – it was a perfect spring day, and we lay on the grass like these couples were doing, watching the sun move slowly over the leaves that shaded us, sipping wine and eating the takeaway sushi Jonathan had brought.

I was lying back on the grass, drowsy with content-ment, loving having him back with me, my mind just catching up with what my heart already knew, when he fed me a piece of tuna and a diamond ring slid down the bamboo chopstick and landed on my front teeth with an audible clack.

My eyes snapped open. I reached up and lifted it up to the light, saw what it was, and started to laugh.

SOPHIE RANALD

"Epic fail," Jonathan said, laughing too. "Most inept proposal ever. That was meant to be all classy and subtle. I was going to put the ring in the chopsticks and... But, you know, will you?"

"Yes," I said, without the slightest hesitation. We never finished the sushi – we were too eager to get home to his flat and consummate our engagement.

Laughing at the memory, I grabbed Owen's hand and said, "What shall we do now, Squidge?"

"Nice cream?" Owen said hopefully.

I hesitated. It was almost noon – if he had ice cream now, he wouldn't eat his lunch. But if he had ice cream now, I wouldn't have to make lunch for him, and go through the frustration of asking him whether he wanted his cucumber in sticks or rings, and having him change his mind after I'd cut it up, and cry inconsolably at my unreasonableness when I refused to start all over again with new cucumber.

I chose the path of least resistance, and when we got home Owen announced that he was full, and I put him down for his nap.

Jonathan was still working, hunched over his laptop in the spare bedroom, which had rapidly deteriorated from the haven of gracious elegance I'd imagined into a kind of man cave-cum-black hole, where boxes of still-unpacked toys fought for floor space with bags of clothes I kept meaning to take to the charity shop or flog on eBay, and Jonathan's ever-growing collection of golf clubs. Looking at the clutter made me cross, so I looked at Jonathan instead.

He was frowning at a spreadsheet, flicking between it and an internet page which I could see was a mass of figures, incomprehensible to me.

"How's it going?" I asked tentatively.

There was no reply.

"What do you think about the terrorist attack on Royal St Andrews?" I said.

"What?" Jonathan spun round so quickly that his wheely chair almost overshot itself and slammed his knee into the leg of the table. He winced and caught his balance just in time, in a way that reminded me of Owen averting an unplanned dismount from his scooter.

"Just joking," I said. "Look, I was wondering what you fancied doing tonight? We haven't spent any time together for ages. I'm sure Darcey's going to want to stay over with Juniper, so once Owen's in bed I'll make us something nice for dinner. And you can make us cocktails. It'll be fun."

"Great," Jonathan said distractedly. "That sounds great, Laura."

"I'll go to the shops then, shall I? Owen's asleep, will you listen for him?"

"Of course." Jonathan's face softened, as it always did when he talked or thought about the children.

"Okay." I brushed the top of his head with my palm, but he was already absent again, his attention focussed entirely on the screen.

I picked up my handbag and left the house. If I was going to cook, there was any amount of stuff in the freezer I could have used, but I was suddenly overcome by cabin fever, and by the need to be alone. Even walking up the hill to the main road, crossing it and joining the throngs of shoppers in our local supermarket felt like a chance to be inside my own head for just a few minutes.

I pushed a trolley through the aisles with no real intent. I'd make a salad – Darcey loved salad, and so did I. But Darcey wouldn't be home. What would Jonathan like? Browsing the shelves as I ambled along, I found myself dropping random thing after random thing into my shopping cart. Chilli Heatwave Doritos. Frozen pizza with pineapple on it. Cherry tomatoes. Wafer-thin ham. A massive pack of Diet Coke. Two bottles of prosecco. Pink Lady apples.

It was only when I caught myself lingering over the small section of shelf devoted to pain-relief and corn plasters, and found my hand automatically dropping two packs of ibuprofen and a giant roll of Elsastoplast onto my trolley that I realised.

I wasn't shopping for my family. I was shopping for Felix and me.

I actually blushed, as if I'd been spotted by one of the school run mums stocking up on extra-strong ribbed condoms. I retraced my steps, putting every-thing back in more or less the same place where I'd found it. Even so, I found myself lingering by the herbs and spices, remembering how Felix and I used to corpse with childish laughter in Tesco, arranging the spices so their labels spelled out rude words.

Basil, oregano, thyme and mixed herbs made 'bottom'. Bay leaves, oregano and sage made 'boobs'. Felix even managed 'spanking' in a particularly impressive effort that required kaffir lime leaves and Italian mixed herbs. It was the most juvenile thing ever, and it used to make as laugh so much we could hardly stand (and we laughed even more when we wondered what possibilities would extend if only there was a herb whose name began with U).

I caught myself giggling like a loon, right there in the herbs and spices aisle.

A passing child asked his mother, "Why's that lady laughing, Mummy?"

"She must be a nutter," said his sister.

"Sssh, Felicia," the mother said. "You remember I talked to you the other day about how unkind it is to make fun of people who are... different."

Even though she dropped her voice discreetly for the final word, I heard it, and my laughter died in my throat.

What was I doing, exactly? Mooning, that's what. Mooning like a teenager with a crush on Harry Styles. Except teenagers were allowed to do that, because – well, because they were teenagers. In a woman of my age – a married woman of my age – it was nothing short of pathetic. And it's not even as if Felix was a legitimate crush, like Robert Webb or Dr Ranj or someone. He was my ex, for God's sake. And he was my ex for a reason.

Think about it for one second, Laura, I told myself. If you weren't married to Jonathan, you wouldn't have your children. Other ones, perhaps, but not these ones, my favourite people in the world. The idea was chilling – if I allowed myself to think this way, wasn't I inviting some sort of disaster? If fate thought I was wishing them away, mightn't it intervene to remove them from me?

The thought gave me the horrors, and I pushed it away, forcing my attention back to the absurd contents of my shopping trolley. This was it. Enough. It had to stop.

I forced myself to retrace my steps, replacing all the random items on the shelves where I'd found them. I started again, putting Aberdeen Angus fillet, potatoes, salad, tarragon, butter and eggs in the trolley along with a couple of bottles of expensive red wine. I'd cook Jonathan's favourite meal for us – it would be the beginning of reclaiming the wonderful joy I'd felt when we were first together.

CHAPTER TWELVE

My resolve to be a better wife and mother lasted well into the evening. I watched a DVD with the children to stop them disturbing Jonathan while he worked, then cooked pasta with pesto and cherry tomatoes for their supper, supervised their baths, read Owen a story and told Darcey she could spend half an hour and not a minute more watching unboxing clips on YouTube.

"I don't like those any more, Mum," she said scornfully. "They're babyish."

I detected Juniper's influence, and felt a pang of nostalgia for the asinine vloggers who'd annoyed me so much just a few weeks before.

"What are you going to do then, before you go to sleep?"

She pulled a stack of glossy magazines out from under her bed. I spotted *Girl Talk*, *Shout* and a couple of others in the same genre – harmless enough.

"Read," she said.

"Okay, Pickle. But only half an hour, remember. I'm going to come up and check."

"Whatever." Darcey attempted a disaffected roll of her eyes, then smiled her sweet smile and said, "Night, Mummy."

"Night, precious." I folded her small, sweet-smelling body in a tight hug and held her until she started to squirm, then kissed her again and went downstairs.

So – béarnaise sauce. How hard could it be? Jonathan had made it a few times for dinner parties and it had been rapturously received. It involved a horrible smell, I recalled, and a bit of stirring. That was okay – I could stir with the best of them. It was about the extent of my culinary skill, as it happened. I scanned the shelf of cookbooks and picked one out by a chef with a French-sounding name. And sure enough, there it was in the index under B. I flipped to the relevant page.

"Know this," the chef declaimed in bold type. "If you haven't made béarnaise before, you will surely fuck this sauce up."

"Well, fuck you too, Anthony Bourdain," I said. "Way to encourage the beginners. Dick."

I scanned the instructions. There seemed to be a lot of faff in the beginning with the butter. What difference would melting it and skimming stuff off the top make, anyway, I thought. Butter was butter was butter – loaded with calories and not very good for you, but I could see no sign of the impurities he was waffling on about in the perfectly ordinary pack of Waitrose Essential unsalted butter I'd purchased earlier. I'd just skip that bit and crack on.

I chopped the tarragon and shallot – well, not shallot, because I hadn't checked the recipe before I went shopping, but Google assured me that a small onion would do in extremis. We had no sherry vinegar either, but even Bourdain conceded reluctantly that wine vinegar would be an acceptable substitute, and there was plenty of that – Jonathan used it for salad dressing, I remembered, not allowing myself to wonder whether making your own salad dressing wasn't a bit weird when you could buy perfectly good stuff in bottles – low-fat stuff even.

"Separate the eggs," Bourdain commanded. I looked at my box of organic eggs. They were already separate, weren't they? Each one in its own little cardboard nest. Baffled, I turned again to Google.

Half an hour and a dozen eggs later, I had the requisite four yolks in a bowl, a stack of potatoes cut into matchsticks – more like firelighters, but who cared – and a salad made. Salad I could do – I'd lived on the stuff for the best part of ten years. It looked beautiful – cherry tomatoes and avocado resting on a bed (see, I thought, I can do the cheffy lingo too) of pre-washed baby leaves from a packet. I unearthed a jar of Jonathan's famous dressing from the fridge and sloshed some over my leafy creation.

Now – back to the béarnaise. I scanned the next paragraph of the impossibly complicated instructions.

"What the actual fuck is a Bain Marie, Anthony?" I demanded. I felt like the chef and I should be on first-name terms, given the tribulations we'd shared.

177

Google again. "Well, if it's a bowl over a pan of hot water, why didn't you just damn well say that, instead of wanging on about Mary's bath?"

I turned on some music, poured a gin and tonic, and turned back to the recipe.

I might not be much of a cook but I could follow instructions, and follow them I did. I whisked like a woman possessed, adding the butter gradually like it said, and to my utter amazement, a few minutes later, a cohesive yellow mass had formed in the bowl.

"Yes! In your face, poncy macho chef man," I said, allowing myself a minor victory dance around the kitchen, the whisk held aloft over my head, ignoring the splatters of sauce that ricocheted off the ceiling on to the floor.

The major hurdle was over. I could cook chips – Darcey went through a stage that lasted a couple of months when she was three when that was literally all she would eat, and we'd run out of frozen oven chips often enough that the deep-fat frier and I were not strangers. At the time, I'd panicked, thinking that my daughter was destined for a life of obesity and an early death from coronary artery disease. I'd even booked an appointment with the GP, taking precious time off work, to discuss my concerns.

"All toddlers and small children go through a picky phase," the doctor said, barely looking up from her computer screen.

"Yes, but chips," I said. "If it was lettuce, or something, it would be…"

"Mrs Payne," the GP said sternly. "Your daughter is a perfectly healthy child, a little underweight if anything. If she's still so restricted in her diet in a couple of months, we'll talk again. In the meantime, you might want to work at addressing your own anxiety about weight-related issues."

And that was me told. So I fried chips then, and I fried them now. I was frying away, watching the potatoes gradually changing colour in the hot oil, when Jonathan came into the kitchen.

"Hello, darling," he said. "Sorry I've been so dull all day. What have you been up to?"

"I'm making dinner," I said proudly. "Look, there's steak from Waitrose, and salad, and I even made béarnaise."

"You what?" Jonathan said, sticking a finger into the sauce. "You did too. That's amazing. I wish I was hungrier, so I could do justice to this."

I looked at him. There were deep shadows under his eyes, which were red with strain. His shoulders looked bowed, too, from spending the day hunched over his laptop.

"You need to eat," I said. "And you need a drink, too. I bought a couple of bottles of red – over there. And then you can help me cook the steak."

"Oh, pinot noir," Jonathan said. The way he looked at the label told me I'd fucked up, but he wasn't going to. "Lovely."

He poured us both a glass, sipped his, and grimaced almost imperceptibly.

"Why don't I clear the decks a bit before we cook the meat?" he said.

"Thanks." I kissed him, then turned my attention back to the chips. Golden perfection – that was the thing. I poked at the hot oil with my slotted spoon, fishing out the bits of potato that looked brownest and placing them tenderly on a mat of paper towels.

Then I heard Jonathan say, "Jesus Christ, what's this?"

"What's what?" I turned around and saw him looking into the kitchen sink, as horrified as if the Loch Ness monster had emerged from its depths. And to be fair, what was there was no less grim in its way.

Steaming water was bubbling up from the plughole, clogged with strands of opaque white... something. Like tentacles. Tentacles with yellow bits. Like a poached egg gone horribly wrong.

Jonathan realised what I'd done before I did.

"Laura, did you put raw egg down the sink?"

"I might have done," I said, feeling like Owen must do when I ask him whether he's forgotten to wipe his bottom after doing a poo. "Why, what's wrong with that?"

"Jesus, Laura. Basically you've made scrambled egg in our u-bend. As soon as I ran hot water through it, it cooked and solidified, and now... Oh, for fuck's sake."

Looking at the overflowing sink, bits of albumen swimming on its surface, I had to admit he had a point.

"Sorry," I said humbly. "I didn't know..."

"Didn't know what? That hot water cooks egg? God, Laura. Sometimes I wonder... Wait, I'll get a coathanger. If that doesn't work, we'll have to get a plumber in. Christ only knows how much that will cost. As if I..."

He stomped off upstairs. I fought back tears, and told myself not to be silly. This was just a blip – I'd made a minor fuck-up, but it didn't have to ruin our evening. Resisting the urge to run upstairs after Jonathan and rally round suggesting that one wire hanger might make a better weapon in the fight against our eggy enemy than another, I cooked the steak, trying to preserve normality as much as I could.

"Well, that's going to have to do." Five minutes later, Jonathan was splattered to the elbows with water and bits of congealed egg. "Our contribution to the next fatberg news story – or rather, yours."

He looked at me so sourly I actually flinched.

"Darling, I'm so sorry," I said, cursing myself for apologising even as I did so. "But look, the steak's done and the chips are perfect. Have some wine, let's eat, and the béarnaise worked brilliantly, didn't it, even though I blocked the drain."

Then I looked back at the puddle of golden sauce I'd been so proud of, and realised I'd left the bowl over the heat. What had been a perfect, smooth emulsion was now a puddle of noxious vinegar in which swam yet more scrambled fucking egg.

I stared at it in horror, feeling as if I might be about to cry. But Jonathan burst out laughing. "Oh,

Laura," he said. "It doesn't matter. I'm sorry I was such a grouchy bastard. You tried to make something lovely for me and a tiny thing went wrong and I was a dick about it."

He folded me in his arms and gave me a huge hug that soon turned into more than a hug, and much later we ate the cold, soggy fries and overdone steak, washing it all down with a bottle of ridiculously expensive red wine Jonathan said was a gift from a grateful client.

When we'd finished, I got reluctantly to my feet. "I'd better sort out the kitchen."

"Leave it a second, Laura," Jonathan said. "I want to talk to you."

I felt a cold finger of fear run down my spine. Could it be about Felix? Had he discovered something? But there was nothing to discover – nothing but the shameful, persistent thoughts of him that kept pushing their way into my head. Reluctantly, I sat down again, on the sofa this time, not on the carpet next to Jonathan.

"Is something wrong?" I said.

"Not exactly," Jonathan said. "But I was thinking, today, when you were off with Owen and I was working…"

I waited, but his words had dried up. "What? We had a lovely time, we just went to the library and the park and had an ice cream."

God, why did I feel so horribly, obscurely guilty, as if he was about to accuse me of something?

"I know," Jonathan said. "Owen told me. We hung out together a bit this afternoon, except he kept wanting to help with work and I was worried he'd mess up my spreadsheet so I stuck him in front of *Peppa Pig* for a quiet life."

"I always feel sorry for Daddy Pig," I said. "It's horribly sexist, don't you think, the way he's portrayed as this hapless, incompetent male who gets everything wrong around the house, and getting called fat and lazy all the time. And Peppa's such a precocious little madam. I'm sure she learns all those snidey put-downs from bloody Mummy Pig. Such negative stereotyping."

Jonathan laughed. "You've clearly watched too much of it if you're starting to analyse its depiction of gender roles."

"It's true though!" I said. "Have you seen the episode where… Anyway. I guess you didn't, if you were working."

"That's kind of what I wanted to talk about," Jonathan said.

"What? Not *Peppa Pig*?"

Jonathan reached over and stroked my bare calf. "Not Peppa bloody Pig, Laura. Although it's kind of apt. No, I wanted to talk about work. I was thinking today, when you were off with Owen – I barely see the kids these days, or you. It feels like you're doing all the parent stuff on your own, and we… I don't know."

He splashed more wine into our glasses.

"It's okay," I said. "We kind of knew it was going to be like this, when you got the promotion. It's one

183

of those things. I wish you were around more, obviously. But you mustn't worry about it. You've worked so hard for it – it's what you've always wanted, for as long as I've known you."

I knew I wasn't being entirely honest. This was my chance to tell him how lonely I felt, in the hours between the children going to bed and him getting home – and even when they were awake. How bored I got and how resentful I sometimes felt. But moments like this, moments when we were alone together, had become so rare and precious. I didn't want to sour our calm closeness by saying anything that wasn't calculated to reassure him. And I didn't want to have a conversation that might lead to my saying something about Felix.

"Yeah, it's what I've always wanted," Jonathan said, although it sounded pretty hollow. "Anyway, I thought… Hold on."

We could both hear it – the insistent buzz of Jonathan's phone ringing in the kitchen.

"That's going to be Peter calling from the New York office," he said, uncurling from the floor. "Hell. On a Saturday fucking night."

I heard him answer the call, then say, "No, no problem. Nothing important. Just let me get the figures in front of me."

Jonathan went upstairs and I heard his study door open and close. I waited a few minutes, then gave up and began to stack the dishwasher.

He was still talking when I got into bed – I could hear the low hum of his voice, but I couldn't make out any words. Clearly our conversation, whatever it had really been about, was over. I turned out the light and pulled the duvet over my shoulder, chilly without his warmth next to me, even on this warm summer night.

I was almost asleep when Jonathan came into our bedroom and said abruptly, "I'm going to have to go to New York for a week in August," he said. "More time away from you and the kids."

I sat up, blinking in the light from the hallway. "Why don't I come too? It's school holidays – Sadie and Gareth can have the kids. It'll be fun."

"That isn't exactly the word I'd use," Jonathan said. "I don't even know how much time we'd have together."

"Go on," I said. "It's my birthday next week – you can give me the trip as a present. We'll be able to do some stuff together, won't we? And I love New York."

I'd only been once, and seen nothing much beyond the inside of a dance studio, but it had been enough to convince me.

"I'll see what my work schedule looks like," Jonathan said, and with that I had to be content.

My birthday that year fell on a Monday – hardly an auspicious start to my thirty-seventh year. It was official, I thought gloomily as the alarm clock went off at its usual horrible hour – I could no longer claim to be in my early thirties. Middle age was fast approaching, it was raining, and I'd plucked several grey hairs from my eyebrows the previous night. I wished for a moment that I could turn back the clock – or even just opt out of the whole process of growing old, keep my children the ages they were, just press pause on the whole depressing business.

But Darcey and Owen were too little to look on birthdays as anything other than exciting opportunities for presents and cake. With Jonathan's help, they'd assembled a little pile of gifts on the breakfast table, together with a slightly battered carrot cake and a vase of overblown roses from the garden. The state of the cake was explained by the Co-op box I spotted in the recycling, a large orange 'reduced to 99p' sticker on it.

"Open presents, Mummy!" Owen said.

"I will in a second, just let me make some coffee first. And you're not allowed cake at breakfast time, you'll have wait for tea this afternoon – and so will I."

I remembered how, as a small child, I would have thought that cake at breakfast-time was the ultimate in heady indulgence. Now, the idea made me feel slightly queasy. When did that happen, I wondered? There must have been a day, perhaps at some point in my teens, when the prospect of cream cheese icing at seven in the morning ceased to seem like a good idea – perhaps round about when I went through my brief phase of eating nothing but apples and rice cakes with fat-free cottage cheese. I'd grown out of that, certainly, but never quite regained the idea that sugary food was a treat rather than something to be regarded with suspicion that bordered on fear.

Sipping my coffee, I turned to the small pile of presents. There was a pair of cashmere socks from Sadie, a card and a Selfridges voucher from Mum and home-made cards from the children, Darcey's encrusted with glitter and Owen's with pasta shapes stuck to it. More works of art to add to the collection on the fridge, I thought. When the children weren't looking, I'd have to get rid of some of the older, more curly-at-the-edges paintings to make room for these.

Jonathan said, "Hadn't you better open mine now?"

"I was saving it for last." I ripped the wrapping paper off the small box, and opened it to find a pair of simple, beautiful pearl earrings.

"Thank you," I said, kissing him and sliding them into my ears. "I'll do the school run in style this morning."

"Don't forget the card," Jonathan said.

I slid a knife under the envelope flap and took out a shiny card with pink roses on it, and "To my wife" in squirly gold writing. I suppressed a giggle – Jonathan had always had appalling taste in cards. Then I opened it and unfolded the A4 printout inside. It was a booking confirmation for a return trip to New York.

Inside the card, Jonathan had written, "We're staying at the Waldorf Astoria. I've upgraded to a suite – you deserve a treat. Happy birthday. I love you."

I felt tears sting my eyes and a lump fill my throat.

"Why are you crying, Mummy?" Darcey demanded, her eyes huge with concern.

"Because I'm happy," I said. It was the truth – but not the whole truth. This time last year, a holiday with my husband to the city that never sleeps would have seemed like the best idea ever. It still did – but there was a nagging sense of doubt and guilt overshadowing my excitement.

"Right, I'd better be off." Jonathan straightened his tie and put his jacket on. "I'll try not to be too late tonight. If I can get away, I'll take you out for dinner."

"Great," I said. "Try and let me know in good time, though, so I can get a babysitter sorted, okay?"

"Of course." He kissed me and wished me happy birthday again, and I thought, not much chance of that, is there?

"Right, come on, you two – time to get ready."

The specialness of the day forgotten, I launched into the morning routine – getting the children dressed, attempting a French plait in Darcey's hair, hunting for book bags and hats and raincoats, which always seemed to get misplaced no matter how hard I tried to find reliable homes for them.

The children dropped off, I knocked on Zé's door, but there was no reply, and I remembered that Monday was the day she worked out with her personal trainer. Disconsolately, I walked home again and made myself another cup of coffee. The day stretched before me – special in name, but in every other way just like every other Monday – and Tuesday, and Wednesday, and…

I fought back tears again, and checked my phone for birthday messages on Facebook to cheer myself up, thanking the magic of social media for allowing people to let you believe they were thinking of you, even if all they'd done was set up an app to send each of their friends an identical "Happy birthday, have a fab day x" once a year.

I went upstairs and put on some make-up, suddenly determined not to spend the day mooning about at home and desultorily doing housework. I'd go into town, I decided, and wander around the make-up counters like Mel and I always used to do, trying endless samples of products and walking out looking as garish as clowns. Maybe I could spend Mum's voucher on some miracle snake oil or other that would promise to make me look five years younger overnight.

So I got the train to Waterloo and then the Tube to Bond Street, and was hovering eagerly outside Selfridges, waiting for a gaggle of tourists to make their agonisingly slow way through the doors, when I felt my phone vibrate in my handbag.

It was a text from Felix. My heart hammered when I saw his name on the screen.

"Happy birthday, Laura. Your challenge for the morning is a treasure hunt. Text YES if you accept."

I thought, what the fuck? How entitled was he, imagining that I was free on the morning of my birthday to play his ridiculous games, and not in a spa somewhere, being pampered? Or away on a luxury weekend paid for by my generous husband? Or spending quality time with my precious children?

But actually, he was bang on the money. He'd seen enough of me in my new life to know exactly what I'd be doing, thinking and feeling. He had guessed, only too accurately, that what I wanted and needed was an escape, an adventure, a bit of mad silliness to make me take myself and my life a bit less seriously.

"YES," I texted back.

CHAPTER THIRTEEN

October 2001: Casting

All through that summer, I felt as if I was under an enchantment. Every morning, I woke up with my body intertwined with Felix's, the sheets tangled and smelling of sex. Even if we'd been out the night before and only slept for a few hours, I sprang up to greet the day and sang in the shower until Roddy laughingly told me to shut up that fucking horrible noise – and then the next morning I'd wake up feeling so happy I'd do it all over again.

Even though I was eating more than I had since – well, for as long as I could remember, really, weight dropped off me. It was impossible to eat dry Ryvitas when Felix was ordering takeaway curry, impossible to say no when he brought me bacon and eggs in bed on Saturdays. But the long Sundays spent slumped in front of the telly with Mel were a thing of the past. Felix and I never stopped moving. If we weren't working, we were out exploring London together, or going to gigs or shagging.

Mostly shagging, to be fair – but there was a lot of the other stuff, too. I was never still, but never tired.

And I was dancing better than I ever had. I'd always suspected, deep in a part of my mind where I never allowed myself to dwell for long, that I was mediocre. I was talented, obviously – that was given, having got as far as I had. But I lacked Mel's instinctive musical ability, Suzanne's creative flair, Briony's athleticism. And until now, I'd been coasting, hoping that my big break would come, but not doing much to chase it.

All that had changed – I was in love, and for the first time in my life I was filled with confidence. I still felt nervous before performances, but I didn't have time, now, to sit for hours worrying that I was going to fuck up, and if Felix saw me looking anxious, he'd distract me by cracking a joke, or taking me up on to the roof for a cigarette and a snog, or buying silly presents and hiding them in the flat for me to find.

Sometimes Roddy tagged along with us on our adventures, laughing with us, getting drunk with us, showing off in clubs by doing the splits on the dance floor. I loved having him around – there was no sense of him being a third wheel. At first, we told Mel where we were off to – a museum, the cinema, rowing on the lake in Regent's Park, checking out a new rock band in Camden – and invited her along. She always said no, though, and after a bit we stopped asking.

That was the only cloud on my happiness. Mel and I had been friends since we started ballet classes together when we were six. Even if it was chance that had brought us together, I believed that what sustained our friendship was deeper than that. When I'd started boarding school at White Lodge, I hadn't been afraid of leaving home, because I knew Mel would be there with me. Throughout our teens, she'd been the one I giggled helplessly with over nothing, confessed the heartbreaking enormity of my crush on Justin Timberlake to, begged to tell me honestly, no really, if she thought I was pretty.

When I was given Mel's part in *Swan Lake*, I knew she'd mind. Of course she would – anyone would, in her position. She'd always worked harder than me; she was the one tipped to be a star, the one our instructors criticised most fiercely and praised most warmly. I was the other one of the two of us, aware that I was thought of as Melissa Hammond's friend, not as Laura Braithwaite.

Mel got over her flu, but it took two weeks. She spent them in bed, morose and miserable, while Felix and I gloried in the first heady days of being together, sleeping together, dancing together. I tried to fuss over her, but she didn't want fuss. I brought home the flowers I was given on my first night, a huge, fragrant bouquet of pink lilies, but she didn't change their water and they withered and died after a couple of days.

I was in love and I loved all the world, but I don't think it's true that all the world loves a lover. When you're swept up in the giddy joy of romance and sex, you think everyone's your friend, revelling in your good fortune as much as you are. But Mel didn't revel. She took the antibiotics she was prescribed for the chest infection she developed, she rested as she'd been ordered to do, then when she came back to work she trained harder than ever to make up for lost time. She was civil to Felix, snappy with Roddy, and almost entirely ignored me.

It hurt. Once I realised that she was blanking me, rather than just still not feeling herself, I made pathetic, puppyish attempts to win her back over. I always put her washing on when I did my own. I offered to sew the ribbons on her shoes for her while I was doing mine, even though she was neater-fingered than I was and would get it done in half the time. I told her how brilliantly she was dancing.

But none of it worked, and in due course I stopped being hurt and started being pissed off. One day, one rare afternoon when Felix and I weren't together because he and Roddy were watching the QPR game in the pub with some of the other guys from the company, I tried to talk to her.

I was lying on my bed, leafing idly through the new issue of *Vogue*, which Felix had bought me as a present because there was a free sample of Issey Miyake scent in it, when I heard Mel's light, distinctive tread on the stairs and her key in the lock. I heard her come in and switch on the kettle. Immediately, I felt the tension, a buzz like static electricity that I'd become conscious of whenever she and I were alone. She mustn't have felt it though – I heard her humming as she opened the fridge, and realised she didn't know I was there.

I got up and padded quietly through to the kitchen. Mel was leaning against the counter, staring out of the window. There was a small, private smile on her face – she looked happy, for the first time in ages. This is your chance, Laura, I told myself.

But how wrong I was.

"Hey, Mel," I said.

The kettle snapped off, and so did Mel's smile.

"Hey," she said stonily.

"Are you making tea?"

"No, I'm doing a spot of origami. What does it look like I'm doing?"

"Make a cup for me, please?" I said. Back in the day, I wouldn't have needed to ask.

Grudgingly, with an almost imperceptible roll of her eyes, she took another mug out of the cupboard and dropped a teabag in it. She added boiling water and a big slosh of milk, even though she knew I liked my tea black. Then she handed the mug to me, without out a spoon and with the bloated teabag still swimming in it.

"Anything else you'd like?" she said.

Now, I'd know to back off, leave her be and not fuel what was certain to turn into a row. But I was so happy – I was incandescent with joy and optimism, and I genuinely couldn't understand why, in this wonderful world that had people as wonderful as Felix in it, she didn't feel the same.

"Mel, I really want to talk to you," I said.

"Do you?" she said.

"Yes. Look, Mel, I'm sorry. I really, really am sorry I got your part. You deserved it more than me – everyone knows that. You would have been heaps better than me. It wasn't your fault you got ill – I could tell during rehearsals that Marius wished it was you he was working with, not me. And you haven't lost your promotion – you're still a First Artist, you'll get a solo when they cast *Sleeping Beauty*."

I hated how needy I sounded. I knew I wasn't in the wrong, so why did I feel that way?

"I already know that," Mel said. "I'm the Lilac Fairy."

This stopped me in my tracks. It was – perhaps not unheard of, but certainly unusual for anyone to be privy to the details of a cast before the list was posted on the notice board, and that wasn't going to happen until tomorrow. I'd been in agonies of alternating hope and despair about what my own role might me – could I dare to hope to be one of the fairies, or would I be relegated to the chorus? But then, Felix was almost blasé about his chances of a leading role, and Roddy had said he clearly had Prince Fleur de Pois written all over him. So why shouldn't Mel be confident too? And one thing was for sure, I didn't want to challenge her, not when she was in this mood.

"That's awesome!" I said. "Congratulations! But how did you...?"

"I don't know, know, obviously," Mel said hastily. I could tell that she was regretting speaking out of turn, revealing her hand too quickly in whatever battle we were fighting in her head. "I just think... I've been rehearsing some of the dances, a bit. Marius seemed pleased."

Marius seeming pleased was akin to anyone else throwing bundles of roses at your feet and then kissing them. Your feet, callused and smelly as they were, not the roses.

"Wow! Did you make him actually, like, crack a smile?" Mel's sudden, relative expansiveness encouraged me to try and recapture the mood of easy friendship that we'd lately lost.

"He seemed pleased, that's all," Mel said stiffly. "Anyway, Laura, I was planning to spend a couple of hours studying the score, so if you've got something you'd like to say to me, why don't you say it?"

This wasn't going according to plan. She'd opened up, then immediately frozen me out again. But I'd made up my mind to try and make things right between us, and I wasn't going to let her obvious reluctance stop me coming out with the script that I realised I'd been rehearsing in my head.

"Mel, you're my best friend," I said. "I'm really sorry if I've done something to offend you, or hurt you. I hate how things are between us at the moment, and I want to make them right again. So whatever

I've done, please let me apologise. I don't know what it is, but I'm sorry. Okay?"

I held out my hands in a pathetic little gesture of supplication, and tea slopped out of my untouched mug on to the floor.

Mel grabbed a cloth and dropped to her knees.

"For fuck's sake, Laura, can't you be more careful? Jesus Christ, living with you is like living with a child sometimes. Or, now that Lawsonski's installed himself permanently in our flat – ours, for the three of us to share, remember – like living with a teenage boy who's just discovered wanking and leaves crusty socks all over the place, like my big brother used to do."

I recoiled from the force of her anger, feeling myself blushing to the roots of my hair.

"Mel, that's really unfair."

She squatted back on her heels on the floor, the tea towel still in her hand. Her face was white and tense.

"Maybe you should think about what's fair when you're fucking at three in the morning and screaming like a banshee. Maybe you should consider how fair it is when you leave condoms floating in the toilet for me to fish out. And just how fair is it when you turn up to class in the morning stinking like a hooker and can't keep in time because you've had no sleep? How fair is it to steal a part you don't deserve and then swan – sorry, *cygnet* – around like you're the best thing that's ever happened to this company? You aren't, you know. You're the only person who doesn't know. People are saying…"

I couldn't listen any more. My hurt had turned to shock and then to rage so strong it made my heart pound in my chest.

"God, you utter fucking bitch," I said. "I thought we were friends, but you only want someone you can feel superior to, and as soon as I do one tiny little bit better than you, you can't handle it. You're just jealous, and bitter. Frankly, I feel sorry for you."

I've never forgiven myself for what I did next. I should have known – I did know, really – that Mel was desperately insecure, frightened and vulnerable, that she saw my success as a threat to her own and my relationship with Felix as an abandonment of our friendship. She must have felt like I'd left her alone on a precipice, with crashing a more probable outcome than soaring. I should have sat down and given her a hug, like I do with Owen when he's having a paddy because life all seems too huge and complicated and the only way he knows to deal with it is to scream about me peeling his banana all wrong.

But I didn't.

I tipped the mug of tea – tepid now, thank God – over the floor so it splashed up on to her face and said, "Clean that up. You've started, you may as well finish."

Then I slammed out of the flat, blinded by tears, and went and found Felix and Roddy in the pub. Through my distress, I was conscious that I needed to get my story of what had happened in first, before Mel could tell hers. I was bitterly ashamed, and said so, but I desperately wanted them to be on my side, to have my back when we eventually returned home to the inevitable fallout.

But in the event, there wasn't any. Not that night, anyway. When we got back, many hours and many drinks later, Mel was gone and so were all her things.

And the next morning, when the cast list appeared and I learned that the impossible had happened and I'd been cast as Princess Aurora, with Felix opposite me as the male lead, it didn't feel like a dream come true. It felt like a nightmare that was about to begin.

CHAPTER FOURTEEN

F elix's response came just a few seconds later.
"There's a stranger in your bed. But there's something waiting for you in the bed outside."

For a moment I felt totally creeped out, then I realised what he meant. The old flat, where he'd fallen asleep in my bed that first mad, drunken night. And the flowerbeds outside the building… He had no way of knowing that I was just a few minutes away from Covent Garden, not at my kitchen table in Battersea. I could play him at his own game, I realised, try and catch him as he laid his clues.

I hurried down Oxford Street, my 'impress the salesladies in Selfridges' high heels impeding my progress as much as the crowds of shoppers who thronged the pavements, even before ten on a Monday morning. Impatient to avoid the throng, I cut down through Soho, zigzagging my way along the narrow streets, regretting my shoes and my decision as I slipped and stumbled over damp cobblestones.

I found the street where we'd lived unerringly –
I could have found it blindfolded. Actually, it
would almost have been easier if I'd been unable to
see, because the block of flats had changed beyond
all recognition. What had been a bit bohemian
and louche (and cheap as chips, and considerably
grubbier) was now gentrified beyond recognition,
the brick planters that had bloomed with empty
crisp packets, discarded cans of extra-strength lager
and the occasional syringe were now filled with
bright summer flowers. Flowers – flower beds – of
course!

But with gentrification had come security. The
courtyard that had been free for anyone to access
back then was now barricaded behind eight foot-high
wrought-iron gates, with a telephone entry system.
I'd have to climb. Then I looked at my impractical
shoes and my skinny jeans and thought, don't be
ridiculous, Laura. If I tried climbing those railings,
the only doubt about the outcome was whether I'd be
impaled, arrested or sectioned first.

I was going to have to blag it. I rang a bell at
random. There was no response. I tried another. A
woman's voice, in a strong Eastern European accent,
said, "Yes?"

"Delivery," I muttered.

"Get lost, chancer," came the reply.

Blushing so deeply I felt even my toes must be
red, I tried another bell. A drawling, actory voice
responded, "Hello, Masterson."

"Darling, it's me," I said, attempting a breathy, distressed voice. "Please let me in."

Amazingly, there was a buzz and the gate sprang open. I paused for a moment, wondering whether Mr Masterson might be watching from an overhead window, would realise that I wasn't the acquaintance he thought was calling on him in her time of need, and ring the police. I had no time to lose.

I pushed through the gate and glanced around the familiar, yet unfamiliar courtyard. The brick planters were brimmed with pansies and petunias in shades of pink, lilac and deepest purple, with the occasional flash of gold. But one splash of colour stood out: a vivid scarlet. I hurried over, all my qualms about the stupidity and recklessness of the enterprise overcome, because, God help me, I was having real, actual fun.

Lying in the flowerbed was a bouquet of half a dozen long-stemmed red roses. It was the sort of thing I'd been given by the hundred when I was dancing – they were literally strewn at my feet after a first night or a last one, and even on middle nights they weren't exactly thin on the ground, either. But this one gave me a glow of pleasure I had never felt when I'd asked the stage managers back then to bundle them up and send them to Great Ormond Street or the local women's refuge. This one had a note attached in Felix's handwriting.

"I know it's ancient history, but think you left something somewhere," it said.

The words made me feel as if I'd been hit in the stomach. It was true – I had. I'd left a whole world behind, and I had no way of reclaiming it, even if I wanted to. For a second, the sense of loss I'd felt earlier in the morning returned in a huge, debilitating wave. I'd left it all behind – I was leaving my thirties behind, or I would be, in just a few birthdays. But then the excitement of the chase filled me again, overcoming my melancholy. I'd left something behind. What did he mean?

I racked my brains. Felix was a total scatterbrain – he was always losing, breaking and forgetting things. But I wasn't. I was meticulous, a control-freak, as Roddy used to say. My laundry was always done on time, my pointe shoes always had their ribbons sewn on if not prettily, at least firmly. I didn't leave things behind – at least, I hadn't then.

Then I remembered. One bank holiday weekend – it must have been August, because it was boiling – there'd been a fire, or a bomb alert, or something. Rehearsals were never, ever cancelled, but that day, they had been. And Felix, being Felix, rather than loafing around the flat wasting our unexpected free time, had announced that we were going to a museum. The V&A. Where I'd checked my bag into the cloakroom along with the cotton scarf I'd draped around my neck when we went out, then taken off because it was too hot. When I retrieved my bag afterwards, the scarf had been missing, and when I realised it was too late to go back, and anyway the scarf was a hideous thing, not worth the couple of quid it would cost to replace, and Felix promised he'd buy me another one sometime.

That must be what he'd meant by ancient history – the museum. And us, of course. As the memory flooded back, I found myself hurrying north towards the Tube station. I boarded a train and was at South Kensington in just a few minutes. I'd forgotten how long the bloody tunnel was. I dodged through crowds of tourists, clutching my red roses, my shoes beginning to seriously pinch my feet, then at last found the entrance.

I barely paused to admire the magnificent marble figures that lined the gallery on either side of me – my eyes were only focussed on the signs. Café, Gift Shop, Roman Gallery, Ceramics, Cloakroom... There it was. Lost Property.

"I left something behind," I gasped to the taciturn woman at the counter.

"Yes? When was that?"

Fuck. I couldn't really say it had been fourteen years ago.

"Just the other day. It's a scarf. My name's Laura Payne."

Immediately, her face softened, breaking into a delighted smile. I didn't know what Felix had done, but his legendary charm had clearly been put to work on this ogress.

"Laura! Yes, I think I have what you're looking for."

She turned to the array of cubby-holes behind her, which were filled with an assortment of random carrier bags and items of clothing. There was even a pair of shoes in one of them. How the hell do you lose your shoes in a museum, I wondered.

"Is this it?"

She handed me a tissue-wrapped parcel. My hands were shaking so much I fumbled taking it from her, grasping a corner of the wrapping, so the paper tore away and spilled out a square of exquisite silk brocade that ran over my fingers like water. It was the colours of peacock's tail – all blue and gold and iridescent and wonderful. I gasped with pleasure.

The scary lady beamed maternally. "Happy birthday, yes? You're very lucky, your husband is a charming man."

I felt my own smile fade. "Yes. Yes, he is," I said. "Thank you."

I turned away, wondering what to do next.

The sensible thing, of course, would be to text Felix, thank him for the flowers and the gift, but tell him that this had to stop. It was only a treasure hunt, though. Just a bit of fun for my birthday, a trip down memory lane. And I still had hours before I needed to collect the children, and damn it, I was enjoying myself more than I'd done for ages. And it was my birthday. And I wanted to know where the next clue would take me – if there was one, of course.

I shook out the beautiful scarf, wondering whether there was any message concealed in its folds, but there wasn't. I inspected the tissue paper, but that was blank and empty, too. Then I felt my phone vibrate with another text. I snatched it out of my bag, stabbing at the screen. There were just five words.

"Some boys never grow up."

I shook my head, laughing. He'd got that right. Staging silly games like this wasn't something any of the grown-ups I knew would do, unless they were doing it for their children. There'd always been something irrepressibly silly about Felix. I'd loved that about him, but it could be infuriating, too. It never occurred to him to get to bed early before an important performance – he'd quite happily head out on the lash with Roddy and his other mates, and try to persuade me to come too, and often I'd say yes, even though Mel made a cat's-bum moue of disapproval. And it never seemed to affect him – however hungover and sleep-deprived he was, he always danced brilliantly, talent and adrenaline making him light up on stage.

There was one time, I remembered, when we were on tour in Manchester, when Felix hadn't actually slept in his hotel bedroom for three nights, carousing until the sun came up before coming to my room to wake me up and fuck me until I could barely stand.

What show had that been again, I wondered, searching the fragments of memory. Of course – *Peter Pan*. It was one of the few times we'd starred opposite each other, and it had only happened because I'd been understudying Suzanne, who'd torn her meniscus. I'd thought of it at the time as a beginning, the first of many ballets in which our names would top the programme together. In the end, of course, it didn't work out quite like that.

But that must be where the clue was leading me. A bookshop? There must be hundreds in London. I tried to remember the name of the street where the Darling family had lived in the original play, but I couldn't, if indeed I ever knew. Was it somewhere around here, near the museums and the park and Kensington Palace?

Of course – the statue of Peter Pan was in Kensington Gardens.

I looped the scarf around my neck and hurried outside into the sunshine.

Five minutes later I was standing beneath the statue, willing it to give up its secrets. It was a beautiful monument – charming and whimsical. Jonathan and I had brought the children here once, when Owen was a baby, planning a picnic, but it rained and Darcey cried and Jonathan was grumpy, and we ended up eating sandwiches in Pret, dripping and disappointed in the failure of the day.

I walked around the statue, searching for clues. Then I noticed something out of place – a glint of silver against the verdegrised bronze of Peter's feet. I looked around. It was high up – I'd have to climb on to the base of the statue to reach it. One got into horrible trouble for that sort of thing – it was probably a crime of some kind. I imagined a posse of park wardens, or whatever they were called, descending on me and arresting me, and Jonathan having to come and bail me out.

But I couldn't stop now. Quickly I climbed and reached, and seconds later I was holding a small silver charm in my hand – a pair of ballet shoes, attached to a delicate silver chain. There was a tag of paper attached to it, which must once have held the price, but now it had writing on it, in a tiny, cramped version of Felix's usual scrawl.

"Care to join Lawsonski for lunch?"

I laughed out loud. If there were hundreds of bookshops in London, there must be thousands of restaurants – tens of thousands, even. But I knew exactly where to go.

Felix and I hadn't had a first date, exactly. We'd gone from being colleagues, acquaintances really, to spending every night together, just like that. There was no discussion, no consideration – from the moment I walked into Studio Eight to rehearse the dance of the cygnets that Monday morning, we were inseparable.

It was only on the final night of the show that Felix had said, "Let's sack off the cast party and go for dinner to celebrate, just the two of us."

And he'd swept us off to Knightsbridge in a taxi to a tiny, poky restaurant where everyone spoke Russian, including Felix, and a bottle of iced vodka was plonked on our table without us ordering it. After that, we went back whenever we could afford it – the place was cheap, back then, but we were skint. Still, we celebrated our one-month anniversary there, and our six-month one, and his birthday and mine, and the manager knew us by name and comped us drinks and seemed proud that his obscure little restaurant was the choice of "famous ballet dancers", as he said in his broken English.

Back then, I would have been able to find the place with my eyes shut, but would I be able to now? I left the park and wandered into the maze of streets beyond. It all seemed different from how it used to be – there was Harrods, of course, and Harvey Nicks, where I occasionally used to go to gaze at beautiful clothes I couldn't afford, before we had the children. I could afford them now, I supposed, if I had anywhere to wear them to. Zé managed not to look like a twat turning up for the school run in Moschino, but I was quite sure I wouldn't be able to pull it off.

I turned left, round a familiar square. If only I could remember the name of the road the restaurant was on, but I couldn't. I took out my phone and launched Google Maps, watching the little blue dot that was me moving slowly along. I zoomed in, and then I saw it, helpfully marked on the map, just a block away. Babushka's. Of course – how could I was forgotten? Felix always used to sing the Kate Bush song by way of suggesting that we go there. I smiled at the memory and hurried on, then stopped, combed my hair and put on some lipstick. I didn't have a mirror so I had to do it by feel – hopefully I wouldn't end up with scarlet teeth.

And there it was, the familiar purple door, the familiar plants in their brass urns on either side of it, the familiar collection of rather creepy dolls lined up in the window.

I pushed the door open and paused. It was the same, but somehow different, wrong. It was the smell, I realised. Back in the day, everyone – but everyone – in Babushka's smoked. The air used to be thick with it. When we went there the first time I thought that the ceiling had been painted a deep ochre colour, then I realised it was just stained by the tar of thousands of unfiltered Russian fags. It had been cleaned now, of course, or painted over, and the room was lighter as a consequence, although the heavy lace curtains were doing their best to keep out the bright July sun, giving the interior a ghostly glow like a misty morning just before the sun breaks through.

I barely had a chance to take it in, though, because seconds later I was enveloped in a huge hug and given bristly kisses on both cheeks and then on the lips by a bearded bear of a man.

"Little Laura! Where have you been all these years? You look just the same, *kotyonok.*"

His smell was so familiar – clearly although he'd complied with the smoking ban in his restaurant, he hadn't imposed it on himself – that, to my relief, his name sprang back into my memory.

"Dmitri! It's great to see you. You look just the same, too, and the place. It's good to be back. How are you? How's business?" I could feel tears pricking my eyes, and gushed platitudes to keep them away.

"Oh, it's bad. So very bad." Dmitri had always been an incorrigible pessimist – to have stayed trading in this area for all these years, he must be coining it. "But we don't talk about that! Happy times, yes? And your birthday, and your young man waiting for you just like before. Come this way."

He led me through the warren of rooms to the banquette at the back, which had always been 'our' table. The gilt chairs were the same, upholstered in the same turquoise velvet, albeit a little more worn. The starched, snowy tablecloth was just the same, as was the elaborate, slightly tarnished ice bucket in which a bottle of vodka was reposing.

And Felix was just the same, too, especially in this dim, otherworldly light. The boy who'd never grow old, slouching in his seat, his brilliant eyes watching me as intensely as they ever had.

Then his face broke into a delighted grin, and I saw again the lines around his eyes and mouth that never used to be there, the new hollows beneath his cheekbones. But still, when he smiled, it was like the sun coming out or the first chords of a favourite song playing on the radio.

"Here she is!" Dmitri said. "I knew she would come. Didn't I say she would?" He broke into Russian as he pulled out my chair, and Felix replied, fluent as ever, as far as I could tell, as if he spoke the language every day.

With a flourish, Dmitri opened the vodka and poured three shots, and we toasted one another and drank. The icy, raw spirit hit my stomach and seemed to teleport immediately to my brain. Simultaneously, I felt a giddy elation and a sense of deep misgiving – what was I doing here? How was I going to pick the kids up from school and nursery reeking of booze? I'd just have the one, I promised myself, and when Dmitri immediately refilled our glasses and said again, "*Vashe zrodovye!*" I joined in the toast but only wet my lips with my drink.

"But what am I thinking?" Dmitri said. "You two need to catch up, to celebrate together."

He indicated the menu in front of Felix and there was another rapid-fire exchange, of which I understood not a word. Then Dmitri nodded approvingly and disappeared in the direction of the kitchen.

Felix and I looked at each other for a long moment, then I saw his face relax into a delighted smile, and realised mine had, too.

"You followed the clues," he said. "I wasn't sure if you would. If you hadn't come, I was going to drink to your birthday on my own. Which would almost certainly have got messy."

"I did follow the clues," I said. "Felix, I… thanks. Really, that was such a sweet thing to do. And the presents."

I gestured at the scarf over the back of my chair, the pendant on its chain around my throat, and the roses, which I'd have to ask Dmitri to put in water before they wilted in the heat. Or not, because then I'd have to tell Jonathan…

"It was fun," Felix said, "wasn't it? At least, I hope you had as much fun being the hunter as I did being the quarry. You caught up quicker than I expected – I saw you coming when I left the clue in Kensington Gardens. I had to hide behind a tree, then leg it. People were giving me some seriously strange looks."

I laughed. "I had a head start. I was in town already when I got your text, so I must've gained at least half an hour on you before I even saw the first clue."

"Cheating! I demand a rematch," Felix said.

"No way! I didn't know, I just happened to be there. You can't set traps for people assuming they'll be sprung to your schedule."

Felix looked suddenly serious. "This isn't a trap, you know, Laura."

"Then what is it, exactly?"

"It's a birthday present. No strings, no conditions. Just something I thought might make you smile. Because, you know, I remember you smiling all the time. But now you don't. Not so much, anyway."

"I smile a lot," I said, not smiling. "I do, Felix. My life is great. It's not what I expected it to be when I was twenty-two, but who the hell's life is, fifteen years later?"

"Mine is," he said.

We were interrupted by Dmitri bringing food, and I realised as I watched him place dish after dish on the table that I'd not only finished the glass of vodka he'd given me a few minutes ago, but another one as well.

Soon our table was piled with silver dishes of blinis, dumplings, smoked salmon, salads, and a small pewter bowl piled with pearls of caviar that were the same colour, and had the same gentle gloss, as the metal that held them.

"Felix..." I began to protest.

Dmitri waved a hand at the caviar. "Is my treat. On the house. Here, we love our old friends."

We thanked him effusively – there was nothing else to do – nothing except make sure every morsel of food was eaten so as not to hurt his feelings. My diet was going to have to be forgotten today, even though I didn't feel like eating at all.

I spooned sour cream on to a lacy pancake, added a morsel of caviar and bit into it. The pearls popped in my mouth like bubbles, releasing a taste of the sea, then a blast of richness and sourness. And all at once, I was hungry – for food, for fun, for sex, for more vodka, for Felix.

We tore into the meal as if we hadn't eaten in weeks, downing shot after shot of vodka, exchanging tastes of things that were particularly good.

"Have you tried this?" Felix said, passing me a fork laden with something that looked like shreds of ruby-red glass.

"It's beetroot, isn't it? I hate beetroot." I looked anxiously around in case Dmitri might hear and be hurt, but he was nowhere to be seen.

"Bollocks you do. You used to love this stuff."

"Did I?" In spite of myself, I parted my lips and ate, and the taste came flooding back. It wasn't like the beetroot I'd convinced myself in the intervening years I disliked, a muddy, depressing vegetable that looked a bit like menstrual blood and was about as appetising.

"Fuck," I said. "More. And tell me how you do it – how you're still living the dream."

Felix forked up the last of the beetroot and passed it to me, then he tenderly spooned the final few morsels of caviar on to a blini and fed me that too. Then he poured as another shot of vodka – the bottle was more than half gone.

"Do you want to see?" he said. "Do you want to know how I do it?"

When Darcey was a baby and didn't sleep – I mean, I know all babies don't sleep, but she never, ever did, she was the world champion of mad, screaming insomnia – I developed a clock in my head. I used to count beats, then bars, and they'd extend into minutes and hours, marking the time until, finally, she gave in and passed out. The habit had stuck, and now, when I got into bed at night, I found myself counting, counting relentlessly away the minutes until I'd be wrenched from rest again. And even when I was awake, I was conscious always of time passing in musical notes. It sounds stupid and pretentious, but there it was. So in spite of the food and the chat and the alcohol, I knew that about two hours had passed since I arrived at the restaurant, and I didn't need to check my watch to know I had three left before I needed to report to the school gate and the nursery door, punctual and ideally sober.

"Yes," I said.

"Come on then." Dmitri appeared with the bill, and Felix paid it, after a short and shouty debate which, even though I couldn't understand a word, I realised involved Dmitri not having charged us for lots of what we'd eaten and drunk, and refusing to do so.

I deliberately dawdled putting on my coat, letting Felix go ahead, and left three twenty pound notes on the table, so that although Dmitri's generosity would be acknowledged, his staff, who I knew worked brutally long hours, wouldn't suffer for their boss's grand gesture.

When we emerged into the shining afternoon, I realised just how pissed I was, reeling a bit and clutching at Felix's arm.

"Are you okay, babe?" he said. "Want me to get you a taxi?"

"No, no," I protested. "I'm fine. Come on, show me what you're going to show me."

"Laura. Are you sure you don't want to go home?"

Felix looked at me, his face swimming slightly in and out of focus.

"No, I don't want to go home," I said.

Felix kept his hand on my arm as we walked to the Tube station. Not like a lover, but not quite like a guide either – it was a gentle, reassuring contact, and I was grateful for it, because the dazzling sunlight was making me feel even more pissed than I had indoors. This is why lunchtime drinking is such a terrible idea, I thought. One of the reasons, anyway.

There was a Piccadilly line train arriving just as we stepped off the escalator and, instinctively, we both hurried forward, squeezing into the carriage seconds before the doors slammed shut.

"Made it," Felix said, grinning.

"We did," I grinned back. "But you haven't told me where we're going."

"It's a surprise." His face had gone still and almost grim, the smile vanished. "Another surprise for your birthday."

In the harsh fluorescent light, I could clearly see the lines on his skin, the faint creases around his eyes and mouth that I'd noticed earlier. As he reached up to grip the handrail, I was sure I could see the outline of ribs through his shirt, and I realised how lean he was – the body I'd known so well years ago had changed, transformed from a powerful, muscular machine into something rangier, more angular.

You're not twenty-two yourself any more, Laura, I reminded myself, conscious of the extra stone I was carrying and hoping that the harsh light wouldn't show that my make-up had gone patchy, my nose was pink from the vodka, and my roots needed touching up. But I knew he'd seen all those things about me, just as I'd seen the shadows on his jaw and the sharpness of his cheekbones.

The train pulled in to Covent Garden station and I moved instinctively towards the doors, but Felix put his hand back on my elbow and stopped me.

"No?" I said. "Not here?"

"Not here."

We thundered on through station after station, heading into what felt like the distant reaches of North London, until after another six or seven stops, Felix said, "Right, here we are."

I followed him up the escalator and through seemingly endless corridors of the unfamiliar station, until we ascended a flight of stairs back into the sunlight.

"Welcome to Finsbury Park," Felix said, "Home to Arsenal Football Club, the first of the great nineteenth-century parks and the best bagel shop in London."

Traffic roared past us along a street lined with fried chicken shops, bookies and huge discount stores selling everything you could possibly want, however tiny your disposable income. There were two rival shops on opposite sides of the street, one of which advertised all its merchandise at a pound, and the second at ninety-nine pence. It wasn't all that different, really, from our high street at home, but here there was no organic butcher, no chichi mum and baby shops, no Waitrose. I wondered what it was like to walk into a shop and see something you needed, then have to walk across the road and see if you could buy the same thing for a penny less, because it would make a difference to how many things you were able to buy.

"It's zone two," Felix said, as if reading my thoughts. "It's a highly desirable area." His fingers put quotes around the words, and I realised he was mocking me.

I felt suddenly ashamed, conscious of the bubble of privilege in which I lived. It hadn't been that long ago that I'd bought Darcey's clothes on eBay and scoured the supermarket for discount packs of nappies. But within just a few years, I'd left all that so far behind I could barely remember it.

Felix turned down a side road lined with what must once have been grand homes for prosperous Victorian families. Now, their stucco fronts were peeling and multiple bells jostled for position at their front doors.

"Nearly there," he said.

Since we'd got off the train, I hadn't said a word. My mouth was dry and tasted sour; I wished I'd accepted his offer to get me a cab and gone home. I could have had a cold shower, made some coffee and been early to fetch Darcey from school.

"Felix, do you mind if I…"

"Here we are," he said. He pushed open one of the heavy front doors, which had an ornate, if tarnished, brass knob at its centre, and led me into a carpeted lobby. There was a makeshift reception desk squeezed against one wall, so tightly that the disinterested concierge sat next to it in a shabby office chair.

"Hey, Danielle," Felix said, and she looked up from filing her nails, her face lighting up.

"Hiya, Felix, lovely day," she said.

"Isn't it? This is my friend Laura. Laura, Danielle."

"Hello." I shook her soft, cool hand, and she gave me a brief smile then returned to her manicure.

Felix led me up the stairs, which were covered in the same worn, figured carpet as the hallway. We hurried up three flights, until my thighs were tired and my lungs staring to burn. It was airless and very hot; a smell of burned toast and unwashed bedding seemed to have seeped into the wallpaper. Then he turned on to the landing and fitted a key into one of three identical, scuffed white doors.

"After you," he said.

Through the fug of vodka, I realised what must be happening. This place – this was one of those hotels you read about that rent rooms by the hour, where people come with prostitutes, or to have sordid, illicit sex when they have nowhere else to go. And the way the woman downstairs – Danielle – had greeted Felix, clearly he was no stranger to this place, or this kind of transaction. My stomach lurched with horror, there was a sudden flood of saliva into my mouth and a rush of sweat down my back, and I realised I was going to be sick.

"Where's the bathroom?" I gasped. "Please, Felix, quick."

"Laura, what's…" The he looked at me, realised, and took my arm again, bundling me upstairs to a half-landing and through a door with a 'Ladies' sign on it.

I fell to my knees on to the cold tiled floor and vomited gruesomely, while Felix held my hair and patted my back. When the first spasms had passed, he said, "I'll be right back," and closed the door behind him.

I straightened up, feeling suddenly much, much better, and glanced in the mirror. God, I was a sight – my skin greenish-pale in the harsh light that bounced off the spotlessly clean white walls, my hair limp around my face. Before I could start any emergency repair work, there was a tap on the door and Felix's voice said, "Only me."

He opened the door a crack and passed me a tube of toothpaste and a brush still in its blister pack, a parcel of wet wipes, a clean towel and a bottle of water.

"Will you be able to find your way back to my room? I'll wait there for you. It's four B; I'll leave the door open, okay?"

"Okay," I said faintly.

I cleaned my teeth, depositing the toothbrush in the bin, cleaned my ravaged make-up off with the wet wipes and smeared some handcream from the tube in my bag on to my tight, flushed skin. I had the wherewithal to do a pretty decent repair job: a sample size of foundation, lipstick, an eye crayon – but what was the point? My dignity was well and truly gone, flushed down the loo along with all the vodka.

So I combed my hair, gulped some of the deliciously cold water and made my way only slightly shakily back to room four B.

I realised as soon as I pushed open the door how wrong I'd got it. This wasn't a room Felix rented by the hour. It was bare and tidy, certainly, but someone lived here. A laptop was open on the bedside table. The hook on the back of the door was laden with clothes on hangers. A stack of books was piled almost as high as the small, wall-mounted telly.

Felix was lying on the bed, his legs outstretched and his hands behind his head.

"Okay?"

"Better," I said. "I'm really sorry. God, I'm so embarrassed."

He held out his arms, and I moved in for a hug, then lay down next to him.

"Laura, please. It's my fault."

"It's not. I drank too much, and then you brought me here, and for some reason I thought…"

"What?" He rested his warm hand on my cold, clammy one.

"I thought it was some kind of… I don't know… flophouse."

I turned to look at him, just in time to see him suppress a wave of laughter. "Flophouse? How retro of you! To be fair, two of my neighbours are on the game, but they don't transact here – they'd be chucked out sharpish if they did. Amour and Summer – which aren't their actual names, obviously. But they live here, and I do, too."

"I know," I said. "I get that, now. But I didn't understand – you said you were living in a hotel, and I thought…"

"What? Malmaison? The Savoy? Sweetheart, you know better than that."

"I do now," I said again, hunching my shoulders and squirming a bit with mortification. "But I was thinking… I kind of pictured you living like we always imagined we would. All glamorous and… you know."

"And I still am," Felix said. "Imagining it, I mean. That's what I wanted you to see. You asked about living the dream – and this is it, right here. I'm living, and I've still got the dream, the hunger I've always had. I'm going to make it big, I know I am. And even if I don't, I wake up every morning knowing something amazing is going to happen to me."

"Really?"

"Hell, yes." Felix laughed, and pushed back his hair. "Let me tell you a story. I went to a casting a couple of weeks ago. My agent said they wanted a guy who could play a wizard, and I thought, great, I can do magic, I can nail this part. So I turned up, and there was a whole row of us sat there, actors like me. And right at the end, there was this bloke with long white hair and a beard down to his waist. And I thought, what am I even doing here?"

I laughed. "Did you get the part?"

"Of course I fucking didn't. But I'm still laughing about it. I'm still standing. And I know I'm ready now, Laura, ready for something huge. The Flight of Fancy *Dream* is going to New York, and they want me to go too – I'm leaving in a couple of weeks. So I don't mind living in a flophouse for now."

"You're going to New York?" I said. "Next month?"

Felix said, "Yes, why?"

Knowing I shouldn't, I said, "I'll be there. I'll be there in August, too."

And I told him the dates.

We lay there on the narrow bed, looking at each other. I'd stopped feeling drunk or sick; I wasn't aware of anything, really, except the sense of infinite possibility Felix said he felt. For a moment, I saw the world through his eyes – a place where dreams could come true, where material things were unimportant, where happiness was found in an alternate reality, on a stage where, for a brief while, hundreds of people loved you more than anything else in the world.

My breathing deepened thinking about it, remembering it. I closed my eyes and for a moment I was back there, on stage, on pointe, applause ringing in my ears. I could even feel rose petals brushing my cheeks.

Then I realised it was Felix's fingers.

"Laura," he said. "Wake up."

I was snapped back to reality as abruptly if an elastic band had twanged my face.

"Shit! What time is it?"

I glanced at my watch, panicked, and called Zé.

"Listen, I'm really sorry, but I've been held up. Please could you collect Darcey and take her back to yours?"

"Sure," she said, as if it were nothing at all. "Juniper was asking if she could come over after school anyway. There's some new YouTube thing, evidently. Want me to give her supper?"

I thanked her over and over, then called nursery and grovelled, saying I'd be late to pick up Owen, too.

Felix watched me silently.

"So, I guess I need to go now," I said, once my calls were made.

"Of course you do. Want me to walk you to the station?"

I didn't. I wanted to stay here, in the surprisingly clean room, and draw the curtains and take him in my arms and for our clothes to magically vanish, and for the dream I'd had and lost to penetrate me when his body did, and for my life to somehow, suddenly, change to one in which there were no kitchen worktops to buff, no shirts to iron, no future to worry about.

"No," I said, "It's fine. I can find my way."

And so I kissed Felix chastely goodbye and walked blearily to the Tube and endured the journey home, feeling sick, anxious and guilty as sin for what I'd allowed myself to imagine. Once the children were in bed and I'd received the expected text from Jonathan saying how terribly sorry he was, he'd been held up at work, and we'd celebrate my birthday properly another night, I made a pot of tea and sat outside in the garden, looking into the darkness, thinking and thinking until I couldn't put off going to sleep any longer.

CHAPTER FIFTEEN

It was the last day of term before the start of the long summer holidays. In just a week, Jonathan and I would be departing for our holiday, leaving the kids with Sadie and Gareth. Instead of last-day-of-term excitement, I was filled with a weird sense of dread that I couldn't quite put a name to. Was it worry about leaving the children? But we'd left them before, when we'd escaped for a weekend in the Lake District last year. They were fine – they loved staying with my sister and her husband.

It was Felix, I realised. He hadn't contacted me since my birthday – I didn't know whether I was relieved or disappointed. What I did know was that I was on a constant knife-edge of tension, my stomach lurching every time I heard my phone ring, my checking of email and Facebook becoming not so much frequent as obsessive.

I checked them now, walking slowly away from the school, but there was nothing – no message, no text, no missed call. Then I heard the sound of pounding feet slapping the pavement behind me, and almost jumped out of my skin.

But it was Zé, in running kit, her hair in a swishy ponytail.

"Laura! I thought it was you. I spotted you from way back – no one else has such amazing posture – and sprinted to catch you up. Come in for a coffee? My machine makes killer espresso."

"I'd love to," I said. "You nearly gave me heart failure – I thought you were a mugger or… something."

She laughed, wiping the sleeve of her top over her sweating face. "If only I could run that fast! Ten k in an hour is about my limit these days. Come on in."

Across the road, I saw Amanda and Sigourney watching us, their heads close together as they whispered to each other. Fuck it, I thought – let them gossip. I was allowed to have other friends, wasn't I? I smiled sweetly and gave them a little wave.

"I'd love a coffee," I said.

We walked back towards Zé's house, and I noticed with envy how quickly her breathing returned to normal. God, I needed to get fit again. But what was the point? I supposed Owen would reach a stage at which he could outrun me in the park, but he hadn't yet, and when he did he'd be grown-up enough for it not to matter.

"Here we are. Shall we sit outside? Then I can have a fag when I've put the coffee on."

"Great idea."

She grinned. "It's reprehensible, isn't it? But I only ever smoke outside. And only after my workout, and when Juniper isn't here. And I don't think she knows. And I can stop any time I like, right?"

"Yeah, right," I said, and she laughed.

"I won't be a second."

I sat on one of the cushioned benches surrounding the small, splashy water feature. Although the house was just feet from a main road, it seemed to be totally silent here. Then I realised, when I listened carefully, I could hear the traffic, but the sound of the water, the rustle of the bamboo plants that lined the lawn, and a chorus of birds from somewhere – had edited it carefully, unobtrusively out. My friend's garden, like her house and her clothes, was a masterpiece of design.

Zé appeared from the kitchen with a tray laden with coffee, steaming-hot milk, a packet of Marlboro Gold and a lighter.

"Breakfast," she said. "Black or white?"

"Black, please," I said, and she passed me a small cup, intoxicatingly fragrant, thick with perfect crema.

"You don't take sugar?"

"Not with this." I smiled and sipped.

Zé sat opposite me, her feet up on the bench, her knees under her chin. The sunlight filtered through the leaves of the magnolia tree and cast soft shadows on her face, still flushed from her run. She lit a cigarette and blew the smoke politely past my shoulder, but I still caught a dizzying whiff of it.

"Are you sure you won't have one?" she said.

"Oh, go on then."

"God, I'm such an enabler," she laughed, then her face became serious again. I noticed lines of tension running across her smooth brown forehead. "Rick didn't come home last night. Again."

"Oh, Zé. Was it work? Jonathan sometimes gets stuck in the office all night – or almost all night." But he never doesn't phone, I thought.

"He wasn't at work. I know, because I rang the office. His PA said he left at seven."

"Was he out for drinks, maybe?" I said, casting desperately around in my head for something I could say that would comfort her. "They seem to socialise loads. Jonathan's forever having dinners and stuff. He loathes it. Or he says he does, anyway. Probably Rick does too."

Zé laughed again, but it was a different sort of laugh, harsh and mirthless. She lit another fag and offered me the packet. I hesitated, then took one too. "I don't even know what he likes or doesn't any more, Laura. We just don't talk. I don't know what he thinks or feels about anything. Since I had Juniper, it's all just shut down. I do my thing, he does his. Not that I even fucking know what his thing is. I presume it's other women. Other men, maybe. He hasn't touched me for years."

"But, Zé, you're so beautiful," I said helplessly. "You're funny and amazing, how can he not…"

She shrugged. "At first I thought it was me having had Juniper. You know – minge like a wizard's sleeve, like sticking his cock out of the window and fucking the night… All that. But I've done more pelvic floor exercises than you can shake a stick at – not that he knows, because we haven't had sex since before she was born."

I tried not to let my face show how shocked I was. Eight years in a marriage with no intimacy at all. The idea filled me with horror. I remembered how lovely Jonathan had been when I had a meltdown after Owen was born, wailing and lamenting about how I'd lost my figure for good and I'd never be the same again, and he'd assured me that I was more beautiful than I'd ever been, and he desired me even more than he had before.

"Have you talked to him about it?"

"I tried to, at first. But we just ended up shouting at each other, so I gave up. I'm lazy, Laura. I'll put up with a lot for the sake of a quiet life. But this – being out all night when I've got no idea where he is – I don't think I can cope with it for much longer. If he's with someone else, I'll deal with it. I'll ignore it and carry on as normal until it passes. Or until he decides to leave me, and then I'll take him to the fucking cleaners. But what if something happened to him? What if he fell under a train or something and I didn't know? That's what scares me. If Juniper were to lose her father like that… He loves her, you know. Even though he doesn't love me any more."

"Do you think you might be happier if you left?" I said. "I hate thinking of you being so miserable, and worrying about him all the time. He doesn't deserve you."

She laughed. "Damn straight he doesn't. But I have it easy. I don't mind that much that I never see him. I get to do my own thing. I have a lovely life, and more importantly, Juniper does."

She lit another fag and stared out across the garden. She looked, suddenly, unbearably sad.

"But I worry that I'll never be in love again," she said. "Never have sex again, never have anyone look at me that way, and look back at them, and – you know. I'm forty-three, Laura. If I wait until Juniper goes to university and then leave him I'll be fifty-three. I'll be ancient. On the scrap heap."

"You won't!" I said. "You never will. You'll always be amazing. When you're ready, there'll be someone who falls head over heels for you, and you with them."

"Yeah, some old codger who can't get it up without Viagra," she laughed and did a little faux shudder. "Not like that lush actor who fancies you."

I felt my face turning hot and scarlet under her steady dark gaze.

"Zé…" I began.

"What?"

"Nothing," I said.

"It's not nothing, Laura. Come on, what's the matter?"

I nicked another of her fags and lit it and, almost against my will, the whole story came spilling out. How I'd met Felix when I was twenty-one, what had

233

happened then, how he'd disappeared from my life for all those years and now come back, bringing with him a torrent of emotions I didn't want to feel but had no idea how to stop. How I hadn't told Jonathan about any of it. How I'd seen him on my birthday and how I'd felt. That I had no idea at all what I was going to do next.

"So there you have it," I finished miserably. "One massive fuck-up waiting to happen, and it's all my fault."

"Life's pants, isn't it?" Zé said. "The way it chucks curve-balls at us and we're meant to find a way of hitting them straight. I can't tell you what to do. I know what I'd do. I'd have a wonderful affair with him, make myself happy, then find a way to walk away before anyone got hurt too badly. But that's me. I don't love my husband. You do."

"But you can't love two people at the same time!" I said. "You can't. Can you?"

"As far as I know, there's no rule against it," Zé said. "We all love lots of people; we just love them in different ways. It's when you love two people the same way that the problems start."

I thought about that for a bit. I didn't love Felix and Jonathan in the same way at all – I was certain of it. Even when I'd met Jonathan, in those first heady days when we were going out and then engaged, I'd felt differently about him from the way I'd felt about Felix. But that was because I was a different person. Now, it was as if my twenty-one-year-old self was back in my head and my heart, bringing with her all the feelings I'd had then.

"I don't know what I'm going to do," I said again.

"Just be careful, Laura," Zé said. "Please be careful. I want you to be happy, but try and be it without causing too much carnage."

In spite of myself, I laughed. "Don't worry. I definitely don't want to cause carnage. I just want – I don't know! I want to make it all unhappen – either what went wrong with Felix and me in the first place, or meeting him again, or – something."

"Well, we both know you can't do that," Zé said. "Take some time to think about stuff, that's all. Don't rush into anything you'll regret."

"I won't," I promised. But there was something I hadn't told her – that when Jonathan and I went to New York in just a few days' time, Felix was going to be there too. And I didn't know if I'd be able to resist seeing him, or what would happen if I did.

I stood up to go, and as I was gathering my things together, Zé's phone rang. "Rick," she said, glancing at the screen.

"Want me to wait?"

"Don't worry. I'll have it out with him, and speak to you later." She hugged me hastily, snatched up her phone and said coldly, "Yes?"

It would have been horribly intrusive to stay. Zé needed to deal with this on her own. So I walked back through the house, let myself out and went home, and when I got there I sent her a text saying how grateful I was for her friendship and advice, and that I was there any time she wanted to talk about things.

The contrast between Zé's serene, immaculate home and our house couldn't have been more stark. The kitchen was carnage. Milk all over the floor, Owen's Marmitey fingerprints on the cabinets rapidly taking on the adhesive qualities of superglue, Darcey's scooter lying where she'd left it in a prime tripping spot by the door, the lamb chops I'd taken out of the freezer for Jonathan's and my dinner looking unpromising in a puddle of pinkish liquid on the worktop.

"Laura, you are a slattern," I told myself. Back when I'd been working, we'd had a cleaner once a fortnight to come in and sort out the worst of it, but now, with me at home all day, there was no way I could justify it. What did I do all day, anyway, when the children were at school and nursery, except drink coffee with Zé, go for walks in the park and daydream? I was meant to be a housewife, but I was neglecting the poor house.

Reluctantly, I pulled on a pair of Marigolds and set to work. Cleaning is meant to be therapeutic, I know, but I've never found it to be so. For every job you do, another seems to appear, like a hydra growing extra heads with each one you chop off. You clean the kitchen cabinets, then notice the fridge needs doing too, then once you've cleaned the outside you may as well do the inside, then you realise that the freezer is clogged with ice so decide to defrost it, then end up with water all over the floor you cleaned earlier. You take the sheets off the beds and then realise all the spare sets are dirty, and you can't wash them until you hang up the wet stuff that's been festering the machine for days. You get out the hoover and discover that its bag needs changing, and the old one bursts when you take it out, scattering six months' worth of dust and crud everywhere. You clean the bath and realise the shower head is clogged with limescale and you'll have to go out to the shop and buy a load of industrial-strength chemicals to dissolve it.

I know, I know – according to Kim and Aggie and their ilk, all you need to turn the most disgusting hovel into a show home is a tub of bicarb and half a lemon. Good luck to them – as far as I'm concerned, the more powerful the chemicals, the less elbow grease is needed on my part.

And it doesn't help that inanimate objects seem to have it in for me. The stairgate that I've walked through five seconds before will mysteriously close and trip me up. The children's car seats are forever breaking my nails out of sheer spite. Even the letterbox attacks me with its lethal brass jaws when I try and remove a stuck pizza menu.

So my blitz on the house took far longer than I intended. When it was time to fetch the children, I still hadn't finished, so I parked them in front of the telly with microwaved frozen pizza (less frozen than it had been when I'd started defrosting the fridge, admittedly) and carried on. I gave them their bath, wondering what the hell the point had been of cleaning the bathroom from top to bottom when they were only going to flood the floor and scatter toys everywhere. I read them a shorter story than usual, put them to bed and returned to my tedious, endless task.

By the time Jonathan got home, the house was immaculate and sparkling. He found me folding the last of the bed linen, which had emerged warm and fragrant from the dryer. I should have been full of Stepford Wifely smugness, but I wasn't – I'd found a video on YouTube showing how to fold fitted sheets into perfect squares, rather than just squashing them into whatever random shape they chose to take on. But the sheets were refusing to co-operate. However many times I watched the tutorial, I managed to pick up the corners in the wrong order and ended up with a misshapen triangle instead.

"Fucking wanker sheets," I muttered. "Sort yourselves out, for God's sake."

"What on earth are you doing, Laura?" Jonathan asked. "Glass of wine?"

"Look," I said, thrusting my tablet at him. "Just look at this. Martha Stewart says you should fold your sheets so they're square, but ours are having none of it. Why have we got rogue sheets?"

I took a large gulp from my glass of wine, and watched as Jonathan played the video, then picked up a sheet and folded it perfectly.

"Have you been fighting with inanimate objects again?" he said.

In spite of myself, I laughed. "All bloody day. But how come it worked for you and it won't work for me?"

"It's not rocket science." Quickly and deftly, Jonathan folded the rest of the laundry. "There. But honestly, how much does it contribute to the sum of human happiness if our sheets are folded into squares? And why are you taking housekeeping advice from a woman who got chucked in prison for insider trading, anyway?"

"It's not just her," I said. "You should see what Anthea Turner says about towels. Apparently you're not allowed to see the edges."

"Have you been drinking, Laura?"

"No! Well, only now." I drank some more wine.

"Who the hell cares if you can see the edges of towels?"

"Anthea Turner, obviously."

Jonathan laughed. "Come here." He folded me into a hug. "Look, as long as the house isn't so filthy we all catch dysentery, no one cares. I don't care. You don't have to spend your time trying to be some model housewife when you could be having fun with the kids, or seeing your friends or whatever. Just because you're not working, doesn't mean you have to turn yourself into some kind of domestic drudge, okay? We can do the cleaning perfectly well together at weekends."

"Okay," I said. Privately, I knew that wouldn't happen – Jonathan would be working, or playing golf, or want to take the children out somewhere. But at least his heart was in the right place. And at least the afternoon of frantic activity had taken my mind off Zé's problems, and my own.

"By the way," Jonathan said, "are you home tomorrow?"

"I expect so. Why?"

"Great. They're delivering my new car."

"What new car? We've got a car."

"Yes, but it's ancient and besides, I wanted…" he looked embarrassed, almost shifty. "I wanted a change."

"What is it?"

He told me.

"Jesus, Jonathan! How much did that cost?"

He didn't tell me that. He said, "I – we can afford it. I got my bonus last month, remember?"

"Why didn't you tell me you were buying a car?" I demanded. "It's a massive decision."

Jonathan shrugged. "I guess because I knew you wouldn't like it. You're such a bohemian, darling. But I'm allowed to spend money on stuff I want sometimes. God knows I work hard enough."

It was true – I couldn't deny that. But I couldn't help resenting that he was able to make such a decision, spend so much money, without even mentioning to me that he was planning to. It felt symbolic of a shift of power in our marriage – a shift from us being equals to him being the one in charge, and I didn't like it one bit.

I thought about arguing with him, trying to explain how I felt. But what would be the point? He wasn't going to change his mind, and it was – as he'd almost but not quite said – his money.

Instead I said, "Shall I cook those chops for dinner then?"

CHAPTER SIXTEEN

November 2001: Backstage

After the announcement on the casting board, there was no more gallivanting for Felix and me. Our day off was spent studying the score of *Sleeping Beauty* until I started seeing seas of black dots in front of me when I closed my eyes. There was no time to go on adventures around London – not when there were endless videos of previous performances to watch. Felix even dialled down his partying and started going to the gym in the afternoons. We were in bed by midnight every night, although I often found it hard to sleep, however exhausted I was, and when I did, I was plagued by dreams of losing my pointe shoes and running through endless corridors looking for them while the stage manager called me over and over again on the PA system.

Roddy kept us sane during those weeks of rehearsals. His good humour never wavered – he didn't seem to know the meaning of nerves. One day he came home with a Jamie Oliver book, announcing that I wasn't eating properly, and he was going to cook us cheap, nutritious meals every night.

"Look at this," he said. "Humble home-cooked beans. Pukka stuff, right? They'll give your jumps added height if you're jet-propelled by farts."

"What's wrong with Heinz?" Felix grumbled. But we ate the beans anyway, because we didn't want to hurt Roddy's feelings, and even though the cooking phase only lasted about a week and we were soon back on our usual diet of toast and coffee, we appreciated the thought.

Mel's room remained empty. Felix was paying her share of the rent and we hadn't had time to look for a replacement flatmate. Every time I came home and saw her closed door, every morning when I walked into the living room and she wasn't there doing her Pilates exercises, I was reminded of the loss of her friendship. And it wasn't just at home – every day at work I was faced with her cold indifference. She refused to speak to me at all, rebuffing my clumsy attempts to apologise until I stopped trying and ignored her back.

At least I no longer had to share a dressing room with her – as a soloist, I'd been given my own. When Anna showed me to the tiny cubicle that was going to be all mine, I immediately started making plans to transform it into a glamorous boudoir worthy of a principal dancer. But that never happened – soon the room was cluttered with make-up, discarded tights and half-drunk bottles of water, and the smell of my sweat and deodorant joined that of its previous occupant.

It was there that Marius came to find me the day before opening night.

In rehearsals, he'd surprised me with his patience, encouraging me to push myself, never missing even the smallest error, yet never raising his voice, and praising and encouraging me when I did well. None of that stopped me being terrified of him, though: I knew that he had the power to demote me as swiftly as he'd promoted me; that my meteoric rise could be followed just as quickly by an ignominious fall.

I was perched at my dressing table in a shabby cotton dressing gown, soaked in sweat from the afternoon's rehearsal but too tired to shower or change into my outdoor clothes. I had no performance that night – Anna had told me to go home and rest. But I needed to prepare my shoes for tomorrow's performance, cutting the satin away from the toes, breaking in the sole, sewing on the ribbons. It would take half an hour – I'd done it so often I could practically do it in my sleep, and right now I was so knackered I might well have ended up doing just that. Wardrobe wanted me to drop in for a final fitting of my costume. I was hungry – I should eat. I needed to file my nails. But instead of doing any of those things, I was just sitting.

There was a tap at the door, but it opened before I had a chance to respond.

Marius wasn't tall, and he certainly wasn't fat, but the room felt much smaller with him in it.

"Good afternoon, Laura," he said, closing the door behind him.

"Good afternoon," I said. I was very conscious, suddenly, that I was naked underneath my robe, and that my nipples were clearly visible through it. At least I hadn't been undressed. But dancers' bodies were nothing to Marius, I told myself – we were just tools, instruments to be analysed, tuned, brought as close as possible to perfection.

"I'm sorry," I said. "I'm a bit of a mess. I was just going to head home and shower."

"You're cold," he observed, glancing at my chest. "You know you're not allowed to get cold. The muscles tighten up, recovery is slowed down – but you know all that." He smiled warmly. "I don't need to tell my newest soloist things she's known since she was six."

"I'm sorry," I said again, "I do know all that, of course. "It's just…"

"You were having a moment of reflection," he said. "It's only natural. How are you feeling, my dear? Nervous?"

I hadn't been, until he said it. "A little. I don't want to let anyone – to let you down."

"Or your boyfriend," he said. "Little Mr Lawson. He's highly talented, as you know, but sometimes I wonder if his attitude isn't just a little lacking."

"He's been working incredibly hard," I said, automatically leaping to Felix's defence. "We all have."

"Oh, Laura," he said. "You are sweet. Like a vixen protecting her cubs. Does he make you happy, then?"

"Yes," I said. "He really does. And he – I mean, I think I've been dancing better, since we've been together. I must have, or I wouldn't have got this part – this amazing opportunity. Would I?"

"It's a remarkable thing to see the flowering of a talent," Marius said. "And it's my privilege to be able to nurture the very best. But it involves taking risks, sometimes, like I've done with you."

"Was I a risk?" My mouth was suddenly dry – my voice sounded croaky. Was he about to tell me I wasn't good enough – that, even after all my hard work, I wasn't going to dance tomorrow night? That Suzanne had recovered sufficiently from her torn meniscus to take the role that would normally have been hers by right?

"You certainly were," he said. "If you could have been a fly on the wall in the meetings when we were discussing casting this show, Laura – you would have laughed to hear me making the case for you. 'Pick her, pick her,' I said. And ultimately it was my decision, so I got my own way. But then, I generally do."

"So I hear," I said. That was the thing with Marius – he expected you to flirt, and however hard you resisted, you ended up doing it anyway – we all did. It was just easier that way.

"Oh, Laura," he said, mock-sorrowfully, "what have they been saying about me?"

I blushed. "Nothing. But of course you get your own way – you're in charge. And you're a genius – everyone does say that."

"A genius with a pair of very sore knees right now," he said. "And I've been here five minutes and you haven't offered me a seat. That's poor manners, Laura. That's a black mark in the book I'm sure you all believe I carry around with me."

"I'm so sorry," I stammered, jumping to my feet. It was true – he'd been standing all this time while I slumped on my dressing-table stool. It hadn't even occurred to me how rude that might seem. "Please."

"There's plenty of room for both of us," Marius said, perching on one end of the seat and patting the worn red velvet next to him.

I hesitated. There was no fucking way I wanted to squeeze myself into ten inches of space right next to Marius. I was deeply regretting lingering in my dressing room – right now, I could be at home, with Felix, perhaps soaking in the closest thing our flat could produce to a hot bath.

"Laura. There's something I need to discuss with you," Marius said.

Reluctantly, I sat down, trying and failing to preserve a paper-thin distance between his thigh and mine.

As he'd done all those weeks before, in what felt like another world before Felix and I were together, before I'd got this undreamed-of part, he raised his hand to my face. But whereas before he'd gripped my jaw between his finger and thumb, almost clinically, now he laid the palm of his hand against my cheek and turned me to face him.

"You're very beautiful," he said. "Not classical. But your eyes are lovely, and you have a charming profile. I think perhaps you could be great, one day."

I could smell his breath, laden with something strong and minty. Up close, the whites of his eyes weren't white at all, and his skin sagged slightly along the razor-sharp line of his jaw. But his hand on my face was terrifyingly strong.

"Thank you," I said.

Marius's hand left my cheek, and he trailed his finger down my neck to my collarbone, then further, brushing my breast through my cotton gown, and down to my waist. In spite of myself, in spite of how much he frightened me, I felt a shiver of something halfway between revulsion and excitement.

"You've lost weight," he said. "That's good. You used to tend to be a bit podgy. Take that thing off, and let me have a proper look at you."

So much for not getting cold, I thought. If he'd done this a year ago, I'd have complied – I would have been too frightened and too flattered not to. But now, the way I felt about my body was different – Felix had changed that. I knew I wasn't just an object to be relentlessly used and disciplined, scrutinised and adjusted. But I'd been conditioned through years of training to do as I was told, and I couldn't find the words to say no; I just sat there, frozen with shock and fright.

"Too shy?" he said. "Then I'll do it for you."

He tugged the belt of my robe loose and pushed the fabric down over my shoulders, and suddenly he was kissing me, hard, his tongue and his breath penetrating my mouth, his hands crawling over my breasts.

"No!" I said, trying to get my hand to his chest to push him away, but my arms were trapped in the sleeves of my gown. I flung my body away from him, toppled off the stool and ended up in a heap on the floor.

Marius laughed down at me. "You really are an innocent," he said. "Pretty girl. Off you go home now and make sure you're fresh as a daisy tomorrow."

He stood up and flung open the door of my dressing room.

"We should do this again soon," he said and walked out.

He almost collided with Felix in the corridor.

I don't remember how I got home that night. Well, I must have walked, of course, as I always did, the few hundred yards through the familiar streets. But I didn't see the throngs of commuters heading down into the Tube station. I didn't see the bright shop windows, incongruously filled with Christmas lights, paper snowflakes and empty boxes wrapped in shiny foil. My eyes were fixed to the ground, but I didn't see the chewing-gum splattered paving stones, either. All I could see was Felix's face – the look of utter shock and disgust he'd given me as he recoiled, turned and ran away.

With no clothes on, I couldn't follow him. I called his name, but he didn't listen. So I retreated into my dressing room, dressed and came home, numb with shock and hurt.

I lay in the bath for almost an hour, long after the water had lost what little heat it had started out with. I scrubbed my skin until it was red and sore, trying to rid myself of the memory of Marius's touch. Even after I'd cleaned my teeth, I could still taste his tongue in my mouth. Eventually, too cold to stay in the water any longer, I dried myself and dressed, shivering, pulling an old jumper of Felix's on over my jeans, as if it could provide the comfort I needed from him. I made tea and sat on the sofa, the jumper pulled over my knees, cradling the mug for warmth. I couldn't drink the tea, though – when I tried to swallow my throat closed up and I felt as if I'd be sick. I dialled Felix's phone over and over, but he didn't answer.

At last, I heard a key in the lock and felt a wave of relief – but it was only Roddy.

"Hey, Laura," he didn't flop down on the sofa, or go into the kitchen, or fling open the fridge and complain that there was never any fucking food in this place, as he usually did. He hovered in the doorway, looking at me.

"Roddy," I said. "Something's happened."

"Yeah," he said. "I saw Lawsonski earlier. He's not a happy bunny."

"It's Marius," I said. "Roddy, he…"

"Laura, don't drag me into this. Seriously, you guys need to sort it out. You're my friends, but I'm not getting involved. Not my circus, not my monkeys."

I gripped my mug harder, shock hitting me like a punch in the stomach. "What do you mean?"

"Look, you aren't the first person to do what it takes to get a part, and you won't be the last. It's just – you guys seemed so happy, that's all. You must've known he'd find out."

"But I didn't!" I said. "Is that what Felix told you?"

He shook his head. "That's what the whole company is saying."

I thought of the hours I'd spent alone in my dressing room, or rehearsing my solos with Felix, and I imagined it. I knew how it worked – our lives were so insular, our days in many ways so repetitive, that any juicy piece of gossip got handed round and chewed to death until it was flavourless and finished, and the next bit of news got started. It had never occurred to me that people would talk about me – invent lies about me and Marius. Just thinking about it flooded with a full-body blush of mortification.

"Roddy, I didn't!" I said again. "Jesus, what do you think I am? He's old, he's disgusting. He must be almost fifty. He's our *boss*."

"All the more reason to shag him," Roddy said. "Because he'd be extra grateful."

"He came to my dressing room and groped me," I said. "It was awful. I didn't know what to do. And then Felix saw us. It was just this afternoon – he never, ever touched me before and I hope he never does again."

My breath was coming in shallow gasps, and I started to cry. Roddy disappeared into the bathroom and returned with a wad of loo roll. He sat down next to me and put his arm around me.

"You don't believe me, do you?" I sobbed.

"Look, everyone knows Marius is a dirty old bastard," he said. "But he's never exactly been short of offers, if you know what I mean. People know what's in it for them. It'll blow over, Laura."

"But I didn't do anything wrong! He... he assaulted me. And everyone's going to listen to a load of gossip and not believe me."

"It's your word against his," Roddy said. "People are going to say you were fucking him and you didn't want your boyfriend to find out, and then when he did you cried rape. I believe you, Laura. But I don't think a lot of other people will. Did he – I mean, what did he do exactly?"

I told him.

"Oh, babe. That's horrible. But you're okay, right? He didn't hurt you?"

I wanted to explain to him how I felt, the crawling horror of Marius's hands invading my body, the shock and helplessness I felt when he kissed me, the shame of knowing that everyone thought I'd offered myself to him in exchange for a promotion I wasn't good enough to earn any other way. But I couldn't. I wished Mel was there – she would understand. Or she would have done, back when we were still friends.

And then, with a sickening lurch, understanding came to me.

"Roddy, Mel started this story about Marius and me, didn't she?"

"I couldn't possibly say," Roddy said. "You know how it is – no one's talking about something, then everyone is. If it was her, you won't be able to prove it, same as you can't prove he did what you're telling me."

I stared at him. His face was full of concern, but his words belied it.

"Are you saying there's nothing I can do about it? Are you telling me I just have to suck it up?"

"No! Well, actually, yes, I guess I am. What's the alternative?"

"I could go to management. Talk to our union rep. Tell Anna. There must be something I can do."

"Laura, if you did that and you couldn't prove anything – which you can't – it'll totally fuck your career. You know that."

I mopped my eyes with the loo roll, which was soaked through with my tears. I knew he was right. I imagined going through months of meetings and tribunals, reliving what Marius had done over and over again, until the telling became more real than the thing itself and I could barely believe myself any more. I imagined having to face Marius and accuse him, and how he'd laugh at me and deny it all. I imagined where that would leave me when eventually it all came to an end – relegated to the Corps de Ballet, until the time came for my contract to be renewed, and then it not being.

And, I thought, if I did persuade Felix to believe me, and he took my side and supported me, he'd be tainted by association, our careers crashing and burning in perfect unison, a pas de deux of failure.

"It would, wouldn't it?" I said to Roddy, outrage and disbelief fighting the certain knowledge that he was right.

"Babe, it just would. None of us like it, but there it is. So there's no point getting yourself worked up about it. Talk to Lawsonski tonight, tell him what happened, kiss and make up. Then put it behind you. Walk on that stage tomorrow and be a star, prove to everyone that no matter what they think, you are good enough. And everyone will move on to the next juicy bit of scandal soon enough. That's my advice."

Roddy was my friend – my oldest and closest, since Mel and I weren't friends any more. I trusted him – I thought I was doing the right thing to follow his guidance. Even with hindsight, it probably was right – or it would have been, had things turned out differently.

"Okay, I guess," I said.

Then Roddy poured me a massive vodka, made me scrambled eggs on toast, massaged my feet and sat with me watching old episodes of *Buffy* until we were both nodding off on the sofa.

But Felix didn't come home.

At midnight, Roddy said, "Sweetie, I need to get my beauty sleep, and you should, too. Want a cuppa before bed?"

"I'm okay," I said. "I'll stay up for a bit, just in case."

"Try not to stress about it. He'll have crashed on someone's floor. He just needs to make a point, and you two can talk about it tomorrow and soon you'll be cooing away at each other again like the lovebirds you are. Listen to Uncle Roddy. I know what I'm talking about."

Roddy might have had lots of sex, but he knew even less about relationships than I did. Still, I was desperate to believe him, and I tried to, but I still couldn't bring myself to go to bed – to the bed that Felix and I had shared for the past eight blissful months, to lie in the sheets where we'd made love the night before, that smelled of him and of us. I didn't know, then, that I'd never sleep there with him again, but I felt a superstitious dread of waking up in the morning and him still not being there.

I took the sleeping bag that Felix had brought with the rest of his meagre belongings when he'd moved in – if you can call turning up with a backpack and a third of the rent 'moving in' – and curled up miserably on the sofa. It was the night before my first ever big part – I knew I should be feeling nervous, but this horrible sense of dread was something entirely different.

I slept fitfully, on high alert for the sound of Felix's feet on the stairs, his key in the lock, but it never came. And when Roddy's alarm clock trilled at eight the next morning, I was already awake, anxiously checking and rechecking my phone for a voicemail or text I knew wasn't there.

There was no pandering to soloists on the day of an opening night. I was expected to turn up for class as usual, so I did. Roddy stuck by me, pretending cheerfulness, greeting his friends and clowning around as usual. But I noticed the glances people gave me, the whispers I couldn't quite hear, Mel's feline malevolence as she glanced towards me without meeting my eyes. I couldn't believe I'd been so oblivious, caught in my bubble of pride and excitement, that I hadn't noticed any of it before.

Felix didn't show up to class, but he couldn't miss our final rehearsal in the afternoon. When I came into the studio after lunch – the lunch I'd been completely unable to eat – he was there, talking to Anna as if nothing had happened.

I waited, silently, and watched. Anna was explaining a point of choreography to Felix, suggesting that his arms might be better in a different shape.

"As if you're moving through water, pushing against resistance," I heard her say.

Felix moved his arms as directed.

"Good, yes, just like that."

Felix nodded and turned away, smiling. Then he saw me, and his features froze again into still indifference.

But his cold composure couldn't hide the ravages of a sleepless night. I'd seen Felix hungover often enough to know the signs: the dark hollows under his bloodshot eyes, the smell of smoke in his hair, the infinitesimal delay in his response to the musical cues.

Somehow, we got through that rehearsal, but as the hour went on, I found my shock and hurt turning to anger. How could he be so fucking selfish? He'd danced major leading roles before, but I hadn't – this was the biggest night of my career, and he'd chosen to jeopardise it. Of course he was hurting – but he could have talked to me about what he'd seen and heard, let me reassure him that I loved him, I hadn't been unfaithful, it was all malicious and untrue.

At last, Anna said, "That will do for now. Go and get some rest."

Felix shouldered his bag and headed for the door, and I followed, desperate to talk to him, explain what had happened and make things right between us.

But Anna said, "Just a moment, please, Laura."

I paused, wanting to ask her if it couldn't wait until later, but the habit of obedience to my teachers was too deeply ingrained.

"Yes, Anna?"

"This wedding dance, Laura, is all about Princess Aurora coming to womanhood. During it, she stops being a coquettish girl and becomes confident and sensual. We've seen that in you, this last few months. That's why I felt you would be perfect to dance the role, and I supported Marius's decision to cast you."

I felt tears prick my eyes – she was absolutely right. But I didn't feel like a confident, sensual woman today, that was for sure. I felt like a frightened, lonely child. I nodded silently, knowing that if I tried to speak, I'd cry.

"We all have times in our careers when we have to overcome adversity," she went on. "When I danced Odette-Odile in *Swan Lake* – a very long time ago – I'd just discovered I was pregnant. Halfway through the run, I miscarried. I missed one show, then the next night I was back on stage. It was the hardest thing I've ever done."

"I'm sorry," I muttered. "That must have been awful."

"I'm not telling you this for sympathy," she said. "I know you're going through a difficult time right now – you think you're hiding it well, but you're not. The sparkle you've been showing, that made your interpretation of this role so magical – it wasn't there today."

I looked down at my feet and shook my head. "I guess it wasn't."

"Is there anything you need to talk to me about?" she said. "Working with you young girls – I think sometimes we focus too much on technique, on developing you as dancers, and not enough on taking care of you."

My eyes swimming with tears, I forced myself to look up at her. Her face was full of concern. I was almost sure she'd listen to me if I told her what had happened – but then I remembered Roddy's advice: talk to Felix, put it behind you, walk on stage and be a star. If I hurried, I would be able to catch up Felix up on the roof smoking a cigarette. On this cold, raw afternoon, I might find him alone.

"It's okay, Anna," I said. "It's just nerves, I guess."

She brushed a tear off my cheek with a warm, gentle finger. "All right, Laura. If that's what you say. I know you'll do your best tonight – I know you have it in you to be brilliant. Have you eaten anything today?"

"Not really," I said.

"You need to keep your strength up." She reached into her bag and handed me a cereal bar. "Eat that, keep warm, and do your relaxation exercises. And don't you dare let me down!"

I managed a smile, thanked her and left the studio, running up the stairs to the roof in search of Felix. But he wasn't there – there was only the faintest smell of cigarette smoke hanging in the freezing air.

CHAPTER SEVENTEEN

I dreamed the dream I had so often: that Owen was crying, and I couldn't find him. He wasn't in his bed, or in Darcey's room. I thought she was asleep, but when I nudged the duvet aside, I discovered a nest of fluffy ginger kittens curled up on her pillow. Panicking now, I ran downstairs, but the ground floor of our house had been transformed into the forest from *A Midsummer Night's Dream*. I could hear Owen's cries growing louder and louder, and ran through the trees searching for him, trying to call his name, but no sound came out. Then a powerful pair of arms grabbed me from behind, pinning my arms against my sides. I struggled, but couldn't free myself. The forest was hot, humid as a tropical jungle. The air was thick and difficult to breathe, cloying my lungs so I couldn't fill them enough to scream, and all that came out was a strangled croak.

"Laura!" Jonathan's voice woke me at last. "Jesus. That was quite a nightmare. I tried to hug you but you just thrashed about."

I opened my eyes, briefly disorientated before I realised – we were in New York, in our hotel room, and I'd taken a sleeping pill the previous night to try and stave off jet lag. It had left me with a banging headache and a foul taste in my mouth – not a great way to start a holiday.

"I dreamed we'd lost Owen," I said, shivering at the memory, even though the room was so warm. "And our house was all weird, with trees growing in the lounge, and there were kittens, I think." The memory of the dream was dissipating even as I spoke, fragments drifting away as I tried to recall them, elusive as smoke.

"Laura, the kids will be fine," Jonathan said. "You know that, don't you? They were as happy as anything when we dropped them at Sadie and Gareth's yesterday."

"Owen was crying," I said. "He was crying when we Skyped them last night."

"Laura, he threw a strop when we told him it was night-time here and we were going to bed, even though they were just having breakfast," Jonathan said. "He was making a principled objection to the existence of time zones, toddler-style. He's fine. They'll both be fine."

"I know," I said. "I know they'll be okay, and Darcey couldn't stop going on about how excited she is about the kittens" – that must be why they'd made an appearance in my dream, of course – "and the pony. They'll have a great time. I just hope Sadie doesn't let them eat too much junk."

"Or what?" Jonathan said. "Relax, darling, five days of fish-finger sandwiches won't give them type two diabetes or scurvy or whatever you're imagining."

"Don't take the piss." I knew he was trying to cheer me up, but I still felt anxious and irritable. "How do we get coffee here, anyway?"

"I ordered it last night, remember?"

Of course – when we got in from dinner, Jonathan had painstakingly filled in the room service card while I got ready for bed, but by the time he'd hung it on the door my sleeping pill had kicked in and I'd been unconscious. There had been no enthusiastic first-night-of-holiday sex for us.

"That'll be it now," Jonathan said, wrapping himself in a white towelling dressing gown and answering the knock on the door. "Thanks very much. I can manage."

He put the laden tray down on the coffee table – our room was huge, more like a suite, really – and tipped the chambermaid.

"Now, we've got bacon, pancakes, toast, pastries, melon, orange juice and, of course, coffee. Name your pleasure, darling."

"Just coffee, please. I'm not hungry – I might have something to eat later, when I've woken up properly."

I watched as Jonathan dressed and breakfasted simultaneously, putting on his shirt, then crunching his way through a couple of slices of toast with bacon between them before doing up the buttons, stepping into his trousers, drinking a cup of coffee then knotting his tie. He always did this at home – reading his emails while he shaved in the mornings, pausing while doing the garden to practice his golf swing with a spade.

He called it multitasking, but for some reason I can't put my finger on I'd always found it intensely irritating. It was irritating me now, so much that I went and had a shower so I didn't have to watch.

The hot water and lavish hotel toiletries made me feel more cheerful – Darcey would love the miniature bottles of shower gel, shampoo and moisturiser, and I made a mental note to steal a generous supply to take home.

"So what's the plan for the day?" I asked, emerging from the bathroom wrapped in a fluffy towel.

"We could do something together this morning," Jonathan said. "A museum, maybe? Staten Island? Whatever you fancy. Then have lunch, then I've got meetings all afternoon, I'm afraid, but we'll meet this evening for cocktails and dinner somewhere fabulous – I'll get the office manager to make a reservation. I'm sorry to have to leave you on your own so much, but you'll be okay, won't you?"

"I'll be fine," I said. "I'll go shopping, or something."

"Great," Jonathan said, but he, too, was looking at his phone, not really listening to me. "That's weird."

"What's weird?"

"Email from Wanda in the office here – she's saying something about the DBMG account. We've not had any business from them for years. Just some admin fuck-up, I expect – I'll clear it up when I meet with them later."

"What's DBMG?" I asked, more to appear interested than because I really wanted to know.

"Energy company. They explore large-scale oil reserves, mostly in South America. That's their version of it, anyway – mine is that they buy and then desecrate huge swathes of rain forest, and when they're done they walk away and leave fucked-up ecology and loads of people without work. Nothing illegal, but highly unethical and exploitative as far as I'm concerned, so I was quite happy to let the account quietly slip away."

"That's horrible," I said.

"It is horrible," Jonathan agreed. "But they'll carry on doing it regardless of who their financial services firm is, so there was an argument for fighting to retain the business, but…" he shrugged.

"You didn't fight too hard?"

"No, I suppose I didn't. But don't tell that to Wanda in the Wall Street office. She's a seriously tough cookie – I'm a bit scared of her. Anyway, we should get going, if you don't want anything to eat?"

I dressed hastily, gulping another cup of coffee while I did my make-up – Jonathan's habits were nothing if not contagious – and ten minutes later we were out in the blazing hot morning, walking hand in hand up Park Avenue.

We wandered through Central Park for a bit, until it got too hot, and then retreated to the Museum of Modern Art and spent a happy two hours exploring the galleries, together but not together. If I stopped to look at a painting, Jonathan wouldn't wait for me, but then a few minutes later he'd come and find me and take my hand, saying, "Come here, Laura, you've got to see this." And I'd go, and we'd talk about what he'd found and then drift apart again.

It was my favourite way to look round galleries with someone – there was nothing worse than feeling you had to wait and stare at something that didn't interest you, or risk looking like a philistine.

It was also, I realised uncomfortably, a fairly accurate reflection of the state of our marriage. But I didn't want to think about that, not now, not when we were happy and having a good time together. So I didn't think – I just looked at the beautiful paintings, and when Jonathan was out of sight, I sneaked off to gaze at the ceramics display, which I knew would bore him. He found me there half an hour later.

"I knew you'd be mooning over cups and saucers," he teased. "I don't know why you bother coming, when you could just go to John Lewis and do the same thing."

"Fuck off!" I laughed. "It's Harrods, at the very least. Look at this, look at the glaze."

"Owen would smash it in about a nanosecond," Jonathan said. "It's gone midday. We should get some lunch and then I'll have to head off for my two o'clock."

I realised I was starving, and thirsty, and my ankle was hurting from standing for so long. But when we drifted back out into the hot streets, we found ourselves doing The Dance of Lunch.

When you've been together as long as Jonathan and I have, even the things that annoy you about each other become games – become mythologised almost. So it was with us and lunch. We'd been out to dinner together countless times, and it was always fine, bar the occasional overdone steak, upselling sommelier or minor row. But lunch was another matter.

The first time it happened, we'd been going out for just a few weeks and I'd stayed over at Jonathan's for the first time. We did all the usual stuff – woke up, had coffee, had sex, showered, and then Jonathan suggested going for lunch, so we strolled down his local high street and assessed the options.

"What's this place like?" I asked as we passed an organic salad bar.

"No idea whatsoever," Jonathan said, "and I don't intend to find out now."

I was slightly taken aback, but thought, fair enough, maybe salad isn't his thing.

"How about Thai?" Jonathan said.

"Really? For lunch? All that rice?" I objected. "There's a nice looking café there across the road."

"No fucking way," Jonathan said. "It's always rammed with families with screaming kids at weekends."

Little did he know that one day, we'd be one of those families. But back then, I had to admit he had a point.

And so it went on. Jonathan put in a bid for Nando's; I said no because their chicken wasn't free range. I proposed a Vietnamese place, but he said the last time he'd been there the waitress was so rude he'd vowed never to go back. After half an hour of this, we decided that the next place we passed would be the one we went to, even if it turned out to be horrid, as of course it did.

And time and time again over the years, the scenario repeated itself, until we came to recognise and fear the Dance of Lunch, which always ended in disappointment and ill temper.

And now, here in New York, city of about a zillion restaurants, it was happening again. Jonathan wasn't in the mood for sushi. The queue at the falafel cart was too long. I didn't want to go to a burger place because I was worried about hormones and antibiotics in the meat. A pleasant-looking Mexican restaurant turned us away because we hadn't booked. And all the time, I was getting hungrier and hungrier and we were both getting crosser and crosser.

I found myself turning to passive aggression.

"Look, we can go to the burger place if you want. I'll just have something else – they probably do a vegetarian option, even if it's not very good."

"No, Laura, don't be a martyr," Jonathan said. "This is your holiday, you must eat something you'll like."

"It's too late now," I said. "We're doing the Dance of Lunch. Wherever we end up will be minging, let's just cut our losses and not be too late to eat anything at all."

"I'm sure there was a place just down the road here that I read about," Jonathan said, getting out his phone.

And then I gave up all hope. Once Jonathan started Googling, I knew we were well and truly fucked.

When eventually we found the restaurant Jonathan had read about, I was feeling sick with hunger and suspected my face was getting sunburned. Jonathan was looking hot and cross in his suit, and snapping at me whenever I feebly suggested that we just pop into the next place we passed.

"Here we are!" he said. "Thank God for that."

But it turned out to be closed for lunch on Tuesdays.

We looked at each other, both equally pissed off, and then we started to laugh.

"Look, this isn't going to happen," I said. "You grab something on the way to your meeting and I'll head back to the hotel and eat there, okay?"

"Hold on, there's another place we can try just down here…"

"Jonathan! No! In about five seconds we're going to have a row if we carry on like this, and I don't want to have a row."

"God, Laura, you're so unreasonable," he said, but he was smiling as we parted, and I saw him hurry off down the road and duck into a sleazy-looking hot-dog joint where I wouldn't have eaten even if I'd been on the verge of slipping into a hypoglycaemic coma.

I went and found a raw food café and happily ordered seaweed and cashew salad and carrot juice, which I knew Jonathan would rather have gouged his own eyes out with a spoon than eaten.

Once I was alone, I felt my good mood evaporating. Jonathan and I were getting on, now, in this brief interlude, but that didn't change anything, really. It didn't change how frustrated I was by our marriage, how I felt he never listened to me any more, how trapped and stifled I felt in the unending sameness of my days at home. It didn't change my restless, relentless thoughts of Felix. And it didn't change the fact that he was here, in New York, now.

"*Dream* doesn't open until the weekend," he'd texted the previous day. "And I've got two days off rehearsals. So I'm all yours if you can get away."

All mine. He might be, for a few snatched hours or one night – but I knew I could never be all his again. In my mind, I'd turned over possibility after possibility. I could – I knew I should – walk away. But the idea of never seeing Felix again made me feel like Darcey would feel if I told her there'd never be another Christmas.

I could have sex with him, get him out of my system and return to my marriage with a spring in my step – and with a horrible, guilty secret I could never, ever let Jonathan discover. I could – I flinched at the phrase – have an affair, let it run its course, let the inevitable discovery happen. And then what? Divorce, or patching things up and enduring a lifetime of bitterness and resentment. Staying together for the sake of the children, or shattering our little family to smithereens like the Christmas bauble Owen had crushed in his chubby hand last year.

Remembering that, remembering how he'd howled with shock at what he'd done, and how tenderly Jonathan had comforted him, I felt tears fill my eyes. I was trapped, caught between what I knew was right and the prospect of something more – excitement, passion, happiness. There was only one name I could put to what I longed for, and it was Felix's.

I paid for my lunch and left the restaurant. I'd said I'd go shopping, so that's what I would do. I needed something – anything – to distract me from the turmoil of contradicting thoughts in my head. I spent the afternoon wandering from one air-conditioned haven to the next, minimising the time I spent on the scorching, humid streets. It had been ages since I shopped just for me, instead of panic-buying jumpers in colours that didn't suit me in between school shoes for Darcey and a new winter coat for Owen.

Now, I could try things on at my leisure, and I made the most of it, sending the helpful shop assistants back for different sizes, spending ages scrutinising my body from all angles, asking for high-heeled shoes to get the full effect, and then finally failing to make a decision and moving on to the next shop.

By the time I got back to our hotel, I'd bought just one thing: a gorgeous, drapey silk dress in an unlikely shade of tangerine, which a sales assistant had made me try on, insisting that the colour was "just, like, totally you". Amazingly, it was. I'd wear it out tonight, I decided – make an effort for my dinner with Jonathan, wherever we ended up going.

I glanced at my watch – it was half past six, so I had masses of time to have a leisurely bath, paint my nails, straighten my hair, and generally make myself look as groomed and glossy as all the women I'd seen in the shops and on the street.

And so I did. I titivated as thoroughly as for a first date, then helped myself to a miniature bottle of champagne from the mini-bar, and texted Jonathan.

"Hey – where are you? What time do you want to meet?"

His reply didn't come instantly, and I felt myself getting faintly annoyed as I sipped my champagne. He'd said cocktails then dinner – he'd said he'd book somewhere. It was getting late – this might be the city that never slept, but he'd mentioned a seven o'clock meeting the next morning, and we wouldn't be able to have much of a night out at this rate.

I'd sipped my way through almost all the tiny bottle of fizz by the time my phone rang. It was Jonathan, and he had his 'people are listening' voice on.

"Laura? It's me. Sorry about the delay."

Automatically, I found myself responding with equal formality. "Hi. That's okay. I'm sorry to have texted, I know you'll have been busy."

"Yes. As a matter of fact, it looks like this meeting's going to go on for a while, and then we're heading out for some food. I don't anticipate getting back much before midnight, if then. You'll be okay, won't you?"

My 'you're in a meeting' voice deserted me as quickly as it had arrived. "Okay? Yes, of course I'll be okay. I'll sit here in our room on my own in the dress I bought especially for tonight and order room service and watch *Sex and the City* reruns on TV. It'll be amazing fun."

"Give me a moment, would you, Peter?" Jonathan said. I heard his hurrying footsteps, then a door slamming. "Laura?"

"What?" I said sulkily.

"I cannot have this, okay? I'm working. Get it – working. I've been having really intense, really unpleasant conversations with my colleagues all afternoon and they're going to carry on all night, most probably. So I'd prefer not to have another unpleasant conversation with you. You're an adult, Laura,

you're perfectly capable of looking after yourself. Go
for dinner, go to the theatre, do whatever you want,
but don't give me a hard time when all I'm doing is
my job, which if you remember is what I came here
to do, not act as a tour guide for you. And before you
ask, yes, this is what it's going to be like every night.
You wanted to come – you're here. Deal with it."

And before I could formulate a reply, he'd ended
the call.

I stared at my phone, waves of shock and hurt
crashing over me. Jonathan never lost his temper like
that. He'd never shouted at me or at the children,
even when they were being their most insufferable.
And back then, he'd been properly shouting. At least
he'd done me the courtesy of leaving the room first,
and not telling me off like a naughty schoolgirl while
Peter, whoever he was, and the rest of his colleagues
listened in, approvingly, while the little woman was
put in her place.

Thinking of this, my hurt turned to anger. I imagined Jonathan walking back into the meeting room,
placing his phone face down on the table and saying, "Right, where were we?" as if I were a temporary
inconvenience, one that had now been dealt with, so
the proper business of the day could resume. I could
cope with him working late at home – I didn't bloody
like it, mind, but I was willing to put up and shut
up, but here? On holiday? And then I remembered
that it wasn't a holiday, for him, it was a work trip I'd
muscled in on. And then I thought, but I wouldn't

mind him doing this on a work trip I'd muscled in on if he didn't do it all the time at home, too. And so my thoughts went, round and round, making me more and more annoyed.

And anyway, what the hell was I meant to do now? I could ring Sadie and try and talk to the children again – check that Owen was all right and had settled down. But when I worked out the time difference, I realised it would still be night-time there – too early even for Sadie and Gareth's countryside hours. A man might have been able to stroll out alone into the streets and pick a bar or a restaurant and eat and drink alone, but I couldn't – not dressed like this, anyway. Maybe if I changed back into jeans and took my Lonely Planet guide, or at least my tablet, as defensive camouflage.

I unzipped the dress and was about to tug it off over my head when my phone buzzed. If that was Jonathan texting me to tell me he'd changed his mind and could come out after all he could piss right off, I thought angrily. But it wasn't – it was Felix.

"Any chance you're free for a drink?"

Well, I was, wasn't I? "Where are you?" I texted back.

"Chelsea." He gave me the name of a bar I'd never heard of, and its address, and within two minutes I was in a taxi on my way there. It was as simple as that.

The bar was hidden away on a quiet side street, so unassuming I thought the cab driver had brought me to the wrong place. I paid the fare and walked anxiously up and down, past a launderette, a school and what looked like a backpackers' hostel. Just as I was beginning to wonder if Felix was playing one of his practical jokes on me, making me come all the way downtown only to send me off again somewhere else, he texted again.

"It's the black door by the hotel. You can't miss it. Actually, I did – about six times! So far, so speakeasy. I'm at a table in the garden."

Black door – I was right there. I pushed it open and a very thin blonde girl in a black dress looked me up and down, gave a false smile, then glanced at her clipboard.

"Good evening, Ma'am. Do you have a reservation?"

Feeling foolish, foreign and overdressed, I said, "No. No, I don't, but I think my friend's here, in the garden. This is Raynes Law Room, right?" Even the name of the place made me feel like I was the victim of some elaborate hoax. But her smile warmed a degree or two.

"Come right this way."

I followed her through the subterranean gloom and out through a door. The light dazzled me briefly, then I saw Felix, sitting at a wrought-iron table in the corner under a shady pergola festooned with fairy lights. Even though the evening was still hot, out here it felt pleasantly cool.

I thanked the hostess, wondering whether I ought to tip her for her thirty seconds of service, but she vanished back inside before I had a chance to decide.

Felix stood up and we kissed each other shyly on both cheeks, then he pulled me towards him for a hug. His body felt lean and taut under his dark green shirt. He smelled like he'd just had a shower. In my high heels, I was almost the same height as him, and our eyes were level as we looked at each other, smiling.

"It's good to see you," he said. "I'm glad you came."

"Me too," I said, feeling a surge of pure happiness as we smiled at each other.

We sat down and he handed me a cocktail menu, which was full of unfamiliar drinks.

"They specialise in prohibition era recipes," Felix said. "God only knows what that means. I thought everyone sent themselves blind drinking dodgy moonshine brewed in car radiators. But apparently not – this is actually rather good."

He passed me his glass for a taste – it was.

"I'll have whatever that is," I said to the waitress, who was hovering by our table.

"Sure," she said. Then she hovered a bit more, and said, "Excuse me, but aren't you Felix Lawson?"

"That's right," Felix said.

"Oh my God, I'm so excited to see you! I'm a drama student. Me and my friends have already booked, like, eight shows of Flight of Fancy's *Dream*. Would you mind… Would it be okay if I took a selfie of us to put on my blog?"

"Not at all," Felix said, and the waitress whipped out her phone, put her arm around him and snapped away for a few seconds, while I watched awkwardly.

"Thank you so much! Now, what can I get you guys to drink?"

She took our order and went away, saying, "My name's Nancy, just let me know if there's anything at all you need."

"God, Laura," Felix said. "Sorry about that."

"It isn't your fault," I said. "Does it happen a lot?"

"Never," Felix said, and I could tell he was pleased, although he'd never admit it. "First time in my life. I'm a nobody, remember?"

"Looks like you aren't one any more."

"I don't know," he said. "The last five years – there were times when I thought I should chuck it all in."

"What, acting?"

He nodded. "There was one stretch where I didn't work for six months. After that you start to wonder whether you've lost the right to call yourself a performer. Whether you aren't really a barman who does a bit of acting on the side."

The waitress brought our drinks, gave Felix a megawatt smile, and went away again.

"Anyway," he said. "Sorry. I'm boring you."

"Of course you're not. It's just – it's hard, isn't it? It wasn't when we were twenty, but it must be different now."

Felix laughed. "Everything's different now from when we were twenty."

Our eyes met and I felt a rush of sadness – a deep regret for what I'd had and lost. Everything was different – except one thing. I still loved Felix. I'd never stopped loving him. The realisation hit me like a bullet – I could almost feel the rhythm of my heartbeat changing, quickening, as if I'd been running up a hill. I felt as if I'd spent the past fourteen years asleep, and now I'd woken up again. My senses were suddenly on high alert – I was conscious of every drop of condensation beading my glass, the distant roar of traffic on Sixth Avenue, the smell of Felix's skin.

The evening felt replete with possibility, but I had no idea what was going to happen – or even what I hoped for.

Felix broke my mood of refection with a laugh. "It's all big talk, anyway," he said. "Ask me again in six months and I'll probably be back mixing cocktails, phoning my agent every day and moaning that there are no parts out there for short, ageing ex-dancers."

"You're not short," I said. "And even if you were – look at Tom Cruise."

"I prefer not to, actually," Felix said.

Nancy came over and took our order for another round of drinks.

"What time do you need to get back?" Felix asked.

"I don't," I said. "We were going to go for dinner somewhere, but Jonathan had to work late, and so there I was, all dressed up with nowhere to go. Then you texted."

Just saying my husband's name felt strange – for a few minutes, it had felt almost as if he didn't exist.

"I'm glad I did," Felix said. "I'm glad you're here. I'm glad we've found each other again."

"Me, too," I said, and he stretched across the table and brushed the back of my hand with his fingertips.

"So what do you want to do? Are you hungry?"

I shook my head.

"We could go dancing? Find a dive bar with live music and throw some shapes?"

I imagined dancing with him again, experiencing the synergy of our bodies, the way we could still move together like we used to. But, more even than that, I wanted to be alone with him. "You know what I'd like? It's so hot. Why don't we go to Central Park?"

"And walk around the lake and look at the stars?"

"Exactly."

So that's what we did. We didn't walk for long, because of my high heels, but we looked at the stars and tried to see how many constellations we could identify, which wasn't many, so we switched to looking at the lights of the city skyline, trying to identify the buildings, but we couldn't get many of those right, either. And, to be honest, I found it difficult to focus on anything except Felix's hand in mine, the sound of his voice, and how much I wanted him to kiss me.

It was after one when I got back to our hotel, and Jonathan still wasn't there. I undressed, hanging the orange dress in the wardrobe, cleaned my teeth and got into bed, my body going through the motions automatically while my mind raced back to Felix.

What was he doing right now, I wondered. I imagined him in a hotel room across the city, kicking off his clothes as I'd seen him do so many times, leaving them in a heap on the floor. I knew how he would look asleep, his long legs pushing the covers aside. I knew the way his body moved when he was dreaming. I knew the way he woke in the morning, instantly alert and eager for the day to begin, not grumpy and muddle-headed before several cups of coffee, like I always was.

I turned out the light and lay in the semi-darkness, the room illuminated by the city's million windows, one of which was his.

When I heard the click of the door unlocking, I felt a leap of shock and hope and sat up – had he come? He hadn't, of course – he wouldn't and couldn't. It was Jonathan, late, cross and a bit drunk, his tie askew and his face shadowed with stubble.

"I thought you'd be asleep, Laura," he said. "Did I wake you?"

I shook my head. "I was awake anyway. Jetlag, I guess. How was your day? And your night?"

"Brutal," he said. "Back-to-back meetings all afternoon, then dinner, then one of the guys had the bright idea of going for drinks afterwards, and we ended up in some sleazy strip joint. I thought that sort of thing went out with the ark, but evidently not."

"Strip joint?"

"I'm sorry, darling. I should have realised, but I didn't. They said they were going on to a club, and would I like to come along, and by the time I realised I couldn't back out without looking like a total prude. Christ, I'm knackered."

"I'm not surprised," I said. "Sounds like an eventful night."

"Laura," he pulled off his tie and sat down on the bed, reaching his arms out to me. "I'm sorry, okay? I didn't realise. And I didn't touch, I just looked."

"Sure you did," I said.

"Oh, for fuck's sake," he snapped. "If you're going to be all passive-aggressive about it..."

"I'm not being passive-aggressive." I was wide awake now. I was pissed off, of course I was, but at the same time I felt almost relieved, as if Jonathan's leering over naked girls was the same as my longing for Felix, and the two things somehow cancelled each other out.

"Yes, you are."

"Look, I'm really not. If you think having some stripper's tits shoved in your face is an appropriate way to do business with your colleagues, who am I to argue?"

"See? Totally passive-aggressive."

"Jonathan, what do you want me to say? For God's sake, it's done now. Either you'll do it again or you won't – you're a big boy now, you can make up your own mind about what's appropriate."

"So you don't care?"

"Is that why you told me? So I'd fly into a fit of jealous rage?"

Jonathan pushed his hands through his hair. Suddenly he looked desperately tired.

"Yes, actually, a fit of jealous rage would be preferable to you apparently not giving a fuck what I do."

"Well, you're not going to get a fit of jealous rage," I said coldly. "I thought we'd be spending some time together while we were here, and evidently that isn't going to happen, but I'm not going to make myself miserable by arguing with you. Presumably you've got another busy day tomorrow – you should get some sleep."

Jonathan didn't say anything more. He went to the bathroom and I heard the shower running. I turned out the light and lay on my side, facing the wall, and when he came to bed I pretended to be asleep.

CHAPTER EIGHTEEN

The next morning, Jonathan was hollow-eyed and sour with hangover. There was no breakfast, because we'd both forgotten to order it the night before, and no coffee.

"Want me to ring room service?" I asked.

"Don't bother on my account," he said. "My first meeting's at seven, remember. So I can't hang about, much as I'd love to."

"Look, I – about last night..." I began, then stopped myself. I didn't want to apologise for our row, which hadn't been my fault. I didn't want to tell him I'd seen Felix, because that would lead to another, worse row – and this time it would be my fault.

"I said I was sorry, Laura. What do you want, blood?"

"I just want us to have a nice time together," I said miserably. "Like we did yesterday, remember?"

I could barely remember it myself – the previous morning seemed like a different world, like it had happened to a different person.

Jonathan's face softened. "We will, I promise. I've got meetings in the diary all day today, and a dinner tonight, but tomorrow's almost free, and we've got another day after that. I'm sorry this hasn't turned out like you hoped. I know it's dull for you hanging around on your own, but I'll make it up to you, okay? I promise."

"Okay," I said, feeling a fresh unfurling of guilt inside me as I kissed him goodbye. I wasn't hanging around on my own. I hadn't last night and I wasn't going to today, either.

While I was in the shower, Felix sent a text. "So what's happening?"

Naked and dripping on the bathmat, I texted back, "J working all day. How about you?"

His reply arrived almost immediately. "I'm meeting a hot woman for breakfast at the deli where they filmed that scene from *When Harry Met Sally*."

I felt briefly bereft, then I realised what he meant. "I'll be there in half an hour," I texted.

I dressed quickly – no heels this time, no designer frock. I just chucked on jeans and a stripy top and flat shoes, because I knew there'd be exploring to do. Felix hadn't said, but it was implicit – we'd be spending the day together. All day, and perhaps the evening too. I felt giddy with excitement as I left the hotel and boarded a subway train.

In the air-conditioned chill of the carriage, I tried to force myself to think. I knew I was approaching a crisis – a point at which I'd have to make a decision. But I wasn't capable of being rational, balanced or reasonable – my heart was so firmly in charge that my head wasn't even getting a look-in. Also, I was fiercely hungry – all the cocktails we'd drunk the night before, plus no dinner, had left me feeling light-headed with desire for food as well as for Felix.

Take a look at yourself, Laura, I scolded. You're turning into an animal. Where's your self-control? But I didn't know, and nor did I particularly care.

Felix was waiting for me in the deli, two steaming mugs of coffee in front of him. When he saw me he jumped up and hugged me so hard he almost lifted me off my feet.

"God, you look amazing," he said.

"You didn't say that last night," I said. "And I spent two hours getting ready. You contrary bastard."

"You hadn't got ready for me then," he said. "Today you have. But you're always beautiful. You always were. Now drink your coffee and I'll get us some food – do you want smoked salmon, salt beef or pastrami?"

"All of them," I said. "But that would be wildly excessive. You choose."

A few minutes later, he returned carrying a tray heaving with food, and for a while we didn't say very much because we were too busy stuffing our faces. When I could eat no more, there was still enough left to feed the five thousand.

"I'm beginning to think you're some kind of feeder," I said. "Remember, you always used to bring me bacon sandwiches on weekends? And that lunch on my birthday, and now this. You'll only be happy when

I'm so huge I can't get up from bed, and the fire brigade have to be called to winch me out of the window."

"It's fuel," Felix said. "We've got a busy day ahead of us. Unless you have to be somewhere else?"

I noticed how, as ever, he shied away from mentioning where I might need to be, or who with.

"I don't have to be anywhere," I said. "I'm where I want to be."

"What, you want to stay here? Shall I order cheesecake, and then make you do that fake orgasm thing so I can post it on YouTube?"

I laughed. "You know that's not what I meant. So, what are we doing?"

Felix had lost none of his ability to plan adventures without appearing to have planned anything at all. That day passed in a blur of sunshine and laughter. It was like all our days off had been, except there was no evening performance to cloud our enjoyment – there was something far more significant, which we didn't even mention.

We took the ferry to see the Statue of Liberty. We went to Ground Zero, and remembered that we'd been together in the flat in Covent Garden when the Twin Towers fell, holding each other and crying, unable to watch the scene on television but unable to turn it off, either. We walked up along an old railway track that had been turned into a park, and when we passed 28th Street, Felix told me about an amazing immersive theatre production we absolutely had to see together next time.

"Is there going to be a next time?" I said.

"I don't know, Laura. I guess that's up to you."

He took my hand, and when I look back, it seems as if, for the rest of the day, he never let it go – although of course that can't be what really happened.

When we'd walked so much I felt like my left foot was about to fall off, Felix said, "Time for a break?"

"Definitely," I said.

"The apartment where I'm staying is about five blocks from here," he said. "We could go there?"

I knew exactly what that meant, but I didn't say no. We stopped at a liquor store on the way and bought a bottle of champagne, then I followed Felix through a glass door and up three flights of stairs, which smelled a bit of unemptied bins. I felt my heart sink, worried that he was stuck in yet another squalid, miserable place. But when he unlocked the door, it was to reveal a beautiful, airy room, filled with the light of the setting sun, with white-painted walls and an air-conditioning unit rattling in the window, making it blissfully cool.

"I borrowed this from a mate who's working in California for a couple of months," Felix said. "It's small, but it does the job. I don't know how long I'll be here – it's possible the show will tank and I'll be back in London before you can say, 'Make mine an Old Fashioned.'"

"It's lovely," I said. I couldn't help but notice that most of the floor space was taken up by a giant four-poster bed, covered by a blinding-white duvet.

I wondered if he'd made it that morning imagining coming back here with me.

I heard the champagne cork pop and Felix handed me a fizzing glass. Then he stood still for a moment, looking down at me, his face grave – almost sad.

"Laura," he said. "I'm only going to say this once, unless you ask me to say it again. I love you. I never stopped loving you. I regret what happened more than I can ever say. I've spent all this time regretting it, wishing I hadn't been such a fucking fool."

I looked at the glass in my hand, then put it down carefully on the floor and wrapped my arms around him. I wanted my embrace to say that I was sorry, too, that it wasn't his fault – to comfort and console him. But the feeling of his body next to mine was too intoxicatingly exciting, and I found myself pressing hard against him, wanting to imprint the shape of him into my flesh.

Seconds later, we were kissing each other, as hungry and eager as we'd been the first time we'd made love in my tiny single bed, our skin still slick with post-rehearsal sweat. My hands moved over his body, discovering the hardness of his chest, the smoothness of his back, the powerful muscles of his thighs under his jeans. His lips moved from my mouth to my neck, then to my collarbone and lower, pushing aside the neckline of my top.

"Take it off," I said, and he did.

I kicked off my trainers, not bothering to undo the laces. Felix carefully unbuttoned my jeans and I stepped out of them and stood in front of him in my bra and pants. He pulled his shirt over his head – I heard a button ping off and bounce on the floor-boards – then held me close again, his naked skin warm and smooth against mine.

For a moment, I rested my face against his chest, inhaling the smell of him. Then he lifted me up, as easily as if I weighed nothing at all, and laid me down on the bed.

This was it, I realised through the haze of my desire – this was the moment, the point of no return. His mouth was pressed against mine, his eyes swim-mingly close, his cock hard against my stomach. I wanted him like I wanted to breathe.

And then I said, "Felix, stop."

He did. He lay down next to me and took my hand, and we both stared up at the ceiling, our breath com-ing in identical gasps. Every part of my body yearned towards him – I could almost feel myself thrumming with desire, like a twanged guitar string.

I turned to face him and said, "I can't do this. Not unless I leave my husband."

Felix looked aghast. "Laura, you can't. Why would you do that?"

"Isn't it obvious?" I said. He put his arm round my shoulder. I could feel his warm breath against my neck.

"I can't let you fuck your life up because of me," he said. "Or your children's lives, or Jonathan's, even though sometimes I'd like to throttle the bastard. I've got nothing to offer you – you must be able to see that. You've got a great life with him. He's what you and your kids need."

"Then why do I feel so trapped?" I said. "Yes, we've got everything we need, if you mean a nice house and holidays and access to good schools. I should be happy – I was happy, until I saw you again and felt just the same as I did before, when we were together. But it's not the same, is it?"

"You love him," Felix said. "If you didn't, we wouldn't be lying here talking."

I looked down at the white sheets and knew what he meant. "I do love him. I do, but it doesn't stop me wanting you. I have since that first time you kissed me – or Oberon did."

"Never in my life have I found it so hard to stay in character," Felix said.

I tried to laugh, but what came out was a sort of choking hiccup.

"I can't cheat on him. It's just so sordid, apart from being wrong."

"I want to fuck you, of course I do. Jesus, Laura, I've been lying awake at night thinking about nothing else. If you wanted me to, there's no way I could resist, even if I knew it could only happen once. But you don't want that. I understand why – it is sordid, it is wrong, too many people would end up getting hurt. But if you left Jonathan for me, you'd never forgive me. You'd feel so guilty about it that you'd end up hating me. You'd regret it for ever."

I thought about that for a second, and I knew that he was right.

"I shouldn't have come here," I said. "To New York, I mean. It's just been a really terrible idea all round."

"Not for me," Felix said. "Even if I never see you again, I'll be able to remember these two days."

"We'll always have Paris?" I said.

"Something like that."

He wrapped his arms around me again. His body was so familiar, so strong. Holding him made me feel safe, but I knew it was an illusion. This was the most dangerous place in the world for me to be. What I wanted to do could never be undone. Even if we never spoke of it again, even though no one need ever find out what had happened in that room, no one would hear us over the roar of the traffic outside and no one could see, I'd know. I'd know, and I'd never be able to forget it, face my husband or respect myself.

I opened my eyes. Felix must have sensed the finality of my decision, because his lips left mine. I looked at his beautiful, familiar face close to mine for a moment, and then I said, "I must go."

"Yes, I think you must," he said. "I'm sorry, Laura, I didn't mean to leap on you. I just –"

"It wasn't only you," I said. "I want to just as much. That's why I have to go."

"I know," he said.

I put my clothes on again, as hastily as I'd removed them. Felix walked with me to the door. We didn't say goodbye – he just brushed my cheek with a fingertip, and I tried to smile, then turned and walked away down the stairs.

I walked all the way back to our hotel, and by the time I got there it was dark and I'd stopped crying, although the hollow feeling of sadness in my chest remained.

It was only when I was in the lift going up to our room that it occurred to me to check my phone. I had twelve missed calls. Suddenly, I felt not just sadness but fear. I slid my key card into the door and opened it.

Jonathan was sitting on the sofa, his back to me.

"Hi," I said. "You're back early."

He stood up and turned to face me. "How long have you been fucking him?" he asked.

I felt blood rush to my face. "I don't know what you're talking about."

"Yes, you do, Laura. He was hanging around you like a bad smell in London, and now he's followed you here. Or perhaps you followed him. There I was worried you were bored, spending your holiday on your own. You haven't been, have you?"

"Jonathan, I..." I sought desperately for the right words. I wanted to tell him it was over, there'd never been anything, really, just a crazy longing in my own head for something from the past, a dissatisfaction with the present. But the habit I'd formed of denial was too strong to break now. And how had he found out? Someone must have seen Felix and me together – but who?

As if he'd read my thoughts, Jonathan said, "I suppose you thought you were being discreet. Shame about your boyfriend's fangirl following. I wouldn't have seen this, except I was looking online for something for us to do together."

He threw his phone towards me, hard. Reflexively my hand darted out to catch it. On the screen was the photo Nancy, our waitress, had taken of her and Felix together the night before. Her face and his were pressed together, smiling, but in the corner of the image was a slice of another face that was unmistakably mine.

"Everyone's talking about the NYC opening of Flight of Fancy's *A Midsummer Night's Dream* this week," the caption read. "So imagine how excited I was to meet one of its stars, Felix Lawson, out in Chelsea with his gorgeous girlfriend."

"Jonathan, seriously, there is absolutely nothing happening. Felix and I met up for a drink, and today we went sightseeing together. That's literally all. I haven't cheated on you, ever, and I never will."

Even though it was the truth, I knew how very, very close I'd come to it not being. My words didn't sound convincing, not even to me.

"Then why did you lie to me? God, you must think I'm completely fucking stupid."

"I don't! Of course I don't. I'm sorry I didn't tell you – it just didn't seem important."

"Oh, I see," Jonathan said. "Honesty isn't important. I guess that tells me all I need to know about how you feel about our marriage."

I stood, still holding Jonathan's phone with its trivial, incriminating evidence. I couldn't deny the truth of what he said: I had lied. I had chosen not to be honest with him – and not because it wasn't important, but because I knew full well how important it was. I'd lied so I could carry on doing what I wanted to do, enjoy the heady sense of freedom being with Felix gave me, imagine a life without commitment and duty and responsibility.

And now, by telling Jonathan that there had been nothing beyond friendship between me and Felix, I had made it even harder for myself to tell him the real truth.

"You brought him into our home," Jonathan said. "My home, our children's home. Did you have sex in our bed?"

"Jonathan, please," I said. "You have to believe me. I didn't sleep with Felix. Not in our bed or anywhere else. I didn't!"

Then I remembered the afternoon of my birthday, Felix's room in London, Felix's bed – and I realised that that, too, was not literally true.

My doubt must have shown instantly on my face, because Jonathan said, "I don't believe you, Laura."

Jonathan's phone vibrating in my hand, then ringing shrilly, startled me so much I almost dropped it. I held it out to him and he glanced at the screen, then swiped it with his thumb.

"Sadie?" There was a pause. "Laura's here. I don't know why she hadn't been answering her phone; it must be on silent. What's wrong?"

I felt suddenly icy cold. This was it – the punishment I'd feared, the fate I'd tempted, was coming sooner than I could ever have expected, and in the most terrible way imaginable.

"I'll tell her," Jonathan said. "We'll get her on a flight tonight; she'll be there in the morning. It's not your fault."

"What is it?" I asked. "Is it Owen?"

Please, please let him not be dead, I prayed. If he is, I'll die too – my heart will stop and never start again.

"It's Darcey," Jonathan said. "She's in hospital. Pack your bag. I'll ring for a taxi and get the office to change your flight. Do it now, Laura."

CHAPTER NINETEEN

November 2001: Performance

Like all dancers, I was used to working through pain. I'd finished the ballet during which I broke my toe, and returned to work after just four days off, which is why it never healed properly. I'd danced with pulled muscles and tendonitis. Most days, I danced with my feet bleeding into my pointe shoes. I was far more used to feeling pain than not feeling it. And now, I was going to have to go on stage even though my heart was breaking, and I was going to have to dance and dazzle and smile, smile, smile.

I looked at my face in my dressing room mirror. I looked white and miserable, and my eyes were red and swollen from crying. Well, that was the first thing I needed to sort out. I poured a stream of eye drops into each eye, ignoring the sting, and while they took effect I did my hair, securing it in its bun with countless pins and grips and a cloud of industrial-strength hair spray.

Then I turned my attention to my face. My make-up took me half an hour: heavy foundation to mask my blotchy pallor, contouring to bring out my cheek-bones, blusher to mimic a healthy glow, layers of shadow to make my eyes look huge and luminous. By the time I'd carefully stuck on my false eyelashes, the face that looked back at me wasn't that of a frightened young girl any more, but a ballerina, confident, serene and beautiful.

Still in my leotard, tights, hoodie and legwarmers, I made my way through the corridors and found an empty studio. I spent almost an hour warming up alone, feeling my body coming gradually to life, my muscles remembering their individual jobs, the residual pain and stiffness receding. I forced myself to concentrate only on my body, preparing it for the task ahead like a mechanic tuning a car. The turmoil I felt in my mind I securely isolated, the way the sports psychologist had taught us. Later, on stage, I could let my emotions take over, when there was useful work for them to do, when they'd add expression to my face and passion to my steps. Now I had no use for the gnawing pain in my heart, so I ignored it.

I was in the best shape I'd ever been, I told myself: honed, trained and rehearsed. I was ready for this. Now all that remained was to put Laura aside and become Aurora, the beautiful princess celebrating her birthday with her doting parents and a court that worshipped her, preparing to meet the four princes competing to make her their bride.

Back in my dressing room, I put on the gorgeous rose-pink costume I'd wear for my first scene. It was a perfect fit – it had been made for me, and the final adjustments had been completed just the day before. I laced up my pointe shoes, tying the ribbons securely around my ankles, and took a last look in the mirror. I was ready – the transformation was complete.

All through the building, I knew, my colleagues would be going through the same process. Alongside the stage manager's calls over the tannoy, I could almost hear the buzz of anticipation building. It was opening night of one of the most popular shows in our repertoire – everyone would be nervous, terrified, excited, but entirely focussed on their own performance. At that moment, I realised, nobody gave one single fuck about the spat between the two principal dancers or the rumours about Marius and me.

The thought gave me the courage I needed to leave the bolthole of my dressing room and make my way to wait in the wings.

I heard the roar of applause that signalled the conductor's arrival in the orchestra pit, then a second, quieter wave of appreciation as the curtain went up and the set was revealed – true enthusiasts know that one should clap for the conductor, but never for the set.

I felt a warm pair of hands of my shoulders and started, then heard Roddy's voice whisper in my ear, "I'm on. You're going to be fabulous. I love you, and so will everyone else after tonight. *Merde.*"

"*Merde,*" I whispered back.

The first scene – the princess's christening, at which the fairies bestow their blessings on the baby, the evil Carabosse arrives and curses her with death on her sixteenth birthday, then the powerful Lilac Fairy mitigates the curse to a hundred-year sleep – seemed to pass in seconds. I felt none of the paralysing stage fright I'd experienced before performances in the past – I was strangely calm, keyed up and eager to get out there on to the stage and get through my first big scene, the horribly difficult Rose Adagio. When my musical cue came, I stepped out on to the stage as poised and eager as any princess making her debut.

All the notoriously perilous balances went without a wobble. Jerome, then Roddy, then Stav, then Tom held my hand in turn, letting me find my balance before releasing me to stand alone, perfectly still, my entire body hovering over the toes of one foot. I could feel my muscles burning with the effort of it, but they didn't let me down, and I knew my face kept its radiant smile throughout. If I hadn't been confident of my performance, the roar of approval from the audience told me I'd nailed it. I was on my way to becoming a star.

My thighs were trembling with fatigue and my feet felt like they'd been dipped in acid, but I was hardly conscious of my body at all as I left the stage. I was floating on a wave of elation and success, made weightless by the bubble of triumph inside me.

Then I saw Mel and Felix, and my joy shattered like the Christmas bauble Owen would squash between his clumsy toddler's palms years in the future. The two of them were standing together in a corner, Felix already in his costume for his grand entrance after the interval, Mel in her lilac tutu, her face masked with make-up, her hair pulled tightly back behind her perfect, delicate face. Felix was looking slightly absurd as male dancers always do until they start to move. His legs in the thick white tights, perfectly muscled though they were, seemed frail and vulnerable under his elaborate brocade jacket, and the bulge his ballet belt created between them was a crude parody of the maleness I knew when we were together, naked in bed.

But it was his face I looked at – his dear, familiar face, normally so animated, laughing or about to laugh. He wasn't laughing now – his head was tilted downwards as he listened to Mel.

I watched them for just a few seconds before they saw me, but it was enough. I knew what she was saying to him, what she was doing. I knew that she was nurturing the seed of doubt and mistrust she'd planted, pouring shit on it so it would grow into a horrible, destructive plant with roots strong enough to destroy the fragile foundations of love Felix and I had built.

I hurried over to them, but I was too slow on my tired legs. Felix glanced over to me, his face haggard with sadness, then turned away. There was no time for me to talk to him – he was about to go on stage again and, unlike Mel, I wanted him to have maximum focus for his big solo.

Whatever Mel had said to him, it didn't affect him on stage. It would be exaggerating to say I never loved him more than when I watched him dance – this was the man who reduced me to a quivering jelly in bed, over and over again – but he was dazzling to watch, graceful and powerful, his technique so perfect and sure that he was free to bring real expressiveness to the role.

I stood in the wings and watched as the Prince's companions disappeared into the forest, leaving him alone. The lights dimmed and Felix danced alone on the darkened stage, every movement expressing his loneliness, frustration and longing. I could have watched him forever, but all too soon my own cue came and I was back on, dancing the image of Aurora, summoned by the Lilac Fairy to persuade the Prince to break the spell of sleep.

Somehow I got through the scene, even though Mel was looking daggers at me and Felix, who should have appeared enraptured by my beauty, refused to meet my eyes at all. As I danced, I felt my confidence ebbing away. Even though I knew the steps perfectly, I found myself ending up in the wrong place several times. My balance was off, the footlights dazzled me and I forgot to spot properly in my turns and got dizzy and disoriented.

At the final moment when Felix was supposed to wake me with his kiss, he still didn't meet my eyes, and his lips didn't make contact with mine.

There was applause for me afterwards, of course, but it wasn't the rapturous outpouring of appreciation I'd heard after my first solo, and I knew that even if the audience hadn't noticed the technical faults in my performance, they could tell that something wasn't right.

When the scene ended and the curtain came down for the interval, I ran to my dressing room in tears. Roddy was there, waiting for me, ready to wrap his comforting arm around my shivering shoulders and towel the sweat off my back.

"I can't go back on," I sobbed. "It's awful, he hates me. We can't dance together like this. I don't know what Mel's been saying to him, but be believes her, not me. I'm going to fuck it up, I know I am."

"You're not going to fuck it up," Roddy said. "Come on, Laura. You're a professional. This is your big night – the only person who can spoil it for you is yourself. Man up, change your costume, drink some water and get back out there and knock their socks off. You can do it."

"I can't." My teeth were chattering so I could hardly get the words out. "I screwed the last scene up so badly."

Roddy wrapped a clean towel around me. "You're freezing. You know we aren't supposed to get cold. Never mind how you dance, you'll be in all kinds of shit if Anna catches you in here shivering."

I managed a feeble smile. "Will you talk to him, Roddy? Find him, and tell him that what she's saying isn't true?"

"Okay," he said. "But only if you promise to get your kit on for the next act, fix your face, and get out there and do your job."

"I promise," I said.

"Good girl." Roddy hurried out, slamming my dressing room door behind him. His tough love approach was what I'd needed. I sipped some water, cleaned off my smudged eye make-up and reapplied it, and stretched the tightness out of my thighs and calves. I forced myself to breathe deeply, to focus, trying to isolate my fear and sadness again, deep inside me where they wouldn't get in the way. It didn't work as well as it had before. The confident princess I'd managed to find within myself before had retreated again, replaced by a frightened girl unequal to the challenge she faced.

But Roddy was right – I had a job to do. Whatever happened between Felix and me, this was the defining moment of my career. If I wasted this opportunity, I'd never forgive myself.

Somehow, I found the strength to pull on my magnificent finalé costume, pin the sparkly tiara to my hair and walk back out into the corridor with a smile on my face.

When I passed Mel, I ramped the smile up a notch and said, "You danced brilliantly earlier." It wasn't true – she'd seemed wooden and lacking in sparkle, but the look on her face, as if I'd slapped her with a sweaty pair of tights, was worth it. Suddenly, my smile felt genuine.

The final pas de deux in *The Sleeping Beauty* is relatively simple, at least compared to the agonising difficulty of the earlier scenes. I knew I'd have to be absolutely precise, but the choreography held no terrors for me. And Roddy had promised to locate Felix in the interval and speak to him, and he'd know there was nothing between Marius and me, that I loved him and was faithful to him. In less than an hour, it would all be over – I'd be taking my curtain calls, holding the red roses Sadie always sent me on opening nights, smiling into the faces of the audience, who I'd be able to see for the first time. It was all going to be all right, I told myself. I just had to get through this final scene, do my very best – which was, as Roddy said, only doing my job.

I waited to make my entrance, still smiling, and when the music told me it was time, I glided out on to the stage at exactly the same time as Felix made his entrance from the opposite wing.

I could see straight away that Roddy's mission hadn't been successful. Either he hadn't been able to find Felix, or Felix hadn't been willing to listen. His face was stony and set. I felt my own smile waver, and for a second I wanted nothing more than to run off stage, run all the way to my dressing room, hide there and cry.

But I didn't. I moved into the familiar sequence of steps, feeling my muscles doing what they'd been trained to do, even though my mind was in a turmoil.

I swept my arms into the choreographed gestures that meant, in the language of ballet, "I love you." Felix's arms echoed mine, but there was no love in his face – none at all. When he touched me, I could feel his hands almost flinching away from contact with mine. He didn't support me for long enough for me to find my point of balance, and I wavered and almost fell.

"Please, Felix," I hissed through my smile. "Please don't do this."

Almost imperceptibly, he shook his head, but if he said anything I didn't hear it, because I'd moved away, instinctively obeying the music.

We moved into the series of lifts – frightening for any dancer, but I'd loved doing them with Felix, because I trusted him so completely. Even though, strictly speaking, I was too tall to partner him, he was so powerful he lifted me effortlessly, making me feel as if I was flying.

It didn't feel that way tonight. His hands on my waist felt unsteady and insecure, and the upward momentum of his arms was slightly out of time with the spring of my legs.

It was on the third lift that it happened. Somehow, we'd got through the first two, but this time I jumped more powerfully, he thrust my body higher into the air, and I felt my weight tip too far backwards, his balance falter, his hands slip away from my body – and then I was falling, the lights a blur as I tried to land safely and failed.

Over the music, over the horrified gasp from the audience, I heard a sickening crunch as my ankle shattered.

For one mad moment, I thought I could get up and carry on dancing. There was pain, certainly, but it didn't feel all that much worse than pain I'd danced through before – not then. Then I saw Felix's face. He was chalk-white with shock – almost green under his make-up. He was looking, horrified, at my left leg.

I looked too – I wish I hadn't. My foot was twisted to an impossible angle. A dark pool of blood was spreading over the floor and soaking my white tights. For a moment, I didn't understand where it had come from – had I scraped myself against something? Then I saw the shard of bone, a different white from my tights, that had torn through the fabric as well as my skin, and I understood what had happened.

With that realisation, the full force of pain hit me like a punch to the face and, almost immediately, I blacked out.

CHAPTER TWENTY

All the dozens of times I'd been on flights before, the ban on phone use had seemed an inconvenience at worst and a welcome respite from the buzzing electronic summons of my mobile at best. Now, it was torture. There was no way for me to contact Sadie get an update on how Darcey was for seven long hours – seven hours for which I was completely unable to sleep, to watch the inflight entertainment or to read the magazines I'd automatically bought at the airport. All I could do was stare at the satellite flight tracker, willing the tiny aeroplane-shaped icon to hurry the fuck up and get me home to my daughter.

I refused both the beef curry that was served an hour after take-off and the wilting chicken wrap they gave us before landing, and, although I would have loved to take full advantage of the bar service, I resisted – I'd need to drive at the other end.

At last, the aircraft began its descent, and the second its wheels thumped on to the runway I was rummaging in my bag and switching on my phone,

SOPHIE RANALD

ignoring the disapproving tuts of the woman next to me.

But when, as I stared at the screen willing it to find a signal, she muttered to her companion, "I don't know what people think is so important that it can't wait ten minutes," I was unable to stop myself snapping back, "My daughter's in hospital in Bristol with a head injury, that's what's so important. So maybe you could stop judging other people for ten minutes."

Her face fell. "Oh my goodness, I'm so sorry," she said, and I immediately felt guilty as hell for biting her head off. "Poor wee mite. What happened?"

"She fell off a horse," I said. "I don't know any more than that. As soon as my sister told me I got on the first flight I could, and when I spoke to her at the airport in New York she was in A&E, waiting to be seen."

"Poor little soul," the woman said. "And poor you, how terribly worrying. I remember when my eldest was eleven, he…" and she embarked on a long and involved tale of her son's many skateboarding accidents, while I switched my phone off and on again in a desperate attempt to get it to find my network. But when at last it did, and I saw a message flash up on the screen saying that I had four new voicemails, I realised that my battery was on its last legs. Before I could listen to them, the seatbelt sign was switched off and in all the fuss of disembarking, my phone died.

After that, everything took on the quality of the sort of dream I used to have when I was dancing, and still do in times of stress. It took ages for our luggage

308

to be unloaded, and my bag was among the last to thud on to the carousel. I wandered around the long-stay car park looking for our trusty Ford Focus before I remembered that we'd come in Jonathan's new car, which I'd never driven before.

At first, I couldn't even unlock it. I walked around and around its indifferent silver body pressing buttons on the remote control, until finally I lost my temper and delivered almighty kick to one of the tyres, shouting, "Come on, you fucking fucker of a thing!" Amazingly, it worked. On the next press, the car bleeped and the doors unlocked obediently, as if to say, "I don't know what you were making such a fuss about. Woman drivers!"

Then I had to figure out how to adjust the seat so it was in the right place for me and not for Jonathan, which took another quarter of an hour and left me sweating and furious. I was still in the clothes I'd put on the previous morning to go and meet Felix – I hadn't eaten or slept for twenty-four hours and, I realised, I was in no state to drive. But there was nothing for it – I needed to get to my daughter.

I gave up on trying to figure out the sat nav. I'd have to get there the old-fashioned way, using street signs and memory. I carefully reversed out of the parking space and headed towards the exit in a series of jerks, my knuckles white on the steering wheel.

By the time I got to the motorway, I'd reached something of an armed truce with the car and my breathing had returned to normal. Just take it slowly,

Laura, I told myself – don't crash, and don't fall asleep, and it will all be okay. Then I realised that Darcey might not be okay, and a fresh wave of panic washed over me.

How could I have abandoned her, gone chasing off after Felix and left my little girl in harm's way? I remembered how, when she was born, I'd looked into her eyes for the first time, and whispered, "I promise I'll never let anything bad happen to you."

I remembered how, in the first exhausted confusion of learning how to look after her, I'd squirted baby shampoo into my own eyes to find out if it really didn't sting. I remembered walking the streets for hours and hours with her in her sling, because that was the only thing that seemed to stop her crying. I remembered when that didn't work and I ended up crying too, thinking that I must be a total failure as a mother if I couldn't even comfort my own baby.

I'd failed her now – and it was through my own selfishness.

Right now, my daughter could be lying in a hospital bed, surrounded by wires and tubes, in pain and frightened. And I didn't even know which hospital she was in, because in my panic to get the latest update from Sadie before I left New York, I hadn't asked, thinking I'd call when I landed. And now I couldn't, because I wasn't even competent enough to charge a phone.

And Jonathan wasn't there. The one person I needed, I trusted to be by my side, a loving, steadying presence, talking me down when I was being ridiculous, making me laugh when I was at my lowest ebb. The person who loved our children as much as I did. If Jonathan had been there, he would have reassured me that it wasn't my fault, that there was no point panicking, that Darcey would be looked after by professionals who saw children with bangs to the head every day. But he wasn't there. He wasn't there because only one of us really needed to be, because he had other responsibilities, and because however much he wanted to, however much he longed to rush back to our little girl, he'd had to do his duty for his employer, trusting me to care for our family.

But I hadn't – I'd placed it all in jeopardy in the worst, most selfish way. I was alone in this crisis, without my husband, and the horrible magnitude of the row we'd had made me doubt he would ever be with me again. Thinking of Jonathan made me start to cry again, and the road ahead of me blurred with tears.

I was still crying when I drove through the redbrick gateposts and on to the crunching gravel drive that led to Sadie's house. I forced myself to pull over, blow my nose and compose myself – I didn't want Owen to see me in this state. I sipped water, snatched a few deep breaths, and drove up to the house, ready to find out the full horror of the news that awaited me.

The first person I saw was Owen, riding a yellow toy tractor across the lawn. As soon as he spotted the car, he jumped off and came running over.

"Mummy!"

"Hello, Muffin," I picked him up and pressed his solid little body to my chest, trying not to cry again. "I've missed you so much. Have you had a lovely time?"

"I got a tractor," he said. "It's a toy one but I rode a real one with Uncle Gareth. When I grow up I want to be a farmer too."

"He can have a job here any time he likes," Gareth said, emerging from the house. "Hello, Laura. You must be exhausted. We've been trying to call you but your phone was off – was the flight okay?"

How was the flight? Never mind the fucking flight, I thought, how was Darcey?

"Sadie spoke to Jonathan earlier," Gareth went on. "I'm awfully sorry we gave you both such a fright. We tried to reach you but you'd obviously boarded the plane already. Sadie and Darcey are down at the stables."

"What?" My voice rose to a shriek.

"Yes, when the hospital checked her over they assured us there was no harm done," Gareth said. "She gave us all a bit of a scare, falling on her head like that, but riding helmets are pretty tough, and she's tough too. We can go and find them, if you like."

Dazed, I followed him round the house and through the avenue of trees that led to Sadie's domain.

She was leaning on a fence post, watching a chestnut pony trotting round a paddock in circles.

"Heels down, Darcey," she called. "That's better. Back straight – oh, hello, Laura. We were expecting you to ring."

"Sadie, what the fuck is my daughter doing on that horse?"

"Rising trot," Sadie said. "She's going to make a lovely little rider, you know. What happened yesterday wasn't her fault at all, or Bumble's. A bird scarer spooked him – bloody things should be banned – and he took off. He's normally pretty bomb-proof but you just never know."

Fury and relief fought for the upper hand in my mind, and relief won.

I climbed through the post-and-rail fence, and walked over to Darcey, trying to assume a calm I didn't feel.

"Hello, Pickle."

"Mummy! Look, I can ride! Auntie Sadie said after you fall off you should get straight back on, so I did. I went to hospital, you know."

"I know you did," I said, through clenched teeth.

"Bumble got a fright and bolted. He jumped over a log, but I only fell off afterwards," she said proudly. "Auntie Sadie says I've got a good seat."

"It certainly sounds like you do," I said faintly. "Come on, why don't you get off and give me a hug?"

"Don't you want to watch me do rising trot?"

"I did just now, Pickle," I said. "You looked great."

"Come on, Darcey," Sadie said. "I think Bumble's had enough for one afternoon. Show Mummy how you dismount."

Darcey took her feet out of the stirrups, swung one leg over the pony's hindquarters and slid to the ground, looping the reins over her arms like a pro. Only when she'd taken off its saddle and bridle and fed it a carrot would she let me hug her.

The sun had brought out new freckles on her nose and lightened her hair. She smelled of saddles and fresh air, and she looked completely happy.

I'd promised to protect my baby girl but, I realised, it simply wasn't going to be possible. However much I longed to wrap her in cotton wool and keep her safe like the precious treasure she was, I wouldn't be able to. She'd have accidents, she'd fail at things she desperately wanted to succeed in, she'd make bad decisions. One day, hopefully a long time in the future, someone would break her heart. But for now, she was confident, courageous and glowing with pride – I couldn't let my own fears for her show.

"Can I have riding lessons when we go back to London, Mummy? Please, please can I? I'll never ask for anything again, ever."

I looked at Sadie and we exchanged a smile. I wanted to wring my sister's neck, but I also loved her for being part of Darcey's discovery of something she adored.

"I'll have to talk to Daddy," I said.

I did indeed have to talk to Jonathan, but it proved to be harder than I expected. Not to get through to him, but to communicate about what, now I knew Darcey was safe and well, was troubling me.

"Laura? Is she okay?" he said, answering his phone on the first ring. "I talked to Sadie while you were flying, but…"

"She's fine," I said. "Absolutely fine. She fell off and hit her head, and she was a bit woozy afterwards, Sadie says, so they took her to be checked out just in case. But there's nothing wrong with her at all. She was back on the fuc– back on the horse today when I arrived."

"That's my girl," Jonathan said. "Can I talk to her?"

I passed the phone over to Darcey.

"Hello, Daddy," she said, suddenly shy.

I hovered and listened while she told him everything she'd told me about how wonderful Bumble was, and how it hadn't been his fault she'd fallen off, and launched an impassioned plea for a pony of her own. Half an hour before it had just been riding lessons – clearly our daughter could sense the thin end of the wedge.

Then Jonathan wanted to talk to Owen, and I heard one side of a long conversation about tractors.

"It's like a fire engine, only better," Owen said, and I wondered how on earth Jonathan and I, the most urban couple in the world, ever, had given birth to two children whose spiritual home seemed to be the countryside.

For a moment, I imagined moving to a little cottage in a village somewhere, with roses growing up the wall and an apple tree in the garden. I'd learn

SOPHIE RANALD

to make jam and cheer my daughter on from the sidelines at gymkhanas. Owen would join the Young Farmers. Jonathan would – no. It was unthinkable. No one needed management consultants in the country. And besides, right now I didn't even know whether I had a marriage any more.

"Can I talk to Daddy again, darling?"

Owen handed my phone reluctantly back.

Sadie said, "Come on, you two, let's go and see how the kittens are doing," and the children ran eagerly after her.

"So, yeah, they're fine, as you can hear," I said. "Listen, Jonathan, we need to talk about stuff."

"We do," he said. "But right now isn't the time, Laura. I'm sorry, but I don't have the headspace for it right now. Things are crazy here. There's – just one second – okay, Wanda, I'll be right there. I have to go. I'll be home on Thursday, we'll speak then."

I said, "Okay, we'll speak then."

He ended the call and I looked at my phone for a moment, wishing that its smooth blank screen could communicate Jonathan's thoughts to me across the miles that separated us. But it couldn't, of course.

And then Sadie came bustling in and said, "Tea's ready, Laura, you must be starving," and I realised that I was.

Over sausages, buttery mashed potato and peas, I gave the edited highlights of my adventures in New York, telling the kids about the subway and the skyscrapers and the horses that took tourists around Central Park in carriages. I didn't mention Felix at all – the time I'd spent with him felt like it had happened to another person in another lifetime. Which, in a way, it had.

By the time Gareth brought a massive dish of gooseberry crumble to the table, to "Oooh"s of joy from the children, I was almost comatose with tiredness. At one point I drooped so much that my hair ended up in my pudding bowl, and I splattered cream on to my face when I jerked awake.

"You lot carry on," Sadie said. "I'm taking Laura up to bed."

Gareth said, "Come on then – who's helping me wash up?"

To my amazement, Darcey and Owen both leapt to their feet, Owen reaching up to grab the crumble dish and almost tipping it over his head before Gareth rescued it.

"You're in here, same as usual," Sadie said, leading me upstairs to the room where I'd always slept during school holidays when I was a teenager.

The bed was covered with the familiar, faded patchwork quilt under which I'd tried, misguidedly, sleeping with my pointe shoes on to improve the flexion in my feet. My suitcase was propped open against a mahogany chest of drawers that squatted in the corner of the room as if it had been there forever – probably because it had. There was even a rosebud in a glass vase on the windowsill.

SOPHIE RANALD

"I'm going to run you a bath," Sadie said. "It won't take long, we've had a new boiler fitted. Unpack your stuff, I'll be right back."

I didn't do as she said. I sat on the bed, too tired to think or move, until my sister returned and practically manhandled me into a tub of scalding scented water, then ten minutes later extracted me from it and took me back to my room.

"I've left you a cup of chamomile tea," she said. "Although frankly you'd sleep if it was quadruple espresso. Gareth and I will put the kids to bed. Don't worry about anything. We'll talk in the morning."

I said, "Thanks Sades. I love you."

"Love you," she said, and even though she was already on her way out of the room, her mind on the dogs or the kittens or her sourdough starter, I knew she meant it.

CHAPTER TWENTY-ONE

For the next two days, I just let myself and the children be looked after. We went for long walks in the sunshine. We ate mountains of Sadie's wonderful cooking. Darcey rode Bumble and Owen rode on the tractor with Gareth. Jonathan Facetimed the children in the evenings, but didn't seem to want to talk to me beyond asking if I was all right, and telling me that he was.

When it was time to go home, we had an extra passenger in the car: the smallest of the kittens, a little biscuit-coloured ball of fluff who Darcey christened Elsa.

The drive to the Cotswolds, when I'd been frantic to get to Darcey, had seemed to take an eternity. The drive back to London passed in no time at all, because I was dreading what awaited me there.

Jonathan had gone straight to the office from the airport, but he arrived home in time to see the children, give them their baths and read them a story before bedtime. It broke my heart to see their excitement at seeing their daddy again, and Jonathan's pleasure in doing the simple, everyday tasks of being a father. The guilt I felt, knowing that our little family might be about to be shattered, and it would be all my fault, was almost unbearable – I couldn't watch as he kissed them goodnight, knowing it might be the last time he did so here, in this house we'd chosen together with so much excitement.

I went downstairs, opened a bottle of wine and sat in the kitchen to wait for Jonathan, the kitten purring on my lap. I'd made up my mind, at some point in the course of one of those long country walks: I was going to tell him the truth. However much it hurt, however much was at stake – I couldn't lie to him any longer. Whatever decision he made about our marriage, he needed to make with the facts, not with the cowardly half-truths I'd told before.

"They're both asleep," he said when he came to find me a few minutes later. "Out for the count. It must be all the country air."

"It did them good, I think," I said. "Apart from Darcey frightening the bloody life out of everyone, they had a wonderful time."

Jonathan sat down opposite me. The kitten regarded him with one amber eye, then jumped on to the table and padded over to him to say hello.

"She shouldn't be allowed on the table, should she?" I said.

"She's a cat," Jonathan said. "She makes her own rules."

He waggled the end of his tie at her and she crouched, tail twitching, then pounced and began savaging it viciously. We both laughed, and for the first time since I'd left New York, we met each other's eyes.

Jonathan looked awful, I saw with shock. There were dark rings under his eyes and his hands were trembling as he lifted his glass of wine and took a sip. His belt was on a tighter hole than usual, and I wondered if he'd eaten at all, or slept, the past few days.

"Shall I make some food?" I said. "We haven't got much in but there's spaghetti, and some jars of sauce somewhere I think."

Jonathan shook his head. "I'll get something later. Laura, I don't think I should stay here tonight. I can stay at the flat in the City we use for clients – there's no one there this week. I think we both need some space."

'Space' – that dreaded word that signals the beginning of the end of a relationship, together with its ominous successor, 'trial separation'.

"Okay," I said. My throat was so tight and dry I could barely get the word out. I sipped my wine and tried again. "But before you go, I want to tell you about what happened with Felix."

"Go on," he said. His voice was hoarse and I knew he felt just the same way I did, strangled with dread and sadness.

"I didn't just meet him a few months ago," I said. "He was my boyfriend, when I was dancing. My first proper boyfriend. And the thing is, you know how normally when you break up with someone, when you're really young, it kind of peters out? You get sick of them, or you meet someone else you like more and realise it's too soon for you to be tied down. You start having rows, and they get worse and worse, and in the end you're miserable more than you're happy, and you call it quits. You know what it's like."

He nodded. "I guess so."

"That didn't happen with him and me. Everything was perfect, it was wonderful, and then it was over. There wasn't any in between bit. So I didn't have the chance to stop loving him then, and I don't think I ever really did afterwards, either."

"Even when you met me?"

I looked down at the kitten, who was washing her whiskers with a tiny white paw. "Even then. Even when I was so in love with you, part of me hadn't let go of him."

"As if he'd died," Jonathan said, and I remembered him telling me years ago, when we first got together, that his last girlfriend had been a widow, a girl called Tash, whose husband had been killed in a motorcycle accident. Jonathan had felt, he said, as if he could never live up to the memory of the man she'd loved and lost, and that's why their relationship didn't work out.

"A bit like that," I said. "And, I know this sounds stupid and pretentious, but there's a saying that dancers die twice: once when they stop dancing, and then

again, obviously, when they actually die. So I was kind
of mourning that, too, because I'd never thought my
career would end the way it did. And I thought, when
I met Felix again, that I could somehow get my old
life back."

"And so you fucked him, and fucked up our marriage, and forgot all about our children, because you
were pissed off about not being a ballet dancer any
more. Jesus, Laura." He shook his head. He was looking at me with utter contempt.

"Jonathan, I didn't. Please believe me. I'm not
proud of what I did – I was unfaithful in my heart,
and that's a terrible thing to have done. And I kissed
him, and that's terrible too. And I didn't tell you what
was going on. But that was all. I promise."

"That's enough for me to be going on with,"
Jonathan said. "What you're telling me, Laura, is that
I'm not enough for you. Our marriage isn't giving
you what you want. So, fine – I suggest you go off and
get whatever it is you do want. And I hope you know
what that is, because I don't."

I stared silently at the kitten, who'd fallen asleep
on Darcey's tablet, curled up in a ball with her nose
tucked under her tail. I felt blindsided by shock and
shame – put like that, what I'd done was unforgiv-
able. Clearly Jonathan wasn't going to forgive me.
The scene I'd imagined – me telling him the truth
about what had happened and saying I was sorry, him
listening and understanding and us moving forward,
reunited and stronger, wasn't going to happen. I

remembered Roddy's advice from long ago: kiss and make up, then put it behind you. It hadn't worked with Felix then and it wasn't working with Jonathan now.

Jonathan had his mobile out and was tapping the screen.

"My cab's on its way," he said. "Two minutes. Anything else you want to say to me before I go?"

There was – there was so much. That I was sorry. That I hadn't wanted to hurt him. And things I wanted desperately to ask, too – was this it? Was this the end of our marriage? What should I tell the children? When would we see him again? But the constriction in my throat had tightened so I couldn't speak.

"We both need time to think," Jonathan said, less harshly. "Tell the kids I'm away with work – God knows I have been often enough lately. They'll hardly notice I'm gone. And I'll call you after the weekend and we'll sort out what to do next."

I nodded mutely. Jonathan's phone buzzed and he said, "Cab's here. Goodnight, Laura."

He didn't kiss me goodbye. He put his jacket on and left the room, and I heard the wheels of his suitcase rattling over the wooden floor, then the slam of the front door. He hadn't even unpacked, I realised – he'd made up his mind to leave before I'd said anything. He would have gone anyway. It felt so horribly unfair that I started to cry, heaving sobs of guilt and self-pity. Felix hadn't listened to me when I told him the truth, all those years ago, and now Jonathan wouldn't believe me, either. Before I'd even been able to explain, he'd jumped to the worst possible conclusion and decided what he was going to do about it. He hadn't even given me a chance to tell him I loved him. I might as well not have talked to him at all.

The kitten woke up and looked at me quizzically, then came over and sniffed my nose with hers. A tear landed on it and she started away, sneezing. It was so comical I started to giggle through my tears.

"Oh Elsa," I said. "I'm so glad you're here, anyway, you daft little thing. What are we going to do, though? What the hell are we going to do? I brought you here under false pretences. You thought you were going to be a family cat and now we aren't a family any more."

I imagined what my future would be like. Saying goodbye to the children one night a week and every other weekend. Seeing them go off to their Daddy, the hurt and confusion they'd go through as they adjusted. They would adjust, of course – children of divorced parents did, like Sadie and I had. And when Jonathan met someone else – which he would do, really soon – they'd adjust to that too. They'd probably even call her Mummy.

And me? Would I be with Felix?

The thought filled me with horror. I couldn't be with Felix – not now, not any more, not ever again. He could have been a dalliance, a brief flirtation with my past, but I didn't want that and neither did he. I was different now – I was a mother with two children and a husband I'd loved and trusted until I'd fucked it up by doing something that broke his trust in me. Felix had wanted to recapture the romance we had when we were young. That was all I'd wanted too, really. The whole thing had been an illusion, a game, a scene from a play. I wanted Jonathan – I wanted my husband back, and now it was too late.

My phone rang, startling me out of my reverie and making the kitten jump too. Please, God, let that be Jonathan, I prayed. Let him have changed his mind and be coming home again.

I rummaged in my handbag and, of course, the second my fingers found the phone, it stopped ringing. I checked my missed calls – Zé. she hardly ever rang me – she texted or sent me messages on Facebook. There must be something wrong.

When I called back, she answered straight away.

"Hi, it's me. Sorry I missed your –"

"Are you back from New York?" she asked, without preamble.

"Yes, we got back the other day. I've been staying with my sister. Is everything okay?"

"Can I come over?" she said. "I need to talk to someone."

"Of course," I said. "I could do with some company too."

"I'll be there in five."

I put another bottle of wine in the fridge. The way she sounded, we were going to need it.

Her appearance when I opened the door shocked me as much as Jonathan's had done. She was wearing a tracksuit and no make-up, and she looked pale, distressed and much older. I could see she'd been crying, and when she saw me she started to again, and so did I. I wrapped her in a hug, took her through to the kitchen and poured drinks for both of us.

"What's happened, lovely?" I said. "What is it? Is there anything I can do?"

"There's nothing anyone can do," she said. "I just needed to talk to someone. I'm so sorry to invade like this."

"Don't be mad," I said. "Come on, tell me what's wrong. Is Juniper okay?"

"She's fine. She's asleep. Carmen's there. I may as well make the most of her while I can."

"Is it Rick, then?"

She nodded, and a succession of nightmare scenarios flashed through my mind. Another woman? But Zé had told me she'd suspected for ages that Rick wasn't faithful, and chosen to turn a blind eye. Could he be ill? Diagnosed with some dreadful disease?

Before I could speculate further, she said, "He's been arrested."

"Oh my God. Is it a mistake? Sometimes that happens," I said, trying to think of an example to reassure her and failing.

"It's not a mistake," she said. "They've got him bang to rights. The stupid, stupid bastard. And I'm stupid too. I had no idea. Literally no idea at all that he was…"

She fumbled in her bag and took out a pack of cigarettes.

"Do you mind? I'll go outside if you like."

"Of course I don't mind," I said. "I'll join you, if you can spare one."

She ripped the cellophane off the pack and tried to open it, but her hands were shaking so much that she tore the cardboard flap. I took the pack gently from her, extracted two fags and lit them.

"Sorry," she said. "My Mum always used to quote some guy who said watching a woman open a pack of cigarettes is like watching a lioness opening an antelope. Who was it, I wonder? Misogynist dick. But he had a point."

I laughed, feeling the nicotine rush to my brain. Even with her own life falling apart around her, Zé had a way of making me feel better about things.

"So what happened?" I said.

"It's been going on for months," she said. "Years, probably. I just didn't see it – all those nights when he was 'working late' and I knew he wasn't really, and I thought there was another woman and I just didn't give a shit. I wish I'd called him out on it, but I didn't. I just couldn't be bothered, as long as I had my nice easy life. I've only got myself to blame."

"Don't be ridiculous," I said. "Of course this isn't your fault. You mustn't even think that way."

I found a saucer for us to use as an ashtray and passed Zé the roll of paper towels to blow her nose.

"He was gambling," she said. "That's what he was doing all along when he told me he was working. Online and in private members' clubs and even on those fucking high-stakes terminals in betting shops. He lost more than a million pounds, Laura. He stole from the firm and pissed it all away."

"He stole from the firm? How?"

"I don't know exactly," she said. "I'm so thick, I don't understand stuff like that, and he won't tell me. He's just denying everything. But he's been sacked, and the police came this afternoon and arrested him. He's going to go to prison, Laura. I know he is. And I hope he fucking rots there, because we're going to lose everything. He borrowed against the house, too. I looked at our bank statements after they'd taken him away. There's debt everywhere, so much of it. I'm so frightened, Laura. What are me and Juniper going to do?"

"I don't know," I said. I put my hand over hers. Her fingers were icy cold.

"I just let it happen," she said. "I never asked him about work, about where he was – I just turned a blind eye and carried on with my life. I never even thought about the future – I just assumed that we'd carry on like this indefinitely, and if he ever did up and leave me for someone else, I'd take him to the cleaners and carry on as normal, without him. I even thought it would be better that way."

"But maybe it will," I said. "You've got a chance for a fresh start. You're so clever and amazing, and Rick wasn't making you happy. Anyone could see that."

"But a fresh start where, Laura?" She took a gulp of wine and lit another fag. It took her three tries before she could get the flame in the right place. "The house will go. Carmen will have to go. We'll end up in some horrible temporary accommodation and I'll have to find a job, and I'm totally unemployable. All I know how to do is be a rich man's wife."

"But you worked as a journalist," I said. "And your blog…"

"Is just a hobby to get me free clothes," she said bitterly. "I haven't worked for ten years. I thought I'd never have to again. I thought the rest of my life was going to be sessions with my personal trainer and going for manicures."

I said, "Let me talk to Jonathan. He'll know what happened with Rick at work, anyway. Once you've got all the facts, it'll be easier to decide what to do next. Nothing will happen for ages, anyway, will it?"

"I'm meeting Rick's lawyer tomorrow," she said. "Apparently he's shit-hot and gets people off who've done far worse things. But shit-hot means expensive, and there's no money to pay him. Where is Jonathan, anyway?"

I thought about pouring out the sorry story of my own stupidity, Jonathan's anger and his coldness, how he'd walked out with his bag two hours before and I didn't know if he'd ever come back. I wanted to confess to her everything I'd done with Felix. But her own problems were so huge and frightening – it would be unfair to add to them by making her worry about me.

"Away with work," I said. "But I'll talk to him as soon as I can, I promise."

"Thanks, Laura," she said. "God, what a mess. I suppose I'd better go home and try and get some sleep. I'm meeting the lawyer at stupid o'clock tomorrow – Carmen will stay with Juniper. I haven't told her what's going on, poor girl. And I'm going to have to tell Juniper, too."

The thought made her start to cry again. By the time she'd stopped, and we'd finished the wine and almost all the cigarettes and evicted the kitten, who'd fallen asleep in her handbag, and hugged each other goodnight, it was after midnight.

But I didn't go to sleep. I switched on my laptop and found my CV, which I hadn't looked at for more than six years. It was time to update it now – time to start thinking about the future. If it wasn't going to contain Jonathan, I was going to have to find a way to manage on my own. I couldn't just wait for him to see the truth – I needed to take charge of my own life and the children's. It was time to stop sleepwalking through my life, time to stop dreaming, however alluring and seductive my dreams had been. I was going to have to make a plan, and it would need to be a good one.

CHAPTER TWENTY-TWO

"**O**uch! Bloody hell, those claws of yours might be tiny but they're sharp, Elsa."

The kitten's pounce on my toes, which I'd unwisely allowed to poke out from under the duvet, jerked me from sleep. I sat up, groggy with hangover and feeling none of the determined optimism I'd managed to summon up the night before. A glance out of the window told me that there'd be no fun outdoor activities with the children – grey sheets of rain were battering the pavement and I could hear minor tidal waves swooshing up from the tyres of every passing car.

Not bothering to get dressed, I went downstairs in search of coffee and managed to drink two cups before the children woke up. I'd definitely ruled myself out of contention for any good parenting awards anyway, so we spent the day on the sofa together, Owen watching CBeebies and Darcey and me playing with the kitten. We found an app that made little fish swim around the tablet screen, and

Elsa was transfixed, batting it with her paws, whiskers bristling with frustration.

I'd like to say that we moved on to a plethora of stimulating and fun rainy-day activities over the next two days. I wish I could claim that we made a tent under the kitchen table, or baked biscuits, or went outside and splashed in puddles. But we did none of those things – like I say, in the parenting league table, I was precisely bottom. Even at the best of times, the kids liked nothing better than slumping in front of screens, and it was about all I had the will for too. And besides, I wanted us to be there, if Jonathan came home.

But he didn't. He didn't even call. All that weekend, we didn't leave the house. We lived on cereal and takeaways and watched mindless crap on YouTube. The rain fell, and we waited.

By Monday, even the kitten had cabin fever. The kids were beginning to complain of being bored (when I say "beginning", they'd been whining about it intermittently since Saturday night) and I was going out of my mind with the need to see something beyond the walls of our house. For the first time since we'd left New York, I blow-dried my hair properly, put on make-up, and dressed in something that wasn't pyjamas. I made cheese on toast for our lunch, but Owen announced that he wasn't hungry.

"Do you want something else? Cereal? Banana?"

"Ice cream," he said.

"You can't have… Oh, all right," I said, conceding defeat and opening the freezer. But we were out of ice cream. We were, in fact, out of just about everything except a bag of peas buried under a mountain of frost, a chicken carcass that had been there for months waiting for Jonathan to turn it into stock, and one lone fish finger in a squashed cardboard box.

"I want ice cream," Owen demanded.

"There isn't any, sweetie," I said. "Look – you can see there isn't."

"Yoghurt," he said.

I sighed. "There isn't any of that, either. We're going to have to go to the supermarket."

"I don't want to," Darcey said. "It's so boring."

"I know it is," I said. "I feel your pain, Pickle. Believe me, the last thing I want to do is drag the two of you round Waitrose, but it's that or starve."

"I want Daddy," Owen said. "Where's Daddy?"

"Daddy's working," I said. "He'll be home in a couple of days, and maybe he'll take you to McDonald's."

"I want Daddy now," Owen said, starting to cry.

I picked him up and tried to cuddle him, but he was having none of it, his feet thudding against my thighs, his entire body rigid with rage. He could probably sense that all was not well, I thought, a fresh wave of guilt and misery battering me. My poor babies – how many more days and nights would there be when they wanted their father and he wasn't there? And how many years did I have ahead of me, coping alone with the house, the children and a job if I eventually managed to find one?

Owen was still yelling when my phone rang. I prayed it would be Jonathan, but it was Amanda.

"Oh dear, someone sounds cross," she said.

"Just a bit," I said. "Actually we're all going a bit crazy. This rain!"

"It's like bloody Groundhog Day over here too," Amanda said. "That's why I was ringing. I've given in to the relentless demands for soft play, and I was wondering if you wanted to join us?"

"I'd love to," I said, crossing my fingers, "but I've realised we're absolutely out of food and down to our last roll of loo paper, so I really need to do a supermarket run. Is there any chance you could...?"

"Believe me, any distraction right now will be welcomed with open arms," Amanda said. "Drop the kids off here and go and do your shopping. I'll take care of them. Hopefully not by drowning the lot of them in the Thames."

She sounded surprisingly human, I reflected, bundling Owen and Darcey into their macs and heading out into the street. If even Amanda, the model parent, was going crazy with school-holiday inertia, I could feel a bit better about my own laxness.

We hurried through the drizzle to Amanda's house, and it wasn't without a certain sense of relief that I handed the children over.

"I'll drop them back off at yours around five, okay?" she said.

"Fantastic," I said, thrusting two twenty pound notes at her. "Let me know if that doesn't cover whatever you do. Take them to a Michelin-starred restaurant, casino, whatever, it's fine."

The word casino made me think of Rick, and Zé, and I wondered why she hadn't been in touch. I'd texted her to say I was thinking of her, and had no reply, and assumed things were just too hectic. I resolved to call her as soon as I got home, or even drop round.

Then Amanda said, "So who was the man I saw coming out of Zé Campbell's house earlier? I only caught a glimpse but he looked vaguely familiar."

Shit, I thought, it must have been a police officer. Poor Zé – already people were gossiping about her, waiting for her downfall.

"I think she mentioned she was having someone to stay," I lied. "Juniper's godfather? Rick's cousin? Something like that."

"Hmmm," Amanda said. "Anyway, good luck with the shopping. See you later."

"Bye," I said. "And thanks so much again."

After being cooped up at home with two stir-crazy children and a bonkers kitten, the prospect of grocery shopping seemed like a blissful opportunity for me-time – the stay-at-home mother's spa day, I thought, as I untethered a trolley from its fellows and pushed it into the vegetable aisle. I remembered the last time I'd come shopping here, how I'd imagined buying groceries for me and Felix. Now, I knew that would never happen, and to my surprise I felt relieved. I wasn't shopping now for an imaginary Felix, nor for Jonathan, but just for me and my children. It was strangely liberating. Salad, fruit, cheese, bread, loo rolls, yoghurt, ice cream, fish fingers, a few random treats, and I was done. This would see us through until I got around to doing a proper online order, involving all the dull and heavy things like tinned tomatoes and dishwasher tablets.

Even so, the carrier bags were not light. I felt my shoulder muscles protesting at the weight of them as I walked out into the street, and noticed it had started to rain again. I had no umbrella, and even if I had, I needed both arms to balance the bags, so it wouldn't have helped.

I thought about waiting for a bus to take me the one stop to home, or even calling a taxi, but then I thought how ridiculously feeble that would be. It was only a few hundred yards; only a bit of rain. So I walked on, but as I did so, the shower intensified to a downpour. My hair was soaked and dripping down my face; the legs of my jeans were sodden.

Reluctantly, I gave up and huddled under a bus shelter with a group of similarly wet, disconsolate shoppers. We looked at one another with a mixture of fellow feeling and hostility – I knew the collective thinking was running along the lines of, 'I'm wet, you're wet, we're all wet. We're all in it together – but what if someone comes along who is also wet and needs this more than we do?'

And, inevitably, it happened.

A woman with a guide dog came down the street, pulling one of those wheely trolleys. She needed one hand for the dog and one for the trolley, and she was soaked through. The dog, of course, looked perfectly happy, trotting proudly along leading its mistress home.

There was a sort of collective shuffle among the bus shelter's occupants, like in a Tube carriage when a pregnant woman gets on. Everyone knows someone should get up and give up their place, but no one wants it to be them. No one meets anyone else's eyes, especially not those of the person who needs a seat.

Except this woman didn't have eyes to meet – well, she did, obviously, but they were concealed behind dark glasses. I had a brief tussle with my conscience, but my conscience easily won. After all, I was wet anyway – how much wetter could I get? I headed back into the downpour and approached the woman and her dog.

"Excuse me," I said. "There's a bus shelter just here, if you want to get out of the rain?"

"Thank you, dear," she said. "That's very kind. Isn't it the wettest August you've ever known?"

"Dismal," I agreed, steering her under the shelter, into the last corner of space. "There you go. I hope you get home safe, when it eventually stops raining."

And, my good deed for the day done, I hurried on towards the house.

But before I got as far as the next corner, I felt a tap on my shoulder and a voice behind me said, "Carry your bags, madam?"

I spun around. It was Felix. At first I thought I must be hallucinating – but no, it was unquestionably him, grinning at me from under his umbrella.

"You're in New York," I said stupidly.

"I came back," he said. "I'll tell you all about it, when we're somewhere dry."

"I live just round the corner," I said. "But you know that, of course."

"I do," he said. "Are you going to invite me back for a coffee?"

Briefly, I wondered whether that would be the stupidest idea ever. Then I said, "Fancy a coffee?"

"I thought you'd never ask." He took my shopping bags in one hand and my arm in the other and, huddled under his umbrella, we walked the rest of the way home.

"I'll make the coffee," he said. "You get yourself dry."

Gratefully, I kicked off my soggy sneakers and headed upstairs. God, I was a sight. My mascara had washed off my eyelashes and spread itself down my face, my hair was drenched rats' tails and my top had gone completely see-through, revealing my red bra. I dried off, changed my clothes and repaired my face, then hurried back to the kitchen.

Felix handed me a mug of coffee and I rummaged in the carrier bags and found a packet of biscuits.

"They're only Jammie Dodgers," I said apologetically. "For the children."

"My favourite," he said, ripping open the pack.

"So, are you going to tell me what you're going here?" I said. "I thought the *Dream* run started last week."

"It did," he said. "But I took a few days off. I'm flying back tomorrow, and I'll be there for the rest of the summer, then I'm back in London, hopefully for the foreseeable future."

"Why?" I said. "I mean, why did you come back?"

"For an audition."

The excitement he radiated told me the answer, but I asked the question anyway. "And you got the part?"

"I did. I totally fucking nailed it. They love me."

"So they should." His pleasure was infectious – I smiled at him over my coffee mug and he smiled back. "What is it?"

"It's a new BBC series, about the Wars of the Roses. Kind of *Game of Thrones* meets *The Tudors*. Big budget, lots of galloping horses and heaving bosoms – you know the kind of thing. It's called *A Crown of Thorns*."

"Felix, that's amazing," I said. "They're not making you play Richard III, are they? With a prosthetic hump?"

"Guess again," he said.

"Whatisname – the middle one? The drunk who drowned in a barrel of wine?"

"Hell, no," he said. "I'm Edward, the hot older brother who gets to shag all the girls. And the male lead, as it happens."

"That's so brilliant," I said. "Do you get to smoulder?"

"Of course," he said, and smouldered.

I laughed. "Congratulations. It's your big break, like you said was going to happen."

"Looks that way," he said. "And even if nothing comes of it, they're planning three seasons so it'll keep me in lunches at Dmitri's for a bit. And if it gets syndicated to the States – but that's thinking too far ahead."

"But why are you here? Not just in London, but here, here?"

"I came for the biscuits, obviously," Felix said.

"No, you didn't."

"Okay, they're an unexpected bonus. I'm staying down the road, with your friend Zélide."

"With Zé? Why?"

"Her mate Anton told her I was auditioning, and she rang to wish me luck. She asked me where I was staying, but I hadn't sorted anything yet, so she offered her spare bedroom. She's having a bit of a rough time – I think she wanted company."

"She told me what happened with Rick," I said.

"And I wanted – I guess I wanted to see you again, Laura. To make sure you were okay, after what happened in New York."

I said, "Jonathan found out about us. He's moved out and I don't know if he's going to come back."

Felix said, "Oh God. I'm so sorry."

The joy had drained out of his face. He didn't look triumphant at all, just shocked and concerned. I sniffed and felt a tear trickle down my cheek.

"Sweetheart, don't cry." He jumped to his feet and wrapped his arms around me, holding me tight. There was nothing sexual in his embrace, and no desire in my response to it. I let him hold me while I wept, but all I could think was how much I wanted another pair of arms around me, another chest to press my face against – the embrace of the man I'd loved and trusted for ten years, whose trust I'd betrayed.

"You really love him, don't you?" Felix said.

I nodded my head against his chest, smearing my newly applied eye make-up all over his T-shirt.

"Then we'll just have to get him back for you," he said.

CHAPTER TWENTY-THREE

November 2001: Curtain

The first thing I said to my orthopaedic surgeon, when I'd emerged from the anaesthetic and she came to see how I was doing, was, "Will I be able to dance again?"

To her eternal credit, she didn't actually roll around on the floor pissing herself laughing. The NHS trains its daughters well.

"Laura, that was a highly complex fracture," she said gravely. "A compound one also, with damage not only to both the medial and lateral maleollus, but also to the surrounding ligaments and tendons, and the skin, of course. You have two screws and a plate in your ankle. I see a lot of professional athletes in my work – and I count dancers among them – and I know you have a better understanding than most people of how your body works."

I nodded. I was still pleasantly goofed out on painkillers. "So it's bad, right?"

"Athletes – and dancers – are, in my experience, highly motivated when it comes to their recovery," Mrs Bhattacharyya went on. "Believe me, what you have ahead of you, for the next few weeks and months, will be highly challenging. How well you recover depends on how well you rise to those challenges."

"Yes, but…" I began, and then I stopped. I didn't need to ask her anything more – her face, and the x-rays she'd shown me earlier, when she was explaining what had been done to me, told me everything I needed to know. I didn't bother asking her whether I'd be able to run down a flight of stairs or whether the pain that throbbed through the cushion of morphine would ever go away, or even whether I'd always walk with a limp. My dancing career was over – that was all that mattered to me.

I said, "Okay. Thank you," and went back to sleep.

I slept for most of the week I spent in hospital – it felt like I did, anyway. The physiotherapist's twice-daily visits were a maddening interruption – more than the pain, I resented her focus on what seemed to me the trivial matter of achieving strength in the muscles surrounding my shattered joint, the minor detail of keeping early-onset arthritis at bay. I wasn't going to be able to dance again, so as far as I was concerned I might as well use a wheelchair for the rest of my life, which I hoped would be short. I was in the grip of shock and depression, and it made me absolutely horrible to everyone.

Sadie visited, bringing flowers, chocolates and heaps of glossy magazines. Her patience was phenomenal – when I snapped at her and asked what the fuck I wanted with chocolates when they'd only make me even fatter than I was going to get anyway, she calmly said, "Fine, I'll have a couple then. They're from this artisan place in the village and they're lovely."

And so she sat on the chair next to me, eating chocolates and reading me bits of scurrilous gossip from *Heat* magazine, and not minding when I snapped back that I didn't give a shit what colour Victoria Beckham's hair was this week. She knew – and I knew – that her mere presence was as healing as even the strongest drugs.

When Roddy came, he was twitchy and overly sympathetic at first, then his flood of concern dried up and I knew he'd come with not only a basket of slightly wrinkly grapes that were going an unappealing shade of beige around their stems, but also an agenda.

"Listen, Laura," he said, shifting from foot to foot, ignoring the plastic chair in which Sadie seemed able to sit tranquilly for hours. "I know you haven't been taking Lawsonski's calls, but…"

"But what?" I said. My ankle was throbbing and I was very thirsty, but I wasn't going to ask Roddy to pour me a glass of water. It was warm, anyway, and tasted stale. And it no longer made any difference to anyone, least of all me, if I stayed properly hydrated.

"But he really wants to see you. He's so sorry, now he knows everything. I tried to talk to him that night, babe, I did honestly. But Marius was with him in his dressing room, and then we got the five-minute call and…"

"Tell him I never want to see him again," I said. "Tell him if he comes here I'll call security and get him thrown out. Tell him I hate him."

And I adjusted my pillows, closed my eyes and pretended to go to sleep.

A couple of days after that, I went home with Sadie and Gareth, because there was nowhere else for me to go. I felt like the worst kind of imposition, with my crutches and my stultifying gloom and my bed in their dining room because I couldn't manage the stairs yet, but I also felt safe, because Felix had never met my family and wouldn't be able to come and find me there.

Mel, however, had and could. I was in the conservatory, lying uncomfortably on a wicker sofa watching the lights flicker on and off on the Christmas tree, when I heard Gareth say cheerfully behind me, "Visitor for you, Laura."

Sadie would never have let Mel past the front door, but she was off coaching a Pony Club rally, and such nuances were lost on her husband. As far as he was concerned, guests were to be welcomed with open arms and given tea and scones. Even as I craned round to see who it was, Gareth was moving a table over and putting a laden tray down on it.

"If there's anything else you need, I'll be in the field just over there, beyond the house," Gareth said. "Or just ring my mobile, obviously." He flushed, clearly not knowing how to cope with Mel, who looked like she'd arrived from an alien planet in her leather hotpants and cashmere poncho.

"Thanks, Gareth," I said, and he hurried away, relieved.

"So," Mel said, sinking down cross-legged on to the floor next to me. Already I envied her casual grace – and I had years of this ahead of me, years of seeing other women do stuff I'd once been able to do, and couldn't any more. "Christ, that's uncomfortable." She stood effortlessly up again. "Want tea? Or one of these scone things?"

"Just tea. Black, obviously," I said, and I took a spiteful pleasure in seeing Mel blush as she remembered the last time she'd made me tea.

She held her cup and mine awkwardly, not sure where to sit, until I moved my legs over to make space for her on my sofa, even though it hurt. She perched her perfect bum on the edge and looked at me sideways through her hair, putting the teacups down just too far away for me to reach.

"I'm so sorry about what happened, Laura," she said. "We all are. The whole company is, like, gutted for you. But you don't need me to tell you that, of course – you must know already that your pain is our pain."

What the fuck was she on about? My pain was my own – I could feel it becoming more intense by the minute as she leaned her insubstantial weight against my foot. I tried to move away and that hurt even more, so much that I hissed involuntarily through my teeth.

"Oh my God, what am I like?" Mel said, leaping up and almost tipping me over onto the floor. "Sorry,

Laura. Look, now I'm up, I won't sit down again. I expect you want to know why I came."

To gloat, I thought. But I said, "Oh yes, I'm avid to know."

Mel ignored my sarcasm and said, after a brief, dramatic pause, "I came to say goodbye."

"Goodbye, then," I said. Pathetic, I know – but my leg really, really hurt and I was really, really thirsty, and also I needed to wee and the sooner she buggered off the sooner I could ring Gareth on his mobile and ask him to help me back to bed. There was no fucking way I was asking Mel.

Mel rummaged in her handbag and found a nail file, and scraped it up and down her thumb a bit. Then she cleared her throat and said, "I'm going to New York. I've been offered a job at NYCB."

"That's nice," I said, hating her.

"And I'm getting married," she said. That made me try to sit up, and, with a bit of hefting from my arms, I managed to.

"What the fuck?" I said.

"Yes," Mel said. She gave the little, subtle tilt of her head that she always did in moments of high emotion in her solos, which she thought was highly affecting and several of my colleagues had told me they found highly annoying, and she added, "To Marius. I know you'll be so happy for us, Laura. He's been offered a creative directorship there, and New York is such a wonderful, creatively challenging environment – I just can't wait. We're so in love."

I was too shocked to say anything for a minute. Then I managed to stammer, "But you... Since when?"

Mel giggled. "We've been together a few months, actually. It was a secret love affair! Marius didn't want people talking about me. He's so wonderful, so considerate. He..."

She burbled on, but I wasn't listening. I was thinking. Suddenly, so many things made sense. How defensive Mel had been whenever Marius was mentioned – she must have been harbouring a crush on him for ages. And then he'd promoted her, and slept with her, and she knew that everyone would say the two things were inextricably linked – which they probably were. So, to deflect attention from what she was doing, she'd started the rumour about him and me. I wondered if she knew what he'd done to me in my dressing room that night. I hoped she didn't – but who knew? Mel was ambitious enough, and presumably still sufficiently in awe of her famous fiancé, to overlook a minor indiscretion like sexual assault.

"But I must skedaddle," she said. "Curtain goes up on *The Nutcracker* in..." she glanced at her watch. I'd never seen it before – it was slim, gold and studded with diamonds. "Four hours."

She swooped down and embraced me, trying to pull me up into a hug, but that made me yelp with pain. Just then Sadie arrived home, took stock of the situation at a glance and rang the local taxi firm, standing guard over me like a Rottweiler while Mel gathered her stuff together and acted all casual.

"Bye, Laura, mwah, mwah," she said, when the taxi finally arrived. "See you soon – maybe on stage!"

Sadie took Mel's elbow and steered her back into the house. From the expression on Mel's face, I suspected my sister might have been using the martial arts techniques she learned as a child, which gave her the skills to cause excruciating pain but leave no mark.

I lay back, relieved to be able to stretch my leg out and equally relieved to be free of Mel's saccharine presence. Then I noticed a WH Smith carrier bag on the floor underneath my chair. A half-litre bottle of Diet Coke was lying next to it, and a copy of *Dance Weekly* had almost spilled out.

I edged carefully around and stretched beneath me, retrieving the Diet Coke first of all. I took a few grateful swigs, then reached for the magazine.

Just a few months before, I would have devoured the gossip pages eagerly. Now, what I read only made me sad. It told me one thing I had known for a while: that Laura Braithwaite, a rising star in the company, had sustained a career-ending injury. It confirmed what Mel had just told me: that the Creative Director was decamping to New York with a select few of his top dancers. And it told me why: that he had been exposed as a serial harasser of women, and that the whistle-blower had confronted Marius, broken his nose, handed in his notice and then boarded a flight back to Moscow, where he was expected to resume his glittering career.

Chapter Twenty-Four

The next day, I awoke to brilliant sunshine. The world had that washed-clean feeling you get after loads of rain, and my brain felt like it had been laundered, too. I was actually singing as I went downstairs to feed the kitten, until Darcey stuck her head out of her bedroom and said, "Mummy, please stop making such a noise. I'm trying to watch *Frozen*."

"Sorry, Pickle, I won't do it any more," I said. "Come on, get dressed, we're going round to Zé's."

But as I helped Owen get his clothes on, I found myself singing again – Jonathan's song. "What shall we do with sleepy Owen?"

"I want Daddy," Owen grumbled.

"I know you do, darling, and so do I. But I hope we'll see him very soon."

I didn't feel as confident as I sounded – not by a long way. But the gorgeous day, as well as the late-night phone conference I'd had with Felix and Zé, made me slightly more optimistic.

Half an hour later, the children were rushing around Zé's garden and she, Felix and I were drinking coffee and eating croissants in the sunshine.

"The thing is…" Zé and I said together.

"Go on," I said.

"No, you first," she said.

"No, please," I said.

"Christ, you two!" Felix said. "Can't you just talk over each other, like men do? What's with the politeness?"

"Okay, then," I said. "The thing is, Jonathan's still not taking my calls. I don't even know where the bloody company flat is. And until he talks to me, I can't sort anything out at all."

"And Rick's not taking my calls either," Zé said. "The fucker. And until he does, I can't tell him that I want him to die a slow, painful death and never see his daughter again. But he'll have to, won't he?" She lowered her voice. "How is this happening to me? How does going to visit your ex-husband in prison even work?"

"You'll find a way," Felix said, squeezing her hand. "I believe there are buses that take you there, full of gangsters' molls carrying rasps hidden in fruit cakes. Or maybe I watched too many of the wrong sort of movies when I was a kid."

"You can piss off, too," Zé said, but she was giggling in a helpless sort of way. "God, I'm so glad the two of you are here."

Then her mobile rang.

"Fuck, it's Rick's lawyer," she said.

"Put it on speakerphone," Felix said, glancing over his shoulder to check that the children were well out of earshot. "We need to know what's going on."

Zé pressed a couple of buttons, then said, "Hello?"

"Is that Mrs Campbell?"

"Yes," Zé said, sounding a bit croaky.

"Please hold for Mr Faraday."

There was a beep and then another beep, and then a plummy voice said, "Zélide? Martin Faraday here."

"Hi Martin," Zé said. "Is there – I mean, have you heard anything new?"

"I've got good news," the lawyer said. "A decision has been taken by the firm to drop all the charges. No further action will be pursued, so long as Mr Campbell undertakes to repay fifty percent of the funds in question. The remaining... er... shortfall is to be absorbed by the partners."

I gasped. That meant Jonathan.

"Mr Campbell has asked me to advise you that he will be travelling to Dublin this afternoon to spend a short period with his brother there, recovering and reflecting on what has occurred," said the lawyer.

"That's probably a wise decision," Zé said. "Because if he came back here, I couldn't be held responsible for what would occur then."

The lawyer cleared his throat. "I understand your distress, Mrs Campbell. Please be aware that I shall be in constant communication with your ex... with your husband, and likewise with the partners at Strachan Delaunay Whitworth. I'll be keeping you informed as and when the relevant documents are signed and the settlement agreement finalised."

"Thank you," Zé said faintly.

"Thank you," Martin Faraday said. "And good day."

"OhmyGodohmyGodohmyGod," Zé said, hugging her knees to her chest and pressing her forehead into them. "It's all still so shit, but I feel so relieved. Why did they decide that? How's he got away with it? I'm so livid with the brass neck of the man, but still –"

She reached her hand into the air and snatched it down again in a triumphant, "Yes!" gesture, then got up and ran out on to the lawn, sweeping Juniper up into a massive hug.

"Mum, don't!" Juniper's clear voice carried easily to where Felix and I were sitting. "God, you're so embarrassing."

I looked over at Felix, my heart hammering. "What now? I really, really need to talk to Jonathan."

"Couldn't be easier," Felix said. "What's his number?"

He had the small, happy smile on his face that he'd always had when he was embarking on an adventure.

"Felix, what are you going to do?"

"Nothing illegal, I promise. Give me his number and you'll be with him this morning."

I hesitated, then decided to trust him and trotted out the eleven digits of Jonathan's mobile.

A few seconds later, over the speakerphone, I heard my husband's voice, sounding so familiar and yet so strange, distorted by the horrible distance that had spread between us.

"Jonathan Payne speaking."

"Mr Payne?" Felix said. "Faraday here."

I gasped and had to muffle a laugh with my hands. Felix had replicated the lawyer's accent flawlessly.

"Yes, Martin," Jonathan said wearily. "What is it? You know I'm -"

"I'm aware of your situation, Mr Payne," Felix said. "But it would be most helpful if you could spare just a few minutes of your time for a brief face-to-face conference."

"Christ. All right then. I suppose you want me to come to your office?"

"I don't believe that would be advisable, Mr Payne," Felix said. "There's the risk of media scrutiny. You're staying at the client apartment, I understand?"

"That's right," Jonathan said.

"Forty-four The Drake, EC2Y?" Felix said.

"Er, no," Jonathan said. "It's eight-one-one Roman House. I'll give you the postcode."

"That's quite all right," Felix said. "My error. I have it here. I shall be with you in under an hour."

He ended the call, just as Zé and the children came running back to the table.

"Can I have a croissant?" Owen said. He pronounced it 'crusty'.

"Of course you can, sweetie," I said. I felt like my insides had been scooped out and filled up with a weird, curdling mixture of relief and trepidation. "Butter or jam or both?"

"Both," Owen said.

"Felix, will you do some magic?" Darcey said. "Please?"

Felix smiled again, the delighted, almost devilish grin I knew so well. "I think I just did," he said.

"Felix will do some magic for you soon, Pickle," I said. "Mummy has to go out."

"Can I come too?" Owen said.

"Not today," I said. "You've got to stay here with Zé and be a good boy."

"I'll call a cab for you," Zé said.

This seemed like a sensible suggestion, but it turned out to be a mistake. Traffic in the city was blocked solid – there was some protest march happening, and we were diverted to Tower Bridge and then got stuck again.

"Let me out here, please," I said to the driver. "I'll walk. It's not far."

But I'd misjudged the distance. I walked for what felt like miles through the streets, growing more and more anxious, the sun beating down on my shoulders and reflecting off the pavement until I was a hot, sweaty mess.

"A midsummer day's nightmare," I said to myself.

At last, I found reached the building, an edifice of glass and steel next to a huge roundabout. The noise was thunderous – traffic roaring past, horns blaring. Poor Jonathan, I thought, staying here. How he must be missing home, the garden, the children. But was he missing me?

I felt as nervous as I ever had before going on stage. We'd tricked him to get me here – he'd made it quite clear that he didn't want to talk to me. He'd probably slam the door in my face, and I'd have to go home and find some way to tell the children that Daddy wasn't coming back. I might as well give up, go down into the Tube station, go back to Clapham and send him an email telling him I accepted his decision – that it was all over, all my fault.

Then a tall woman in a suit emerged through the glass doors, and I felt a blast of air-conditioned chill. She held the door open for me, and my feet carried me, almost without my bidding, into the chilly lobby. I'd sit down for a few minutes, cool down, then make my way back.

But I'd reckoned without the presence of the concierge, who smiled politely from behind his desk and said, "How may I help you, madam?"

It was too late – I was here, I'd have to go through with it.

"I'm visiting number eight-one-one," I said. "Jonathan Payne."

"May I take your name?"

Shit. What if he refused to let me in? I was going to have to stick with the script for now. "I'm from Faraday and Partners," I said.

The concierge gave me a raised-eyebrow scrutiny that said, quite clearly, that he didn't know what law firms today were coming to if their staff arrived to appointments in flip-flops, sweating and scarlet in the face. But he picked up a handset, pressed a few buttons, and said, "Your visitor from Faraday and Partners is here, Mr Payne."

"Thank you," I said.

"Through the glass doors, the lift is on the right. It's the eighth floor, last door to your left."

I thanked him again and let my trembling legs carry me to the lift. As it swept me upwards, I looked at my reflection in the mirror and confirmed that I looked just as terrible as I'd imagined. Well, it was too late to do anything about that now. If Jonathan turned me away, it wasn't going to be because I had no make-up on and the humidity had made my hair frizz, that was for sure.

I waited for a long moment in front of the door, then lifted my hand and knocked. Jonathan opened it almost immediately – he must have been hovering in the hallway, waiting for his solicitor.

I'd expected him to be shocked when he saw me, probably angry. But to my amazement, he looked relieved.

"Hello, Laura."

"Hi. I'm sorry about blagging my way in, but you weren't answering my calls. We need to talk," I said.

"You'd better come in," he said. "Would you like a coffee?"

"Just a glass of water," I said.

Jonathan gestured towards a white leather sofa. "Have a seat."

Jesus, I thought, this is awful. It felt like the worst kind of business meeting, when you know the person you're there to see doesn't want to see you. Jonathan hadn't even touched me – even the most unwelcoming client would have shaken my hand.

Jonathan returned with a glass of water and put it on the glass coffee table in front of me, then sat down on a twin white sofa on the opposite side of the room. He rested his elbows on his thighs and stared down at his hands – or at the hideous abstract design on the black and yellow carpet, I couldn't tell for sure.

"How are the children?" he said.

"They're fine," I said. "They miss you."

"I miss them, too," Jonathan said, his voice catching in his throat. "I miss them so fucking much. And you, too. I was going to come home, but then –"

I sipped my water and waited for him to carry on.

"I was too ashamed," he said. "After what happened."

"You were what?" I said. "But you've done nothing wrong. It was Rick who stole the money."

"Yes, it was. But I let it happen."

"How?" I demanded. "Of course you didn't."

"He put all the fake claims through the DBMG account," Jonathan said. "Remember, I told you about it? It's been dormant for years. I should have shut it down, or at least kept an eye on it, but I didn't.

It all came out when I was in New York. Rick was putting through travel expenses on his personal credit card, allocating them to that account, then cancelling and claiming the money back. If I'd been doing my job, it would never have happened. That's why I've resigned. It's over, Laura. I don't have a job any more."

"But they've decided not to prosecute him," I said stupidly. "I don't understand."

"Because I persuaded them not to," he said. "Not that it took much doing – they were pretty keen to close ranks and avoid the scandal. But someone had to take the hit, and it was me. It was thinking about Darcey's friend that made me decide. That little girl – what would her future be like if her dad went to prison?"

"You did the right thing," I said.

He shook his head. "I did the only thing. But now – don't you see, Laura, what this means for us?"

"What, you not having a job? You'll find another, won't you?"

"Not in this industry," he said. "I'm a marked man now. And to be honest, I don't want to do this any more. I fucking hate it – I've hated it for years. The hours, the corporate bullshit, the immorality, the dick-swinging competitiveness, never seeing you or the kids. It's a miserable life. I've been miserable."

"Why didn't you say?" I asked, but I didn't need to. I remembered that he had once tried to tell me, and anyway – I knew.

"Once you're in it, you can't get out," he said. "Not the job, the whole life. The house, the holidays, the car, you being able to stay at home... I couldn't let you all down, Laura. And I couldn't talk to you about it, because – well, because we haven't exactly been talking about stuff, have we? And now I have let you down, and I can't even give you all those things. Maybe you'd be better off with that smarmy actor anyway."

"Jonathan," I said. "Look at me." And for the first time, he did. His face was haggard with tiredness and stress, and I understood for the first time how heavy the burden was that he'd been carrying, all alone, unable to put it down or share it with me.

"None of that matters," I said. "I don't care about the house. We were happy before we moved there and we could be happy somewhere else. And I hate not working. I've been bored stupid. That's why this thing with Felix happened – not that anything actually did happen. You believe that, don't you?"

He nodded. "I've thought about it over and over," he said. "I was wrong to doubt you, Laura. I know how you feel about us – about me and the children. I know you wouldn't chuck it away. And I so nearly did, because I was jealous. I'm sorry."

I said, "I've been thinking about it too. It wasn't about Felix, really – it could never have worked between him and me. I knew that all along. I never wanted to leave you, not for one second. But I thought

I could somehow get my past back. That never works, does it?"

Jonathan shook his head. "You can't get the past back," he said.

"And I don't want to," I said. "What good is the past to me? It didn't have the children in it. It didn't have you. You're what I want."

"You know what I want?" Jonathan said.

"What?"

"I want to take you out to lunch. I'm starving."

"Don't be mad," I said. "We'll only end up doing the bloody dance of lunch."

Jonathan said, "But there's this fab street food place that does burritos…"

I said, "Or how about the raw food bar up the road?" There wasn't one – I was just making shit up. But it was worth one last, tiny lie to see the expression on his face – he'd rather eat his own feet than raw food, but he wanted to make me happy.

"Um… Or maybe sushi," he said, throwing in his last bid.

"Jonathan," I said. "We've got the rest of our lives to argue about lunch. How about now we go to bed?"

And he stood up from the sofa opposite me and we sort of flung ourselves against each other, and I felt what I hadn't felt when Felix hugged me the night before, hadn't felt for the longest time, actually. I knew I was in the arms of a man I loved and trusted completely, a man who'd make a dangerous, difficult choice because it was the right thing to do. I knew that this was the right place for me to be.

It sounds weird, I know, but we had a tiny honeymoon in that horrible, sterile corporate flat. And when we surfaced a couple of hours later, the sheets sweaty and tangled around us, I felt that we'd changed the place, as well as ourselves.

"I should drop the keys off downstairs," Jonathan said. "It's time to go home."

I said, "We're already here. Anywhere you are is home."

CHAPTER TWENTY-FIVE

"Zé Campbell's looking awfully pleased with herself lately, isn't she?" Amanda said, as we dropped off Darcey and Delphine, who were bundled up in their winter coats, scarves, woolly hats and the mittens that constantly seemed to be getting lost.

"Isn't she?" I said. "It's wonderful that she's so happy."

I'd realised that the way to deal with Amanda's attempts to drive a wedge between Zé and me was simply to pretend that she wasn't. I knew full well, though, that in her view I'd backed the wrong horse – picked the wrong friend. In Amanda's world, a woman like Zé, a woman who'd recently divorced her husband, sold her house, moved into a two-bedroom flat and been reduced to buying her groceries at Tesco, ought to be looking devastated and ashamed, if she dared show her face at the school gate at all.

But Zé hadn't obliged. She turned up looking as gorgeous as always, thanks to the fact that her blog was garnering more free clothes than ever (even if she did have to flog them on eBay after a couple of wears). A new warmth and energy had replaced the brittle languor she'd had before. She glowed with contentment. And Juniper, too, seemed utterly unfazed by their changed circumstances.

Just the other night, when I was kissing Darcey goodnight, she'd said to me, "Mummy, Juniper says being poor is the best fun. Will we ever be poor?"

"Juniper isn't a bit poor, Pickle!" I said, horrified, and embarked on a lengthy lecture about food banks and child labour and what poverty actually was, and how Juniper and her mother's perfectly comfortable life bore no relation to it at all. I was still going strong when I realised my daughter had fallen asleep.

I must have been smiling at the memory, because Amanda said, "And you're looking very cheerful yourself, Laura. We've missed you at book club, so it's nice to see you doing the school run for a change, instead of your hubby. Has he – I mean, is he back in work again?"

"He's at a meeting this morning," I said. "A new client. It's amazing how much demand there is for advice on ethical management. He's having to turn work away, because he likes being around at home for the children. And the kitten, of course. She's much harder work than they are."

Amanda sniffed. "Well. I'm delighted it's working for you... I know how difficult it is when men find themselves suddenly cast in a caring role. It's so emasculating for them."

"Is it?" I said, unable to suppress another smile at the memory of Jonathan and me last night, on the sitting room floor, when I'd got home slightly pissed after meeting Zé in the pub. The meal he'd made for us had ended up burnt to fuck, but we didn't care. "I'm not sure whether Jonathan feels emasculated. I'll have to ask him."

"Yes, do," Amanda said. "It's so important to keep the channels of communication open in a marriage."

She was preaching to the choir there, I thought. Over the past few months, Jonathan and I had talked and talked until it felt as if we had no words left, and then we'd cried, and after that we'd talked some more. We'd endured a few sessions with a relationship counsellor, complete with more talking and more tears.

It had all made me understand a lot of things a lot better. I understood why Zé and Juniper were so much happier without Rick, even though when he was there he mostly hadn't been. I understood why, in spite of his flaws, Juniper went off eagerly for her weekends with her father (although Zé had promised to tear him limb from limb if he so much as looked in the window of Ladbroke's on those weekends).

I understood the full scale of the decision Mel had made all those years ago to marry a man she didn't – she couldn't possibly – have a proper, loving future with, in order to further her career. I remembered how I used to envy what she had: the fame, the curtain calls, the body that could withstand the demands she placed on it. Now I realised the price she had paid for it. I wondered whether she thought it was worth it, but I knew I'd never find out.

And most of all, I understood how close I'd come to losing the thing that mattered most in the world to me: the life Jonathan and I had built together, the days and weeks and years stacking up into something that was strong and full of joy – or had been, until it wasn't any more.

It's not like I woke up, the way the fairy queen did in the play, and went, "OMG, I dreamed I was in love with a *donkey*!" But I did realise that, even though Felix still had a place in my heart and always would, I loved him in a completely different way: as a part of my past – a part that helped make me the person I am now. As a memory of who I used to be before I grew up and made a life I can live until its end. And some day, perhaps, as a friend.

Amanda interrupted my reverie by pressing an envelope into my hand. "I do hope you'll be able to join us for our pre-Christmas drinks party on the twenty-second," she said. "It's become a bit of a tradition. Mulled wine and champers and nibbles for a few of our closest friends – there'll be about a hundred and twenty people there. Thank God I managed to snap up that nice Carmen when Zélide had to let her go. The woman's a wonder with the children, and in the kitchen too."

"We'd love to come," I said, quailing slightly at the prospect, but recognising it as the offer of a truce of sorts. "I'll check with Jonathan. I'm sure we can make it, although we're leaving the next day to spend Christmas with my sister." Where, no doubt, Darcey would be spending every waking moment sitting on the back of a horse – which was better than lying in a heap on the ground next to one, I supposed.

"And do you have any plans for New Year?" Amanda asked.

"Actually, we're going to Dublin for an old friend's wedding," I said. "Just Jonathan and me."

As part of my new-found urge to make peace with my past, I'd sent Roddy a friend request on Facebook. He would have been quite entitled to ignore it, or block me – but he didn't. He accepted straight away, and we spent many hours catching up with all that had happened in the years since we last saw each other. Roddy's life had turned out to be far more exciting than mine. He'd worked all over the world, happily moving on when he got a better offer or itchy feet. It was in Australia, he told me, that he'd met Fintan and fallen in love. The two of them had moved back to Dublin together to be closer to Fintan's family, and Roddy was working at the National Ballet of Ireland, planning to retire and move into teaching in a year or two.

"As soon as they changed the law here, I asked Fintan to marry me," Roddy had written, "And guess what he said? So you must come to the wedding – it's going to be the mother of all parties."

Knowing Roddy, I was sure it would be.

He'd invited Felix too, and told him to bring a partner. To my surprise, I'd found this out the previous night, not from Felix but from Zé, over a bottle of wine in the pub.

"So this wedding you're going to," she said. Then she paused and blushed. I'd never seen her blush before. "Um… Felix has asked me to go with him. We've been out for drinks a couple of times, but I guess this is… I don't know. Something more. I haven't said yes. I wanted to talk to you first, in case you minded."

I thought about it for a moment, and realised I didn't mind at all – all I felt was excitement that two people I cared about might find happiness together.

"And how's your work going?" Amanda said. "You poor thing, it must be awfully hard being away from the little ones."

"Actually, I found it much harder being at home with them," I said. "And Flight of Fancy are a great employer – they're very flexible. I have to be, too, of course, because of all the late nights doing press launches and stuff. It's brilliant being back in a creative environment after so long."

I could have carried on forever about work and how amazingly lucky I felt that Flight of Fancy had been looking for a PR person at the exact time when I'd speculatively sent Zé's friend Anton my newly polished CV, but I made myself shut up. I could tell that my refusal to deliver any bad news wasn't going down well with Amanda.

SOPHIE RANALD

I could understand her frustration. She wasn't an unkind person, I knew that. But she liked the world to conform to the rules she'd laid down in her head, rules of a game she'd invented, in which she would inevitably emerge victorious. Unfortunately for her, it seemed I didn't know how to play. Still, if she could afford to be magnanimous, so could I.

"I'd better rush, or I'll be late," I said. "But it's been lovely chatting to you. Do bring Delphine round for a playdate some time soon. Let Jonathan know when would suit you."

"Before you go, Laura, there's just one thing." This was it, I realised – she was about to produce her trump card.

"Go on," I said.

"It's about the school nativity play," she said.

"Yes? Darcey's going to be a donkey, she's absolutely thrilled about it."

"Oh," Amanda's face fell a bit, but then she rallied and said triumphantly, "Delphine has been cast as Mary."

I don't know how I did it, but I managed to keep a straight face until I'd said goodbye and turned away from her. But then I burst out laughing, and didn't stop until I got to work.

The End

ABOUT THE AUTHOR

Sophie Ranald is the youngest of five sisters. She was born in Zimbabwe and lived in South Africa until an acute case of itchy feet brought her to London in her mid-20s. As an editor for a customer publishing agency, Sophie developed her fiction-writing skills describing holidays to places she'd never visited. In 2011, she decided to disregard all the good advice given to aspiring novelists and attempt to write full-time.

It Would Be Wrong to Steal My Sister's Boyfriend (Wouldn't it?) was published in August 2013, followed by *A Groom With a View* and *Who Wants to Marry a Millionaire?*, originally entitled *The Frog Prince*.

You Can't Fall in Love With Your Ex (Can You?) is Sophie's fourth novel, and she also writes for magazines and online about food, fashion and running. She lives in south-east London with her amazing partner Hopi and Purrs, their adorable little cat. Follow Sophie on Twitter @SophieRanald, or like her Facebook page for updates and random wittering about the cuteness of Purrs (there will be pics! Even videos!).

Acknowledgements

Readers familiar with the stunning, large-scale immersive theatre pioneered by Punchdrunk will recognise their work as the inspiration for Flight of Fancy's *A Midsummer Night's Dream*. Felix Barrett, Maxine Doyle and all the performers who captured my imagination and stole my heart over the hours (too many to count!) I spent exploring the worlds of *The Drowned Man* and *Sleep No More* deserve my eternal gratitude. So, too, does my wonderful friend Helen Taylor for planting the seed of my Punchdrunk obsession, and for being the perfect travelling companion in New York.

The phenomenally talented Paul O'Shea was kind enough to meet me and talk with unstinting honesty about what life as a working actor is really like. Thank you, Paul, for that and for those unforgettable moments in the Gatekeeper's office.

Being tone deaf and cursed with two left feet, it was harder for me to get to grips with the world of classical ballet. I stumbled and giggled my way through a term of adult beginner's classes at Trinity Laban Conservatoire of Music and Dance, and I'd like to thank my teacher, Chloe Stone, for her patience and good humour. I also found a wealth of information and inspiration in Darcey Bussell's autobiography, *A Life in Dance*, and Toni Bentley's fascinating memoir, *Winter Season*.

Having learned so much and written so much, it felt at times as if I would never finish this novel. Then I spent a week with my sister and her partner, who live just outside Johannesburg. Jassy and Dion's company, the cats and horses, the beautiful countryside and cauliflower wraps all worked their magic, and the book was done. Thank you, my most amazing sister and brother-in-law – I love you both, even if Morris the cat was delighted when I left.

Back at home in London, Lizzie Coulter shared her knowledge of legal matters to help me come up with high-finance shenanigans that I could never have dreamed up on my own – thanks, Lizzie. The incomparable Peta Nightingale and her colleagues at LAW have provided me with endless support and advice – I can never thank you enough. Amy Tipper and Victoria Innell at Amazon have done so much to help my books succeed, and I'm enormously grateful for all your hard work. Tash Webber has produced another gorgeous cover, and Catherine Baigent has found and fixed flaws in my writing to make me look better than I deserve – thank you both.

Finally, and always, my darling Hopi and my precious Purrs have made me laugh and given me cuddles when I've needed them most. You're the best.

Discover more sparkling romantic comedies
by Sophie Ranald

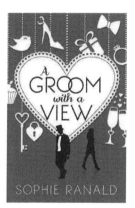

If you enjoyed *You Can't Fall in Love With Your Ex
(Can You?)* why not read *Who Wants to Marry a
Millionaire?* for FREE?

Sign up to Sophie's newsletter at sophieranald.com
to claim your copy and receive updates and news
of future giveaways!

Made in the USA
Middletown, DE
07 September 2022

73474941R00227